more praise for
IN SOME OTHER WORLD, MAYBE

"Shari Goldhagen writes with a special, effortless kind of magic—her characters (even when they're movie stars) feel real: maddening and beguiling, funny and heartbreaking. This novel is a story about coincidence and connection, about lives spinning in and out of control over decades and across the globe, but it's also about people who seem like friends, people we desperately want—no matter how badly they screw up—to turn out all right." —Christopher Coake, author of
You Came Back and *We're in Trouble*

"This is a wonderfully rich story of what might be and what might have been. Goldhagen writes with authority about show business and popular culture as she tells this ageless and all-too-human tale of the mistakes and the compromises that we all make for the sake of love. This book will entertain you, perhaps even titillate you, but above all it will touch your heart." —Lee Martin, author of *The Bright Forever* and *Break the Skin*

"*In Some Other World, Maybe* is a sprawling novel about growing up and setting off on your own, about going to Hollywood but remembering your beginnings. Goldhagen has given us memorable and appealing characters, and their stories all moved me. By the last page, I felt like we had become friends. I already miss them."
—Christine Sneed, author of *Little Known Facts*

"*In Some Other World, Maybe* is nothing less than an exploration of our hearts, the surprising places they lead us, the ways they break, and the infinite ways they can heal. And it is an absolute delight of a novel, spilling over with questions of fate and choice and characters so richly drawn and sympathetic that the loves and struggles of an interconnected group of men and women felt as real and as essential to me as my own. I read this book practically nonstop for four days straight. *In Some Other World, Maybe* hijacked my life and vaulted me completely into Shari Goldhagen's world." —Lauren Fox, author of
Still Life with Husband and *Friends Like Us*

"*In Some Other World, Maybe* makes the glamorous seem strikingly familiar and the mundane sparkle with new possibility. Goldhagen spins a lyrical saga that finds an unusual balance between hip and wise, with unforgettable and utterly human characters at its heart. I will not soon shake this book."
———Jillian Lauren, *New York Times* bestselling author of *Some Girls* and *Pretty*

"*In Some Other World, Maybe* is funny and deft and moving and sweet, at least till it's harrowing and disturbing and plain dangerous. It's tender then explosive, sexy then raw, a dozen points of view coming together to tell a story no one character alone could possibly have a handle on. Shari Goldhagen is a writer of force and intelligence, humor and warmth, heart and heartbreak, darkness and light, and this novel has it all."
———Bill Roorbach, author of *Life Among Giants*

praise for
FAMILY AND OTHER ACCIDENTS

"Real life with snappier dialogue . . . reminds you that simply paying attention is one of the things literature can do best."
———*The New York Times Book Review*

"Engrossing, beautifully written."
———*People*

"A lithe, living text . . . Goldhagen has charted a compelling, believable course of true brotherly love."
———*San Francisco Chronicle*

"Delicately mines the complexities of how loved ones seem close and far away—often at the same time—and how the smallest word uttered has the power to unravel or save."
———*Entertainment Weekly*

"Immensely assured."
———*Booklist*

"Unsentimental and emotionally riveting."
———*Publishers Weekly*

also by shari goldhagen

FAMILY AND OTHER ACCIDENTS

in some other world, maybe

other

world,

maybe

shari goldhagen

ST. MARTIN'S PRESS ❧ NEW YORK

IN SOME OTHER WORLD, MAYBE. Copyright © 2014 by Shari Goldhagen. All rights reserved. Printed in the United States of America. For information, address St. Martin's Press, 175 Fifth Avenue, New York, N.Y. 10010.

www.stmartins.com

"History of Flight" originally appeared in *Prism International,* Volume 41, Fall 2002.

Designed by Anna Gorovoy

Library of Congress Cataloging-in-Publication Data

Goldhagen, Shari, 1976–
    In some other world, maybe : a novel / Shari Goldhagen.—First edition.
        p. cm.
    ISBN 978-1-250-04799-1 (hardcover)
    ISBN 978-1-4668-4829-0 (e-book)
    I. Title.
    PS3607.O45415 2015
    813'.6—dc23

                                                    2014032132

St. Martin's Press books may be purchased for educational, business, or promotional use. For information on bulk purchases, please contact the Macmillan Corporate and Premium Sales Department at 1-800-221-7945, extension 5442, or write to specialmarkets@macmillan.com.

First Edition: January 2015

10 9 8 7 6 5 4 3 2 1

for my family

in some other world, **maybe**

1 three blue-eyed girls go to the movies

Adam Zoellner has 266 days left.

The first day of kindergarten at Coral Cove Elementary, Adam shoved Sean Dooley into a wall of cubbies when Sean called him a bastard. He wasn't entirely clear of the word's meaning; he just knew his grandfather sometimes used it when arguing with his mother after everyone thought he was asleep, knew it was somehow a slam on his mom. Sean pushed back, and Adam's nose smashed into oatmeal-colored concrete—blood droplets splashing on linoleum flooring. Adam was biting Sean's forearm when Mrs. Krass rushed from the art easels to intervene. The school didn't have a full-time nurse, so a teacher's aide walked Adam, nose pinched with a brown paper towel, to the assistant principal's office.

The bleeding had long stopped, but at the assistant principal's insistence, Adam was still sitting with his head back when his mother charged in a half hour later. Wearing a monogrammed butcher's apron from her parents' ice cream shop, she was twenty-five and ludicrously beautiful. Anger coloring the apples of her cheeks, she scooped Adam into her arms.

"Ms. Zoellner." The assistant principal stood, and even at five, Adam recognized the hint of desire in the man's voice, a different tone entirely than the one he'd had when lecturing Adam about using words to resolve conflicts.

"And for your information," his mother said, as if it were the next logical beat in conversation, "you lean forward for a nosebleed; otherwise, you can choke on blood."

She whisked Adam out before Mr. Clark could even apologize. Adam didn't realize how upset she was until his mother was fastening him into the passenger seat of his grandparents' station wagon, her light fingers examining his face. More than the silent tears dampening her face, it was the panic in her eyes that pulverized everything inside of him—the first time he understood the awesome responsibility of being someone's whole world.

"I'm okay, Mommy," he lied, pushing a smile. "It doesn't hurt."

His mother calmed, called him her "good boy." Her terror abated, and her eyes reverted to their normal sad gray as she asked what happened, and he made up a story about fighting with Sean Dooley over the good crayons.

"I'm sorry," he said.

That was the moment Adam realized he was good at pretending, at convincing people he felt things he didn't—the moment he decided he wanted to be an actor.

It was also the start of his internal countdown. The years, months, and weeks until he could leave their drowsy little Florida town forty-five minutes east of the beach and an hour southwest of Disney World.

The next day at school, Adam played nicely with the girls in the housekeeping area, avoided Sean altogether, and paid rapt attention to the alphabet exercises, even though his mother had already taught him to read. He did everything in his power to guarantee she *never* came racing into the assistant principal's office again.

Thirteen years, he kept it up. Every aced test, drama club performance, and fly ball caught in left field became one more rung on the ladder out of Coral Cove and the pressure of meaning too much to someone.

He has 266 days left.

A fat packet with his early admission agreement and scholarship information arrived from New York University two days ago, and classes start September 7—266 days.

Wearing his own monogrammed Sally's Scoops apron, Adam is behind the counter at his grandparents' ice cream shop on a Friday in mid-December, rereading the glossy college brochure for the fifth time and contemplating how he's going to tell his mother.

On the ancient television in the corner, *Nightly News* shows images of president-elect Bill Clinton, and Adam can't help but relate—boy from a small town gets out, a boy with a single mother.

She'll understand; she tried to leave once, too.

So distracted, he almost doesn't notice the rustling of red and green tinsel on the door when Molly Kelly walks in.

"I was hoping you'd be working." Molly smiles and threads black hair behind her ear. Two years ahead of him at Coral Cove High, Molly had played Sarah to his Sky in *Guys and Dolls*, Gwendolen opposite his Jack in *The Importance of Being Earnest*. He'd had a crush on her dating back nearly as far as the escape-plan countdown; she'd been dating Sean Dooley's older brother almost as long. "It's been, like, forever."

Sliding the packet of NYU information underneath the register, Adam lets Molly give him an awkward hug across the counter and asks how things are going at the local community college where she's studying something.

"I'm actually taking this semester off." She shrugs, clavicle delicate in a blue cotton top that matches her eyes. "Working full-time at the diner, trying to save up and move out of my parents' place."

Adam nods, says nothing about Kyle Dooley, and makes her a waffle cone of rocky road. It had been her favorite when she used to come by so they could run lines while he worked.

"You still qualify for the friends-and-family discount," he says when she tries to pay.

"Aww, you're too sweet." She takes a quick lick. "Speaking of free stuff, it's, like, totally last minute, but do you wanna see *Eons & Empires* tonight? My manager's kid got sick, so he gave me his tickets."

"I always liked the comics," Adam says, though he may be the only teenage boy in the entire Western world who's never actually read one.

"Yeah, I'm kinda curious, and you and I haven't hung out in a while."

He's seen her exactly twice since she graduated—an impressive feat in a town of only twenty-five thousand people. A year ago she'd served him a turkey club at Coral Cove Diner, and then, a few months later, he'd spotted her making out with Kyle behind the hardware store next to Sally's Scoops.

"It's the eight o'clock show," Molly is saying. "I know I'm giving you, like, tons of warning."

The store closes at ten, and Friday is the biggest night of the week—kids from CCH and the college branch campus, couples on dates, and all the weekend tourists en route to the beach or amusement parks who wander into the shop to use the bathroom and stay to buy sundaes and Florida-shaped magnets. Closing even a few hours early will likely cost the store several hundred dollars. In all the years he's been working at Sally's, Adam has never complained that his grandparents pay him minimum wage, never yelled at unpleasant customers or pocketed money from the till; no one could ever say Anna Zoellner's bastard son wasn't responsible.

But it's *Molly Kelly*, maybe the only thing he's ever wanted that wasn't a thousand miles north or three thousand miles west.

And if he goes out with Molly, he can delay going back to his grand-parents' house, having to walk past his mother reading one of her fat Russian novels on the couch. He won't have to tell her about NYU, won't have to tell her that he's leaving.

"Sure." Adam grins; enough complete strangers comment on his smile that he's pretty sure it looks good. "Let's go to the movies."

Two hours later, Adam and Molly are in the third row of the sold-out one-screen theater three stores down from Sally's, and he's hyperaware of three things:

First, he *hates* the film—all special effects and nonsensical sci-fi about alternate Earths, with an Academy Award–winning actor wearing a bald cap and growling overwrought lines as the draconian Captain Rowen.

Second, Sean Dooley followed them from Sally's and is seated behind him, eyes boring into the side of Adam's skull. This could be because Adam is out with Molly (who may or may not be dating his brother) or Sean might still be pissed about last baseball season, when Coach put Adam in at third base after Sean was suspended for cheating. It may honestly be a holdover from that first day of kindergarten. Sean is quite possibly the only person out of Coral Cove's twenty-five thousand who doesn't like Adam.

Third, Molly seems oddly engrossed in the movie, hand stalling midway between her mouth and the popcorn bag on the armrest between them.

Everyone in the theater collectively gasps at something happening on-screen. Molly taps her foot to his and wrinkles her nose. So very pretty. He nudges her foot back, notices the curve of her calf, and has absolutely no idea what happens during the rest of the film.

It's after ten when the movie ends, and they follow the crowd into the parking lot toward Molly's twelve-year-old Honda. Keys in hand, she makes no effort to unlock the driver's side door.

"Do you wanna grab coffee or something?" he asks, even though the only places open are the diner where she works and Captain Ahab's Bar, where everyone will know they're not of age because everyone knows everyone's business in Coral Cove.

"It's such a nice night." She inhales deeply. "We could go to the beach?"

Molly fueled most of his masturbation fantasies in ninth grade, and though he's not particularly proud of it, he was thinking of her when he lost his virginity to Dana Mott after homecoming sophomore year, thought of her all last spring when he was dating Abby Patterson. This time his smile is unconscious.

The drive takes nearly an hour, and they recount their performances on the CCH stage—the sanitized strip club from *Guys and Dolls*, how they took all the dirty words and cigarettes out of *Grease*.

"How about Nikki Summer, our pregnant Hot Box dancer? Like, I kept expecting Ms. Smithfield to make her drop out when she started showing, but no." Molly is shaking her head.

"It probably made for a more realistic strip club," Adam jokes. "Or so I've heard."

Even though Molly is laughing, Adam senses her brewing melancholy. She may have had a lovely voice and an amazing figure, but Molly never really was that great of an actress.

From the rearview mirror, her class of ninety-one tassel dangles: 266 days.

His mother will understand; she left after high school, too.

The closest beach isn't the nicest, but when they arrive a few minutes past eleven, it's still a haunting mix of inky sea and inky sky. Slipping off flip-flops, they walk for a while, close enough that their arms occasionally bump. When they reach the lapping fingers of the surf, they stop and stare at the vanishing point on the horizon.

Adam reaches for Molly's hand.

She looks surprised, as if she hadn't brought him here for exactly this.

"Whad'ya think of the movie?" she asks, but holds his fingers when he tries to let go of hers.

"It was really big," he says diplomatically.

"Yeah." Molly looks at the cycling waves. "My favorite part was when they showed all the different lives of the Snow sisters in all those other universes. Like how they got to be princesses and movie stars and doctors."

Adam doesn't remember this but bobs his head in agreement.

"I mean, how cool would it be to get to do so many different things?"

Then he does recall the montage, a series of costume changes for the two lead actresses, their differing hair colors—one red, one gold—standing in for character development.

He wonders if the reason those scenes didn't stand out to him is because, since the second day of kindergarten, he's always *been* everything to everybody in this universe. Only eighteen, and he's already played a million different roles—class clown, class president, probably valedictorian in June. He can get high with the guys who grow pot in their basements as easily as he can make his grandmother laugh with a clean joke. Teachers are so charmed, that he's pretty sure they don't even look at his work anymore before stamping an A, and tourists at Sally's Scoops always pronounce him "such a nice young man." Nobody could ever say Anna Zoellner's bastard son wasn't an all-around good kid.

But apparently not everyone had that same jack-of-all-trades existence.

"It was like those girls had constant do-overs," Molly is saying.

"You just turned twenty," Adam says. "What do you need to do over?"

She shrugs, mumbles something about different experiences, which he assumes means not dating Kyle Dooley exclusively for centuries. "I dunno, maybe work harder in school, go away to college."

"You can do that. Just ace a semester at community and transfer."

"Nah, that stuff never came easy for me," she says. "I can't, especially now."

He doesn't ask what "now" means. It's after midnight; he's only got 265 days.

Apropos of nothing, she brightens. "You were always good at everything," she says. "Are you headed to Gainesville next fall?"

Wouldn't that be easier? If he went to Florida or Florida State with the other kids at CCH who actually leave town to attend school full-time? He could come home on weekends to keep his grandparents' shop in cheap, honest labor, could still eat China One takeout with his mother and talk to her about books when she got home from her job at the hospital, could continue making sure she never looked terrified over his well-being again.

He hadn't applied anywhere within three hundred miles.

"I actually got a scholarship to NYU." It's the first time he's spoken this out loud.

Her happiness is so genuine, any annoyance he had over being dragged to the beach to *not* make out dissipates. "That's amazing," she says. "You're really going to do stuff, aren't you?"

"Molly." He takes both her hands in his, squeezes; he's always been good at convincing people of things that aren't true. "You can do anything you want."

These must be the magic words, because when he leans in to kiss her, she doesn't stop him but opens her mouth and hooks her fingers in the belt loops of his jeans to draw him closer.

"I always thought you had a thing for me," she says in the fractured seconds when their lips and tongues aren't touching.

"Guess I didn't hide it well."

She smells like sand and strawberries and baby powder. Yards and yards of silk skin under her flimsy tank top.

"Thought you were really cute, too," she says.

This is a bad idea.

Not because she may still be with Kyle Dooley—the Dooley brothers are the kind of overathletic assholes who pepper John Hughes films. And not because Adam has been on a few dates with Joy Keller, and Joy might not realize he's simply marking time.

It's a bad idea because Molly clearly wants *something*, and he's got only

265 days. Because 265 days is still a lot of time—enough to fall in love and apply to state schools and end up a teacher at Coral Cove High, directing musicals or coaching the subpar baseball team.

But it's *Molly Kelly*.

Cock so hard it hurts, his eyes flutter closed. In the darkness the tide sounds the same as cars that pass on the highway facing his bedroom window, everyone on their way to somewhere better.

"Always liked you." Molly's words muffled in the ever-diminishing space between them. Words he wanted seven hundred days ago, when he was a sophomore and she was a senior, when he didn't have the escape route mapped out yet.

Hands beneath his shirt, she runs fingers across his stomach, around his sides. He trembles as she dips below the waist of his jeans. Does he even have anything? He's not in the habit of bringing condoms to the ice cream store.

"What the fuck, Molly!" Two hundred feet away, a shout.

Confusion.

And then Sean Dooley—who's got four inches and fifty pounds on Adam—is yanking him apart from Molly, while Kyle Dooley, who is even bigger, is standing next to her looking as though he might cry.

"What are you doing here?" Molly sounds truly outraged, which makes Adam feel slightly less used.

"You're going out with freaking Zoellner?" Kyle says Adam's name as if it's a genital fungus and reaches for Molly's elbow. "The punk who stole third base from Sean?"

"You had your idiot brother follow me to the movies, didn't you?" Molly bats Kyle's hand off her arm.

"It's not like that. I was worried—"

"Leave me alone," she says.

"Molly—" Kyle looks monumentally sad, but Adam steps forward anyway.

"Look, she said she wants to be left alone—" he starts.

Sean cuts him off. "Zoellner, shut the fuck up!"

Adam does; 520 days ago he would have fought for Molly's honor, staked a claim, done something. Tonight he tries not to sigh and waits to see how badly the situation will deteriorate.

"We'll figure this out," Kyle is saying to Molly.

"I already told you what I want to do," she says, but sounds much less convinced.

"Can we just talk about it?" Kyle asks, and Molly lowers her eyes. "Lemme give you a ride home."

The rolling of the ocean.

"I can't." Now she's completely lost. "I drove, and Adam won't have a way back."

"Sean can take him, can't you?" Kyle asks.

The younger Dooley offers a creepy smile. "Sure, Mol. You and Kyle go back in your car, and I'll make sure Z gets home."

"You would?" She looks to Sean, then seems to remember Adam is the one she needs to check in with. "No, I should take him home."

"I'm closer to Z's house anyway," Sean offers.

"I don't know," she says again, close to tears.

"It's fine, if that's what you want," Adam says, always good at convincing people of things that aren't true.

"You're sure?" she asks, and he nods. "Okay, I'll give you a call tomorrow?"

Adam would bet his scholarship that he'll never hear from her again.

With arrangements finalized and keys exchanged, the two groups start in different directions. When Molly and Kyle are no longer visible, Sean stops walking, and Adam realizes what should have been obvious ten minutes earlier.

"You're not really giving me a ride," he says flatly.

Sean snorts. Adam sighs.

Burst of pain as Sean's knuckles crack across his nose.

Adam's eyes close, and he must bring his hands to his face, because there's nothing blocking Sean's fists from a series of quick jabs into his left side.

Swinging back blindly, bare feet slipping in the sand, Adam fails to connect with any part of the larger boy.

The last fight he was in, ironically with Sean Dooley, was thirteen years ago, and Adam is amazed at how stunningly bad he is. Apparently he's not good at *everything*.

"Who's the better third baseman now?" Sean demands.

If the statement weren't immediately followed by a fist to his cheek, Adam would find it hysterical. There was never any question of who the better third baseman was. Adam was simply the third baseman who didn't get caught with a crib sheet during a trig exam.

By sheer serendipity, Adam manages to duck the next body blow but trips on nothing, lands flat on his ass.

He must look extraordinarily pathetic, because Sean's anger extinguishes to cold fear, perhaps realizing that assault is more serious than cheating on a math test. It's a moment Adam *could* take advantage of. Sure, he feels like crap, but he can tell his injuries aren't serious. He could kick Sean's legs from under him or spring to his feet and exploit the element of surprise.

But he's got only 265 days; Adam doesn't need to prove shit to Sean Dooley or anyone in Coral Cove anymore.

So he stays down.

Blood falls from his nose, darker than the surrounding sand.

"Stay away from her," Sean says, but it seems halfhearted. He doesn't bother kicking grit at Adam, doesn't mumble "bastard" under his breath; he simply walks away.

Inching back on his elbows, Adam eases down until his head touches the ground. He concentrates on the throbbing pulse on the left side of his face, experimentally shifts his jaw, runs fingers over bruised ribs.

A slight chill in the air, it's no longer hot at night. Florida *does* have seasons, but he's never owned a winter coat, has seen snow only on TV.

Part of *Eons & Empires* had taken place during a nuclear winter, where survivors trekked through falling ash and dead earth, everyone bundled in scarves and boots. For all its faults, the movie did a really good job of making it look cold; the New York University brochure is full of vibrant pictures of students walking the snow-covered city campus.

She'll understand, she's probably known for a long time.

After high school his mother had left to model or wait tables or go to school. She'd made it as far as Atlanta, lasted four years, and returned with a two-year-old son and no explanation. Anna Zoellner moved back into her parents' house, worked at their store, got a nursing degree and a job at the local hospital, and never talked of leaving again.

Not sure how long he lies on the beach, Adam feels water licking his fingers when the tide comes in. His nose has long stopped bleeding when he finally stands.

It's a fifteen-minute walk to the road, another ten before he finds a sports bar with lights on. Five minutes more of holding a quarter in the phone booth before he musters the courage to dial his mother.

The restaurant is family-owned, and it's a brother and sister a few years older than him closing up. They hand him a paper cup of crushed ice for his rapidly swelling eye and let him sit in a booth while they flip chairs up onto the tabletops and break down the soda machine.

Dagger of guilt over the ice cream shop he abandoned what seems like years ago.

Adam offers to buy something, but the siblings—both round and freckled—give him a plate of French fries, ask which school he attends.

And he wonders if his whole world would be different if his mother had ever dated anyone seriously (even with Adam, she got asked out constantly but rarely went), ever had other children. A sister to work alongside him at Sally's Scoops? A brother to tag-team-battle the Dooley boys? Someone to stay behind so his mom won't be all alone with her books and aging parents, with whom she rarely agrees.

In her old VW Rabbit, his mother arrives in forty minutes flat. Her full lips thin when Adam slides into the passenger seat and she sees his face. He's again five years old with a bloody nose.

"Baby?" she asks.

"It's not as bad as it looks," he says, trying not to wince as she examines his cheek.

"I can run you to work—get X-rays to be on the safe side?" she asks, and he shakes his head. "Have you been putting ice on your eye?"

Adam holds up the cup of slushy water.

"Well, keep it on for ten minutes, then off—"

"I'm okay, really, Ma, it doesn't even hurt," he says, as convincing at eighteen as he was at five.

She drives in silence, and he rests his arm on the door, leans out the window so he won't have to look at her.

"Thank you for coming," he says over the rush of air. "I'm really sorry."

"What happened?"

"I got into a fight, dumb high school stuff."

The car eats miles.

He shifts in the bucket seat, moans when the shoulder belt strains against his rib cage. His mother sighs.

"Sure you don't want to go to the hospital?"

He shakes his head. "Do you maybe have any Advil?"

She hands over her purse, and he rummages through the contents—worn copy of *Ulysses* from the Coral Cove Library, pens without caps, dingy plastic picture holder with his Sears portrait as a toddler in denim overalls. He knows that behind that first photo is his school picture from every year. Finally, the white container with the blue label.

"If you can wait, there's stronger stuff at home," she says.

"This is great." Shaking out three caplets, he starts to dry-swallow them but feels her eyes on him and takes a sip of the melted ice to wash them down.

Thirty-eight and she's still so beautiful, even with her black hair pulled back in a messy ponytail and her makeup long faded.

Other than their slate-gray eyes, Adam and his mother look very little alike, his dimples and Roman nose genetic hand-me-downs from some man he's never questioned her about; no one could ever say Anna Zoellner's bastard son wanted more than the parent he had.

Molly Kelly is pregnant.

The realization hits so hard, he jerks upright and has to bear another worried glance from his mom.

At twenty, Molly is the same age his mother was when he was born. And he has a vision of his mom alone (or maybe not alone) in an Atlanta apartment, deciding to have him, deciding to keep him. He wonders why but knows he'll never ask, the same way he'll never ask why she came back to Coral Cove, a place where she probably didn't fit in long before she was a single mother.

"Ma?" His voice wobbly.

Concerned again, she turns, clicks her tongue.

"I got into school in New York," he says like he's choking, *feels* like he's choking. "And I qualify for this big scholarship—covers everything."

"That's wonderful." Tone light, but now she's the one avoiding eye contact, gaze locked on the stretch of highway ahead of her.

The ache in his head and pain in his side are nothing compared to the sudden crush of his lungs, like he's breathing through cheesecloth.

"I'm gonna go," he says.

He doesn't realize he's shaking until his mother pulls over to the shoulder of the road, unhooks her seat belt, and reaches across the gear console to run the back of her hand down the side of his face that isn't purpling and unnaturally warm.

"Of course you are. You know how proud of you I am, right?"

"I . . . I'm so sorry."

"Shh, shh, s'okay, baby." Her fingers are cool on his cheekbone. "You're my good boy."

CINCINNATI

The movie credits are still rolling when Sharon Gallaher, tears streaming down her face, decides she's going to see *Eons & Empires* again.

Wiping her nose on the sleeve of her denim jacket, she checks her Swatch. It's 2:15 P.M., thirty minutes before the next showing. She could probably hide in the bathroom and sneak into the theater without paying admission again, but she's already skipped school; the last thing she needs is an irate manager calling her parents. So Sharon goes back to the box office and buys another ticket with the last five dollars in her wallet.

Afternoon on a Friday, this showing is more crowded than the first, and it takes a few minutes before she finds a spot in the back near two older boys talking about how the film probably won't be as good as the comic books.

"Ed Munn didn't want anything to do with the movie," the blond guy is saying. "He wouldn't even let them list him as the creator."

He's wearing a Walnut Hills ring, and Sharon realizes the boys are seniors at her high school. The dark-haired one's locker is down the hall from hers—he sometimes wears a *Star Trek* shirt that says BEAM ME UP, SCOTTY.

Bob of panic in her esophagus that they might recognize her. Then Sharon remembers she's a freshman with only a handful of friends (most of whom are really only friends with Laurel Young—the daughter of her father's business partner). These upperclassmen would have no idea who she is.

Still, the nervousness lingers as she settles into her chair and a preview starts for *Jurassic Park*. She worries the film will be less special this time with these reminders of her own reality so near. The sensation begins to fade when the film opens with bald Captain Rowen and Commander Bryce fighting over the Neutrocon (which makes alternate-universe travel possible) as their plane plummets toward the desert sand. Sharon is completely absorbed by the time Rowen throws open the aircraft's hatch and jumps out, sans parachute, at the last minute.

Two years earlier Sharon read her first *Eons & Empires* comic book the way most twelve-year-olds probably examine their first *Playboy*—locked in a bathroom, heart tangling in her throat, fearful of being caught in the act of something naughty.

The couple next door had a weekly date night on Fridays (so completely different than Sharon's own parents, who were far too practical for such an extravagance), and Sharon babysat the Robbins' four-year-old son. After putting Elliott to sleep, Sharon would rummage through the Robbins' bookcases, crowded with volumes crammed three deep—thin pamphlets of poetry, hefty Victorian novels, some books new, others with covers softened by age or notes marking specific passages. Her own house had only her father's accounting textbooks and a handful of mass-market paperbacks by Mary Higgins Clark and Dean Koontz. Sharon told her friends (well, she told Laurel) that she took the babysitting gig because she needed money, but the truth was she actually preferred reading the Robbins' books to going anywhere kids her age were headed.

That particular Friday, Sharon was putting back *Lady Chatterley's Lover* (which she'd heard was scandalous but had found boring) when she noticed the stack of comic books behind *Shakespeare's Collected Works*.

Eons & Empires, Issue 1: Rowen Rising was on the top of the pile in a clear plastic sheath. The cover was a washed-out gray with dozens of striking blue Earths of different sizes seemingly bouncing around the edges. In the foreground two women—one a blonde and one a redhead—clung to each other while a bald man in black and a buff guy in white clashed swords. The title and Ed Munn's name were written in crimson across the top.

In the same way everyone knows a little about Spider-Man or Wonder Woman, Sharon had a passing familiarity with *E&E*. Knew Captain Rowen was the bad guy, Jason Bryce was good, twin sister scientists were in the mix, and it had to do with parallel universes and nuclear war. Still, she'd never actually seen the comic books, and holding the decade-old first issue from 1981 gave her a rush of warmth she couldn't explain.

Even though it was date night and the Robbins wouldn't be home for hours, Sharon tucked the issue into her purple book bag, went to the powder room, and bolted the door. Before reading the text she studied each panel—the artwork minimal and haunting, all grays and blacks in World 1, the other universes each a different color palette. It read like a book (a more interesting one than *Lady Chatterley's Lover*, anyway). All about Commander Bryce and the Snow sisters traveling to the parallel Earths in the hope of stopping Captain Rowen from blowing up North America in their own world. Midway through volume one, Sharon realized she was dizzy from holding her breath.

It wasn't that she could identify; it was the exact opposite. The world-hopping struggles between Rowen and Bryce had less than nothing to do with her own life in the suburbs. With her friends (well, Laurel and Laurel's friends), whose universe was all about ballet flats and grades and getting asked to school dances. With her parents, who were still married to each other, had one cocktail at precisely 6:30 after work each night, paid their taxes, and were absolutely adequate and innocuous in every meaningful way. In *E&E*, things mattered, decisions had consequences, character was tested.

And Captain Rowen—wonderful, tortured Rowen—who wasn't so much evil as misguided, who loved Cordelia Snow with all his heart no matter what universe they were in. Rowen was infinitely more interesting than any of the boys Laurel and Laurel's friends found attractive.

For the next eighteen months, Sharon read and re-read every issue at the Robbins' house on date night, even after Laurel and her friends began including Sharon more and more on trips to the mall and slumber parties. When the Robbins moved to Minneapolis, Sharon stole new *E&E* comics from the library or the racks of the Waldenbooks at Northgate Mall and hid them in plain sight among the mess of papers and clothing in her room. It wasn't that she didn't have the money to buy them—she'd saved almost everything from her babysitting gigs—it was about not wanting to share *E&E* with anyone, even cashiers and librarians. Talking about the comics had the potential to make those worlds less real, to weigh them down with the boredom of Cincinnati.

Two months earlier, Sharon, Laurel, and Laurel's friends had seen *Candyman* at the Esquire Theater, and there had been a preview for the *E&E* movie. As the screen filled with the ash of nuclear winter and the dashing Jake James appeared dressed as Commander Bryce, Sharon had felt naked and exposed, everything in her digestive system chugging to a halt.

"Jake James is so hot," Laurel had whispered in her ear. "We should see that."

Sharon had made an affirmative sound. Movies Laurel's friends saw were never about the film but were about going to the bathroom in pairs to apply sticky pink lip gloss, about which of the older kids with a driver's license might give them a ride to Pizza Hut or the Busy Bee afterward. Sharon understood and even had fun when the girls helped her apply blue shadow that matched her eyes or used their curling irons to give her straight black hair body. But the thought of seeing *her* Captain Rowen battling Bryce and his passion for Cordelia Snow while Laurel and Laurel's friends discussed the attractiveness of the boys behind them was intolerable.

That was when Sharon began planning today. Taking a map from the glove compartment of her father's Taurus, she plotted a course to the mall and checked *The Enquirer* daily in case the matinee listings changed. She'd even pretended to feel a little sick at school yesterday so her absence wouldn't come as a surprise.

Though her parents were usually busy getting ready for work when she left to catch the bus, Sharon made a point of saying good-bye and going out the front door. Instead of heading to the bus stop, she wandered the wooded area behind the house until both their cars were gone, then ducked back inside to call the school attendance office. She'd tried to take on her mother's slight Midwestern accent as she pretended to be Joan Gallaher explaining why Sharon wouldn't be coming in.

Cincinnati isn't a city designed for walking—even downtown, and especially in her suburb right outside the limits—but the trip to the theater wasn't bad. Before she and Laurel had quit Girl Scouts, Sharon had earned all the badges for reading maps and using compasses, and most of the journey had been a straight shot along the highway. It was an unusually nice December day, where a jacket was sufficient, and although she brought an umbrella, she hadn't needed it. The whole walk had taken little more than an hour; it was quite possibly the most daring thing Sharon had ever done.

As she watches the movie again, Sharon notices subtle details. The film-makers had kept the color palette the same as in the comics, and much of the dialogue was lifted verbatim as well. She could have recited it along with the actors. And the boys from her high school are plain wrong; the movie is actually better than the comics.

When the credits begin after the second show and she wanders back into the mall, with its glittery holiday decorations and Victoria's Secret smell, Sharon is not crying but bone-crushingly disappointed, pining for that world where everything is significant. That it will be another year and a half before the sequel comes out is as horrifying a thought as three more years of high school.

Even through the spray-can snow on the mall's glass doors, Sharon can tell it's darker outside than it should be at 4:30 P.M. Further inspection reveals that it's pouring rain, the fat drops a little like the nuclear fallout in the film.

At some point she must have lost track of her umbrella. She's mentally retracing her steps when there's a tap on her shoulder.

"You go to Walnut, right?" It's the beam-me-up senior from her school. A few feet behind him, his friend is talking to a trio of girls in Country Day uniforms.

"Yeah, I'm a freshman. I wasn't feeling well this morning, so I didn't make it in." Bites her tongue; sometimes, when she's nervous, Sharon talks too much.

"Thought I recognized you. You've got those pretty eyes." The boy is tall and lean, has soft-looking ears and a fascinating mix of stubble and red bumps on his chin. She wonders what a girl like Laurel would say in return, what a girl is supposed to say.

"Did you like the movie?" he asks, and Sharon can hardly breathe. She can't talk to him about Rowen and Cordelia's tragic love story and the struggle to find the right universe that will allow everyone to save World 1, not here, where things are safe and comfortable, where the Gap is having a sweater sale and a Muzak version of "White Christmas" blends with the fountains.

"It was pretty good," Sharon mumbles, grabbing the door. "I need to go. My ride is waiting outside for me. It's my parents here to get me."

She's at the edge of the parking lot before registering how much colder it's gotten since the afternoon and how hard the rain is coming down. But even if she had enough money for another umbrella, she'd run the risk of bumping into the guy again. Pulling the front of her jacket tighter, she hunches over and trudges toward the highway.

As she follows the grassy path along the shoulder of the road, everything feels slower than on the way there. There's more traffic this time of day, so she moves farther from the highway, the ground mushy and hard to navigate. Water soaks through her sneakers and socks, every step like squishing cold Jell-O. In ten minutes the saturated denim of her jeans goes from annoying to debilitating.

She thinks of Commander Bryce and the Snow sisters in the movie leading groups of survivors through the cold ash and burning sun of nuclear winter, and even through her own discomfort, there's that stab of longing to be out of this world and in a more unpleasant one.

Another ten minutes and her teeth are chattering, hands stiff and numb.

She flirts with the idea of calling her parents. Obviously they'd never understand about *E&E* and Captain Rowen, but she could invent a story about a fight with Laurel and Laurel's friends at the mall after school. Her mom especially seems to like it when she "gets out there" and does "normal" teenage things.

No phone booths anywhere.

Rain stings her eyes, and she realizes she can't keep going, might not even make it to the exit ramp thirty yards away. So Sharon just stops and feels sorry for herself.

An old station wagon with wood-paneled sides pulls to the shoulder of the road. The driver leans across the passenger seat to roll down the window.

"Where you headed?" asks a man, maybe fiftysomething, with a salt-and-pepper beard.

She tells him Reading Road.

"It's on my way," he says. "I can drop you."

He pops open the door.

For years, after-school specials and PSAs have spouted reasons *not* to get into cars with strangers, but none of them are as compelling as getting out of the freezing rain. Sharon slides in, instantly creating puddles on the cracked vinyl seats and floor mats.

"Thank you," she says as welcome heat blows at her face from the vents.

So relieved, Sharon takes a few seconds—until the car is zipping at fifty miles per hour—to notice her surroundings. Smell hits first, something long past ripe and decaying. Then she glances behind her, where the whole hatch of the back is filled: yellowing newspapers and plastic IGA grocery bags, oil-soiled rags, gardening tools with clumps of dirt clinging to sharp edges, what looks like the blade of a chain saw. On the dashboard there's a saint figurine, and rosary beads dangle from the rearview mirror along with a military-looking medal.

"Don't worry, little lady," the man says when he notices her looking. "I'm not a religious zealot or anything."

"I wasn't thinking that," she says politely, though his mentioning it makes her shiver again.

This close, she can see how dirty the driver is. Younger than she originally thought, but unkempt, with a brown, indiscriminate substance under ragged fingernails.

"This used to be my wife's car, and she'd take it to church sometimes." The man is leaning toward her, familiar scent on his breath—the Scotch her father pours himself each night after work. "Lot of good all that praying did her, right?"

Sharon nods and tries not to let her mind wander to the tools and possible chain saw in the back, not to make any unfounded connection between them, the presumably dead wife, and the smell.

"I'm only saying religion didn't help her," says the man.

Through the windshield the world is eclipsed by curtains of rain and a fog of condensation from heat on old glass.

Get out of this car.

Shame strikes before fear. Her grades have always been okay—solid B's with A's in history and English, despite her inability to spell—but as far back as she can remember, Sharon has always harbored a secret sense she was smarter than most people in some less tangible way. That all that time reading about other worlds and making up stories had to count for life experience, even if the experienced life might not be her own. Had she been reading a book where the young heroine accepted a ride from a stranger, Sharon would expect the girl to end up raped or murdered or tortured in some horrible, imaginative way. She would have dismissed the character as too dumb to warrant concern.

Get out of this car.

"Sir, it's okay if you drop me off here," she says, trying to determine through the steamed windshield where exactly *here* is.

The man continues talking, as if she's said nothing.

"You know that old saying, 'There are no atheists in foxholes'?" he asks. Though she's never heard it, Sharon nods again.

"Well," the driver continues, "I was in the war, dodged sniper fire, had a gun held to my temple, and I can tell you, for damn sure, I was the atheist in the foxhole."

"Thank you for your service," Sharon says, without knowing which war the man is talking about. Her father, who joined the National Guard to avoid being drafted during Vietnam, says the phrase whenever they walk by uniformed soldiers.

"Sweet girl." The man looks at her directly for the first time, revealing a red bulb on the end of his nose and cracked lips with dried saliva tamped in the corner of his mouth. "Such exquisite eyes."

"Thank you." As stealthily as possible, Sharon inches her butt toward the door, but it's hard, because her jeans are wet enough to stick to the worn vinyl seats. "Really, it seems like the rain is letting up. You can just drop me off here, that'd be great."

"Still looks like cats and dogs to me," says the man. He's right, of course, thick sheets of water smacking the windshield. "Reading Road is on my way; it's no trouble."

Her back finally against the side of the car, Sharon cautiously lets her right hand search for the door handle.

Eyes on her, not on the road, the man smiles, his teeth crooked but whiter than she expected. "It wouldn't be right of me to leave a pretty little girl like you on the side of the road in this weather, now would it?"

Captain Rowen pulling open the hatch of the crashing plane and jumping without a parachute—the lesser of two deaths, the one with autonomy.

Her fingers finally find the metal latch.

Get out of this car.

Sharon squeezes, releases when she feels it give.

A tickle of icy air on her back.

And then she hurls herself against the door.

Falling backward isn't easy. It goes against every human instinct to grope for the seat belt or the console, to cling and cling and cling to the known.

Let go.

A crash of pain in her left thigh like nothing she's ever felt before when she hits the asphalt and tumbles away from the highway down the grassy shoulder. Hurts like hell, but she can tell her leg isn't broken, knows it will still work even if it's unsteady.

Forty minutes later, when she opens the door to her house, soaking wet and bleeding from small cuts on her hands and cheek, she'll think about how fortunate it was that she landed the way she did, realize it could have gone another way.

When her parents look up from the living room couch in confusion, then rush toward her, she'll realize that she could have cracked her head open or been crushed by oncoming traffic. Or maybe something minor, a broken wrist or collarbone, an injury that would have slowed her down or dulled her reflexes.

Again and again throughout her life, she'll recall the luck of her landing. When she gets her acceptance letter to NYU, and when she kisses a boy she's falling in love with in Washington Square Park. When she burns her novel manuscript or gets her first byline in *The New York Eye.* Over and over, she'll contemplate that there but for the grace of Captain Rowen she'd not have the opportunity to screw up this new thing, to move forward, to breathe.

But when she hits the pavement at fifty miles per hour and rolls down the soggy grass, she's not thinking of possibilities and failures in other universes; she's thinking only of getting up and running home to the safety of the world she knows.

CHICAGO

Technically, Phoebe Fisher kisses Oliver Ryan first.

They're in Evanston Township High School's cafeteria, where they've been eating lunch together for two months, theoretically so he can help her with physics. Neither one of them has actually brought up anything about motion laws and vectors for the last few weeks, though. Instead they discuss their teacher's proclivity for plaid pants, Oliver's summer at U of I engineering camp, and how Phoebe wants to move to LA and become an actress after graduation. He tells her she'll blow them away at her audition for the school's production of *The Importance of Being Earnest* next week, and Phoebe, almost unconsciously, leans over their plastic lunch trays and brushes her lips against his.

Luckily, Ollie seems amenable to the idea and kisses back. She'd locked lips with plenty of guys at her old school in the western suburbs, but none had worn glasses; she likes the feel of the rims as they slide down Oliver's nose and bump her cheek. As far as kisses go, it's fantastic, and the two of them simply grin at each other for a solid thirty seconds after. Finally he asks if she wants to go to the movies that night.

"Braden and I were gonna see *Eons & Empires*," he says, "but I'd rather go with you—you're a lot prettier."

Even though *Eons & Empires* is definitely more her fourteen-year-old brother's kind of film, Phoebe thinks this might be the first *really* good thing that's happened since she moved in full-time with her dad and transferred schools.

The feeling evaporates when she notices her brother and a few of his freshman cross-country buddies staring at her across the room. Raising dark eyebrows at Chase twice, Phoebe asks what his deal is, using the language of facial expressions they've shared since they were little. Chase rolls blue eyes back and returns to his friends.

Phoebe watches him for a few seconds, but Chase doesn't look up; things are just so weird now that they're both in high school. Eventually she relaxes and again thinks that the date with Oliver might be a good idea.

She feels this way all through trigonometry cosines and the *Heart of Darkness* discussion in twelfth-grade lit. Is still excited about it as school lets out and she gets into the passenger seat of Nicole Green's BMW, Evie

Saperstein sprawled in the back. Then Nicole turns onto the street where all three of them live and suggests they go to her place and hang out for a few hours.

"Can you just drop me at my dad's?" Phoebe asks.

"What, you got a hot date?" Evie glances up from the CD liner notes of a new band she's into—Pearl something.

"Kinda." Phoebe stares out the window at the large stone houses, realizes she's nervous.

She's known these girls for years, has seen them on the weekends when she and Chase would stay with their father and stepmother. Their families all went to the same synagogue, and the three of them had sleepovers after all the bar and bat mitzvah parties. But Evie and Nicole have been her everyday friends only since September, when Phoebe's mother took a job in Hawaii. Though the girls had seemed excited to have her—Nicole convinced the dance corps to give Phoebe an audition, and Evie had gotten her involved in drama club—they're still strangers in many ways. Phoebe doesn't know how they'll react.

"I'm going to see a movie with Oliver Ryan," she says.

"Who's that?" Evie asks from the back.

"You know *Ollie*." Nicole conveys exasperation while staying focused on the road (perhaps the reason she passed the driver's test on the first try and Phoebe is scheduled to take it for the third time next week). "Braden Washington's friend, with the red hair and cute glasses, sorta quiet."

"*That* guy?" Evie sighs. "Have you looked in a mirror since the swelling went down, Pheebs? You're, like, way too hot for that guy."

Automatically Phoebe's fingers float to her nose. In a particularly skillful maneuver, she'd convinced her parents that if she *had* to move across town for senior year, the least they could do was let her get a nose job—a fresh start, a better chance to be noticed by modeling agencies next year. Stunningly, they'd agreed, and a plastic surgeon with an office in the same medical complex as her father had taken out the bump and thinned the tip. It looks amazing—the perfect complement to her heart-shaped lips and high cheekbones—but she hadn't thought it would make her feel so weird. She wonders if she should tell Oliver about it, if it counts as lying if she doesn't.

"I mean, these braids are a little Pippi Longstocking." Evie reaches around to yank the long black pigtails hanging nearly to Phoebe's waist. "But you're the prettiest real person I know."

"I like Ollie." Phoebe shrugs. "We've got the same lunchtime, and he's been helping me with physics."

"I could have helped you, Pheebs." Nicole sounds hurt, a phenomenon Phoebe is discovering occurs with great regularity.

"Ollie *is* nice," Nicole continues, "but his dad is a pilot and almost never around, and his mom died in the eighth grade."

Nicole offers the last bit of info as if it's a character flaw on Oliver's part. Phoebe doesn't mention that her own mother is alive and well and just abandoned her children for Maui. She wonders what Evie and Nicole say about her when she's not there.

"Yeah, he mentioned that," Phoebe says, relieved Nicole is pulling into the circular driveway of her father's house.

"Dave and I were gonna see a movie later. Want us to come with?" Nicole asks. "Might be fun?"

Nicole's boyfriend is perfectly amicable, but he and Nicole started dating in junior high and spend whole weekends looking at high-rise condos downtown, planning which one they'll buy when Nicole is done with law school and Dave is a doctor. It seems too intense for her first date with Oliver.

While telling Nicole the offer is sweet, Phoebe suggests, in an undefined way, that they might see each other at the theater.

"Wait, we're all going as a big couples' thing?" Evie leans over the bucket seats. "Fine, I'll ask that drummer from Fresh Delicious."

Phoebe can see exactly how this will go: Nicole and Dave planning a lifetime of couples' dates for them; Evie making smart-alecky, hypersexual comments—everyone doing their damnedest to make sure Oliver Ryan never asks her out again.

"Let's play it by ear, and maybe we'll see each other there," Phoebe says, trying not to offend Nicole but to also get out of the car and into the house before any more bad plans can be fashioned.

"Call me," Nicole is saying as Phoebe shuts the door.

Through the foyer, with its dramatic stairs and heavy chandelier, the chatter of afternoon talk shows and smell of baked goods draws Phoebe to the sprawling kitchen as if she were a cartoon dog. Wearing an apron over an extremely tight sweater, like a sexed-up Betty Crocker, her stepmother pulls a tray of snowman-shaped sugar cookies from the oven.

"You're not hanging out with the girls today?" Gennifer pulls off oven mitts to fluff her mane of honey-colored hair.

"No, I've got a date," Phoebe says. "But don't tell Dad. It's the first time we're going out, and I don't want to answer a zillion questions."

"I'll make him take me out to dinner to get him out of the house." Gennifer smiles, and Phoebe can almost feel the wave of sisterhood she's projecting. Six years ago Gennifer was a twenty-five-year-old temp entering patient records at Phoebe's father's cardiology practice. That her father and Gen fell into the un-ironic love of Lifetime movies would have been an unbearable cliché if Phoebe's mother hadn't been the one who had left the year before. "So who is this guy?"

"He's a senior, too. He's been helping me with physics." There's no point in lying; Gen has proven capable of keeping secrets. "Tall, red hair. Not Jewish."

Winking a green eye, Gennifer touches the Star of David Phoebe's father gave her for completing conversion classes, asks where Phoebe and her "mystery man" are going.

"We're seeing a movie at Old Orchard." Phoebe helps herself to one of the cookies, which presumably are for the holiday party at her father's office the next day. "The *Eons & Empires* thing."

"Oh, hon." Gennifer bites her lower lip. "Not the seven thirty-five show?"

"Yeah, why?"

"Your brother and his friends are seeing that."

Chase, who had morphed from the sweet baby brother she used to play dress-up and board games with into a hormoney teen with acne and mood swings. Chase, with his pals who gawk and whisper at her, who sneak into his room with stolen copies of *Playboy* and *Gentleman's Prerogative*.

"Maybe it's a big theater?" Gennifer offers hopefully.

And once more the date seems a monumentally poor idea.

Phoebe's bedroom is three times the size of the one she'd had at her mother's house in Palatine, and in the center is a huge canopy bed that she'd really, really wanted when her father got it for her twelfth birthday. She doesn't have the heart to tell him she now thinks it's ridiculous. Her closet here is also twice the size, and she selects a blue baby-doll dress that makes her boobs appear slightly larger than the barely B's they are.

Remembering Evie's Pippi Longstocking comment, Phoebe undoes her braids, smooths the ebony waves with her fingers. Oliver is tall, so she slides on Mary Janes with a three-inch heel that make her five eleven. Dots gloss over her lips and applies a light coat of mascara. Even before the nose job, everyone told her she should model, and at her old high school she got all the cute-girl roles in plays. Still, it's different now. She always looked like her mother—pale skin, dusk-colored eyes—and their noses had been almost identical. With her new upgrade and her mother working halfway around the globe, it's as if Phoebe has lost that entire world.

She wonders if Oliver would have liked her as much with her old nose, if he would have been so eager to help her with physics.

The doorbell rings, and she glances out the window at Oliver's red hatchback parked in the driveway. One final check in the mirror, and she grabs a peacoat, jogs down the steps.

Ollie, despite what Evie said, looks plenty good standing in the foyer, hands shoved in his pants pockets. Less attractive is that Chase (wearing a Captain Rowen T-shirt) apparently answered the bell and is deep in conversation with her date—something about the *E&E* comic books.

"Hey, you found it." She smiles at Oliver, angling Chase out of the way.

He grins back and tells her she looks nice; her brother remains frustratingly close.

Ollie asks if she's ready. Phoebe nods enthusiastically, and they head out.

Chase follows.

Spinning to face him, Phoebe rolls her eyes to the left and raises her right brow in furious communication.

"Ollie said he'd give me a ride." Chase shrugs.

Phoebe raises her eyebrows again.

"It seemed dumb to make Gen schlep to the mall when you were already going, so I told her I had a ride, and she went to meet Dad for dinner."

"Did you tell her your ride was with me?" Phoebe's desire not to appear a spoiled brat on her first date with Oliver is all that keeps her from screaming.

"I didn't think that was important."

"It's really no big deal," Ollie says politely.

She's about to protest again but concedes. Turning so only her brother can see, Phoebe mouths, "Fine, but we're not taking you home."

Chase shrugs again. Phoebe takes a deep breath and tries to remember that she's excited to be on this date, that it may be the first truly good thing that's happened since she switched schools.

In gentlemanly fashion, Oliver opens the passenger door for her, but the gesture loses something when Chase crawls in the back.

Surprisingly, Chase doesn't say much on the ride, though Phoebe occasionally feels his eyes on her. Oliver asks about the rest of her day and tells her about a crazy sub he had in calculus. She's almost forgotten Chase is in the car at all until they pull into the packed mall parking lot and her brother points out the window at Nicole and Dave getting out of her BMW.

"Look," he says. "It's your married friends."

Oliver gives Phoebe a curious glance, and she bows her head. "Yeah, Nic mentioned they might see the movie."

Ten minutes later, they're in a roped-off line waiting to enter the theater. Chase is ten people ahead with a handful of ETHS underclass boys, who occasionally look Phoebe's way and whisper. Phoebe focuses on ignoring them. Nicole suggests that they go to Maggiano's for dinner after the movie, and Phoebe again tries not to commit to arrangements while not offending. Dave makes mindless small talk with Ollie about an AP math test.

They've been there twenty minutes when Evie, dressed in ripped black fishnets and a tight ribbed dress, arrives with a college-age dude wearing almost as much kohl eyeliner as she is.

"Sorry we're late; we were fucking," Evie says in the tough-girl persona Phoebe is never clear how seriously to take. Dave gives a choked laugh, and Nicole's eyes narrow into the mother of all withering glances. Phoebe looks at her shoes.

Evie starts to pull up the rope to join them, but Nicole crosses tiny arms over her tiny body and informs Evie that line jumping is rude.

"Seriously, Nic?" Evie's face ices over, and Eyeliner Guy looks tragically bored. "What's the BFD?"

Then, as everyone else just stands there, Evie and Nicole proceed to have one of their stare-down fights, the result of having been best friends forever and ever, long before Phoebe joined them full-time.

Mercifully, the theater doors open, and everyone shuffles forward.

But conditions don't really improve inside. The only row with enough open seats to accommodate them is in the very front, and there's awkward chair hopping as the group determines the best configuration of couples. When they've finally settled, Dave asks Oliver if he wants to go to the snack counter, and Evie suggests she and Phoebe hit the ladies'.

"I'll wait until you guys get back. Someone has to hold all these seats," Nicole says, more forty-seven than seventeen.

Staring into the wall of mirrors above the bathroom sinks, Evie applies burgundy lipstick to already burgundy lips, blots on a paper towel.

"So Oliver seems cool," she says, apparently having forgotten that Phoebe is way too hot for him. "How far do you think you'll go tonight?"

Embarrassingly, it takes Phoebe a half second to realize what Evie is asking.

"I don't know." She tries not to sound rattled. "Guess it depends what time the movie gets out."

"This is the fifth time Reed and I've hung out, and he's older." Evie sprays perfume on her ample cleavage, teases tawny hair. "I'm pretty sure he's expecting the works," she says with a hint of sadness.

While Phoebe figured that Dave and Nicole were probably sleeping together, and that there may have been a slab of truth in all of Evie's talk, she's never actually told the girls she's still a virgin—that the pinnacle of her sexual experience was giving a pretty cruddy handjob to Jared Wells after junior prom. And she realizes Evie and Nicole may have just assumed she's more experienced than she is, either because she's pretty or because her old school had a high rate of teen pregnancies. This discovery is so completely isolating and unnerving that Phoebe ducks into one of the toilet stalls, leans her head against the plastic divider, and just breathes for several minutes until Evie asks if she fell in or needs a tampon.

As the girls are leaving the bathroom, Evie bumps into Chase, who was apparently standing directly outside the ladies' room.

"Careful there, mini-Fisher," Evie says.

Phoebe tries to communicate to Chase with her eyebrows that he should let this go.

Based on her brother's bizarre behavior all day, Phoebe fully expects that Chase will take umbrage at Evie's ribbing, but he apologizes and starts back toward the theater.

Spotting Oliver and a tub of popcorn at the condiment stand, Phoebe hustles over to help.

"Hey there," she says, and he stands even taller, handing her the diet soda she'd wanted.

"Hey yourself," he says.

For a second they have their familiar ease from the school cafeteria, and this date once again seems a brilliant idea. She leans close, and he takes her hand; this time he's the one who initiates the kiss. They're doing that smiling/staring bit when she notices Chase standing next to them.

"What?" Phoebe asks, caring less and less about appearing a spoiled brat in front of Oliver.

Chase doesn't have an immediate answer, but when she raises her right eyebrow, he says, "I was gonna get a Coke, but Gen left before giving me my allowance."

Phoebe contemplates telling him off, but at this point she's willing to pay a bribe and reaches for her purse.

Oliver stops her. "I got it," he says, unfolding bills from his own wallet. "Is ten dollars enough?"

Thrusting her arm out in the universal motion for stop, Phoebe prevents the exchange. Ollie's talked at lunch about saving for college (her own father has not only volunteered to foot the whole bill but is currently trying to sweeten the prospect with a new car if she ever passes the driver's test). "You shouldn't give him money," Phoebe says to Oliver gently. And then, not at all gently, to her brother, "Don't you dare take that."

"It's fine," Ollie insists.

Chase thanks him, tucks the cash into his jeans pocket, and finally leaves.

"I'm so sorry," Phoebe says. "I don't know what his problem is today."

"He's just worried about you." Oliver shrugs. "Wants to make sure I'm a good guy."

It's a nice thing to say, and Phoebe wonders if it's true.

"Haven't you noticed he's been following you around all night, and the whole business with the ride?" Oliver continues. "It's kinda sweet; I never did that stuff for my sister."

Maybe Chase *is* looking out for her? She tries to recall the last time the two of them did something together, decides she'll go to his track meets in the spring and will drive him to school if she ever gets her license.

"Well, I already know you're a good guy." Phoebe tries to sound sexy, to channel a little of Evie, wonders what Oliver's expectations are about how far they'll go tonight.

"I'm glad you think so."

Before they can discuss Oliver's merits in more detail, Dave, his own sodas and tub of popcorn in hand, comes over and tells them the movie is going to start soon.

Back at their seats, a preview for *Jurassic Park* rolls. Evie and Reed start making out, and Nicole and Dave melt into cuddle positions. Evie's question from the bathroom still bouncing around her head, Phoebe notes, with regret and relief, that two inches of air separate her leg from Oliver's and their hands are occupied with soft drinks and snacks.

The theater darkens further, and images of a violent plane crash fill the screen. Seated so close, Phoebe is instantly nauseated by the loud pops and whirls and jumpy camera work.

Vomiting on Oliver *would* definitely answer the question of how far they'll go tonight. Closing her eyes makes it a bit better; perhaps she can remain like this for the whole two hours.

Breath on her shoulder makes her shudder. Oliver in her ear: "Let's get outta here."

They hunch over, but still their backs cast shadows on the screen as they get up. A few people, probably her brother's friends, boo at them.

As they slink past, Nicole gives Phoebe the kind of challenging glance she usually reserves for Evie fights, and Phoebe mouths, "Headache." Face softening, Nicole whispers, "Call me tomorrow." Still kissing Reed, Evie pats Phoebe's arm as she goes by; Phoebe squeezes back in confirmation. Chase catches her eye as they walk by his row, and he starts to climb out. Using their eyebrow communication, she lets him know it's okay, that Oliver is a very nice guy. Giving her one last look, Chase nods, eyebrows that he'll get a ride home with his friends.

Phoebe and Oliver continue to the exit and find themselves in the courtyard of the outdoor mall, where leafless trees are strung with Christmas lights, and the air is crisp and not terribly cold for December in Chicago.

"That was a little crazy, right?" Oliver says. "I hate the front row, too."

"Did you *really* want to see the movie?" Phoebe unconsciously twists her fingers and presses them to her chest.

"Naw, I mean, I used to read the comic books, but it will be out on video in six months. We can rent it then."

"Just the two of us?" she asks.

"That would be really, really awesome." He laughs. "Do you wanna get ice cream or something?"

"There's a good bakery on Sheridan," she says. She used to go there with Nicole and Evie back when this wasn't her regular mall, when it was a place to go on weekends with friends who weren't everyday friends. When Evie and Nicole had known and dismissed Oliver, never suspecting he was someone Phoebe might like. When her brother was too young to worry about whether or not she was dating good guys. When most of her life was a world and the western suburbs away. But this world is kind of cool, too. "Maybe I can treat you to a cookie?"

Halfway to the car, he takes her hand.

"I had a nose job," Phoebe blurts. "Last summer before I transferred."

Oliver looks at her bewildered.

"I didn't want you to see a picture of me and think I lied about it. And I had it done because I wanted to, not because I broke it in an accident or anything."

"Oh." He still seems perplexed. "I like your nose. I probably would have liked your old one. Your nose really isn't the reason I asked you out."

Technically she kisses him first, but Oliver is quick to kiss back.

2 we still don't have a winner

Phoebe is surprised Adam is registered to vote in California at all, let alone in their district. He'd only moved into the second bedroom of her Studio City apartment in December, and for the last few months, he'd been so obsessed with whether the pilot he'd filmed would be picked up that she couldn't imagine he'd gotten around to filling out the forms.

The more surprising thing Phoebe discovers, when she wobbles from her bedroom at 9:00 A.M. on November 7, is that Adam is awake, showered, and dressed in something other than the NYU T-shirt and track pants he's been wearing every day since CBS *officially*, officially passed on *Goners* three weeks ago. Adam *is* wearing gym clothes, but clean gym clothes, like he might actually work out, as opposed to getting drunk or high and insulting the TV and all the actors who *do* have on-air sitcoms.

"Is this that hotel off Lankershim?" he asks, gray eyes alert, no longer drugged and dilated, as he studies the Department of Elections mailer.

"Yeah, the ExecuStay." Phoebe's not even sure she's still registered, but it's good to see Adam off their secondhand couch, so she tells him to give her a few minutes and she'll come along. "Just lemme brush my hair." She starts to run fingers through her short black bob, but he reaches for her hand.

"Don't—it's sexy like that."

It is; she knows.

After he booked the pilot and they started sleeping together, Adam had suggested she chop the heavy, straight hair that had hung halfway down her back since sixth grade. He'd said it would accentuate her features, make her more distinctive. Following the cut, she'd booked two crappy local print ads through her crappy modeling agency and had gotten even more phone numbers slipped to her at the hostess stand at Rosebud. But it's been weeks since she and Adam have had sex and, as they never bothered discussing what it meant when they started screwing, they'd certainly not gotten around to analyzing what it means now that they're not. Phoebe's been waiting for him to say *anything*.

His hand still on her arm, him noticing she looks good—this could be that moment.

He lets her wrist go; it's not.

"When I was in high school, they let everyone over eighteen leave early to vote." His voice takes on the gauzy nostalgia it has had since *Goners* was pronounced a no-go and he started idealizing the small Florida town where he grew up. "I don't think my grandfather's ever forgiven me for going for Clinton."

She'd still been seventeen in November 1992, but Oliver had been of age, and when they were in love and telling each other everything, he'd confessed that he'd been confused by the punch cards in the voting booth. Kissing him, she'd whispered they should go back to her dad's house, because she'd "never fucked a voter before." (She'd actually never fucked anyone at that point but was trying on her sexuality and liked the way it sounded.) Now that's the kind of line she'll throw out at an audition to show she's tougher than she actually is, something to say when flirting with the bartenders and waiters so they'll remember to tip her out at the end of a shift. With Oliver, it had been different—eight years ago, sex had been a concept linked to love.

Adam suggests they walk to their polling place, since it's just down the street.

"*Nobody walks in LA,*" she sings in her best New Wave voice, and when he laughs, she feels herself smile, excited she made it happen.

The natural light in their basement apartment is so limited that, stepping outside, she's temporarily blinded by the sun. Tripping over broken concrete, Phoebe grabs Adam's biceps for support. He pats her fingers. Neither one lets go when she's stable.

"Are you going home for Thanksgiving?" he asks. "Your father *and* your brother called again last night."

"So everyone can tell me I'm wasting my life? No thanks."

Adam shrugs. "I like your parents."

The feeling wasn't entirely mutual. Six weeks ago, her father and Gennifer had been in town and taken Adam and her to The Palm. While Gen had squeezed Phoebe's arm in the ladies' room and pronounced Adam "a doll," her dad had barely contained a grimace when she'd said Adam was an actor, and he'd taken strange issue with Adam calling him "Dr. Fisher" instead of Larry.

Phoebe doesn't mention this. Nor does she ask if Adam is going to Florida. In February, after he shot the *Goners* pilot and he and Phoebe were hooking up, Adam had flown his mother out to visit, but he never goes home.

She tells him Melissa, another hostess at the restaurant, is having an orphans' Thanksgiving in Culver City (doesn't ask if he slept with Melissa, who had asked Phoebe for his number last year after Phoebe and Adam's acting class had come in for drinks).

"We can do that if you stick around," Adam says, and she thinks this might be his way of asking her to.

"That'd be fun."

Still arm in arm, they walk the remaining ten minutes in silence. In her vampire life of afternoon auditions and Rosebud shifts all night, she's rarely out in the world this early and is surprised by the sheer number of people (in cars, mostly in cars) being productive. A lot of them are actually lining up to vote at the hotel lobby.

"We could skip this and get coffee." Gently she squeezes his shoulder, sinewy muscle under cotton. "Gore's winning California with or without us."

"You trust someone else to make decisions for you?" He grins; he may not be the best-looking guy in LA, not even the best-looking guy in their queue (it *is* Studio City), but when he smiles, she'd challenge any jaded person in this whole jaded city not to turn to microwaved butter. It's the first time she's seen it in a long time, and she wonders if this means Adam is off the couch for good, ready to take his rightful place as the only aspiring actor in this ghetto of aspiring actors she's certain will make it. Wonders if tonight she'll be fucking another voter.

The election has all but been called for Gore by the time Phoebe pulls open Rosebud's famous bronze door around six.

Other than the sleek television sets above the bar, the place looks almost the same as it does in the pictures from the forties and fifties, when Humphrey Bogart, Sammy Davis Jr., and Marilyn Monroe used to sip champagne cocktails and nibble veal chops in red leather banquettes.

"Hey, dollface." Burke—the flamboyant fan-favorite bartender—waves her to the bar lining one wall of the enormous restaurant's front room. "Try this." He hands her a tumbler of something fruity-smelling and brown.

Taking a sip, she shudders.

"It's a Tennessee—rye whiskey, cherry liqueur, and lemon juice," he says. "Looks like Gore's gonna win, so I figured we needed an appropriate cocktail."

Two hours and 180 tables later, things are beginning to look a lot less sure for Gore, and Burke is mixing a drink called Texas Tea. On the TVs mounted between the shelves of liquor bottles, the NBC political guy is doing something wonky with a whiteboard every time Phoebe peeks over. By ten the place is packed, everyone maudlin. From what she gathers between seating guests, Florida has now been given to Bush.

A cheer erupts around eleven, but she doesn't have time to see what's going on because Jake James, Commander Jason Bryce himself, sashays past four waiting parties and requests a table for his group of six stoned-looking dudes in jeans and T-shirts. A check of the book isn't necessary; Phoebe knows he doesn't have a reservation, and all the large tables are booked until the kitchen closes at midnight.

"We'd love something outside," Jake James says without actually looking at her. It's a consolation that in her four-inch heels she's taller than him.

His last few movies were box office and critical roadkill, and Jake has done his tour of the rehab circuit, but he's still the biggest name in Rosebud at the moment, and Jerry, the manager, will be pissed if she can't instantly accommodate him.

"We're a little busy now," Phoebe says lightly, signaling for Melissa to help pacify the grumbling customers. "Gimme a sec, and I'll get you set up in our garden area."

"Awesome. What's your name, honey?" He continues before she can answer. "You must be new; I know all the hot girls here."

Phoebe smiles, doesn't mention she's seated him twice in the past year, each time without a reservation.

Busboys install a makeshift table in the restaurant's garden—prime real estate that remains out of paparazzi range while still boasting a view of the Hollywood sign. A four-top and a six-top have to be repositioned, customers midway through meals suddenly crammed into spaces far too small to adequately maneuver a knife and fork. Luckily, both tables are groups of tourists excited all the stories about Rosebud in the guidebooks are right—*the stars do eat here!*

Fifteen minutes later Melissa returns from seating a studio head outside and hands Phoebe a glass of criminally overpriced champagne.

"From Mr. James." Melissa rolls her eyes conspiratorially, but there's also an edge of jealousy. With long blond hair and an intense suntan, Melissa is the opposite flavor of Phoebe (if choices are limited to attractive, white would-be actresses). "He wants you to join him in a toast."

Returning the eye roll, Phoebe takes a sip, though it's strictly against Rosebud policy to drink on the clock. Weaving her way through the obstacle course of tables, plants, and people, she feels excitement build in her throat, decides she should give Jake her number when he asks, even though all the tabloids say he's a prick and still dating that redheaded pop tart who sings "Chasing Nothing," even though Phoebe kind of wishes Adam wouldn't want her to.

Jake waves her over and takes her hand while the tourists and regulars all stare.

"I know you used a little magic to get us out here, so thank you," he says, then raises his glass. The guys at his table follow. "To indecision."

As they clink flutes, she's starting to think he might not be the cad he's always made out to be, then he leans in, whispers in her ear, "Downstairs men's room. Second stall, five minutes."

It's not as though she has to go. Jerry may take care of celebrities, but that doesn't include whoring out unwilling staff. And boning Jake James probably won't help her career—a lesson she's learned over and over in the seven years she's been in LA. But on the off chance it might . . . she's slept with worse for less.

Which is how she ends up in the semisecret basement bathroom, back pressed against a stall divider while the actor who saved countless worlds in the *Eons & Empires* movies jacks his fairly unformidable penis and squeezes her left breast so hard she worries the implant might pop.

When she was eight, she'd crashed her bike and needed fifteen stitches in her calf. Watching the doctor sew her up was disturbing, and she twitched and screamed until her father told her to imagine the whole family at Disney World. Before she knew it, the doctor was finished. Over the past seventeen years, the fantasy has morphed from Chase and her on the Dumbo ride to Oliver and her in her high school bedroom, but the idea is still the same.

She checks back in with her body just in time to avoid getting jizz on her thigh when Jake James finishes. He stops panting long enough to kiss her neck.

"Rock and roll, right?" he says. She can't imagine there's a required response, wonders if she's hit some rock bottom of starfuckery.

In a startlingly chivalrous move considering what's just happened, Jake stands guard at the door while she reassembles herself, then checks the hallway to make sure the path is clear. As little more than one boob was involved in the whole shebang, a quick yank to straighten her dress is all it takes to be presentable and back at the hostess stand.

"Soooo?" Melissa asks, and for a breath-catching second, Phoebe worries someone saw them in the bathroom. "Did you give him your digits?"

"He didn't ask."

And Jake James continues not to ask, doesn't even say good-bye when his group slithers out the famous door to a waiting SUV an hour later.

They're so slammed, Phoebe doesn't understand that Jake's toast was about the presidential race until after 1:00 A.M., when she and Melissa are sitting on bar stools, sipping Texas Tea, aching feet discreetly slipped out of high heels.

"Your hottie roommate coming?" Melissa asks.

"Probably not," Phoebe says; the mention of Adam is a rabbit punch, even if her five minutes in the bathroom with Jake James was hardly a

betrayal. Before he decided a better use of his time was screaming at the
TV, Adam had tiptoed back in plenty of mornings smelling of sex and
another woman's perfume—even *after* he booked *Goners* and he and
Phoebe started sleeping together. "He's really into this election."

"Bummer," Melissa says.

In terms of hours logged, Melissa is probably Phoebe's best friend in the
city. Hired by Jerry on the same rainy Thursday two years earlier, they've
double-teamed through horrible shifts, covered for each other so they
could make auditions, and danced with Burke at every gay club in West
Hollywood. And yet Phoebe had never mentioned when she started
hooking up with Adam and isn't about to bring it up now. But she finds
herself thinking about her long-ago life in Chicago, of Evie and Nicole, of
her brother making sure that her dates were good guys.

It's after 3:00 A.M. by the time Phoebe is fumbling with her lock, hands
fat and dumbed by the dull sick that comes from hovering on the brink of
drunk. On the other side of the door, Tom Brokaw is on the TV offering
commentary, and Adam is talking back.

"Thiz—iz my fault," Adam slurs, standing less than a foot from the
screen. He waves a drunken finger at her. "I'm from Florida, should've
staaaaayed." Then he adds a variation on his mantra since the network said
they were no longer considering *Goners* as even a midseason replacement.
"Not like I wazzz doing anything here."

He's in the same clothes, though there's no evidence he made it to
the gym. Eyes half closed, he sways, catches himself on Brokaw's two-
dimensional chin. If she *was* his girlfriend, Phoebe would probably be
required to deliver a lecture, but she rents, doesn't own.

"Your one vote would have changed everything?" In a few hours she'll
understand this is oddly close to the truth.

"Thaz right."

Spinning on the toe of the expensive running shoes he'd gotten with a
bit of the *Goners* money, Adam staggers to the hall closet and removes his
not unformidable penis from his pants. Phoebe quickly grabs his arm and
leads him to the bathroom, where he recognizes the toilet and continues.

Not trusting his aim or stability, she leans against the sink, watches his clear ninety-proof spray into the bowl.

Turning toward her, he offers the goofy version of his kilowatt smile, asks, "Wanna hold it?" The hand on his dick follows his eyes, and she jumps to avoid the arc of urine.

"Adam!"

A repentant bad puppy, he bows his head to the task at hand, offers rambling apologies. Even after he's retucked, he doesn't look at her, and she feels guilty for snapping.

"It's okay." She forces a laugh. "I've got good reflexes."

"No, iz not okay. I . . ." Adam's still not looking at her, but lays one hand on her shoulder, the other against the tile wall for support. He ducks so his forehead touches hers, and she feels blood pulsing through him where their skin meets. A bead of his sweat skis down her cheek, tastes like alcohol.

Phoebe had been hesitant to let Adam move in when her old roommate packed up and went back to Iowa. She knew Adam wanted to sleep with her and figured that if they were living together, they might get drunk or bored and things would end badly (he'd already boned half the girls in their acting class). But when he booked the *Goners* pilot and they actually *did* hook up, it had been nothing like that at all. Adam's agent had called with the news, and when he'd gotten off the phone Adam had looked beatific, so otherworldly happy, that Phoebe couldn't *not* touch him.

"Phoebe," he says with something that sounds like gravitas. Maybe now he's going to apologize for the way he's been for the past few weeks, acknowledge he's lucky to have her. Maybe tell her he wants to give them a real try as a couple. Or not, tell her he wants to go back to being friends.

Nope, he's going to fall into her.

He's too thin and a good two inches shorter than the six one his head shots claim, but it's still 165 pounds of deadweight boy suddenly in her charge, and she stumbles against the wall.

"Adam, come on," she says, shaking him back to consciousness.

And she wants to tell him he can't do this, not because she wants to be his girlfriend, but because she read the *Goners* script and it was shit—he deserves better than an asinine frat-boy character making PMS and date-rape jokes. Because it's one dumb setback and he's so close (so much closer than she's ever been), and so many untalented people make it, all the truly gifted ones who keep trying *have* to. Because before he walked into Thetta Tunney's workshop buzzing with the kind of commanding energy that felled trees and whistled teakettles (the kind that Jake James mustered to get her into that bathroom), she'd forgotten a lot of things, had started believing she'd come to California to seat starlets, go on dates with cheesy millionaires and washed-up actors, and irk her cardiologist father by not enrolling—even part-time—in one of the many area schools. Because when she and Adam put up their scene from *Cat on a Hot Tin Roof* in class, he was so good it made her better, made her remember why she was enduring the city's smog and traffic in the first place.

Of course she can't say any of this now. So she oversees the unsteady mission to his bed, pulls off his shoes, and flops down beside him. As she plays with Adam's sandy hair, the last thing she hears before falling asleep is Katie Couric's cheery voice on the *Today Show* three hours ahead in New York. "Good morning, America. We still don't have a winner."

The country hasn't elected a president and Phoebe hasn't decided about Thanksgiving a week later when she nearly trips over Jake James outside the Dan Tana's restrooms after puking up fifty dollars worth of meat.

"We meet again." Jake smiles, and Phoebe can tell he has absolutely no idea who she is or why he knows her. After exchanging pleasantries, she leaves him to ponder and goes back to her date—an entertainment lawyer she met at Rosebud who's polite enough to stand when he sees her approaching their table.

Lawyer is a bit on the quiet side, but she's always been good at drawing people out, at getting them to talk, and soon she has him chatting about his work, joking about his high-maintenance clients. Lawyer asks softball questions—where she's from, her family, and career. She talks about the print work and the industrial films, the local television commercials, and the Dannon spots five years ago that had seemed the gateway to something bigger but never amounted to anything more than six months of royalty checks.

"So do you think we'll have elected a president by January?" she asks during a lull in the conversation. "Maybe we were just given two crappy choices."

Inching his hand closer to hers, he agrees. "Isn't that so often the case?"

Another bottle of wine, drinks at a nearby bar, and Lawyer takes her hand as the valet brings around his silver Maserati. He waits until they're on Santa Monica Boulevard before asking her if she'd like to check out the amazing view at his place.

"I'm sure it's stunning," she says, "but I can't sleep with you tonight."

"I didn't mean to imply . . ." He looks stricken she made that assumption, takes the turn onto Sunset toward her apartment. "I . . ."

"You don't have to apologize." Unhooking her seat belt, she slithers across the console to his lap, tells him to pull over, which he does without question.

If she *really* liked Lawyer or planned to see him again, Phoebe would start by unbuttoning his shirt, then lick circles around each nipple, travel down his stomach, spend a good few minutes teasing his inner thighs with her breath until he squirmed and moaned. She doesn't plan on seeing him again, but he seems a fundamentally decent man, and she's encountered so many less-than-decent men since moving to LA. Men who pushed her head into their crotches or dropped pills in her drinks. Strong men who got rough. Drunken men who probably thought the sex was more consensual than it was. Lawyer isn't one of those men, and he deserves a reward for that. So for him she does this: runs her fingers down the shaft of his cock, tongues the head, swallows him down. The gearshift pokes her hip, and his grasp on her hair borders on pain, but Lawyer doesn't take long, remembers her name when he comes.

"Oh, Phoebe." Shuddering, he strokes her cheek. "Sweet, sweet girl."

His semen in her mouth is powdery bland as he drives her home. She wonders if he tastes it when she kisses him good night.

Blue light from the TV flickering across his face, Adam is still boneless on the couch when Phoebe gets in after midnight; the tinge of unwarranted guilt.

"Do we have a president yet?" She leans on the doorjamb to pull off her shoes.

"Your lipstick's smeared." He's so nonchalant he could be telling her he changed a lightbulb. "Silver Maserati get lucky on the first date?"

"Do you care?" No anger, she actually wants to know, is *desperate* to know.

He turns back to the screen. She follows, reads the ticker scrolling along the bottom: FLORIDA SECRETARY OF STATE KATHERINE HARRIS ANNOUNCES BUSH LEADS GORE BY 300 VOTES.

Thinking Adam won't answer, Phoebe starts toward her bedroom, stops when she hears him stand.

"I used to," he says evenly. A half-full bottle of Corona is on the coffee table, but his eyes are sharp. He isn't drunk, isn't high. "Not so much lately."

"Because you don't care about anything? *Goners* didn't go, so nothing will ever matter again?"

"Things like you?" Voice hemorrhaging sarcasm, he's next to her—too close, really—she can smell her lavender body wash on his skin spiked with sweat. "Because what we had was *sooo* meaningful?"

"Whatever, go back to your pity party."

She actually feels the change in temperature as his pupils narrow.

"Poor, poor Princess Phoebe," he says with a venom she's only heard once, in their scene from *Cat on a Hot Tin Roof*, his Brick berating her Maggie, smoldering yet calm. "I apologize. I realize I haven't been telling you how beautiful, how fucking special you are. Aphrodite herself, rising on the half shell."

She remembers Adam's mother's visit, how Anna Zoellner mentioned her son had been a National Merit Scholar and gotten a full ride to college, remembers Adam is smarter than she is.

"Frankly, I thought I'd earned a reprieve," he continues. "Thought maybe some other poor bastard could pick up the slack. But I was wrong. I'm not allowed to be upset about *my* life, because you need your favorite toy."

"I know you've had a rough couple of weeks—"

"No, I don't think you understand, *princess*. This is all I've got. I don't have the option of shilling yogurt or marrying well because I'm so very, very pretty—practically perfect since the new nose and fake tits." He taps the bridge of her nose, pulls his finger back before she swats it away. "People don't just give me things on the off chance I might sleep with them."

"Says the great wandering womanizer. Stop."

"You should be an escort; it would be more honest."

The terrifying thing that will haunt her is that this moment, with her blood furious and heart in hyperdrive, could go either way. Sure, she wants to slug him. But she also wants to slam him to the wall and devour his mouth, wrap her legs around his hips and carve hieroglyphics in his back with her nails while he fucks her.

Her palm stings after she slaps him.

His hand balls into a fist. For a fractured second that's more interesting than scary, Phoebe thinks he's going to hit back, channel all that energy into a weapon, wonders what it would feel like to have her nose broken again, this time without anesthetic.

But he's still Adam, taught by his grandparents to call people "sir" and "ma' am," to hold doors open, say "please" and "thank you," and never, ever contemplate striking a woman.

Not physically at least.

Exhaling something between a laugh and a sigh, he unclenches his fist and runs fingers through his hair—a gesture she knows means he's stressed. Under the pink of her handprint, he's ashen, purple half-moons beneath his eyes; she's about to apologize.

"You'd never actually need to be an escort, though, would'ya, *princess*?" he says, placid and deadly. "Wouldn't it save everyone a lot of hassle if we admitted your daddy is the one I actually owe two months' rent?"

Tears stinging her sinuses, she's in her room, door shuttered, before he can say anything else.

A smash.

Peeping through the gap in the door hinges, she notes there's a hole in the living room wall and Adam is muttering, shaking his hand. It looks like it hurts; she hopes it does.

According to the Rolex her dad and Gennifer gave her for graduation, it's ten past four, six in Chicago. She catches her father before he leaves for his daily jog.

"It's a little early out there," he says. "Everything okay, princess?"

Poor, poor Princess Phoebe.

"I was just missing you guys." She tries to sound normal. "Can I come home for Thanksgiving?"

The next morning (noon, really) there's still a hole in the wall, but the entire apartment has been scrubbed, scoured, and swept. Shoes she kicks off in the living room (all those fancy high-heeled sandals she can afford because her father still supplements her income) neatly lining the wall outside her bedroom.

Though he's not in it, Adam's room, too, has been cleaned, mounds of dirty clothes and wrinkled issues of *Variety* gone. The only thing not filed or folded away is a new box of résumé paper and a cartridge of printer ink on the slim desk by the window. Laundry detergent smell as she sits on his bed and picks up a framed photograph from the nightstand—Adam and his mother at the base of the hills, the Hollywood sign in the background too iconic to be real. Phoebe had taken the picture and gotten it framed for Adam's birthday.

After he filmed *Goners*, Adam had paid for his mother to come to LA and then slept on the couch for a week so she could have his bed (a completely alien notion to Phoebe, whose own parents would never contemplate staying anywhere less than a four-star hotel when they visited). Worn and achingly beautiful, Anna Zoellner looked a decade older than Phoebe's mom despite being ten years younger. Every aspect of Anna had fascinated Phoebe—from the mystery of Adam's father ("I've never met him," the only thing Adam ever said on the subject) to the fact that Anna brought Proust's *Remembrance of Things Past* to the beach—it was intangible, a lesson locked in the lines around Anna's eyes and the white threads in her raven hair, how looks and intelligence apparently didn't guarantee shit. So Phoebe had tagged along when Adam took his mother to all the touristy places—the Walk of Fame and Santa Monica Pier—places Phoebe hadn't been since Oliver drove out with her after high school. As she was leaving for the airport, Anna hugged Phoebe, whispered in her ear, "Take care of my baby." Phoebe had to swallow back tears; it was the first time in twenty-five years anyone trusted her to do anything more important than look pretty.

What a fabulous job she's doing.

Adam isn't home by the time Phoebe leaves for work. Not there when she returns nine hours later, feet knotted, dress stained with spilled soda. But the hole in the wall has been plastered, a slight discoloration the only in-dication anything ever happened. That's been painted when she gets home the next night, and there's a bowl of the pears she likes on the kitchen counter with a note advising her to help herself. Adam's door is closed, lights out. Pressing her palm to the paneled wood, she can't decide if he's snoring or not.

Phoebe doesn't actually see Adam again until the next afternoon, when she catches a glimpse of him leaving the bathroom, towel around his waist. She doesn't talk to him until the day after that, when he calls Rose-bud at the start of her shift. Melissa hands her the phone.

"Sorry to bother you at work." He sounds normal, if a bit hesitant. "Your friend Evie called and said she needs to know about a reservation on Wednesday night. She made it sound important, so I thought you might want to call her back before you got slammed."

Next to Phoebe, Melissa mouths, "Invite him here."

"Oh, thanks." Phoebe lowers her eyes, as if he were in front of her and she couldn't look at him. "I, um, I'm going home for Thanksgiving, and my high school friends are planning this dinner."

"When's your flight?"

"The red-eye Tuesday night."

"I'll take you to the airport," he says.

To get him off the phone, she agrees, and then avoids him for the next three days.

Tuesday Phoebe ignores a note on the refrigerator from Adam reminding her he'll take her to the airport, and then nurses a latte at Peet's Coffee until it is actually time to leave. At the apartment, she grabs her bag, calls a car, then doubles back to Adam's room, hesitates before entering the half-open door. Clearly he hadn't meant to fall asleep, pretzeled in a torturous angle on his still-made bed, a few copies of his résumé—not the one with his acting credits but the one he uses for temp agencies—littering the com-forter. She wants to slink out without saying good-bye, or maybe write a note—something benign and cowardly: *Have a good weekend!*

Instead Phoebe runs her fingers along his forehead. He jerks and makes a small, helpless sound that purees her major organs.

"What time is it?" Propping himself on an elbow, he blinks away eye gunk.

"Ten fifteen."

"Oh." Sitting up, he takes in Phoebe's jeans and hoodie, duffel bag over her shoulder. "Lemme get my shoes and I'll take you."

"I got a cab," she says and watches his face fall. Something in her heart catches, and she wonders how they got into this horrible place of unclear outcomes. "It's on the way."

"That's silly." On his feet now, grabbing a sneaker. "I'll drive—"

"It's not a big deal." She sighs. "You know me, I'll put it on my dad's credit card anyway. I just wanted to wish you a happy Thanksgiving."

Outside, a horn.

Adam follows her to the living room, holds her arm.

"Wait." His eyes blazing into her, she wants to look away. "I'm sorry."

She starts to say the taxi is easier, but they both know that's not what he's talking about.

Phoebe should say she's sorry, too, but she's unclear what to apologize for. For slapping him? Blowing Lawyer? Jake James in the men's room? For occasionally pretending Adam is Oliver, not during sex, really, but when she lay in his arms afterward—fantasizing that Adam feels about her the way Oliver did? For not keeping her promise to his mother?

"No worries." On tiptoes, she brushes lips across his brow because saying anything else might cause Adam to look sadder than he already does, and she feels like she's having an asthma attack, needs to get outside and into Adam-free air immediately.

"At least let me carry your stuff—"

She waves his hand away. "It's really light."

"Well, call to let me know you got in okay."

It's a weird echo of what her father always says as he drops her at O'Hare, of what she asked Oliver to do seven years ago when he headed back to Chicago for school. But no one calls to say they got in all right; the reason to call would be *not* getting in okay.

"Yeah. I'll try you later."

She actually does want to call Adam almost immediately after landing at eight in the morning, when she bumbles off the jetway to find not her father or Gennifer waiting at the gate, but her brother. Though it takes her a few seconds to recognize Chase. He's shaved the goatee that had been a permanent fixture since he started at the University of Wisconsin five years ago, and instead of his usual ironic T-shirts—Oscar the Grouch or bald and menacing Captain Rowen—he's wearing tailored slacks and a jacket she's almost certain is Prada.

"Where's Dad?" She sounds accusatory, and Chase grins, universes older than she remembers, as if six months at a New York investment bank has turned him into her senior.

"We were already up for our run, and I never get to drive anymore."

The "we" stops everything. Busy contemplating new Prada/professional Chase, Phoebe hadn't noticed the brunette next to him in a smart leather trench coat, pantyhose, and stacked heels no less than five inches high.

"Sharon Gallaher, only one G," says the woman. "It's great to finally meet you. I've heard so many stories."

Yes, a few weeks ago (or was it months; time in her vampire life is nebulous), Chase had mentioned he was dating someone, but he was always dating someone—usually a blond someone—and he'd never brought any of the someones home before.

"You're even more luminous than in the Dannon commercials." Sharon is still talking. Despite the grown-up clothes (early in the morning on a day no one works), she's probably not more than twenty-three, cheeks round and dewy in a way that's never natural past twenty-five. "I love the bob."

Unconsciously, Phoebe's fingers go to the blunt edge of her hair. Sharon sounds sincere, which isn't always the case; shards of blame are often tucked into compliments from other women.

"It's really short," her brother says, sounding almost clueless enough to be pre–Wall Street Chase Fisher.

Although as kids they could communicate whole schemes behind their parents' backs using nothing more than eyebrows, when Phoebe tries meeting her brother's gaze to ask who this girl is, Chase offers no explanation, just takes Phoebe's bag and throws it over his shoulder. And she remembers all the messages she didn't return because she was so caught up in her non-relationship with Adam. All those things that she could never tell her brother because he'd been protective of her long before there was anything to protect her from.

"You ready?" Chase frowns. "Did you not bring a coat?"

And in case there was any doubt, it socks her in the gut—like the frozen Chicago air will a few minutes later—that she's not in LA anymore.

In the breakfast nook three hours later, Gennifer is clearing platters of bagels, whitefish, and sturgeon that cloyingly thoughtful Sharon brought from New York; Phoebe's father and brother are beaming at Sharon's election analysis; and Phoebe is staring into her coffee mug as if it contains vital information.

"Florida aside, Gore should've had this in the bag," Sharon says, still in the heels. After extensive contemplation, Phoebe determines that Sharon's round face is pleasant but forgettable, save for killer Columbia-blue eyes about 15 percent larger than normal. Phoebe's not sure if she doesn't like Sharon for real or simply because the girl is dating her baby brother—flash of Chase following her and Oliver around on their first date.

"The problem was that he separated himself too much from Clinton." Sharon is still talking. "Monica, Whitewater—people still love Bill Clinton."

Having watched Adam watch CNN for the past three weeks, Phoebe could jump in at several points in the conversation but doubts anyone would hear. It turns out being ignored by her family might be more hurtful than being pitied for not having a career and living with a too-polite aspiring actor.

Phoebe learns, mostly through Chase's glowing recaps, that he and Sharon met at a wash-and-fold in the West Village, where he wooed her by carrying her laundry bag up four flights to her apartment. Sharon had graduated from NYU a year early, majoring in English and something called American Studies, and now she's working on a master's in creative writing. She is, in fact, twenty-two, which would have made her a freshman when Adam was a senior. Phoebe has no desire to ask if they knew each other.

"Have you been to Chicago before?" Phoebe asks when everyone else has stopped talking about Al Gore and she hasn't said anything in a really long time.

"Oh, yeah." Sharon nods. "I grew up in Cincinnati, and we came here a lot. I *adore* Chicago."

"Sharon's setting her novel here," Chase offers, unsolicited.

"Umm-hmm, I *adore* the architecture; it's the perfect backdrop for the story I want to tell," Sharon says, and quick as that, any thought that Phoebe's hair clog of dislike for this girl was unwarranted slides down the drain.

"You're writing a novel?" Phoebe's father sounds intrigued, not likely to tell Sharon it's a idiotic pipe dream and ask if her father sends her checks, too.

"She's published a bunch of short stories and is considered the best in her program," Chase is saying as Sharon blushes, the color lovely on full cheeks.

"How exciting. Where can we read them?" Gennifer, who had also sat out the political portion of the conversation, is back in her comfort zone. "I read everything."

"Do you write from your own experience or make it up?" Phoebe's father, who has never once asked if Phoebe is a method actor, never coordinated a West Coast trip to see one of her workshop showcases.

Right then Phoebe decides she'll never take another cent from her father. When she gets back to LA, she'll demand they promote her to bartender at Rosebud, or she'll get a second job or sell some of her shoes.

Before Sharon can explain how she spins words into poetry and poop into gold, Phoebe puts her coffee cup in the sink, says she's going to take a nap.

"Aww, you must be tired." Gennifer loops toned arms around Phoebe, her absurd mane of hair tickling Phoebe's nose.

"You feel okay, princess?" Her father looks up, bushy eyebrows pup tents of concern.

"I'm fine." Sullen and childish perhaps, but physically tip-top. "Something about planes wears me out."

"I was going to show Sharon around Evanston a little later if you wanna come," Chase says.

"Yeah, maybe," Phoebe says, though the thought of tagging around as her brother and Sharon cuddle and coo is slightly sickening.

Satisfied, everyone nods and returns to Sharon and Chase and their fabulous life in Manhattan as Phoebe heads up the stairs.

It would be wrong to call Phoebe's room her childhood bedroom because she really only lived there full-time for a year. It *does* look exactly the way she left it seven years ago. Framed photos of her and Oliver at prom, her long hair whipped into an updo with side curls. With Nicole and Evie on Santa's lap at Old Orchard Mall, aware of without fully understanding the power of their sex—three good-looking teens playing little girls, wiggling on a grown man's lap. Phoebe and Chase visiting their mother in Hawaii, everyone wearing leis and looking unhappy.

It's barely 9:00 A.M. in Los Angeles, but Phoebe calls her apartment.

"You've reached Phoebe Fisher and Adam Zoellner. We can't come to the phone right now, but if you leave a message, we'll return your call as soon as possible." Her voice on the machine is an octave lower than normal and official sounding, in case the caller is an agent or casting director or someone else of importance.

"Hey, Z," Phoebe says, even though she never calls Adam "Z." That's a nickname used by guys on his softball team and girls he remains friendly with after sex. "Wanted to let you know I got in. Give me a ring when you can."

The television on her dresser still has cable, and she turns to CNN. As she's falling asleep, she sees, not without satisfaction, that Sharon was actually wrong about the date the Florida court set to certify election results.

When she wakes up, VP candidate Dick Cheney has apparently been taken to the hospital with chest pains, and the sun is already setting just after five.

Across the street, lights are on in every room of Evie's parents' house. Dinner isn't until seven, but she can go over a little early. Scalding shower, another short black dress, and heels as high as Sharon's but much less sensible, with an open toe. Hair so shiny it appears metallic, bronzer dusted across fine bones, lips the deep sangria that's become her signature. It's enough that her parents, Chase, and Sharon all stop watching the news when she comes downstairs. The finished product is somewhat compromised when Gennifer insists Phoebe wear her fur-trimmed puffy coat because it's thirty degrees outside and Phoebe forgot her own jacket.

"Let us know if you go out somewhere after dinner," Chase says. "Shar and I might join you for a drink."

Phoebe nods, and Gennifer walks her to the door, gives her another hug, somehow more motherly now, when the fourteen years between them should barely be significant. "It's good you're seeing the girls," she says. "You three were so close in high school."

"Phoebe *Fucking* Fisher." Evie has inexplicably acquired a slightly British accent despite moving to Manhattan after graduating from Bennington. She gives a double European cheek kiss to hammer home this point before taking Phoebe/Gennifer's coat. "You're so thin! Please don't tell me you've become one of those ano LA bitches."

"Nope, I'm good," Phoebe somehow manages with a straight face.

"Your boobs look amazing." Evie looks as if she might grab one.

"I had a good doctor." This may or may not be true, but unlike her rhinoplasty, Phoebe did *not* use a friend of her father.

"You didn't go too big, that's the key. Everyone in my industry goes too big."

Evie does PR for a record label and often sends packages of unlistenable CDs; Phoebe can't recall any specifics about artists' breast sizes. Evie's hair is the same shocking maroon it was when they were bridesmaids at Nicole's wedding two summers ago, when Nicole kept bemoaning how dumb it would look in the pictures. But Evie's hair doesn't look silly anymore. With ebony eyeliner and her own short black dress, it works, and Phoebe feels young and old and out of place again.

"Thank *God* you're finally here," Evie continues. "I've been back three days, and I'm not sure I'll last the week without killing Nic—wait till you see her; she looks like she ate Dick Cheney. And I'll bet you a doughnut she never goes back to work once she has the kid."

"I'll pass on that bet."

They sit on a couch in the sunken living room Evie's mother has re-done four times in ten years. Currently it's beige with burgundy accents and goes perfectly with Evie's hair. Bending forward as if someone might be eavesdropping, Evie says that yesterday she saw Chase getting the mail. "That boy grew up mighty nice."

"He's in New York now." Phoebe shrugs, making no reference to Sharon or their potential post-dinner drink.

"Reeeeeeee-allly."

Evie's mother shuffles in, says hello, and tells Phoebe she's gorgeous. "So everyone still talks about the yogurt commercials." Evie's mother can't stop staring at Phoebe's boobs. "What are you doing next?"

Wanna hold it? Sweet, sweet girl. Rock and roll, right? You should be an escort.

Phoebe forces a smile. "I've got a lot of balls in the air."

By the time Phoebe parks her father's sedan in a downtown garage and she and Evie walk three blocks to the restaurant, they're late, and Nicole is already at a banquette in the back (apparently this hostess doesn't know not to seat incomplete parties). In an Empire-line dress, Nicole does indeed look as though she might have eaten Dick Cheney, but other than the massive stomach, she's the same elfin person she's always been. She presses her lips into the same condescending look she's always given—as usual, directed more toward Evie.

"You *live* downtown." Evie rolls her eyes, and they could be back at ETHS. "Pheebs and I had to trek all the way from Planet Evanston."

The once-and-future feeling continues as Evie picks a bottle of wine from the list, ignoring Nicole's protest that she can't drink. Someone orders an artichoke Parmesan dip that probably contains a week's worth of fat. Phoebe doesn't partake but keeps a tortilla chip in hand, lest Evie accuse her of being anorexic again.

"Pheebs's brother is bangin' and in New York and she's going to set us up." Evie breaks a chip in half so she can double scoop.

"For real?" Nicole bumps Evie's shoulder. "You'd eat Chase alive in a week, E."

"Bitch," Evie says, but she's smirking, likes that they acknowledge she's all steel and sharp points, the girl she always wanted to be back in high school.

And really Nicole, too, is likely the kind of person she'd hoped to become. She may have graduated top of her class at University of Chicago Law, but the fact that she married Dave and is well on her way to leaving a job at the city's top litigation firm to change diapers really wouldn't shock anyone from school.

"So who are you fucking these days?" Evie turns to Phoebe.

"E!" Nicole says.

"Come on, you want to know as badly as I do. You get off on our *Sex and the City* stories."

"I do." Nicole smiles in a way that's warm and inviting and makes Phoebe want to hop a plane back to her dysfunctional Southern California life as soon as possible. "*Are* you dating anyone famous, Pheebs?"

"It's not like that," Phoebe says, but because Nicole looks thoroughly disappointed and is growing a human being, she adds, "Jake James bought me a glass of champagne the other day."

"*No!*" Nicole.

"The good stuff?" Evie.

"Cristal." Phoebe allows herself a grin.

"*We* should get champagne." Evie flags down a waiter as Nicole explains, again, pregnant women can't have alcohol.

Evie and Phoebe are finishing off a bottle of sparkling wine that's decidedly *not* Cristal when Dave arrives to take Nicole home. In the years since the wedding, he's chunked up considerably and has to be the only twenty-six-year-old in the Chicagoland area with a receding hairline; by the time he's a doctor, he'll be completely bald.

Hugging Phoebe and Evie, Dave sighs as if genuinely content. "It's good to see the witches of Evanston together again," he says.

Maybe it's the half bottle of not-Cristal, but Phoebe's choked up as she watches Dave help Nicole into her coat. And she wonders what would have happened if she hadn't stopped returning Oliver's phone calls her first year in LA. Would her life mirror Nicole and Dave's? Would she and Oliver have a town house in the up-and-coming West Loop?

After Phoebe makes her post-meal bathroom trip, Evie suggests the two of them grab a drink at the Leg Room; it seems as good a plan as any. There's a crowd of assholey-looking guys at the door, but the bouncer quickly ushers Phoebe and Evie through the velvet rope. Inside it's not even crowded, and they commandeer a red velvet chaise longue, blow off more assholey guys, and sip martinis equally as overpriced as those in LA and Manhattan. Phoebe talks about her auditions, and Evie says she wants to move to California, handle PR for people who actually want to be famous instead of mopey emo musicians. "Of course I'll give you a discount on my services," she says, nudging her shoulder to Phoebe's.

"I still can't afford you."

"It would be a really big dis—" Evie cocks her head toward a table in the corner. "Is that Braden *Fucking* Washington?"

Still built like an underwear model, Braden it *is*, and Phoebe's heart bounces in her chest. She's here with Evie, so maybe . . .

Then Oliver is next to her with different black glasses and the same strong jaw.

"Hey, Phee," he says. "Long time, no see."

Three hours later, Evie and Braden have split a cab home, the bartender has announced last call, and Phoebe and Oliver have told each other everything and nothing about their lives (Phoebe leaving out things like shagging Adam and bad bathroom romps with past-their-prime famous people).

Oliver offers to drive her home, and she turns over the keys to her father's car, despite being completely sober. Too soon, the ride ends, and she invites him in like she's seventeen again.

Leaving the lights off, she brings him upstairs to her old bedroom, hand in hand, and wiggles free of Gennifer's puffy coat while trying not to abandon contact. The sun is already rising, so it's bright enough that she can read a Post-it note on the nightstand in Chase's aggressive handwriting: *Adam called twice, said to call back when you get in.* She sets Oliver's leather jacket directly on top of the message, and they sit on the canopy bed she'd wanted so badly as a child.

In hushed voices, they talk more about everything and nothing until they stop, and he takes off his glasses.

"I don't know what to say, Ollie," she begins as he leans in to kiss her. "Something happened, and after a while, I thought you would hate me."

"Shhhh." He runs a finger along her throat. "Things happen; I could never hate you."

That is another bet she probably shouldn't take.

Phoebe finds herself on her back as Oliver Ryan unzips her dress for the first time in years. He dusts her neck with his lips, presses his legs against hers. She wonders if he'll say anything about her implants, but he doesn't. Licks each breast, wanders down her belly. Moves he didn't have when they were both virgins. With an irrational sting of jealousy, she wonders who taught him. When they're through, he covers her like a blanket, and she strokes his shoulder blades until she realizes he's asleep.

Maybe they wouldn't have been exactly like Nicole and Dave but perhaps like some other kind of couple who successfully transitioned from children to adults? There's a good chance Oliver would have transferred from Northwestern to UCLA or Cal Tech if she'd asked, if she'd returned his calls.

But she hadn't. Not when he left messages straining so hard to sound like his world wasn't splintering glass because she wasn't calling him back. Not when she finally changed her number so she wouldn't hear his voice on the machine on those evenings she'd come home feeling like used Kleenex after dates with those not so fundamentally decent men, or from auditions that weren't *really* auditions but men wafting promises in front of her in exchange for something else. Not when she came home drunk and sore, a wad of cash in her clutch making her wonder if she'd accidentally changed careers. On that night, she'd taken a pen and written Oliver's phone number on the underside of her wrist—like the numbers tattooed on her grandfather at Buchenwald—traced them until the ink smeared, but she still didn't call.

It's too warm in her bed, in Oliver's arms, and she should call Adam back.

Untangling herself, she goes downstairs, follows faint TV voices to the den where Sharon is on the couch. There's a stack of computer printouts on her lap—most likely her novel set in "adorable" Chicago.

"Jet-lagged, too?" Phoebe asks.

"Not really." Sharon politely sets the papers aside. "I get my best work done at night."

She's wearing a pair of Chase's boxers and one of his Mr. Bubble

T-shirts (a few must have survived her brother's Manhattan makeover). The heels are gone, and Sharon looks young and dopey in owl-like glasses that keep sliding down her nose. In a brief glance at Sharon's work, Phoebe spots two typos, which is inherently endearing. Phoebe can imagine her all-grown-up brother with *this* person, reading the paper or shouting out *The Price Is Right* answers like he used to do with Phoebe on snow days.

Sitting in the love seat, Phoebe gestures to the TV, where the same loop of never-ending election footage is still running. "What did I miss?"

"They're halting the Miami recount and something about dimpled chads. Oh yeah, and Dick Cheney had another heart attack."

"Good to know."

The images on screen change to Al and Tipper Gore alongside Bill and Hillary Clinton at the Democratic National Convention.

"It's funny the way that Tipper and Al are so ridiculously gaga about each other." Sharon pushes the glasses back up. "It's like the opposite of the Clintons. Like, he might make a crappy president, but I guarantee you, if Gore pulls this thing off, we won't have another Monica incident. That man *adores* his wife."

It occurs to Phoebe that the reason she stopped returning Oliver's calls wasn't that she hadn't loved him. She had. Loved that he knew how cameras and engines worked, the way he shoved his hands in his pockets when he was nervous, loved the splattering of freckles on his chest and the copper curls of his pubic hair. It was simply that she had also loved the promise of a different life, and it had seemed impossible that the two worlds could work together—incongruous to imagine coming home to Oliver after flirting (sometimes more than flirting) with casting directors for one-line parts or selling some form of sex at the restaurant. Impossible because she was no longer the girl who Oliver helped with physics, and she hadn't wanted him to discover that.

Adam, though, he understands those things. Understands her not really eating dinner to save the calories for alcohol or spending a year's worth of tips on breast augmentation. Understands dyeing her hair or learning Latin phrases for a part she's got no shot at but wants so bad she can feel it in the back of her throat. Adam knows what it's like to be told "no" so many times that the word becomes meaningless background noise—the whoosh of traffic from the 405.

"Honestly." Sharon is still talking. "Hillary will quietly leave Bill the minute he's out of office."

"No, she won't," Phoebe says with more force than intended. "He could screw a dozen more interns and she would stay."

Sharon looks at her with those killer eyes wide. "Why?"

Phoebe smiles, on sure footing for the first time in weeks. "She won't ever leave because she believes in him."

3 history of flight

It's after noon on Thanksgiving Day by the time Phoebe Fisher pulls into your driveway. Killing the engine of her father's car, Phoebe smiles at you not unlike the way she used to smile at you in high school—when you loved her so much it actually felt like an anvil on your chest when you had to go home (to this very same house) for the night.

"Ollie," she says.

"Phee."

And then you both laugh at the weird time warp you've tripped into.

"So yeah, I leave on Sunday," she says.

Even though that's three days away, you're fairly certain that the time warp ends here, that you won't be seeing her again this trip, maybe this decade.

Kissing her cheek, you tell her how glad you are to have run into her at the bar, and she says the same.

"Well, you know where to find me," she says, though that hasn't been the case for so very long. You were the one who was always easy to access, the one who stayed. For seven years you didn't know where to find her, and for a while you'd thought that might just kill you.

But seven years is a long time, and all of that hurt has eroded, so you don't call her on the irony; you simply nod.

You start to open the passenger side door, and she takes your hand briefly, smiles again, and lets it go. "Ollie, don't you ever get tired of that gray Chicago sky?"

Sure, you've seen other skies—visiting your mother's family in the east, a handful of trips to see Braden in Boulder, the one time you made it out to your sister's place in Salt Lake City. And of course, you spent a summer under Phoebe's California sky, the one all the songs are written about—but this has always been your home. Everyone else in your life had their various flight patterns in and out of Chicago, sometimes only leaving. Always, you stayed. And something about Phoebe's question ignites a small flame of anger and makes your whole interaction last night less bittersweet and more bitter.

Shaking your head, you open the door, tell her, "Take care of yourself, Phoebe."

Your father:

It can probably all be traced back to your father. Really, to the plane when you were seven.

Your dad was never around much—first as an Air Force captain, then as a pilot for United—and you used to think of him as a sort of superhero, zipping about the globe to save the world like Batman in the Bat-plane. Wherever he went, he brought you back T-shirts, wood toys, and snow globes, all obviously picked up last minute at some airport gift shop. This only strengthened the image of him trying to maintain his alter ego. When he was in town, he'd tussle your red hair, call you "champ."

But the day he took you up in his buddy's Piper Saratoga—a similar model to the one JFK Jr. would crash into the Atlantic eighteen years later—was the day everything changed.

"You're going to love this, Ollie," your father had said, taking your hand and leading you to the hangar. "It's the greatest feeling in the world."

For him it probably was. Your father was one of the world's few happy people who decide early in life what they want to do and actually go on to do it. It would be eleven years before you met Phoebe Fisher, ran your fingers down the inside of her thighs, and realized what the greatest feeling in the world *really* was.

"Are you excited?" your father asked, strapping you into the copilot seat.

You'd flown with your mother and sister to visit various relatives, and you hadn't liked it, but you knew the answer to your father's question was an enthusiastic "yes." Your mother hadn't been diagnosed with cancer at that point, but your father had given up on her and your older sister years before because they didn't love the sky the way he did. So you smiled against the whirling of the engine as the plane began its furious race on the runway, but at your sides, where your father couldn't see, you dug fingernails into the flesh of your palms, leaving half-moon indentations in your lifelines.

"This is it," your father said with finality as the plane broke through low clouds of thinly stretched cotton. "It's like birth, like being born."

Trying to hide your fear, you nodded. If he was Batman, maybe you could be his Robin.

"Come on, champ." Your father offered the controls, as if bestowing a great gift. "Give it a go."

Tentatively, you took the yoke, a strange W-shaped interface that felt far too cheap and plastic to have any real impact on your defiance of gravity. A bright kid, you suspected your father probably wasn't giving you a grave responsibility (seven-year-olds, you knew, were rarely placed in positions of grave responsibility). You figured it must have been like the old-fashioned cars you'd ridden in with Braden and his family the summer before at Great America, where there had been a steering wheel but the cars were on a track, their course determined without your actions. Still, you thought the plane began to plummet. Screaming, you threw your hands into the air like a girl, like your sister.

Your father easily took back the controls.

"Don't worry about it," he said, but after that he looked at you differently. You were not Robin to his Batman.

He wouldn't call you "champ" again for eleven years—not until your appendix ruptured and Phoebe Fisher and *her* father took you to Northwestern Memorial Hospital because your mother was dead, your sister was married in Utah, and your father was flying to Sydney and hadn't thought to leave any contact numbers. Phoebe called the airline to track him down, and when he finally got back to Evanston, he hovered over your hospital bed, guilt wrinkling his forehead.

"Don't worry about it," you said, words thick with morphine. And you thought you meant it, that you didn't care about his absences or opinions anymore—not with Phoebe down the hall.

But hidden away somewhere, all of that must have still mattered, because first semester of your engineering Ph.D. program you found yourself drawn to aeronautics research with a strange mix of guilt and excitement, like it was something taboo.

It must have still mattered, because three years after your appendectomy you heard about a little girl, Jessica Dubroff, who wanted to be the youngest person to fly across the United States. You were on the leather sofa in your father's house trying to file your taxes while your half sister, Natasha, napped in her playpen and your stepmother folded laundry on the floor, her thin shoulder brushing against your calf in a way that made you uncomfortable, even though nothing sexual had happened yet. Maura had the news on, but you weren't listening until you heard the phrase "child pilot."

"Would you look at that," Maura said to the TV. "She can't be more than eight."

Mid-calculation, you turned stony, eyes locked on the screen. The solar-powered calculator dimmed, but you didn't notice; you needed to see what a child pilot was *supposed* to look like.

There she was, a golden-haired girl in her Lilliputian bomber jacket and the baseball cap with WOMEN FLY printed across the top.

One of the reporters asked her if she was scared of crashing.

"Nothing is going to happen," Jessica said, smiling into the camera. "It's simply an airplane."

And you hated her in a way you hadn't hated anyone since you tried to drown Braden Washington in the community pool when you were a junior in high school.

"No, no," you said, forgetting about Maura, who looked up at you, head bent in confusion.

For the next two days, you devoured every media snippet about Jessica and her impending flight—you got on the Web and did a search for newspapers in her hometown and were glued to CNN, even though they played the same clip over and over. When twenty-four hours into her flight Jessica's plane crashed into a driveway near Cheyenne, Wyoming—killing all three people on board—you were inappropriately giddy. You felt you'd gained a greater understanding of the world, as if her crash confirmed a hypothesis you'd developed a long time ago. By then you were an honor roll student at Northwestern, but the plane crash was one of the few times you ever felt truly smart. It was the first time in years you wanted to talk to your father. To call him in whatever corner of the world he was temporarily located and say "I told you."

Your mother:

You never doubted that your mother loved you and did her best and all of those basic things, but it likely says a lot about your relationship that your clearest memory of her is the day she found the Neiman Marcus catalogs under your bed when you were thirteen. It was two years before she surrendered to cancer but months after the diagnosis, when she was already lying around waiting to die.

"Ollie," she called to you from the beige couches in the living room, when you got home from school. "Do you need new clothes?"

You were in a hurry. The Washingtons were taking you and Braden to see *The Princess Bride,* and you wanted to change, dump your books, and go back to Braden's house, where his mother, Alicia, smelled like heaven—garlic and lilacs—as she prepared dinner.

"New clothes?" you asked, walking through the hallway to the living room, the *Days of Our Lives* theme weeping in the background. "No, I don't think—"

And you stopped talking, stopped breathing, because on the couch your mother—not really fat but bunchy in the hips and thighs—was reading *Redbook* and wearing your old *Eons & Empires* hat with the *E&E* crest. She must have noticed the horror on your face.

"Is it okay that I'm wearing this?" She touched the brim.

"Sure," you said. But it wasn't really okay; you were pretty sure the hat had been under your bed along with the Neiman Marcus catalogs, where Alicia Washington modeled fur and sportswear. On nights when you couldn't sleep, you'd jerk off to the pictures of Braden's mom. "It looks good."

"Thank you." Your mother sat up a little. "I found these catalogs under your bed, and I was wondering if you needed school clothes."

There they were on the oak coffee table atop the pile of women's magazines and self-help books that your sister kept bringing her.

Staring at the department store's skinny regal font, you felt your face turn as red as your hair, and a bomb detonated in your lungs.

"Is everything all right?" she asked.

You didn't say anything because you didn't have the kind of relationship with your mother where you discussed things like that . . . ever.

It's not that you didn't love her, you just don't think about her on those Hallmark-card moments like Christmas and graduation—the times when your sister gets flubbery, holds your arm, whispers she wishes Mom were still around.

Instead, your mother's image came to you when you were eighteen and driving from Chicago to Southern California to help Phoebe Fisher move into a studio apartment in a not-so-great neighborhood south of Wilshire Boulevard. In one of those glorious Western states that's simply a colored box on the map, you stopped at a Cracker Barrel knockoff. Sliding into an orange vinyl booth (on the same side as Phoebe, because you were *that* kind of couple), you examined the gravy-stained menu. "Food like Mom used to make," it read.

Your mother's memory washed over you then—the smell of Chinese takeout and frozen pizza burning in the oven, scents that filled your house growing up.

"I'm thinking tuna melt," Phoebe said, her thigh—bare in short shorts—pressed against yours. "You?"

All at once you missed your mom so much your eyes blurred and you had to take off your glasses, rub the bridge of your nose.

"You okay?" Phoebe twisted her fingers together and pressed them to her chest.

And you were suddenly devastated that your mother never met Phoebe Fisher, wished you could have corked Phoebe in a bottle, hopped back in time, and shown her off—*This is my girl, Mom, isn't she great?*

———

Your older sister:

Your sister largely avoided you for the first thirteen years of your life, but when your mother got sick, Karen, three years older, became a great revisionist of history, framing the two of you as grand old chums. This meant doing things like taking you gym shoe shopping at Old Orchard Mall.

Over greasy waffle fries in the food court, she said you could tell her "anything." In a bed at Northwestern Memorial Hospital down the road, your mother was reading magazines and waiting to die, and your father was somewhere over Asia.

"And I do mean *anything*." Karen patted your hand across the table. She looked a little like your mother, only she was pretty, but that might have been nothing more than a combination of youth and aerobics classes. "Sex, drugs, whatever. I want you to know, I'm here for you, Ollie."

"Sure," you said, running a fry through a puddle of cheese sauce and ketchup. Never in a thousand years did you contemplate telling her about Alicia Washington and the catalogs you'd put back under your bed and still used some nights. "I'll keep that in mind."

Karen looked at you, amber eyes so wide and earnest, you felt guilty. It was clear that she was genuinely trying to help.

"I've been wondering about birth control," you finally said, even though you hadn't been. Braden had found his father's Trojans in the bathroom, and the two of you had examined them thoroughly, despite the fact that you hadn't even kissed a girl and wouldn't meet Phoebe Fisher for another four years. "What do you use?"

Lips curling into a knowing smile, Karen leaned even closer, the ends of her long red hair brushing your paper plate, said she'd wondered all about those things when she was your age.

"Mark and I waited to make love until I was sixteen, but I was really nervous about how the condom was to going to work," Karen began . . . and continued with stories about other boyfriends and blowjobs and a pregnancy scare.

It was way more information than you'd ever wanted, and was slightly creepy, but it was also the first real conversation you'd ever had with her, and it led to many more. When Karen left for college in Arizona eighteen months later, you were surprised by how much you missed her.

On Sunday nights she'd call and tell you about each new Mark or Ron or Bob and finally Gary, whom she married her junior year. You never told her about Braden trying to kiss you or Phoebe blowing raspberries on your stomach, certainly not about your stepmother, but it was still nice to have someone to talk to.

The day before your father and Maura's wedding, you picked Karen up at O'Hare. She'd left her baby girl with her husband in Salt Lake City, and when she hugged you, you felt the swell of baby number two.

"So this is nuts, right?" Karen began. "This woman is, like, young enough to be our sister."

You agreed, even though Maura was only ten years your father's junior. At forty she was twice your age at the time.

"Don't you think she's uncannily pale?" Karen asked. "It's like she's an albino or something."

Maura always seemed perfectly pleasant, but that obviously wasn't the response Karen was seeking. "She might be a vampire," you offered.

"I know, right?"

The luggage carousel jerked to life, and Karen asked about school. "I can't believe you didn't want to get out of Evanston; you couldn't have paid me to go to Northwestern."

Karen hadn't actually gotten into NU, but you didn't mention that, just explained again that they had a strong engineering program.

"And that girl never returned your calls?" Karen asked of Phoebe.

You shook your head. "How are Gary and Maxi?" you asked, bending over the rotating belt to pick up Karen's blue roller suitcase.

"You'd know if you ever came out to visit," she said.

Your best friend:

Braden Washington had been your best friend since Mrs. Stewart's kindergarten class, but by sophomore year of high school, the muscles in his chest and arms had swollen, and you occasionally hated the defined V of his torso, the girls who asked you if he liked them, and the Big Ten and Big East recruiters who had already contacted him about college football.

"Do I look any different?" he asked as the two of you stood in line for the high dive at the community pool. It was the summer before junior year (after your mother had finished her dying and your sister had started college in Arizona). Braden looked the same as always, almost goofily handsome, with his mother's perfect cocoa skin and mahogany hair.

"Why would you look different?" Even before the words were out of your mouth, you knew what he was going to say, and your lower body seemed to liquefy. Fifty yards away, Braden's girlfriend tanned with her friends. In a bikini of little more than strings and triangles, Josie was the quintessence of high school—blond with green eyes, a member of student council and the dance team. "You guys did it, didn't you?"

Braden flashed his aw-shucks grin, and a white-hot poker stabbed you between the eyes. It would be a year before you met Phoebe Fisher and got beyond first base.

Still, you must have said something a normal person who didn't abhor his best friend would have said, because the conversation continued. But all you could think about were the Neiman Marcus catalogs you still had under your bed.

Behind you, a pack of skinny, wet middle-school kids screamed that the two of you were holding up the line, so Braden started up the ladder.

"What should I do?" he asked.

You told him to do a back flip because you could do it better, and you needed to be superior at something.

Fisting your hands so tight your knuckles turned to white knobs, you held your breath and hoped Braden wouldn't be able to complete the dive. Still, you were utterly amazed when he twisted awkwardly around and crashed, almost completely prone, into the water. You were even more surprised when he didn't come up.

The lifeguard—a senior at your high school who constantly bragged about bedding the girl guards—stared on from his chair in disbelief, paralyzed by what to do in the face of an actual emergency. So you were the one who dove in. As you reached out for him, Braden's head bobbed up and broke the surface of the water. Gasping and thrashing, he looked at you and went under again. You grabbed his shoulders, broader and more filled out than yours.

Instead of pulling him up, you held him under. In your hands, his body jerked, and you felt a rush of excitement that you were really doing it. Chemically treated water filled your nose, your mouth, your ears.

One, maybe two seconds.

The pool was on an approach pattern to O'Hare, and a plane flew overhead—a stiff white bird in the blue, blue sky.

Just like that, and it was over. Once again you were Oliver Ryan, the boy the Washingtons referred to as their "other son." Yanking Braden up, you swam with his body to the side while he sputtered and choked. With help from the gathered crowd, you pulled him out of the water. His arm slung over your back, you took him to the locker room, where he sank into one of the toilet stalls and threw up pool water and snack-bar nachos. "Brade?" you asked, kneeling next to him.

He nodded. "Thanks, Ollie, I owe you."

"Any time," you said, feeling sick from the smell of chlorine and vomit and thoughts of what you'd been doing. If there was a hell, you were pretty sure you were going there—and it was probably that moment right before takeoff, when the plane picks up speed.

Braden looked at you for a long time. And then you felt his mouth on your own, lips soft and warmer than you would have expected.

Shoving him away, you asked why, even though it wasn't really all that earth-shattering. And then you didn't hate him at all but felt inconsolably sorry for him.

"I'm not—" you started.

But he shook his head. "Don't say it, please."

And both of you sat there, hands between your knees, until the locker room door swung open and three boys—towels flung over their shoulders like capes—clomped in complaining about adult swim.

The two of you never talked about it again, which made you feel even sorrier for him and the girls he dated. But senior year, when Phoebe Fisher transferred to ETHS, all of those things didn't seem to matter much anymore.

Braden played QB at the University of Colorado for a few losing seasons but injured his shoulder junior year in a skiing accident. As soon as Alicia Washington called you from the hospital, you flew out from Chicago, even though you had finals the next week.

"All these girls and his teammates, they all wanted to come, but you were the only one he wanted." Alicia hugged you in the waiting area while surgeons tried to put Braden back together again. Even though she hadn't been in catalogs for quite some time and her hair was probably only mahogany from dye, she still smelled so good. "He's so lucky to have you, Oliver."

Remembering the slick feel of Braden's hair when you tried to drown him, you looked away.

That whole first week you stayed at his off-campus apartment. You went to his classes, took notes for him when he couldn't go, lugged his backpack for him when he could. A part of you thought he would shatter, break down completely, but the closest he ever came was six days after surgery when the two of you were carrying groceries home.

Most of the bags were in your hands, but Braden insisted on taking a few. "I've got a gimpy arm; I'm not an invalid."

At his front door, Braden tried to balance the bags on his bad arm while searching for his keys. The thin plastic straps slipped from his grasp, and a jar of Prego tumbled out, cracking on the chipped tile. Marinara sauce oozed out, and you felt it, all of it—your obsession with Alicia, the jealousy in high school, the undiscussed kiss—in the expanding red puddle on the floor.

"This isn't right," you said, bending down to clean up the mess. "You . . . this shouldn't . . ."

"Don't worry about it; it's spaghetti sauce." Braden adjusted his elbow in the sling.

Shaking your head, you said that wasn't what you meant. Braden blinked and nodded.

"It's cool, I wasn't gonna go pro anyway." He shook his head. "Now it can be the thing I blame everything else on. I can blame my whole life on a wrong turn down the bunny hill."

That wasn't what you had meant either, but you thought about the plane with your father when you were seven, wondered if everyone had some origin story they used to justify and rationalize and validate.

Two days later you went back to school, took your makeup exams, and did fine without the hours of studying you normally would have put in. Braden, likewise, went on being Braden, even though he had six pins and limited mobility in his right shoulder.

Your stepmother:

You suspected it was going to happen with your stepmother years before it actually did. A senior at Northwestern, you were home for Christmas playing Mr. Potato Head with your two-year-old half sister, who kept chewing on the assortment of noses.

Behind the two of you, Maura collected crumpled red and gold foil paper from the living room carpet and menacingly shoved it into a drawstring garbage bag.

"Maura?" you asked, and she looked away.

"It's not even noon yet." Though not the albino your sister claimed, Maura did look as if she were painted in watercolor. Everything about her was nearly translucent, from her flaxen hair to her blue eyes, so light they almost appeared to have no color at all. "And Christmas Day, Christmas Day. I can't believe he *had* to leave."

No one in the world understood that better than you.

Setting aside the plastic potato Natasha had put you in charge of decorating, you touched Maura's slender shoulder and offered a sympathetic half smile.

"You're so good with Natasha." Maura put her hand on yours.

And you knew what was going to happen even before she let her hand fall to the small of your back, even before you got the fellowship offer from Northwestern's graduate program and Maura and your father suggested you live at home to cut down on expenses. And you thought it would be the thing that secured your place in hell, but you didn't really care, because you never believed in hell, not even when you were a kid and your mother had made you go to Mass. You didn't care because Phoebe Fisher still haunted your dreams, even though you hadn't talked to her since freshman year.

It actually didn't happen with Maura for three years. Not until you left your undergrad apartment on Sherman and Noyes and moved back into your father's house. Not until you spent a bunch of nights on the couches (new couches, not the ones where your mother had waited to die) in the living room watching *The Late Show* and jotting down sketches for a generator while Maura folded laundry on the floor. It didn't happen until you started bringing Giordano's pizza home for dinner and picking Natasha up from the sitter's house on days when Maura had to close the animal shelter where she volunteered.

Even on the night it actually happened, it wasn't until after you went to a Cubs game with Braden, who was in town from Boulder, where he'd gotten a schmoozy consulting gig. It didn't happen until after you chugged seven Styrofoam cups of Old Style because you could hardly find anything to talk about with Braden anymore, and you remembered how he used to be closer to you than any real members of your family. It didn't happen until after you stumbled in from the game and found Maura, translucent and sad, drinking cabernet and watching a *M*A*S*H* rerun.

"There's Leona's leftovers in the fridge if you're hungry." She muted the volume.

You told her you'd had a hot dog at the game, but you'd take a glass of wine. The remote fell off the coffee table when she got up. Both of you knelt to retrieve it, and the back of your hand brushed her breast. She clasped it there and held it. That was how it finally happened, on an Oriental rug your father had brought back from China.

It wasn't particularly good or bad, but you fucked like people who needed to. Pressing yourself into her was the same feeling you'd had when you'd almost drowned Braden—surprise you were actually doing something so dark and sticky, so tangibly wrong, you had to question if you were like other people in the world.

Afterward, Maura kissed your forehead, and you were close enough to see the blue veins under her see-through skin. Before she died, your mother had had a road map of lines crossing her body from the operations where they cut into her and took things out piece by piece. At forty-five Maura was older than your mother had ever gotten to be.

You thought it was going to be a one-time thing but weren't surprised when Maura knocked on your bedroom door a few nights later. You let her in, and you kept letting her in. Though you never told anyone about it, you could almost hear your sister's commentary: *"Ollie, you must realize that this is about Dad. About your need to be close to him . . . to connect."* That may have been true, but you pushed the idea away, didn't really think about it until five months later, when you were sitting at the kitchen table eating pancakes with Maura and Natasha, and under the table Maura tapped her knee to yours, the way Phoebe Fisher used to.

"We should take Nat to see the tree lighting tonight," she said.

You said Natasha was too young to like that, and traffic would be a nightmare.

"Nonsense, my father took me in Cincinnati when I was half Natasha's age." Maura put her hand on your thigh under the table. Natasha was concentrating on eating only the chips out of her chocolate chip pancakes, but it still made you uncomfortable. "We can take the 'L.'"

The year before, Maura had redone the kitchen, and the light blue flowers of the wallpaper were the same washed-out shade as her eyes. The weight of her small hand became oppressive on your leg, and you felt crushed by the faded blue all around you. You wanted to tell Maura you weren't Natasha's father and had no desire to be.

"Is Dad going to be home tonight?" you asked, brushing her hand away.

Maura recoiled, and you looked out the window to avoid her eyes and the wallpaper and the hurt that you knew you were causing her.

"I think he's going to be in Beijing until Tuesday," she said.

Your first love:

Phoebe Fisher was assigned as your physics lab partner senior year. She broke a lot of bell jars, got a 39 percent on the kinetics test, and asked you to tutor her. Because her lips looked like satin, and she was nicer than you thought someone like her needed to be, you agreed. For weeks you sat with her in the cafeteria during lunch, trying to explain how to measure velocity. Though she stared at you intently, it became apparent she would never master distance and displacement, so you wrote big on the tests and let her look across the table at your answers.

You still had lunch with her, and one day she leaned across her tray of tuna salad to graze those satin lips against yours.

"I just wanted to do that." She giggled afterward.

"I wanted you to do that, too," you said, wishing you'd been the instigator, that you hadn't made her make the first move.

After four months of snuggling, all-night phone calls, and slightly painful handjobs, she took you to her father's house and laid you on your back under the white lace canopy over her bed. Lowering herself on top of you, she guided your cock between her thighs. It went fine until you heard the rumble of an airplane outside—your father, the Piper Saratoga when you were seven—and went limp before even entering her.

"No worries, sweetie," she said, kissing your shoulder and stroking your red hair. "It'll be better next time."

It was.

Afterward, she put her mouth on your stomach and blew out air, lips vibrating against your skin.

And the two of you were happy ordering Thai food and watching classic movies on the couch. Happy going with Phoebe to her brother's track meets and helping her stepmother set the table on nights you stayed for dinner. Happy watching her play Emily in the school production of *Our Town* and going on double dates with her friends, even though you'd gone to school with Evie and Nicole for years and never talked to them before Phoebe came along. You were happy until the third week of May, when your stomach started hurting.

"What's wrong?" Phoebe asked when you twitched in pain on the couch, your arms and legs tangled with hers.

"Nothing," you said.

You knew you should see a doctor, but you weren't about to see a doctor, because that was how it started with your mother: First her stomach hurt, then she was waiting to die.

Though you didn't die, the next day you did crumple over in the Nordstrom at Old Orchard while Phoebe was trying on bathing suits. She called her father, and they took you down the road to Northwestern Memorial (your mother's hospital), where a perky brunette surgeon sawed into your abdomen and suctioned out the remains of your ruptured appendix.

Everyone knew Larry Fisher, so they let Phoebe stay past visiting hours. After Braden brought your homework assignments, Chase Fisher brought you magazines, and your own father finally arrived, guilty and groggy from Australia, Phoebe climbed into your elevated bed and squeezed your arm. For the first time, it hit you that she was really leaving, not just going down the road like you. Feeling the tingle in your nose and eyes, you turned away because you didn't want her to see you cry.

"Do you want me to get that nurse for more pain stuff?" she asked nervously.

The only thing you could say was "Don't go after graduation."

She laughed, which would have seemed a lot funnier if something in your chest didn't cave in every time you caught sight of the back of her head in the hall between classes.

"Ollie, Ollie, Ollie." She moved her hand from your shoulder to your thigh, the warmth of her palm seeping through the thin fabric of the sheets. "It'll work out. You'll see."

And you trusted her.

So you helped pack her little dresses and movie posters into her Camry, and the two of you drove across the country. College didn't start for you until mid-September, so you played house for a couple of months in her studio apartment. The afternoons were spent touring the different neighborhoods so Phoebe could learn the city. You went to Grauman's Chinese Theatre and drove into the Hollywood Hills with a star map from a street vendor; other than a few blondes who may have been models, you didn't see any celebrities.

Just as in the gum commercials, Phoebe cried and clung to you long after the flight attendant at LAX announced it was time for your row to board when you had to go back.

"I love you, Oliver," she mumbled into the fabric of your T-shirt.

"Phoebe." You started to say you loved her, too, but stopped. For months you'd been telling her that, and you needed to say more. "I want to write your name in the sky."

"Like the Tom Petty song?" She smiled, mascara streaks on her cheeks.

"Sure," you said. But that hadn't really been what you were thinking, it had just seemed the most relevant thing to say.

The first few months at Northwestern, you talked to Phoebe every night while your roommate would dramatically slam the door and head to the communal lounge. Phoebe rattled on about the auditions her low-budget modeling agency sent her on and all the almost-famous people she met at parties. You told her about your new friend Chris, who was nice but made you miss Braden, and about the introductory engineering classes you liked.

Without warning, one day you found a hardness in her voice.

"People here are so different than people in Chicago," she said.

"Yeah," you agreed. "College isn't ETHS."

"It's not the same." It wasn't what she said but how she said it. When she told you she loved you at the end of the conversation, it didn't have the conviction it had at the airport two months before.

And then Phoebe's calls dwindled to twice a week, to once a month, to never. You left messages, but she didn't return them. During the week of your midterm exams, her number was disconnected. You drove down to her father's neighborhood and circled around, just to see if her car was there. It wasn't, nor was it there the ten subsequent times you went back to check.

"It will be better in the long run," your new friend Chris told you over beers bought with fake IDs claiming you were twenty-two and from Kansas.

"It will be better in the long run," Braden told you when the two of you saw the *Eons & Empires* sequel over Christmas break.

"I never liked that girl much anyway," Karen told you on the phone. "I know you don't want to hear this, but it will be better in the long run."

But they were all wrong; nothing about it was better. Not the ache you felt in your solar plexus every day you came home and your roommate smirked and told you, "No, she hasn't called," not the girls you dated at Northwestern or seeing Phoebe eating strawberry yogurt in a Dannon commercial. Not fucking your stepmother.

Years later, when you didn't consciously dwell on being over her but occasionally it occurred to you that you didn't think about her every day, Phoebe Fisher finally did reappear. The Wednesday before Thanksgiving, Braden was in town and wanted to hit some of the swanky bars on the Gold Coast, which was fine because your father was home and you didn't feel comfortable being there with both him and Maura anymore.

It was one in the morning, and Braden was chatting up some Loyola senior when you saw her with Evie Saperstein. Her black hair was cropped close to her chin, and she was thinner, but she was most definitely Phoebe. And because you were twenty-six and not eighteen, you went over and set a hand on her shoulder.

"Hey, Phee," you said, as if you hadn't spent the last seven years wondering about her. "Long time, no see."

The truly remarkable thing was how happy Phoebe Fisher was to see you. At her urging, you slid into the booth beside her, and the two of you talked until the bar closed and shards of gold light started to streak the sky.

Finally, you drove her home in her father's car, and she took you upstairs, where you talked more in her gauzy white bedroom that looked the same as it had in high school. She told you about the commercial she did for a used-car dealership in Orange County, and you told her about your work with Advantage Electric and the undergrad courses they let graduate students teach at Northwestern. Then neither one of you spoke for a long time.

Setting your glasses on the bedside table, you went in to kiss her. Phoebe stopped you and began to offer the apology that you'd desperately needed eons and empires ago. But you didn't want to hear it anymore. It couldn't change all that time you had stayed in the Chicago suburbs while everyone else left.

"Shhhh." You traced her collarbone with your fingers. "Things happen; I could never hate you."

Making love to Phoebe after so many years of wanting to make love to her—all of her body parts alien yet familiar—everything seemed meaningful and slow motion. The only light was the eerie orange glow of Chicago from the south-facing window, and you wondered if the two of you were real at all or if you were ghosts haunting a glitch in the space-time continuum.

You fell asleep, her bare, pale back against your chest.

And you were happy in the time warp, until the next morning, when she told you she was only in town a few days.

"I didn't even bring a coat." She melted in velvety laughter, very different than her old giggle. "That's how long I've been gone."

She was still spooned into you, and you spun her around, had sex with her again, less gentle than before. Maybe you *did* hate her, just a little.

Afterward, Phoebe walked you downstairs to the kitchen, where her father and stepmother, who looked exactly as you remembered, were eating breakfast at the island.

"Oliver." Her father nodded, and Gennifer asked if you still took your coffee with cream and sugar, as if their daughter bringing her old boyfriend down from her bedroom on Thanksgiving Day was a completely normal occurrence.

Phoebe's kid brother, who had grown into his features and looked *nothing* like you remembered, gave you a huge hug and asked about your life with authentic interest. Next to him was a girl in a slim skirt and heels. With her blue eyes and black hair, she could have been the Fisher siblings' younger, less exotic cousin. But from the way she leaned into Chase, you knew they were lovers. You suspected that the girl, who introduced herself as "Sharon Gallaher only one G," cared more about Chase than he for her. It was subtle, the way her body tilted into his while he faced straight ahead reading the *Tribune*'s business section. Feeling an instant kinship with Sharon, you wanted to warn her what it felt like to love and lose a Fisher.

By the time Phoebe drops you home, it's nearly one, and Maura and your sister are bringing holiday dishes (dishes that had been your mother's, even though she never used them) to the dining room table.

"Nice of you to join us," your father says, which is so ironic you briefly forget to feel guilty about Maura.

"Fun night?" Karen jokes, setting down a plate of sliced turkey and licking gravy from her thumb. "I ask because your shirt is on inside out."

From the kitchen you can feel Maura's colorless eyes on you. Not once during the entire meal do you look directly at her.

Three days later—when your encounter with Phoebe feels like a fever dream, your father is back in the sky, and you still haven't talked to your stepmother—you're in your bedroom trying to grade student papers when the outline of Maura's slippers appears through the slit of light under your door.

"Ollie?" she whispers. "Are you awake?"

It occurs to you that you don't want to deal with avoiding Maura anymore, that she's your father's anchor to Evanston, not yours. That you don't care about thrust and hydrostatic lock and helping other people jet off to faraway places nearly as much as you thought you did. That maybe you *are* sick of the gray Chicago sky and of unconsciously waiting for everyone else's return.

Holding your breath until Maura is gone, you take the backpack from the back of your closet, fill it with a week's worth of jeans and T-shirts, and call a cab to the airport for 6:00 A.M.

"What airline?" the middle-aged driver asks as he makes the turnoff to O'Hare.

United offers free standby tickets to pilots' families, but you can't run away from home on your father's airline.

"Maybe Delta?"

"Sure 'bout that?" the driver asks, and you tell him you are. Domestic or international, he wants to know, and you desperately wish you'd had an occasion to get a passport at some point in the past twenty-six years.

The terminal is busy, swarms of travelers scurrying to make early morning flights; other than a guy in a Bears sweatshirt, they could be people from anywhere going anywhere. You line up for a ticket agent, studying the electronic board above the counter listing times and gates for departing flights. Anchorage, Atlanta, Cleveland, Rapid City, Seattle—all the different varieties of the country. Places you never go because you've been stuck in a permanent holding pattern in Illinois.

Across the terminal a tall airline pilot strides by in a navy blue uniform. It's not your father, even at this distance you can tell, but something about the man reminds you of him—confidence.

After twenty minutes in the queue, a uniformed clerk smiles at you, asks, "What can I help you with today, sir?"

"What's the farthest place from here I can go right now?"

Her brow crinkles, and she asks if you're kidding.

Taking out a credit card, you smile with all the authority you didn't have in the Piper Saratoga when you were seven. "Yes, I'm ready for a change."

4 we don't get today

A stitch in her side.

Sharon Gallaher doesn't actually enjoy running, but she adores Chase Fisher. And she loves that even after a year together, he still asks her to go jogging in the mornings before work, as if his routine would suffer if she weren't beside him.

Well, almost beside him.

Ten minutes into their run, when she was out of breath and he'd barely broken a sweat, she told him to go ahead. A quick kiss and he blazed off with all the speed he'd been holding back. That happens most mornings, too, and she's touched that he still asks for permission, that they still do all these things together like the couples in books and TV shows she always assumed she'd never be a part of when she was reading all those books and watching all those shows alone in junior high and high school.

Chase is out of sight, a good two or three blocks away, so it's probably a fine time to stop and pant and wait for him to come back through Washington Square Park. Then the two of them can shuffle back to the apartment on Bleecker she shares with her roommate from NYU.

Well, roommate for a few more weeks.

Three nights ago, over Chinese takeout at his new apartment on Twenty-ninth Street, Chase asked if Sharon wanted to move in. Pouncing on him, she'd agreed, and they'd rolled around on the chocolate leather couch, making cracks about how she could pay her share of the rent with blowjobs and back rubs.

Her roommate, Kristen, had been complaining about Chase staying over so often and his stuff's gradual takeover of their cramped bathroom, so Sharon hadn't thought she'd care. Still, Kristen got petulant yesterday when Sharon said she wouldn't be renewing her portion of the lease.

"I never thought you'd get serious with some finance guy," she'd said. "You always talked about marrying an artist or another writer when we were in school."

"College was a long time ago," Sharon had said, and she feels that way now back among the students at the park. All lumpy backpacks and hooded sweatshirts, they're getting out of their 7:30 A.M. classes, milling around the central fountain, talking about professors, papers, and off-campus parties—everyone still buzzing with the excitement of an untarnished new school year.

Though Sharon only finished her master's and got the job at *Living* magazine last spring, it seems decades ago that she was one of these kids, and she finds herself slightly embarrassed to still be loitering by the arch.

She decides she's happy to be moving in with Chase. Even if his new neighborhood is a bit sterile, the apartment is on the thirty-fifth floor and has a view of the Chrysler Building. And there's no law that aspiring writers have to live in crumbling walk-ups below Fourteenth Street. Sharon still fully intends to be the first person from her grad school class to sell a novel (no matter what Kristen might think).

She decides she's happy dressing up each morning and heading to the *Living* offices at Rockefeller Center with the other commuters. Even if the magazine is mostly bright photos of celebrities and a lot of her duties are more secretarial than editorial, it's still kind of fun, and there's a lot of downtime when she can work on her book. Plus Chase's friends, and especially their girlfriends, think it's cool she knows which famous people eat at which restaurants.

Maybe she's simply happy in general?

Shoelaces on her left sneaker undone.

Hunching over to tie them, she doesn't see the impact of the plane two miles south. She hears it, though, as well as everyone's collective gasp.

SOMEWHERE OVER THE PACIFIC OCEAN
FORTY-SIX MINUTES PAST SOME HOUR

"He needs to get out." Phoebe is shaking Adam's shoulder, dragging him back from the cusp of sleep.

Even before he's fully aware of what's going on, Adam unhooks his seat belt and stutter-steps into the aisle. Phoebe follows, and the man in the window seat manages to exit the narrow row without tripping over their bags, no longer stowed neatly under their seatbacks.

"How long was I out?" Adam flexes stiff legs and arms.

"Four hours, maybe." Phoebe shrugs. The economy cabin is paradoxically quiet and loud, and he can barely hear her over the ambient roar. "Just ten more and the International Date Line to go before the fun starts."

In complimentary airline slipper socks, she looks small and sad, and Adam is glad he agreed to accompany her halfway around the world to visit her estranged mother at the Four Seasons Hong Kong, glad he can help her in this way.

"Pheebs, it's gonna be fine." Adam squeezes the closest part of her—upper arm—in a gesture he hopes conveys sympathy, hopes he's speaking the truth.

"I know I'm being a baby." She sighs. "It's just, when I was little she was like a *mom* mom, and then all of a sudden she wasn't. Now she's even farther away."

Adam sort of understands but often wishes his own mother would run away, see all the places she only reads about. When he'd told her he was going to Asia with Phoebe, his mother had sounded so vicariously misty on the phone that Adam vowed to send her on a round-the-world vacation if he ever really made it (not a recurring voice role on the *Go Go Trons* cartoon made it, but *really* made it).

The man in the window seat returns, gives the perfunctory nod of strangers sharing intimate spaces, and the three of them file back in. Adam reclines his chair, hoping to go back to sleep.

"Do you think Chase is right to blow her off?" Phoebe asks.

"Your brother's busy." Adam wrestles a yawn. Chase had been in LA for business a few months ago. The kid had dressed like Patrick Bateman, offered a challengingly firm handshake, and religiously checked his cell phone. That probably equated to busy. He'd also spent a chunk of time subtly and then less subtly questioning Adam's intentions toward his sister; apparently none of the Fisher men were ever going to like Adam. "I'm sure he'll go see your mom soon."

"Oh." Phoebe perks up. "You missed the food." From her seatback pocket, she produces a packet of Pepperidge Farm Milanos, two mini bags of pretzels, and an apple. "I saved you these."

And like that, his reservations dissipate. "Thank you." He opens the cookies, offers her one.

"I'm good; I ate a lot of something they told me was chicken."

Scrunching in his chair, he rests his head on her shoulder, smells vanilla lotion and Anais Anais perfume as she leans into him.

They haven't *slept together* slept together for more than a year, since before he punched a hole in the wall around last Thanksgiving, but they've gotten in the habit of literally sleeping together—a mostly platonic tangle of body parts on the king-size pillow-top mattress he got after doing a three-episode arc on *ER*.

So much easier this way.

From the moment he'd seen her in Thetta Tunney's workshop, Adam had thought Phoebe Fisher was breathtaking, even if he hadn't realized how astute she was until she picked the scene from *Cat on a Hot Tin Roof* for them to put up, knowing, long before he did, how perfectly the vicious dialogue would highlight their strengths. Even if he hadn't realized how sweet she was until the first night he fell asleep on their couch and woke up covered in a quilt, pillow under his head. But the few months they *were* sort of together, Phoebe had stomped around hurt and put out, as if everything connected to him was an epic failure. It had felt claustropho-bic, like he was back in Coral Cove—the last time he meant too much to someone.

And there are plenty of breathtaking women in LA.

This time he can't hide the yawn.

"Sleepy?" Phoebe asks.

Adam nods into her clavicle. "Aren't you? What time is it?"

"Who knows? We get in, like, two days after we left." She burrows closer. "We don't get today."

CORDOVA, ALASKA
5:03 A.M. AKST

In four hours you and Liam Wing are supposed to head out into the Prince William Sound on the *Jezebel Jones* for the last salmon voyage of the season. If the monthlong trip is anything like the others, you'll be lucky to get three hours of sleep a night between twenty-hour days of grueling labor that cramps your hands and hunches your back. But in the bedroom you and Liam share in the Lake Avenue house, you're lying awake because in his half of the room—separated by a sheet hung from the ceiling—Liam and his on-again-off-again girlfriend are packing for her trip back to Seattle.

Actually, you've been awake since 2:00 A.M., when Liam and Tina decided that the two times they'd had sex that night were not enough.

Since arriving three days ago, everything Tina has done has been loud and frustrating in your shared quarters. You haven't said anything, though, because you've had a soft spot for Liam since you met on the deck of your first seiner last spring, when he'd pointed to the cold, open water and called it the "last frontier."

"Ollie," Liam had said, "we're astronauts." And you'd felt a little like an astronaut, signed on as a deckhand thousands of miles from home. When you'd fled Chicago, you'd told the Delta agent to send you as far as she could without a passport. You'd ended up in Anchorage and followed the job postings and college kids looking for adventure on the ferry to Cordova. But even that far away, Liam's enthusiasm reminded you of Braden (if Braden had a half-Macanese doppelgänger), and there was something nice about that familiarity; you can put up with Tina a little while longer.

"Was the pilot blind?" Tina is saying, her high-pitched baby voice floating above the low hum of the television and through the sheet. "How can you hit a building?"

You roll onto your side so you don't have to see their silhouettes—his short and compact, hers long and lithe.

"I wonder if this will screw up my flight," Tina is saying.

"You can always stay here." Liam at a fraction of Tina's volume.

Sounds of shifting bedding as they make their way down to Liam's futon on the floor.

Rubbing the long red beard you haven't shaved since coming to Alaska, you resign yourself to the fact that they're going to have sex again.

"Oh, you'd like that, wouldn't you?" Tina says through the sheet.

The sudden dropping of something.

An intake of breath.

Liam's muffled voice, "Holy shit."

And then the illusion of the wall explodes as Liam pushes aside the divider. "Ollie, you said your dad was a pilot, right?"

Tucked under Liam's arm on the futon, Tina is quietly crying. For reasons you cannot explain, her tears are more horrible than any of the horrible things blowing up and burning down in real time on television.

Liam gave you the cordless phone half an hour ago, but each time you dial your father, you're dumped straight to voice mail.

Every thirty seconds or so, you remind yourself to breathe.

A downed plane is found in rural Pennsylvania. Tina twitches underneath Liam's arm.

In your hand the phone cries to life.

Glancing at the caller ID on the console, Liam tells you it's a 312 number. Though it could be Maura (whom you haven't spoken to in the ten months since you left), you answer before the end of the first ring.

"Ollie?" your father says. "Thought you might be worried, so I figured I'd give you a call and let you know that I'm fine."

He doesn't sound fine, though; he sounds like he did when he finally got to the hospital after missing your emergency appendectomy—old and out of his element.

"I'm really glad," you say, enormously relieved to actually mean this. You may have been fucking your father's wife, but you're not quite Oedipus. "I sorta knew those weren't your usual routes, but still."

"Everything okay?" Liam mouths over Tina's head, and you nod, step back into your half of the room and the illusion of privacy.

On the line your father is apologizing for missing your earlier calls, saying he spoke to your sister in Utah but had to search through old e-mails to find the number you'd sent after you were long gone.

"Maura took Nat to her parents' in Cincinnati for a few weeks, but I got through to them a while ago, too."

A pause.

"Who would have thought?" His voice is ramshackle.

And you remember how gray he'd looked the last time you'd seen him almost a year ago at Thanksgiving. With Phoebe's reappearance and Maura's hurt eyes, you'd been distracted, but even then you couldn't help but notice that he wasn't the fierce, imposing superhero he'd been in your youth. In the handful of times you've called since leaving, Maura has never been home. Her being in Ohio is probably significant.

"Who could have imagined," your father says, "airplanes as weapons?"

You knew. You always knew, but for maybe the first time since the Piper Saratoga when you were seven, you don't want to say that now, don't need to be right or prove a point. You want to give your father a hug or a back pat or something normal family members do to comfort each other. You want to be Batman to his Robin.

But you're not there. For once you're the one who's gone, holed up in a far-flung corner of the world, while he's in the Chicago suburbs trying to locate the people in his life.

"Dad," you say, "I'm really sorry."

5 scraps of things she used to know

Maybe she missed it?

For the fifth time in forty minutes, Sharon checks her cell phone to make sure it's not accidentally turned off or on mute. That she hasn't missed any calls or texts or smoke signals.

Chase *had* promised he would call.

But there aren't any messages, only the time—9:07 P.M.—glowing in the flip phone's window.

Setting her cell on the bathroom vanity, she takes another swig from Chase's bottle of Grey Goose—warmth blazing down her throat to her empty stomach—and runs her hand under the stream of bathwater to test the temperature.

Kristen's apartment in Queens doesn't have a tub, only a narrow stall shower with a cracked floor. This might be Sharon's last chance to take a bath for a while.

No, Chase said he would call.

And if (*when!*) he does, she's simply going to say she's sorry and she loves him before she has a chance to mess things up anymore. He'll say he's sorry, too, and she can rent another U-Haul, go back to Queens, and retrieve all the boxes of clothes and books and papers that she had hauled to Kristen's that afternoon. No need to figure out how everything would fit in Kristen's windowless second bedroom/closet. No need to drop a change of address card in the mail or find a dry cleaner in Astoria. She could simply bring everything back to the thirty-fifth floor of the Madison Plaza and take a bath *with* Chase when he gets back from Chicago.

The night she moved in, three years earlier, they'd taken a bath. Chase had filled the tub with bubbles, lit candles, put some cheesy love song on the stereo—like all those couples in books and TV shows.

Another swig of vodka.

She's never really been much of a drinker, but it feels good, keeps her pounding heart and the nagging thought that Chase might *not* call at bay. Plus, it's his favorite and makes her feel close to him.

Another phone check.

There's a Dorothy Parker story about a woman bargaining with God for her beau to call. Sharon had laughed out loud when she read it while babysitting for the Robbins on date night; it seems much less funny now.

She strips off her dirty clothes: sweater, T-shirt, jeans, bra and panties made of the silky material Chase prefers, even though she's worn cotton for the better part of a year, even though Chase had gone to his parents' house so he didn't have to watch her move out.

Setting her stuff on the toilet, Sharon notices a utility knife and Sharpie marker in the space between the tub and vanity—moving supplies that must have fallen.

Squatting, she picks up the knife, absently slides out the blade.

Somewhere she'd read something. If bathwater is warm enough, you can slit your wrists and bleed out painlessly. Blood flowing from your arms like the antithesis of a water birth, a death made easier on the dier. Some famous Greek or Roman emperor went that way, didn't he?

Nero?

Then the more concrete notion that's been weighing Sharon down for the past six months, since the rejection letters from agents started pouring in and Chase started spending more nights out with the sell-side analysts: There was a time when she used to know all kinds of things about history and literature and . . . stuff.

Setting down the knife, she notices something else tucked in the tiny space. A yellow Post-it note. In Chase's rigid, heavy handwriting: *Had to go to work, Shar, but I love you very much.—C*

Until she took them down yesterday, there had been a half-dozen little notes like this stuck all over the apartment walls. It had been one of the little lovey things that Chase used to do when he was leaving early or coming home late. They'd charmed Sharon so much she left them up. It's been months since he posted a new message (well, except for the night of the fire). This one must have fallen off the bathroom door when she was packing.

He still might call.

Chase had promised her as much when he left last night.

"You're sure you don't want any of the furniture?" he'd asked as he quickly packed a leather hanging bag.

Since their fight he'd been sleeping on his office couch, and it was the first time Sharon had seen him in days. He'd had the decency to look haggard—black hair greasy and no longer neatly parted, pretty face puffy and sallow. Initially, Sharon had taken solace in that, thought if he looked so upset, surely he'd change his mind. But he'd spoken only a few words to her since rushing in, and none of them had been about calling off their breakup. His appearance, she conceded, was probably the result of his office's lumpy couch and lack of a full-length mirror.

"Kristen has furniture in Queens," Sharon said.

At the mention of an outer borough, Chase flinched. "Like I said, if you want to stay in Manhattan, I can help with rent for a while." He had the same expression he got when talking about how his sister was wasting her life as a bartender in LA.

"I don't need your charity."

"It's not charity; I care about you. Is her neighborhood even safe?" Chase massaged his eyes again—a telltale sign he was getting a migraine.

Without thinking about it, Sharon went to the bathroom and got the large bottle of Advil. "Take some now before it gets worse," she said.

It was something she'd done probably fifteen times in the past year alone, one of those small moments of intimacy long-term lovers take for granted. But then Chase did look up, and it seemed evident his dishevel-ment was very much because of their split.

"Thank you." Lightly, he touched her shoulder.

It was a crack, maybe the first since their fight. Sharon closed the inches between them and pressed her lips to his.

"No," he'd croaked. Then he kissed back, hard, before pulling away.

After that he just looked at her. Some echo of the way he used to, like she was his birthday and favorite dessert stuffed into the body of a pinup girl.

"Chase—" She started to say something but stopped like she should have stopped when they were arguing earlier in the week, like she was never good at doing when she was nervous.

"Shar." Still holding her shoulders, he shook his head and told her he was already late for his flight.

"Please."

"I'll call you when I get in," he said, and his tone suggested it might be the kind of call that changed everything. "We can talk then."

"Promise?" She bit her tongue to keep from saying more.

He rubbed his temples again. "Yeah, I promise."

Grabbing his bag, he was gone, the heavy metal door closing securely behind him.

Yes, Chase had said he would call, and while in the course of breaking up he'd told her he didn't want to marry her and didn't really know her anymore, he'd never been a liar.

Maybe he'd call the landline no one ever uses? Before getting in the bath, Sharon should get the cordless from the kitchen, just in case.

He doesn't even know you're here!

Sharon had told Chase she'd be moved out by the afternoon. Technically she is. She's only back because she'd left her wallet, and it was late by the time she took the N train back to Manhattan and found it.

Maybe Chase is trying to call her at Kristen's?

Except Kristen doesn't have a landline, and Sharon can't think of any reason Chase would know her college roommate's cell number.

Another chug of vodka; maybe he thought she wasn't moving out until tomorrow?

Better get the phone.

Naked, Sharon walks from the bathroom to the main room, means only to grab the cordless, but the peach blur of her reflection in the window catches in her peripheral vision. Already looking out, she can't escape the compulsion to find the Chrysler Building in the jagged Manhattan skyline. Nearly three years she's lived here, but every time—even now—she still cocks her head northeast, seeking out the steel crown.

She'd never seen it before college, but Sharon had known the Chrysler Building from movies, and of course as Captain Rowen's World 1 head-quarters in the *Eons & Empires* comics. But the first time she saw the building for real—on a city tour her second week at NYU—she'd been struck with an awesome sense of déjà vu. The sensation was something she'd felt comfortable sharing with Chase Fisher on their third date. It had been the first thing Chase had shown her when he moved here from the West Village. Taking her out on the terrace, he'd pointed right: "There it is."

Now, because it might be the last time she has this exact view (*No, Chase still might call*), she walks toward the window, her reflection getting clearer and smaller as she approaches the glass. Pressing her palm to the mirrored version of herself, she finds the building where it always is.

Five blocks due north, the Empire State Building is bigger and closer. To the west, the still incomplete New York Times Building and the tower with the weird red light on the top that she's always wondered about but never bothered to look up. All the skyscrapers so bright it's never truly dark in the apartment, no matter how many expensive blinds Chase hung.

Up until the last six months, when she'd started getting rejection letters from every literary agent in the city, Sharon's life had seemed to be on a great upward trajectory. Though high school had never been as engaging as in John Hughes films and QT Network shows, it had steadily gotten better. Laurel Young had kept her around, even after their fathers' account-ing firm fractured, and eventually Sharon became almost friends with Lau-rel's group of girls and went on dates with the buddies of boys Laurel was seeing. Though she often looked at those high school dances and backseat make-out sessions as character research for a story, wearing Nicole Miller dresses and having young men pin corsages on her wrist made her mother stop asking if she was "having trouble fitting in."

College had been a marked improvement. Friends, like Sharon's freshman roommate, Kristen, had come so much easier, and her creative writing classes allowed her to be legitimately good at something for the first time. After years stashing stories in her sock drawer and pretending she'd rather be on a date than reading, she was finally rewarded for her proclivities. She wrote the student newspaper's arts and entertainment column and got paid (albeit very little) to go to shows and readings. Professors encouraged her and offered to show her work to this literary magazine or that agent when she finished her novel. Fellow students turned to her for advice, and sophomore year she gave her virginity to a boy from fiction workshop who wrote a horrible song based on a short story she'd written about a girl obsessed with robots. By the time she graduated a whole year early, she'd published three pieces in small journals with good reputations, which her parents probably didn't read but proudly displayed on their bookcase next to the paperback mysteries. Practically the entire NYU faculty guaranteed her a slot in the master's program, which seemed to impress her folks, even if they didn't understand what she was studying or wanted to be.

And then the pinnacle, three weeks into her second year of grad school, the magical meeting with Chase Fisher at the laundromat on MacDougal. Sharon was stuffing dryer-warm T-shirts and panties into her laundry bag when she noticed Chase at the counter picking up wash-and-fold. Normally she was annoyed by people who deemed themselves too important to do their own laundry, but when she saw him paying for his perfectly pressed and folded clothes, she'd felt a wave of recognition, a whispered "of course."

It wasn't that he looked good. He did (though with fine bones and thick, coal hair, he was probably too feminine to be considered conventionally handsome). It was that when he glanced over at her, she was struck with the distinct feeling that she already knew him. The same way she'd felt seeing the Chrysler Building four years earlier.

Her romantic experience at the time was limited to a handful of forgettable guys from college, but the moment Chase noticed her, it was a foregone conclusion that he would come over and offer to carry her laundry. It was completely inevitable that Sharon would accept and let him haul her bag up the four floors to the apartment she shared with Kristen on Bleecker.

"That's so cool you're a writer; I could never do anything like that," Chase had said on their third date as they wandered around Washington Square Park after pappardelle and osso buco at Il Mulino.

Sharon smiled and explained how her novel was about a young woman kidnapped and murdered after hitching a ride.

"I'm sure you'll be on the *Times* Best Sellers list," he said, and she'd blushed but hadn't disagreed. Her life was turning out so much better than she'd envisioned that she genuinely believed things were destined to go that way. A year later the two of them were living in this apartment looking at the skyline.

Through the window, the city is the same. But the inside of the apartment seems eerily the same, too, even though her things are gone.

There's the same rich brown leather couch and love seat, the same large TV mounted to the wall, and Chase's rarely used Gibson guitar in the same corner, no more likely to be played. The only indications of the years she'd lived here are the empty chunks of space on the bookcases and patches of a faint sticky residue from the Post-its Chase used to write her. It's as if this place has already erased her.

Back in the bathroom with the cordless phone in hand, Sharon picks up her cell, checks it in case she somehow missed a call.

No messages.

Her heart starts racing again.

Another chug of vodka to slow things down.

She needs to stay calm. Chase said he would call, and there's no sense in jumping down his throat the minute he does. Better to be relaxed. Tell him she loves him and she's sorry.

Setting both phones within easy grasp, she eases into the tub. The water has cooled a bit but is still hot enough that goose bumps dot her arms.

Seeing the utility knife in the corner, she thinks again of Nero.

It wasn't only that Roman emperor who slit his wrists. Artists, too. Mark Rothko, or was it Jackson Pollock? And the woman who did the creepy photographs—Diane something.

All those scraps of things she used to know before her brain was full of celebrity gossip from *Living* (not full enough for a promotion, though).

More vodka and the world smudges, though it's probably not possible to take effect that quickly, might simply be her melodrama.

Picking up the knife, she slides out the blade.

Wonders what made those others actually follow through.

There had been the day of the fire four months ago.

She'd been halfway through consuming a sleeve of saltine crackers waiting for Chase to get home from the hedge fund (which had been taking longer and longer lately) when Rodney—the youngest of the doormen—rang her bell with a package. The return address was a prominent literary agency in Midtown where Sharon had sent her manuscript. That it was a package seemed promising, like a thick letter from a college meant you'd been accepted. It was nice to feel hopeful; over the past two months, she'd exhausted all the agents of friends and professors, as well as a whole slew of the listings on *Publishers Weekly*. She'd even convinced Kristen, who had worked in the NYU Office of Annual Giving since sophomore year, to slip her a list of alums in publishing.

The optimistic feeling was short-lived. Tearing open the box revealed not an acceptance letter, but her original copy of the manuscript bound with the same rubber bands, as if it were so toxic that agents didn't even want to throw it in their own recycling bins. Whereas the other rejection letters she'd gotten had contained glimmers of praise—"Ultimately too melancholy, but some artful language"; "a little too depressing for us, but extremely well written"—this one simply read: "Thank you for letting us consider your work. This is not a project we would represent." No one had even bothered to sign it.

Only two years earlier, Sharon had been the toast of her MFA program. Now she was the one getting form letters from literary agencies.

In hindsight, burning the manuscript was a poor idea. At the time it felt wonderfully symbolic to get the big copper pot from the cookware set

Chase's stepmother had given them, place the manuscript inside, and throw in a lit match. Only the first few pages got a satisfactory char before the smoke alarm sounded and she took the whole thing out on the terrace.

The title page and prologue had begun to curl when the wind kicked up and improbably swept a lit page to the next unit's balcony without extinguishing the flame. The neighbor, whom Sharon had never actually spoken to but disliked because she often wore nothing but a sports bra and low-cut yoga pants, had a deck chair, apparently coated in turpentine and lighter fluid, that actually ignited.

For a brief moment, Sharon simply stood there watching the small fire singe the seat of the chair. It seemed likely the tiny flame would quickly be put out by the wind.

That proved not to be the case.

Burning pot of novel in her hands, Sharon ran inside and doused the book in the sink, then raced to the neighbor's door. After gently knocking, then gently pounding and getting no response, she hurried back to her own apartment. Dumping the burned pages, she filled the pot with water and scurried to the balcony. Balancing precariously on her own patio chair, she tried to heave the water in the general direction of the not-so-raging fire twenty-five feet away. The diminutive wave moved horizontally a few inches at best, but inertia caused Sharon to bumble forward.

Instinctively she dropped the pot and reached for the guardrail. Her breathing was heavy and ragged as she watched the pot hit the pavement with a clang muted by thirty-five stories.

That's when the thought flittered across her mind.

Jump.

Follow the expensive cookware down to a dramatic end.

One leg on top of the six-inch-thick railing, Sharon slowly brought up her other foot. It wasn't hard to balance on the thin metal strip. Gingerly, she eased away from the wall until the only points of connection were her feet on the railing and the tip of her left index finger on the brick.

Maybe she would have taken the leap into nothing or maybe she wouldn't have. But when she glanced down, Sharon noticed a Rodney-esque form examining the copper pot remains on the sidewalk.

The trance was broken.

She remembered sports-bra neighbor's smoldering deck chair and the novel remains in the sink. Remembered she had to come up with story ideas for the *Living* magazine all-staff meeting the next morning.

Stepping down to the safe enclosure of her own balcony, she called downstairs to the front desk. Her recounting of events must have sounded nonsensical, but the terms "fire" and "next door" got Rodney's attention. A minute later he was at her door with the set of master keys and a fire extinguisher. Sharon followed him into Sports Bra's apartment (surprisingly, there was a series of fierce, non-Zen oil paintings on the wall). The fire was basically out, but Rodney sprayed it aggressively anyway. The hole in the canvas seat that remained was the kind of thing that begged an explanation.

"I think it's your responsibility to repair this." Rodney offered a sad look as they walked back to the hallway. "I can check if the building insurance will cover it."

Sharon was assuring Rodney she would get the new chair when the elevator dinged and Chase stepped out, already looking confused.

"Was that one of the pots Gen sent us downstairs?" he asked.

Perhaps sensing an impending lovers' quarrel, Rodney quickly ducked into the open elevator car.

"I dropped it," Sharon said, without further detail.

Shaking his head, Chase walked into their acrid-smelling apartment and examined the soggy burned manuscript.

"What is with you lately?" he asked.

The rational part of her realized she owed him an apology. An unfamiliar spiteful and malicious side (maybe the part that wanted to jump) suddenly found it exasperatingly unfair that Chase was kicking ass at his new gig as a portfolio manager, while she was still an editorial assistant at *Living* who'd been rejected by all the major (and several of the minor) literary agencies in Manhattan.

"I know it's impossible for you to understand, but not all of us have the perfect life," she'd said and stormed out.

He didn't follow. With no destination in mind, she went to Dewey's on Fifth and ordered one of their beers on tap, even though she rarely drank, and never beer. When she got back, Chase was already in bed so he could get up and go running at six (it had been a long, long time since she'd gone with him). There was a Post-it note on the closed bedroom door saying he'd paid for the neighbor's chair. Sharon crumpled it up and walked out to the terrace, dropped it over the side. For a while she leaned over the edge, not searching for the Chrysler Building at all.

Even fuzzy from the alcohol and the no-longer-hot bathwater, Sharon can see the time glowing in the window of her cell phone: 11:00 P.M.

Only ten in Chicago!

But no, it's becoming clearer and clearer that Chase *isn't* going to call.

In fact, when she's being completely honest with herself, Sharon has actually called his cell phone . . . not obsessively, but once right before getting the truck and again when Kristen was in the bathroom. It had gone straight to voice mail both times.

Maybe he forgot to turn his phone on after his flight? She's done that. When she and Chase had visited his mom in Hong Kong last year, Sharon had been so taken with the escalators and buildings growing from trees, she'd forgotten to switch it on for two days.

Even so, he's not thinking about you. Not making you a priority.

Picks up the knife. Pushes up the blade.

Arbus.

Diane Arbus—that's the creepy photographer who slit her wrists. Nicole Kidman is supposed to play her in a movie.

Taps the tip of her index finger to the sharp point. Presses until she hears the faintest pop of flesh (maybe it's actually soundless, but she thinks there's a pop).

Chubby dot of blood.

Sucking it off, she remembers standing on the railing.

Runs the blade across her left wrist. Not even enough pressure for a scratch.

Maybe she simply hadn't hit rock bottom four months ago.

The start of the end began five days ago at the *Living* all-staff meeting when the executive editor announced that Julie—the other editorial assistant, who was four years younger than Sharon and had been at the magazine half as long—was being promoted to assistant editor.

Sharon had swallowed over a squawk.

With its focus on celebrities and their shoes, *Living* was far from her dream gig, but Sharon had thought she'd been doing a decent job of ordering lunches for the editors and writing the dry front-of-the-book captions (even if she did work on her too-depressing novel during the downtime). Julie, on the other hand, seemed to spend huge amounts of her day badgering editors for longer pieces to write and volunteering to cover events if the reporters were too busy—apparently that wasn't annoying, that was ambition.

It was Sharon's first acute and painful realization of the day: She was twenty-six, still in an entry-level position, and all she had to show for it was a stack of rejection letters from the finer and less fine literary agencies in New York.

The second acute and painful realization came exactly two seconds later, when the editor noted Julie had two reasons to celebrate since she had gotten engaged over the weekend.

Blushing, Julie joked, "Well, Daniel and I *were* coming up on the two-year mark." On her finger was a round diamond-and-platinum ring that looked exactly like all the rings young women in the office were constantly coming in with after holiday breaks.

A taut spring of anger and anxiety, Sharon spent the next few hours hiding in the ladies' room. That no one noticed she was gone probably spoke volumes about why she'd been passed over for a promotion. At exactly six she put on her coat and, without any memory, took the subway the three stops to the Madison Plaza.

She didn't turn on the television or her computer. Didn't pick up a book or skim Chase's *Wall Street Journal.* Just sat on the couch and waited for him to come home. He must have been out with some of the sell-side guys, because by the time he opened the heavy front door it was after nine, and he smelled of beer and money.

"Hey." Chase nodded in her general direction and set down his messenger bag. "Did you eat?" Without waiting for a response, he opened the refrigerator.

"Why aren't we married?" Sharon demanded.

"What?"

"It's been years. Are we ever getting married?"

Shutting the crisper, he'd rubbed his eyebrows, as if he were getting another migraine. "Do you even want that?"

"You know I do," she said, though she wasn't entirely sure her behavior over the past few months had made that evident.

For a long time, he didn't say anything but studied the grain in the granite counter. Finally, he looked up with the same tortured expression he had when discussing his sister's lack of direction and poor choice in men.

"I'm sorry, Sharon." He said it gently, which made everything more real and a thousand times worse. "I don't want to marry you."

"But we live together, and we used to talk about that stuff all the time. . . ."

"I know." He massaged his forehead. "I wouldn't have asked you to move in if I hadn't thought we were going in that direction. But we've been unhappy for a while now—a ring won't fix that."

She asked how he could say that, but she knew exactly how. It was all those nights they didn't go to bed together, when she stayed up tweaking her novel or pouting over a rejection letter. The weekends where she'd wave away his questions about how things were going on her rewrites or her agent search and turn back to her laptop. The evening just a few weeks ago, when he'd come home with a whisper of the old excitement in his eyes and told her he'd read that the QT Network was working on an *E&E* origins show, and she hadn't bothered to look up from her computer, just snorted a "so."

"I feel like I don't really even know you anymore." He shook his head, as if it might improve the situation. "I'm sorry."

Maybe if she had cried or apologized or said she wanted to work on things, it might have been different. Maybe if she kissed him or swore she was still the person he had fallen in love with. Maybe if she had simply said nothing.

But he was one more person, in a seemingly endless line of people, telling her that she wasn't good enough. Her writing wasn't good enough to represent, her performance at work wasn't good enough for a promotion. Now she wasn't good enough to marry.

"If you feel that way, if I'm so horrible, why haven't you broken up with me already?"

"I don't know. I kept hoping things would get better once you got past this book thing." He said it honestly, but she'd laughed, cruel as she could muster, wanting to transfer her hurt and failure.

"You know you're a fucking coward," she said.

"Stop."

"Seriously, if you're too much of a pussy to dump me, I'll do it for you."

"Shar—"

"Poof, we're over. You're free. Go run back to your fancy friends, and I'll get back to really writing."

That night Chase had slept in his office. Sharon called in sick to work for the next few days and asked Kristen if she could stay with her for a while. When she e-mailed her plans to Chase, he'd told her he'd go to Chicago so he wouldn't be in the way when she moved.

It made Sharon think of that first Thanksgiving she'd gone home with him, when he'd been thrilled to show her off to his family, about how she'd been so nervous she couldn't stop talking about the election. She thought about the way she and Chase used to send each other myriad daily e-mails about genuinely mundane things—"Tried some gummy vitamins at work, yummy!"; "Got the worst paper cut, will definitely need kisses"; "If you could only have egg rolls or pizza for the rest of your life, which would you choose?"—about how they used to speak in a hybrid of baby talk and shared references that would have caused his finance friends to explode into hysterics. How excited he'd been to find her waiting for him in Central Park at the end of the New York City Marathon, and how after business trips to LA he'd rest his head against her shoulder and lament his deteriorating relationship with his sister.

Stuff like literary rejection and sucking at work didn't seem so all-consumingly important then.

And she desperately wanted a Neutrocon so she could hop one universe over and redo their conversation.

Things are very underwater in her head.

Her head, too, must have been underwater at some point, her face and hair wet.

Bath is cooler now.

Chase isn't going to call.

Even if he thought she was moving out tomorrow. Even if he forgot to turn his phone on.

She won't get her chance to say she's sorry and she loves him.

Picking up the Post-it, she reads his year-old message again.

Had to go to work, Shar, but I love you very much.—C

Ink swelling and blurring from her wet hands.

With the Sharpie, she writes her own line underneath his words.

I love you, too. I'm sorry.

Maybe he'll see it when he returns Sunday night.

Maybe he'll call then.

Setting down the note, she picks up the knife.

Was what she wrote more than a simple apology?

No, you don't have the guts, just like on the balcony.

Presses the blade deeper into her left wrist this time.

Red unfolds like a ribbon.

Not painless.

Stings like a motherfucker.

Looks like a lot of blood, but with all the bathwater, hard to tell how much of it has been diluted. Hard to tell if she's serious. If she means it.

Presses harder.

A ring.

The sound she's been waiting for for nearly thirty hours.

So surprising, it takes her a moment to recognize that's what it is: the rarely used landline.

Caller ID shows "Blocked"—the Fishers' unlisted number.

Everything slick with blood and water, she drops the phone twice.

"Chase, I'm sorry, I love you," she says, depressing the talk button, trying to sound stable, sober, and sane.

"Sharon, it's Phoebe Fisher." The voice on the other end doesn't sound stable or sober or sane. "My brother is . . . on the plane . . . aneurysm . . . he's de . . ."

"Thank you," Sharon says.

Get out of this car.

A clatter, and Sharon realizes she's thrown the phone across the bathroom and it's in pieces on the floor.

Get out of this car.

Props herself out of the tub and reaches for a towel. She throws open the cabinet under the sink, yanks out the first-aid kit. Breaking the seal on the bottle of Ipecac, she swallows it in one gulp. Within minutes she's puking up vodka and vodka and maybe everything she's ever eaten. Shivering and sweating. Blood from her arm mixes with the bathwater and splashes on the already damp floor. Shaking, she wraps her left wrist tight in gauze, binds that with surgical tape.

In the bedroom, the phone that she didn't hurl at the wall is ringing. The machine picks up and Chase's voice announces that they can't come to the phone right now. Then his model sister is leaving a message that Sharon doesn't hear.

Get out of this car!

Still soggy and bleeding, Sharon pulls on her clothes in the reverse order she took them off—silky bra and panties, jeans, T-shirt, blue sweater, socks, and snow boots—everything instantly damp.

Phone ringing again.

Grabs her purse from the living room floor. No checking around, no taking any last-minute things she forgot to pack from this life. Before Phoebe Fisher can leave another message, Sharon is gone, the heavy metal door shutting behind her.

She needs to get away from this apartment, from this floor, as soon as possible. No time to wait for the elevator. Sharon pulls open the door to the stairs and hurries down thirty-five flights. Lurching out the side entrance onto Twenty-eighth Street, she's swallowed into the cold, cold city that's too lit up to ever truly be dark.

6   i've never been, but i hear it's righteous

"I'll shave my balls if they want."

That's what Adam told his agent when the producers of a basic cable *Eons & Empires* origins show offered him the role of a young Captain Rowen on the condition he shave his head—no bald caps. It had been nearly four years since the *Goners* pilot didn't go. Years of voice-over work and five-line spots on bad sitcoms. Years of sheepishly asking Phoebe for the odd bartending shift when things got *really* dry. He would have shaved his balls and dipped them in alcohol, repeatedly, had it been a contractual sticking point.

But it's the fourth day of shooting outdoors in Vancouver, and without hair, Adam is fucking freezing.

Seventeen hours earlier the makeup artist had straight-razored off last night's growth of sandy stubble (again) and spent no less than two hours applying elaborate airbrush foundation and details—including Rowen's famous crescent moon birthmark at the base of his skull. While he can *carefully* be helped into a thick overcoat by a PA between takes, the makeup is too delicate for him to wear a hat, and it's really, *really* cold.

So cold he's forgotten the seemingly permanent knot in his right thigh and the continents of fading bruises along his torso from wire work, where producers probably should have sprung for a stunt double, but Adam was too happy to be working on something that didn't suck to say anything.

So cold he's stopped worrying about the pained whine his cell phone kept making and turned it off, accepting it will be on terminal roam for the duration of his time in Canada.

So cold his first instinct is to say no when Cecily Beissel—Cecily of the Jericho Jeans ads—asks him to grab a drink and talk about their upcoming love scene when/if they finish shooting for the night. Of course it's entirely possible she's not asking him out and he's simply suffering hypothermic delusions.

"I figured it would be a nice way to break the ice before we have to put on body stockings." Cecily has a hand on his shoulder. "I've"—she lowers lovely brown eyes—"never really done anything like this before."

Yep, a model with a jeans-ad-caliber ass is asking him to talk her through their sex scene, off the clock, and he doesn't want to because he's chilly. He realizes this would not be the response of the average twenty-nine-year-old heterosexual male. He also realizes it probably has less to do with body heat lost through his naked head and more with the way he'd left things with Phoebe in LA, somehow weirder than the way they usually left things in their long history of leaving things weird.

"It doesn't have to be a big deal." Cecily slides a long red hair behind her ear. "There's a little divey place by the hotel. They serve cheese cubes and crackers."

Adam has to be shirtless and waxed in their love scene; cheese is far from a selling point.

"I'm not . . ." he begins.

He would be shocked if he's slept more than forty hours total since he arrived for preshoots twelve days ago, and because of the head-shaving/makeup applying, his call is a good two hours earlier than everyone else's. He should go back to his room, eat something other than craft table pretzels, rest, figure out the cell phone thing—a blocked number has been repeatedly trying to call.

But . . . he only has one scene near the end of the day tomorrow, and he's so alive and excited from working on a project that might be good that he probably wouldn't sleep anyway.

"Please." Cecily smiles.

Which is why two hours later he's at a bar called Polly's Cave throwing a flightless dart at a faded board. He hits the bull's-eye again.

"I get the feeling you've done this before." Cecily laughs and retrieves the darts. She's changed from Cordelia Snow's white robes into a pair of jeans and a fitted T-shirt with a pink pig on the chest. Pigs seem to be a big thing for her. Yesterday she'd worn pig earrings, and there's a pig on the bag where she keeps her knitting supplies; she's been working on a sweater between takes. "I feel like I'm being hustled."

"I grew up with my grandparents." He sips a local microbrew she'd picked out, Enchanted Ale. "I kick ass at shuffleboard and minigolf, too."

They're two of a handful of customers, and Polly's Cave definitely lives up to the moniker, with poor lighting, wood-paneled walls, and a mothbally odor. For added oddity, the bartender, who radiates dislike for Adam, has a black patch over his left eye. They do, in fact, serve cheese and Ritz crackers in lieu of snack mix.

Popping what must be her fifteenth cheddar chunk, Cecily manages to land a single dart on the target. And because they're in a bar, playing a bar game, and an attractive woman is performing poorly, Adam is required, by bar law, to advise her, position her hips in a better stance, adjust her throwing arm—her creamy skin in his still-cold hand. She's losing less badly when they abort the game and take seats at the long counter.

"Thanks for doing this with me," she says, as if the evening has truly been a hardship. "It's just, we haven't had much time together, and I wanted to know I was pronouncing your last name right before I had to lick your head."

"Is that actually in the script?" He grins, realizes he's having a good time, points to her empty bottle. "Can I get you another?"

She nods and excuses herself to the ladies' room.

The second she turns, it's as if his off button has been hit. Instantly he's so tired the simple act of being upright feels Olympian, and he sags into the bar stool, thankful it's not backless. He needs sleep and a thorough scrub—he'd washed off all the makeup in his trailer, but he hasn't showered since dawn. And he's still freezing, even in the sheepskin jacket he bought his first hour off the plane, when he'd been cold but still had hair.

Staring at his beer bottle until his eyes blur, Adam peels the label off in thin strips wet with condensation. He wonders if Phoebe's behind the bar at Rosebud.

She'd taken Adam to the airport, hugged him good-bye so tight he could hardly breathe, Anais Anais and vanilla-scented lotion heavy around him. Lips against his ear, Phoebe had whispered, "You know how proud of you I am?" He was only going to BC for three weeks, but it felt like a good-bye for longer, and it dawned on him that it would be *much* longer if the show got picked up. Still in Phoebe's death grip embrace, he'd turned her body ever so slightly, until his mouth was on hers. It wasn't that she didn't respond, she did, even ran fingers through his hair (he'd still had hair then) to bring him closer. But when she pulled away, there was something about her smile—it was the pouty practiced one she used on auditions and with customers at Rosebud. Like a line drive to the nuts, he realized he might very well end up just one more guy Phoebe Fisher had known in LA, realized that would bother him.

At this bar, in Canada, the bartender gives him a look, and Adam sweeps the shredded beer label off the counter into his palm, dutifully orders another round.

"So are you some famous actor or millionaire?" the eye-patched bartender asks. "I mean, I know who *she* is." He cocks his head toward Cecily on her way back from the bathroom. "Should I know you?"

There's blatant accusation in this guy's question, and Adam is so beat he doesn't ask if the bartender has seen *Graphic* or *Super Temps* or any of the other movies in which Adam has had small parts. Doesn't tell the bartender he might recall his voice from the *Mortal Warrior* video games or the *Go Go Trons* Saturday-morning cartoon series. No one *ever* recognizes Adam, and it seems like an awful lot of words to get through.

"Me," Adam says, "I'm nobody."

Bartender smirk-sighs. "Well, Mister Nobody, I'd watch myself if I were you; men turn into animals around a girl like that."

"I'll keep that in mind."

As Cecily makes her way back, Adam physically *pushes* all remaining energy to the surface, like squeezing final dollops from a toothpaste tube. Unslouching, tightening muscles, turning so she'll be facing the left side of his face, the cheek with the dimple.

"Did you read the *E&E* comics growing up?" he asks when she's next to him at the bar, her chair closer than before.

"Never." She dips her head to his as if sharing covert information. "Honestly, the first time I even saw the movies was after my screen test. Don't tell."

"I'll take it to the grave."

"How 'bout you?"

Adam tells her he had a passing familiarity with the comics but actually bought several of the collected volumes before he auditioned.

"They're incredibly dark, like the ending scene in the first issue is the same from the movie, Rowen blowing up the whole East Coast while Cordelia begs him to stop." He shrugs, tries to gauge if she's actually interested; her attention is unexpectedly rapt.

"I'd love to see them sometime."

"I have them at the hotel." The words are out of his mouth before he recognizes how suggestive they sound. Behind the bar Cyclops Bartender realizes too, shakes his head.

"Are you inviting me to your room?" Her hand on his shoulder again.

Adam's got just enough bravado left to smile. "Would you like me to invite you to my room?"

She nods, and he sets a twenty on the bar.

As Adam helps Cecily into her leather jacket, Cyclops Bartender looks at him with equal parts envy and anger. And he can't resist.

"Adam Zoellner," he says, taking Cecily's extended hand. "That's my name."

Thank God for hotel cleaning staff.

When Adam left that morning before 6:00 A.M., it looked as though his suitcase had exploded, something he completely forgot until the moment he's sliding the key card into the slot, Cecily indecently close behind him. But when he opens the door and taps on the track lighting, everything is in perfect order, clothes folded neatly on the luggage rack, shoes lining the wall, the *E&E* graphic novels and the sides for the next day stacked on the desk.

Out of long-established habit, he takes off his coat and empties his pockets on the dresser—keys to his car and apartment (both in LA and completely useless), wallet, spare change, phone. Fuck, he's missed two more calls.

"Your room is bigger than mine." Cecily walks toward the window, pulls aside quilted drapes to reveal the shimmering skyline. "Your view is better, too."

He contemplates saying it's a better vista now that she's in it, rethinks, and joins her by the glass. It's frigid here, too, and he fights back a shiver, shudders freely a half second later when Cecily runs fingers down the back of his neck, rubs her ridiculously soft cheek against his.

"I have a confession," she whispers. "I've seen everything you've ever been in. Like, I even tracked down a tape of *Goners*."

"I'm sorry you had to see that." He smiles, cock fighting viciously against his pants, because, yes, it *is* a turn-on when a model tells you she's seen your obscure work. "There's a reason some pilots don't go."

"I think you're talented."

"Do you now?"

Kissing, kissing, more kissing. Against the window, cold glass on his bare head. Against the wall, her hands fisting his sweater. She's got him in the plush chair, hovering above him. Then she's in his lap. When she finally breaks contact, her lips are swollen.

"I'll be right back." She struts toward the bathroom.

Moving toward the bed, Adam starts to take off his thin gray sweater but pauses at the blinking message light on the hotel phone, glances at his cell.

His grandparents *are* getting older; he should probably check.

Five messages from Phoebe on the hotel phone, the initial one placed mere minutes after he'd left. In the first two, her voice is too wet and raw for Adam to understand what she's saying. Crush in his guts that she's been trying to reach him *all* day and he's been playing darts with a jeans model. Midway through the third message, he's almost pieced events together, when Cecily reappears wearing a lace thong and a matching bra. His expression makes her face fall. Sitting on the chair, she crosses her legs.

Phoebe's fifth and last voice mail, left two hours ago, is clear: "The funeral is tomorrow at two. You don't need to come or anything. But, I dunno, maybe you could call me?"

On the nightstand the alarm clock reads 2:15 A.M., which he thinks puts things after four in Chicago.

"Your girlfriend?" Cecily asks flatly.

"Not really . . ."

"Don't worry, it's late anyway—"

"Her brother, he's, um . . . dead."

The words take a second to register. "Oh, God." Bones in Cecily's face shift, and he realizes her beauty is a tad north of freakish, absently wonders if she was teased in high school. "I'm so sorry."

"The funeral's tomorrow—today, I guess . . . I should. I have to go."

On her feet (still in her underwear, but on her feet), Cecily is talking him down, explaining there probably aren't any flights leaving for a few hours, telling him to pack a bag. He must look confused, because she offers her knitting satchel with the pig on it, starts removing balls of yarn and needles. Finally he nods, throws in a change of underwear, nothing close to a suit, but he has a pair of black pants and a different gray sweater, phone charger, dress shoes.

"Um, when's your call tomorrow?" Cecily is miraculously back in her clothes.

"Not until four; I only have the pool scene."

"I can explain to Mick and the crew, but maybe you should have your agent call somebody." The way she's saying this, Adam realizes leaving could really, *really* screw up his career. "I mean, especially if you're not back by Friday . . ."

Friday, where he has what's slated to be another fourteen-hour day of filming, is all of twenty-one hours away, and Adam has no idea how long it will take to get to Chicago from Vancouver. Still, he nods, tells Cecily he'll have Marty reach out, that he'll fly in for the day and then take a red-eye back. She looks less than convinced about the quality of this plan. Still, she calls a car service and rides the elevator down to the lobby to wait with him for the black Lincoln.

"Good luck." She squeezes his hand, adds, "Godspeed."

———

As Cecily predicted, the entire airport is on skeleton crew when he arrives shortly after three. It takes a while to locate an airline employee who can sell him a ticket, and she yawns apologetically through the transaction. Adam will have a layover in Phoenix, Houston, or Salt Lake City. If he can wait until two, there's a direct flight to Chicago.

"I wouldn't take that one, though," the yawning clerk advises. "It'll probably get canceled; they're expecting weather in the afternoon."

Salt Lake leaves earliest and seems his only chance at getting in anywhere near the time of the funeral. So Adam plunks down his credit card for a ticket costing more than a month's rent. After that, it seems prudent to find a phone booth, call his agent, and see if it's possible *not* to get fired.

Knowing Marty will be royally pissed when he hears of Adam's misadventures, and also knowing Marty won't be in the office until ten, Adam leaves the message for him there and hopes everything will magically be resolved by the time he lands in Utah.

The voice mail picks up at Phoebe's parents' house, so he leaves a message, saying he's on the way and will call during his layover.

"I'll be there soon," he says. And then he's hurrying through the nearly empty security line and echoey terminal, as if that could help him keep the promise.

Ninety minutes and a spectacularly uncomfortable nap on the floor later, he's nodding absently at the woman in 16A as he stows Cecily's knitting bag in the overhead compartment and collapses into 16B. Seat belt buckled, impotent cell phone switched off. There's pressure in his ears as the plane speeds up and propels into the brightening sky. Still in his coat, still freezing, Adam tries to rest his head on his shoulder in a way that won't result in a neck kink, closes his eyes.

Darts with Cecily only they're not darts, but arrows he fires from a giant bow, and it's not the bar, but a grand venue where crowds cheer.

Sharp squeeze of his hand.

Adam pops awake and finds the girl in the window seat is gripping his wrist on the armrest they share. Blushing, she lets go.

"I'm so sorry," she says. "I don't fly a lot."

Even half asleep Adam knows he should say something about air travel being extremely safe.

"It's just a little turbulence," he says, and Jesus f-ing Christ he hopes he's been turning in better performances on set. "They haven't even turned on the 'fasten seat belt' light." Adam points to the panel above their heads. His finger is still in the air as the pilot comes on the speaker announcing they've hit a patch of rough air and he's turning on the seat belt sign.

Adam smiles. "Now you can panic."

The girl laughs. She's cute, nymphlike. "I'm Callie."

"Adam."

"So, are you starting out or heading home?" Her voice is still shaky, eyes terrified and wide, so he tells her that he was working in Vancouver but has to go to Chicago for a funeral, labels Phoebe his "best friend," which *is* true. Callie says appropriate conciliatory things, and once she determines the dead person was not someone personally close to Adam, asks polite questions about what he's working on. She reacts with genuine enthusiasm when he tells her he's an actor and they're making an *E&E* origins show. She even claims to have watched a few episodes of *Go Go Trons* with her nephew.

"Wow, that's wow." She lowers her lids, then raises her eyes in a way he's pretty sure she intends to be seductive. "I'd have flown more if I'd known you could meet TV stars."

The stewardess comes by offering plastic tumblers of soda and pretzel packets, and Adam realizes his jaw isn't clenched anymore and he's no longer shivering, that he's momentarily forgotten how tired he is.

Before Callie even sips her Diet Coke, he's devoured his snack, remembers the last thing he ate was a different handful of pretzels fourteen hours ago.

"Here." Callie hands him her own pretzels. "I stopped for breakfast on the way to the airport."

As he eats, she tells him about Salt Lake City, jokes it's not just Mormons. Originally Adam thought she was barely into her twenties, but as she talks it becomes evident she's not a girl but a woman who knows how to work personal space—a light touch of his elbow, subtle bump of her shoulder to his. Perhaps it's just habit, but he finds himself flirting back.

Callie explains she's an assistant in a dermatologist's office and writes the name of a lotion on a cocktail napkin when he tells her how the Rowen makeup makes his head itch. "This stuff is a godsend," she says. "It'll keep you ageless."

As the plane begins its descent, she asks when his connection leaves. "If you've got time, we could grab a coffee?"

So totally something he would have been up for yesterday, or last week, or any number of days before Phoebe's messages.

Since it's only thirty-seven minutes before his next flight, Adam doesn't have to lie.

"That's too bad." She sighs. "Well, maybe you'll come back for a proper visit, or I'll get out to California one of these days."

"Yeah, that'd be fun." He nods but doesn't give her his info even when she says she wrote her number on the napkin.

Stuck in a holding pattern, they land fifteen minutes late. Hurriedly handing Callie her bag from the overhead bin, he calls a quick good-bye and sprints down the jetway. Behind him he can feel her deflate.

Ultimately there's no need to rush; monitors list his connection as canceled. As is the flight to Chicago scheduled two hours later. In fact, several flights to Midwestern cities he's never been to—Milwaukee, Detroit, Minneapolis—are no-gos.

Callie appears next to him, roller suitcase in tow.

"There must be bad weather," she says.

As if further proof is needed, CNN Airport Network is showing a puffy-coated reporter braving wind and sleet above the headline: SNOW-STORMS PUMMEL THE MIDWEST.

They both stare at the screen.

"You can stay with me," Callie offers. "You're not going to make the funeral, and I don't have to work until Monday. I can show you the city."

There's something creepy about the offer, but also sweet.

"That's really nice, but I need to get to her. Maybe I can fly nearby and drive the rest of the way?"

Callie opens her mouth as if she's going to protest but changes course. "I'll stick around until you're rebooked, just in case."

"You don't need to do that—"

"It's no big deal."

Protesting more will achieve nothing, and a line of grumbling passengers is already forming at the United counter, so he agrees and gets in the queue.

"This way you'll have a place to crash if you end up shipwrecked in Salt Lake."

Flash of what it would be like to stay with this girl. Blond hair splayed across pink sheets, golden throat under his lips, a lacy negligee he'll pull up to expose her breasts, let it cover her face like a veil.

He shivers, cold again.

Clocks all over announce it's almost 10:00 A.M., noon in Chicago, he's pretty sure. Adam starts to run fingers through his hair but hits skin and remembers that, in addition to likely missing Chase Fisher's funeral, he'll soon be late for work. Work on a project with hints of brilliance hidden behind its too pretty cast, a project where he beat out hundreds of other actors for an iconic role. He needs to call his agent.

Apologizing to Callie, he checks voice mail on his finally working cell phone.

Four messages from Marty in varying degrees of distress, each first relaying the calls and exaggerations he's made thus far on Adam's behalf, then insisting Adam call immediately. One message from Cecily, asking if he got in okay. Another from his mother he simply skips.

There's a message from Phoebe, voice pebbles and blood, telling him not to worry if he doesn't get there in time for the funeral, giving directions to her father's house and the cemetery. "Thank you, Adam, I . . . thank you."

Callie's eyes on him.

For the second time in a dozen hours, a very pretty girl is looking at him expectantly, and all he can think of is the tender flesh of Phoebe's earlobes and the way she braids her fingers together and clasps them to her heart when she's sad. Phoebe, who over the years he's hurt countless times, countless ways. When, he wonders, did it become his lot in life to disappoint beautiful women?

Finally he's at the desk where a rep tells him there's no way he's getting to Chicago until tomorrow morning. Callie lays a hand on his elbow.

"Please, I have a funeral, is there anywhere within driving distance?" Adam asks the clerk.

The man presses lips together and nods, as if to convey that he feels bad as Adam is probably bald from chemotherapy and all, but he's not the only person trying to get somewhere. "Right now we're still going to Cincinnati; I think it's about a six-hour drive."

"Perfect," Adam says, feels Callie stiffen.

"Did you check a bag?" the clerk asks. Adam shakes his head. "Good, I'm going to put you on the eleven forty-five, which gets in at four ten."

Right around the time Adam would conceivably be filming his lone scene for the day and just late enough to guarantee there's no way he's making his 5:00 A.M. call tomorrow.

"So I guess you're off then?" Callie says. His flight isn't for another hour and a half, and Adam says a silent prayer to various deities that she won't insist on waiting with him.

"Yeah." Burying hands in his coat pockets, he looks at his feet. "It was really nice meeting you."

"Is it wrong I'm bummed you're not staying?" she asks, young and timid, like when she was scared on the plane. "Is this chick in Chicago really that much hotter than me?" She forces a laugh but seems authentically injured, and it breaks his heart a little.

"Callie." He brushes his lips to her cheek; he's always been good at making people believe things that aren't true. "She's got nothing on you."

By the time Adam boards Flight 568 to Cincinnati, the fact that he hasn't slept in thirty hours is becoming increasingly evident. It takes considerably longer than it should to find his row, and he almost sobs when he sees a girl wearing an Unaccompanied Minor badge in the leg-roomier aisle seat.

The kid might be the most striking he's ever seen—perfect red curls down her back and skin the color of the vanilla ice cream he used to serve in his grandparents' shop. This doesn't make the prospect of sitting next to her for three hours in the cramped space by the window any more appealing.

"I would actually prefer the window, if you would rather have the aisle," the preternaturally pale child says in the polite, perfect English of no young person he's ever heard.

"I'd like that." As they shuffle into their places, Adam decides she might be the best kid ever.

"Natasha." The girl extends her hand, offering a surprisingly firm grip. "A pleasure to make your acquaintance."

Adam expects her to begin a conversation like Callie, and frankly he's so grateful for the extra legroom, he'd happily oblige. But Natasha says nothing, only removes items from a pink backpack: a book of Japanese anime with its wide-eyed schoolgirls in short skirts, a bottle of water, and a Ziploc bag of homemade trail mix that looks significantly healthier than the too-sweet Cinnabon he'd eaten about a third of at the airport in between leaving messages for Phoebe and taking the incredibly cowardly route of calling his agent's assistant and telling her he was about to get on a plane before she could patch him through to Marty.

Eyelids heavy as anvils, Adam can't quite fall asleep, so he skims the in-flight magazine and learns he can watch *My Big Fat Greek Wedding* and that he will have his choice of Coca-Cola products.

When they finally do take off, a full hour and a half late, the air is too choppy to focus on the words. Things get disturbingly rough an hour in. A major dip knocks his coffee from the tray, spilling it onto the sleeve of the jacket he's still wearing. Remembering Callie's fear, he smiles at the girl in the window seat. "It's nothing to worry about," he says. "Just a few bumps."

"I know. My father's a pilot, and my parents divorced when I was six. I fly all the time." She points to him wiping coffee from the sleeve of his jacket. "I can fix that. I'm good at laundry."

Dipping a napkin in her water, she dabs lightly at the stain until it's gone, not even damp.

"Which of your parents lives in Cincinnati?" he asks after he thanks her.

"My mother and her fiancé." Her nose crinkles with dislike. "Are you from the area or just visiting?"

"A friend's brother died," he says. "I was trying to get to the funeral, but . . ." His watch says 1:15 P.M., though he has no idea what that means in conjunction with their current position above the Earth. "I'm pretty sure I'm missing it."

"I'm sorry," Natasha says.

"I didn't know him very well." He shrugs. "Actually, I think he kind of hated me."

"But you love your friend?"

Lowering his head, Adam nods, heat on his cheeks—troubled to admit this even to a complete stranger, to an unaccompanied minor.

"Does she know?"

And he wonders if Phoebe *does* know, know he thinks too much about her oddly chubby fingers and the way she can't say "milk." Know she's the best friend he's ever had, and that he can't quite reconcile that with the times he's fucked her so hard her inner thighs were bruised. Know the reason he's never suggested they give things a shot for real has more to do with how much he *does* care than with any great desire to sleep his way through Los Angeles.

"I hope so," he says.

Natasha doesn't need to say Adam could tell Phoebe, just raises ginger eyebrows in a way that makes him forget she is only a child, makes him feel like the one who's underage.

They fly the remaining hour in companionable silence, eating nuts and M&M's out of her trail mix.

As they start their landing, the turbulence picks up; Adam grips the armrest.

"It's like birth," Natasha says. "My father says it's the closest thing to being born that we ever experience."

It's a weird concept, but he likes it.

The Cincinnati airport (which is inexplicably in Kentucky) is massive, and par for the day's course, he's at a remote terminal galaxies from the rental-car kiosks.

After a shuttle bus, three stops on a light rail, and a gigantic escalator (plus a brief detour to meet Natasha's equally pallid mother and pony-tailed stepfather at passenger pickup), Adam finds himself checking his voice mail in the Avis line.

Marty's messages, all five of them, simply say, "Call me now." There's one from Phoebe detailing specific directions to her father's house. "Don't worry about it being late. I'll wait up for you." Her voice is so defeated, it wrenches Adam's chest.

Behind him a strung-out-seeming girl with enormous blue eyes and what looks like a bloodstain on her sleeve grumbles, and he realizes the clerk is ready for him.

Driver's license shown, credit card charged. Yes, he knows dropping off in Chicago will cost more; yes, he will return with a full tank of gas; no, he doesn't want supplemental insurance; fine, he'll take the supplemental insurance.

"Do you maybe have a map?" he asks, and the clerk, whose ID badge reads Vayu, gives him a slightly nervous look but reaches under the desk. The strung-out bloodstained girl audibly sighs.

As soon as the map is unfolded, Adam realizes he has no fucking clue what the middle of the country looks like. What he thought was Illinois is actually Indiana, and Missouri is way farther south than he would have guessed.

With a yellow highlighter, Vayu draws a path from the airport up and left to the edge of Lake Michigan—which doesn't look at all close. "From what I hear, they have pretty nasty weather up there," the man says. "I'd wait until tomorrow; the winds won't be against you then."

Adam nods and heads out to find his indistinct American compact in the shadowy lot. It's not yet snowing in Cincinnati (or Kentucky, wher- ever the hell he is), but he can feel it in the air.

For the first half hour navigating out of the airport and through a series of connecting highway ramps, Adam is perched and alert. Ten miles out of the city limits, he starts to drift as the first fat snowflakes fall. Flipping on the radio, he finds a Matchbox Twenty song he can't stand but some- how knows all the words to. To stay focused, he sings along.

Everything the same—mile after mile of flat nothingness—uniform in the darkness.

His mother. Beautiful and always so sad. "You never called me," she says. "I gave up my whole life for you and you never came home, couldn't even return my calls." Her look is not surprised, only disappointed. "I'm sorry, Ma." Reaching for her hand but can't grasp her, as if she's no longer flesh and bone.

Screeching blast of a horn.

Adam jerks awake.

Instinctively firming his grip on the wheel, he steadies the car in the middle lane. Behind him the sound fades, but his heart continues to slam against his chest. Rigid and hyperfocused, he's sweaty from the blowing heat but freezing as well. Checking the mirrors, he changes to the right lane, slows to twenty-five miles per hour, and follows the exit signs.

There's a truck stop with a minimart, lights illuminating the gas pumps, so Adam pulls over. A pack of dopey stoned teenagers cluster around an ancient pickup truck. One of them starts toward Adam as he's getting out of the car. The stench of marijuana hits three feet away.

"Hey, mister." The kid extends his hand motioning Adam to stop. Maybe it's because he's still shaken from his almost accident, but Adam actually obeys. "We were thinking maybe you could help us out. I left my ID at home." The kid—who really is a kid, maybe five years older than Natasha, and skinny under a heavy oilcloth coat and droopy corduroys—gestures to his group. "And I promised we'd bring a couple of six-packs to my girlfriend's party—"

"I'm not buying you beer—" Adam stops, notices another smell under the weed: chemicals and cat piss. And God, he hates meth—gives him the shits and tremors and reminds him of Coral Cove—but it also keeps him awake for days. People high on crank don't fall asleep on the highway.

"Dude, come on, don't you remember—" whines the teen.

Adam cuts him off. "Maybe we *can* help each other out."

Five minutes and several misdemeanors later, the kids have twenty-four cans of Natural Light stashed in their truck, Adam and the world's largest coffee are back in the crappy rental car, and the lead teen is slipping him a baggie of highly questionable uppers through the window. "My girlfriend's place is right down the road," Lead Teen says. "You can come party with us if you want."

Making a silent promise to donate his first *E&E: Rising* paycheck to some keep-kids-off-drugs charity, Adam thanks Lead Teen but explains he needs to get to Chicago.

"That's cool." Lead Teen nods. "I've never been, but I hear it's righteous."

Caffeine and chemicals gnaw a hole in his guts but manage to keep Adam awake-ish for two and a half hours of more flat nothing. The roads aren't crowded, but the thickening snow and slick pavement limit the speed of traffic to thirty-five miles per hour.

After Indianapolis, when the map indicates he is to do nothing but remain on 65 North for another 120 miles, he feels himself teetering on the edge of unconsciousness again, chugs the rest of the lukewarm coffee. He tries calling Phoebe but gets the machine. Cracking the driver's side window, he's hit with a rush of air so glacial, it feels solid slicing through his light jacket and naked scalp.

Ten miles later the snow has picked up and traffic is at a crawl. He reaches into his pocket for the phone, the terror of returning his agent's calls an instant pick-me-up.

"Where the fuck are you?" Martin Minerva demands without any of his usual pleasantries.

Adam is explaining he's somewhere outside of Indianapolis before realizing Marty didn't mean the question literally.

"What're you doing, buddy?" Marty sighs. "This is what we've been trying to get you for years." Since Adam says nothing, Marty keeps talking. "I've been on the horn for you all day, but I'm not a god. Rex Stern isn't returning my calls, which, frankly, is a pretty bad sign." Another sigh. "Maybe if the dead guy had been your own brother."

"I really had to—" Adam doesn't bother finishing the sentence. It's not really true and he's too worn out to lie. "I'm sorry; she's important to me."

"Your hot roommate? I didn't even think you guys were together."

"Look, I'll just show up, tell her I'm sorry, and head back first thing in the morning."

"It *is* morning," Marty says, and indeed the dashboard readout claims it's 2:15 A.M. "You sound like shit. When's the last time you slept?"

"I have no idea, time zones—"

"You gonna smash the car and kill yourself?"

"Not the plan."

"Seriously, Z, if you're falling asleep, pull over and nap for an hour."

"I can't." If he stops, he will never start again, will be buried under the snow for some future generation to discover: early twenty-first-century man in shitty twentieth-century rental car. "I know it's late, but can you . . . can you just talk to me for a few minutes?"

A sigh more defeated than Marty's first two sighs. "Sure, buddy, what do you want to talk about?"

"I dunno, tell me about your kids," Adam says.

"You wanna know about my kids?"

"Yeah." Surprisingly, he does.

And tales of Elmo and Disneyland and hanging the children's "crappy" paintings in the bathrooms carry Adam through most of the great state of Indiana, until he starts to see signs for Gary. Carry him until the connection begins breaking up. Taking the phone from his ear, Adam sees the battery outline in red—no power left.

"You gonna make it, buddy?" Marty asks.

Adam nods, because the screen is blank, the phone a lump of useless metal in his hand.

An hour later he slams on the brakes, feels the car skid, and narrowly misses becoming the seventh vehicle in a six-car pileup—twisted metal like a multiheaded monster.

It seems a good time for a piss, so he follows the exit ramp to a gas station with a smiling sun on the sign—utterly ridiculous in the current weather conditions.

Teeth literally chattering, Adam can hardly unzip his jeans in the icebox of a bathroom. It's dirty, smells of dumps past, everything eerily lit from a bare bulb's abrasive light. But he leans against the grimy, uneven drywall . . . a few seconds . . . maybe . . .

Shakes his head. Splashes cold water on his cold face.

Urine probably isn't supposed to smell exactly like coffee.

Yet the first thing he does when he's in the dingy store is head for the thermos of hours-old brew, pumps it into a Styrofoam cup, dilutes it with half-and-half and sugar. He should probably get food to counter the caffeine-eating-through-stomach phenomenon, but the flat, depressing cheeseburger on a warming rack is far from appetizing. Grabbing another bag of pretzels, he heads out into the tempest.

The service station attendant had said Chicago was forty minutes away, but going so slowly, it's another two hours before the city's majestic skyline appears, seemingly to grow out of crumbling high-rise housing projects. He's never been, but Adam recognizes the buildings from movies and the stories Phoebe sometimes tells. By the time he makes the turn onto Lake Shore Drive, he's crying. Part of it is simple fatigue, and maybe a side effect of the drugs (a similar, much more humiliating incident happened during an NYU psych exam freshman year after he'd pulled an all-nighter). But it's something else as well. This is *her* city, and for better or worse, Phoebe Fisher is the closest thing he has to a home.

As he enters Evanston Township, the houses become squat stone mini-mansions, with sculptures and snow-covered trees. Phoebe's address is written on the back of his first plane ticket, and he rolls the window down the rest of the way to better read the street numbers.

A startling slap of what can only be called dread when he finally finds it.

The driveway is circular, but he parks on the street, kills the engine, and releases a breath he hadn't realized he was holding. Through the open window, the car rapidly loses heat.

Adam has sneezed and scratched through all the childhood illnesses, had impacted wisdom teeth removed. He's sprained wrists, strained muscles, and woken up missing two days after three lines of very suspect cocaine. And yet he's never felt like this—completely depleted, like someone scooped out everything inside of him, leaving only empty skin and greasy remnants.

It has taken more than twenty-five hours from the time he left the hotel in Vancouver to get here. Hours of motion, of inertia, of knowing the instant he stopped, everything in him would simply shut down like the dead cell phone in his pocket. But he's here now. All he has to do is go inside, and he can be warm and still.

But he's so profoundly afraid.

A significant chunk of him wants to drive back to Cincinnati, fly to Vancouver by way of Atlanta or Berlin or whatever arbitrary hub through which the airline sees fit to route him. Because going inside will be an acknowledgment of things he's been fighting not to fully acknowledge for a very long time.

Leaning forward, he rests his head on the steering wheel.

In an indoor desert of fake sand, throwing punches that fell men twice his size. Roundhouse kicks, warriors in armor, and shields from no particular century or nation. Spinning and spinning, all the moves from the E&E fight scenes, only real. A giant with gnarled hands. A wooden horse twelve stories high. Flaming arrows launched from somewhere in the distance. Something tossing him, turning him about.

A hand shakes his shoulder through the open window.

"Adam." Phoebe's father in a wool coat, face pinked from the subzero temperatures.

It must have been at least an hour since Adam drifted off. Snow has blown in, dusting the wheel, the sleeves of his jacket, his hands—which are alarmingly red and aren't responding quite right to commands from his brain.

"Dr. Fisher?" Adam blinks snowflakes from his lashes.

"Larry," Phoebe's father says, as though it's a reflex—a retread of every other time he's met Adam and tried to dismiss formalities. But this *isn't* like every time he and his wife have swooped into Los Angeles and taken Phoebe and Adam to Nobu or Mr Chow. This is different.

"I'm sorry for your loss, sir," Adam says.

Phoebe's father doesn't acknowledge the statement, instead opens the driver's side door (not an easy task with the wind) and extends his hand. Adam can't seem to get his fingers working, so Dr. Fisher tugs him to his feet by the forearm.

The change in position causes diamond flecks to flash in Adam's peripheral vision, outshining the whirling white. Closing his eyes, he sags against the side of the car, takes a deep breath of ice.

"It's okay, son. I gotcha." Dr. Fisher slings Adam's arm across his shoulders and steadies him at the waist, leads him to the house, even though Adam is stable after the first few steps.

Through the grand entrance, where a crystal chandelier dangles from a two-story ceiling, he sets Adam on a bench by the door and slides his arms from the sopping wet sheepskin coat. Momentarily disappearing into a hall closet, Dr. Fisher returns with a hooded sweatshirt he helps Adam pull over his head. Soft, worn fabric against his scalp feels brilliant, until Adam glances down and notices the University of Wisconsin crest on the chest. A flip in his already unsteady stomach; he's wearing a dead guy's clothes.

"Let me see your hands," Phoebe's father says.

Adam obediently presents his fingers—they seem back online now, still angry red but more steak knives and straight pins than numb. Dr. Fisher frowns and asks about the small blisters on the left ring finger and pinkie.

Adam is still exhausted, still shivering, still not functioning anywhere near optimal, but he's becoming cognizant enough to realize how odd this situation is. Remembering he doesn't know Phoebe's dad well and the man never seemed to like him much. Remembering that he's here to see Phoebe, even if he's scared of what that means.

"Really, I'm fi—" he begins.

A tag on the sweatshirt tickles the back of his neck, and Adam understands. This is a man who lost a child, a doctor who couldn't save his own son but can warm the hands of a cold friend of his daughter's. A friend who fits into the dead kid's clothes.

"Thank you," Adam says and allows Phoebe's father to wrap his hand in a warm towel, wiggles his fingers on command.

It would be wrong to say Adam has never wondered about his own father. Of course he has, but not for years. Tonight, though, he wonders. Wonders about how different things could have been with someone like this in his corner.

Apparently satisfied Adam will live, Dr. Fisher nods. "She's upstairs," he says. "Second door on the right."

And Adam feels as if he should do or say something big and meaningful, some bold gesture. But he's got nothing. So he just returns the nod and starts up the dramatic stairs, feels Dr. Fisher's eyes on him the whole climb.

Phoebe's bedroom is probably bigger than their whole shitious apartment in California. Bookcases, a desk and vanity in a blond wood. Everywhere there are framed photographs of Phoebe, hair still long, posing with all the people in her life. Adam knows he could spend hours studying them, placing faces to the names, and that scares him the same way he was terrified in the car.

In the center of the room is a magnificent canopy bed, and in the middle of that bed is a heap of Phoebe Fisher. She's on her side, and in the limited light, he can't tell if she's asleep or awake, can barely make out the back of her head with its glossy black bob.

This is probably the last moment he could leave, run back down the stairs and out the door. Take the same way out he always takes.

Toeing off his shoes, he doesn't bother with anything else—not his belt or jeans or the gray sweater he's been wearing for days. Not Chase Fisher's sweatshirt. On hands and knees, he crawls into bed and molds his body against Phoebe's spine, drapes an arm over her waist. Whether she's awake or asleep, she doesn't take his hand or respond to his touch at all. Whether she's awake or asleep, she still smells of vanilla lotion and Anais Anais perfume. Whether she's awake or asleep, he realizes what he's known for years, what an unaccompanied minor on a plane had to clarify.

Eight hours later, several things will be different. The storm will have passed, sun bright and harsh over the frozen city dipped in snow. O'Hare Airport will be open, departures running nearly on time. There'll be a first-class ticket in his name on one of those flights—a 4:00 P.M. direct to Vancouver—and several messages from Marty telling Adam that he *needs* to be on that plane. But the humor that wasn't there when Marty was keeping Adam awake and alive all through Indiana will be back. "You must be doing something amazing out there, buddy," Marty's message will say, full of unabashed pride. "Fucking Rex Stern's exact words were: 'The kid's worth holding up production a couple of days.'"

Eight hours later, his muscles won't feel tangled and tight; he'll be starving and truly warm for the first time in days.

In eight hours, he'll still be wearing a dead boy's shirt.

First, though, Adam sleeps, deep and dreamless, wakes to find Phoebe hovering over him. The smile on her lips—the real one, not the one she's perfected for auditions and customers at Rosebud—is both right and wrong with her skin doughy from crying and eyes road-mapped with red lines.

"Hey," he says, shifting onto his back to look up at her. "Sorry it took me so long to get here."

Her grin widens. With her weird chubby fingers, she traces the three-day-old stubble on his scalp.

"I didn't think you would," she says, "but you look good bald."

7 in another country

Phoebe has a historical novel that Gennifer recommended, but instead of reading, she studies the other passengers flying from LA to Vancouver, wonders if they were like the ones on her brother's flight. Wonders if this collection of people would react the same way if a young man were to suddenly collapse on the way to the lavatory. If there would be a doctor or a nurse (like on Chase's plane) to come forward and help. If those efforts, too, would be in vain.

There's a middle-aged man with sable hair in the exit row. Maybe because he looks like her father, Phoebe thinks he might be a doctor. Maybe the outcome here would be different.

She has to pee when they land, but after disembarking and going through customs, she walks past the ladies' room toward the line of pay phones mounted on the wall, dials her brother's apartment in Manhattan, and feels a rush of relief that, for whatever reason, the phone company hasn't disconnected the line, that Chase's recorded voice clicks on after the third ring.

"Hello, you've reached Sharon Gallaher and Chase Fisher. We can't come to the phone right now, so leave a message."

Phoebe's last actual conversation with her brother had been an argument over vodka and Adam five months ago. In LA for business, Chase had insisted on taking her to an overpriced, less-than-stellar sushi place one of his NYC colleagues had recommended, even though she'd lived in the city more than a decade and could have written a dissertation on better sushi establishments in the greater Los Angeles area. The service sucked, the food was worse, and Chase kept checking his BlackBerry and stepping outside to take phone calls that he explained away with the term "portfolio review." Afterward they'd gone to the bar at his hotel, and he'd ordered a Grey Goose martini, extra dirty.

"With that much olive juice, you can't taste the difference and could just order well vodka," she'd said. It was true, but nothing like that could be spoken aloud at Rosebud, where the markup on top-shelf alcohol accounted for a giant percentage of revenue.

"Relax, I'm picking up the check." Chase had bumped his shoulder with hers, raised his eyebrows twice—an echo of the lost nonverbal language of their youth. There'd been creases around his eyes and a few white hairs sprouting at his temples, as if portfolio review had made him the older sibling. "And why do you care if I'm overpaying for drinks?"

"I'm a bartender." Phoebe shrugged. "I'm telling you there's no difference except for the price."

"I *can* taste the difference," he said. "And if I don't order by name, *bartenders* always make martinis with gin." Chase stretched out "bartenders" into something accusatory.

The mood was already strained when he asked, "So what's the deal with you and your roommate; are you, like, together now?"

"We're friends."

"Really?" Chase said with flat disbelief. "You brought him to Hong Kong."

"I don't want to talk about it," she'd said. "It's complicated."

"Pheebs, I'm not trying to be a dick, I just don't want you to get hurt." She'd told him she could take care of herself and asked when he and Sharon Gallaher were going to get married.

"I don't know." He'd looked down. "Lately she's been . . ."

"Complicated?"

"I guess."

He'd tried to give her cab fare, but she'd brushed his money away, insulted and injured. Still, as she'd hugged him good-bye, she promised to get out to New York to see him in the next few months.

Three weeks later Chase had been on a plane to Chicago when an undiagnosed brain aneurysm ruptured; he was dead before the plane hit the ground.

Now Phoebe listens to his voice on the answering machine instructing callers to provide information he'll never receive. She hangs up without leaving a message.

As an afterthought, she enters the code and checks the voice mail at her apartment in California. Her stepmother has left a message asking Phoebe to come to Chicago soon. "I think it might be good for your dad," Gennifer says, reactivating the geyser of guilt Phoebe's felt since she went back to LA ten days after the funeral. "Have fun this weekend, and give Adam our love."

Hanging up, she finally goes to the ladies' room, briefly contemplates putting on makeup but settles for a dab of ChapStick instead. Her hair needs a cut. It's almost to her shoulders for the first time in years.

At baggage claim it takes Phoebe a few seconds to find Adam in the crowd. He's paler than she's ever seen, a stocking cap covering his bald head, torso bulked from a hefty jacket. And the dozen red roses he's holding, presumably for her—that's definitely not consistent with the guy she's shared an apartment with for five years.

"Hey, pretty lady." Adam hands her the flowers, folds her into his arms, and kisses the crown of her head. "Have a good flight?"

She nods against his chest. It's not just the coat. He feels different, more filled out. A few weeks ago he'd mentioned that he'd started working out with Ron Brosh, who plays the show's hero and whose prior claim to fame was being the sexy shirtless guy in an RC Cola commercial.

"I wasn't sure if you'd be hungry, so I made a reservation at this famous place in the West End, or we can order room service if you're tired." Adam takes her duffel bag from her shoulder and leads them toward a waiting black Town Car outside. "If you're up for it, pretty much all of Hollywood North hangs out at the hotel lounge, like, the director of a Mandy Moore movie was there last night and Jennifer Love Hewitt."

Obviously this is what Adam wants, so Phoebe says it might be fun, though it sounds patently awful and she *is* tired, even though it's not yet 10:00 p.m.—something about airplanes.

"A lot of deals are made at the Gerard." Adam is smiling now, looks more familiar. "Who knows, maybe your Lana Turner soda fountain moment will take place in BC?"

It's been so long since her last audition, Phoebe takes a solid second to figure out Adam is talking about her "acting" career.

"Yeah, would be pretty funny if I put in all these years at Rosebud only to be discovered here," she says, but even before Chase died, Phoebe had stopped going to open calls, and when her modeling agency folded last August, she'd made no attempt to find another.

Adam squeezes her hand and points out a few attractions through the car's tinted windows. Everything gray in the drizzling rain, it could be Chicago. From her lap, the smell of the roses tickles her nose.

At Chase's funeral the flowers had been white; orchids and lilies blending with the falling snow. The blizzard hadn't hit yet—not what it became hours later when Adam was driving from Cincinnati—only fat flakes everyone kept shaking off their coats at the graveside. The part of her hair not covered by a black cap had been wet by the time Phoebe had thrown dirt on the lowered coffin. Sharon Gallaher hadn't been there.

"Hey, Pheebs, we're here." Adam, in the car, in Canada, gently nudging her. "You okay. You kinda zoned out for sec."

"Sorry, I'm plane fuzzy," she says.

"We can go straight to bed." Feather kiss on her lips, stroke of her hair.

"No, I want to meet your friends." She tries to mean it. "Will the guy from the RC commercial be there? He's smokin'."

"No sleeping with my mortal enemy." Adam smiles. Then oddly serious, adds, "I don't want to share you."

Half an hour later they're in the famous lounge, designed like an old English club with tapestries and lit fireplaces. Adam insisted she looked great, so Phoebe hadn't changed from the jeans and Converse sneakers she'd worn on the flight—the kind of outfit she wears a lot these days.

Cast members from Adam's show are clumped around the leather-backed bar stools. Ron, the smokin' RC guy; a willowy blonde who introduces herself as Avery Lane; and the redhead from the Jericho Jeans ads, who stands to give Adam a hug.

"You must be Fiona," she says, extends her hand. "Z talks about you all the time. I'm Cecily."

"Phoebe, actually." Phoebe smiles politely, knows Cecily said her name wrong intentionally, but doesn't take the bait and say Adam must not talk about her *that* much.

Light apology, and Cecily is saying she's been to Rosebud a few times for meetings, suggests they might even have seen each other. Phoebe nods, doesn't say she would have remembered, that the Jericho Jeans billboard off Sawtelle had been a favorite of Jerry the manager.

"I love your Chuck Taylors." Cecily, who's wearing stilettos with her jeans and Miss Piggy T-shirt, points to Phoebe's shoes. "You're so lucky you're tall."

Phoebe smiles again. Adam drapes a protective arm around her back—so different from the way they used to be.

Everyone starts talking about filming, Adam and Ron doing their best to fill in the blanks for Phoebe. It reminds her of Evie and Nicole trying to catch her up on the first three years of ETHS when she transferred senior year.

"I swear, Mick—one of the directors—really has it in for this guy." Ron gestures toward Adam. "Seriously, how many takes did he make you do that fall?"

"Had to be fifteen." Adam caresses Phoebe's neck. "Wait until you see this bruise."

"Yeah, makeup's gonna have a bitch of a time covering *that* up for our next naked scene," Cecily says, more toward Adam than anyone else. With Adam's arm still on her shoulder, Phoebe finds she's only mildly annoyed, not threatened, and excuses herself to go to the ladies' room.

Remembering a phone booth by the bathrooms, she ducks inside and calls her brother's apartment. Faithfully, the recorded message comes on after the third ring.

When Chase died, her father and stepmother had been busy filling out official reports and tracking down relatives, so Phoebe had been the one to call Sharon Gallaher. Sharon picked up on the first ring, assumed the caller was Chase, and began apologizing with such raw hope that the bottom fell out of rock bottom.

"Thank you," the girl had said after Phoebe told her. She hung up before

Phoebe could relay information about the funeral and burial. Seven times, Phoebe called back and left the details on the machine. Then she called and just listened to the outgoing message. Sharon never answered again.

On her way back to Adam and his friends, Phoebe passes a group of men and women in business casual clothes and good watches. They look vaguely American, but they're talking about Afghanistan and Iraq in a way that even liberals in California wouldn't, calling them "America's wars." And Phoebe remembers that even though it was only a three-hour flight, she's still in another country.

Adam is at the bar closing his tab, everyone standing around him with their backs toward Phoebe, unaware she's returned. She wonders what they know, what Adam has told these new people in his life about why he fled in the middle of filming the pilot.

"You're really going up so early?" Cecily whines. "Tomorrow's our first day off in *forever*."

"She's tired." Adam tucks his credit card into his wallet.

"Well, put her to bed and come back down." Cecily gives a light tug on Adam's elbow, as if thousands (millions?) of men hadn't whacked off to the Jericho Jeans ad where she was topless, long red hair all that covered her breasts.

"I'm pretty sure he wants to go to bed *with* her, Cese," Ron quips, and Phoebe takes that as a cue to step in close, take Adam's hand, nod when he asks if she's ready to leave. The type of thing she'd never venture before, the type of thing that still feels strange.

Their kisses are reflected in the mirrored elevator doors; pretty people but different from when they met. Different kisses, too, the kind where he strokes her hair, brushes it from her face; years ago he used to pull it. He leads her down the hall to his room, natural gravitation to the bed. More kissing, more hair stroking.

Pulling off his shirt, she fights a gasp. He's always been fit, always put in hours at the gym, but whatever he's doing lately has caused a fundamental shift—the landscape of his body is all hills of lean, defined muscle, waxed smooth and hairless for his role as Captain Rowen. And of course the softball-size bruise on his left shoulder that everyone was talking about at the bar.

Tracing her fingers on the edges that are already changing from purple to yellow, she tells him it's okay if he wants to go back down to his friends.

"I don't." He turns his head, touches his lips to her fingers.

"Cecily seemed disappointed."

"There's nothing to worry about with her." His gray eyes are solemn. "When I first met Cese, maybe there was something, but we're just friends now. I love you, Phoebe."

"I know." For the first time since he came into her life, she's really not concerned about the other women vying for his attention. "It's fine."

"Fine?" Adam aims for mock flabbergasted but can't quite conceal his hurt as he flops back on the bed. "Not exactly the response I was hoping for."

And she realizes this is the first time he's told her he loves her, realizes how much she'd wanted him to say this in some distant, before time in LA—in her country.

"I meant I know you're not sleeping with her." Following him down, she rests her head on his chest, rubs the hairless skin of his stomach, and feels his abdominals tremble. "I know you love me. I love you, too."

"Really?" he asks like a boy, not at all right with his new body, not at all like five years ago. "So are you, like, my official person?"

"Yes, Adam, I'm your girlfriend."

"Good." He rolls slightly so they're facing each other, smiles wide. "I actually already listed you as the emergency contact on all my paperwork."

Had Sharon been her brother's emergency contact? Sharon, who couldn't show up for the funeral, couldn't send a note or make a donation in Chase's name.

And when was the last time Phoebe had to write down those numbers? The last time she'd started anything new? They hadn't made her update her information at Rosebud when she demanded the promotion to bartender four years ago.

Here, in Canada, Adam's lips on her forehead, her nose. She closes her eyes and he kisses the lids. Finally her mouth.

———

The morning after Chase's funeral, Phoebe woke up and found Adam in bed beside her wearing her brother's college sweatshirt. Grimy and bone-weary from having traveled hours and hours to get to her, he'd still been half asleep when she began an all-out assault on his mouth. Brutal kisses with teeth, her tongue eager to learn any remaining things she didn't al-ready know about Adam Zoellner. She'd dug fingers under the offensive University of Wisconsin hoodie and the sweater underneath, raked her nails over his sides. Sticky with a film of dried sweat, he smelled as though he hadn't showered or applied deodorant in days (he hadn't). It didn't mat-ter; she bit the flesh of his neck hard enough to taste blood, made him cry out in a combination of pain and surprise. He was still rubbing the bite when she changed course and reached for his pants, yanked open the belt. Flipping her so he was on top, Adam had held her arms and tried to soothe her. He probably would have stayed like that all day, ca-ressing her, dotting her skin with kisses so tender they made her want to cry. But she'd been crying for three days and wanted to feel different. She'd arched her back so her pelvis rubbed against his cock swelling in his jeans.

In the end he'd won, though, making love to her gently, slowly, even when she tried to ratchet up their rhythm. Afterward he'd held her until he had to go back to BC that afternoon. The network went ahead and or-dered a full twenty-two episodes of *E&E: Rising,* but Adam came home the weekend she got back to LA and made love to her that same way.

The way he does now, as if she's made of Fabergé eggs and blown glass and might shatter. Not at all like the girl he used to throw around when they were just fucking a million years ago.

When they're done, she curls into his side, and he dots her spine with drowsy fingertips, tells her about all the things he can show her tomorrow—Granville Island and Gastown, Stanley Park, maybe sneak her onto the set—places of his universe without her.

"Or we can stay in bed all day," he murmurs as he drifts. "Whatever my *girlfriend* wants."

He starts to snore, something she'd forgotten about in the weeks they've been apart, the weeks of secretly calling Chase's machine and wearing Converse. Running her fingers across his chest, she makes his breathing shift. She'd forgotten about that, too, and about how warm it is to sleep next to him.

Kiss on his collarbone, she whispers, "I really do love you."

At the airport three days later, he sets down her bag, puts his hands on her hips, and asks her to stay the week.

"Come on, Pheebs, my shooting schedule is pretty light. Whad'ya say?"

He doesn't ask what she's rushing back for, but it's a valid question. Back to traffic and smog and martini shakers. To the too-stylized Rosebud patrons and the next generation of hostess/actresses who look at Phoebe as a tragedy, convinced they'll never work their way up to bartender because their big break must be mere days away.

"I can't, sweetie." Phoebe rubs Adam's cheek. "I'm sorry."

"Okay, but promise you'll come back in the next few weeks? My treat."

"I may have to go home and see my parents first."

"Of course," Adam says apologetically. "If you can wait a little bit, I can come with you, maybe."

"That'd be nice," she says, knowing it won't matter; his filming is solid for the next two months.

She checks in, and he walks her to the security line. He tastes like toothpaste when they kiss.

"I love you," she says, and is struck with the memory of seeing Oliver off after he'd helped her move to LA eleven years ago, when the world had been dewy and hers for the taking, when she'd never met Adam Zoellner and Chase was still in high school.

"I love you, too, Phoebe Fisher," he says. "Stay snuggly for me."

Sweet and charming, trying to cram her into the remaining spaces of his new world.

Los Angeles without Adam is more quiet than lonely.

Rosebud is loud and bustling as always, but it's mostly background noise. Clinking glasses and drink orders, superficial conversations of people trying so hard to skate on the surface—designer labels, pilot season, which people in the bar they want to screw.

Adam orders Phoebe a cell phone with a Canadian plan and calls several times a day. Sometimes it's because he needs a prescription refilled or a crucial piece of paper faxed; other times he has a few minutes between takes and wants to check in. Usually he'll ring her from the hotel to say good night, but that's when Rosebud is getting slammed. None of their conversations last more than half an hour. When she's not working or talking to Adam, all the other minutes of her day are quiet.

Dating, it turns out, had eaten a large chunk of time, and now that she's not accepting invitations from men at work or coffee shops or bars, her interactions are quicker and more perfunctory. The space around those moments quiet, too.

Jerry, the manager at Rosebud, acquires a new girlfriend who's allergic to his bull terrier, so Phoebe volunteers to take Kraken on nights when the girlfriend stays over. Pretty soon she's keeping the dog on nights when Jerry's girlfriend isn't sleeping over, and then after Jerry and the girlfriend break up. Finally Jerry asks if Phoebe is interested in keeping the dog permanently. Because she loves Kraken's velvety head and the way he licks her calves after she puts on lotion, Phoebe happily agrees. Occasionally Kraken pants, and he'll bark on the rare times the doorbell rings, but generally he's also quiet.

Quiet time still passes. She calls her brother's apartment, listens to his voice, and wonders about Sharon Gallaher, who could seemingly delete Chase from her life. She goes through Adam's mail and sends him what's important, skims his NYU alumni magazine, paying heightened attention to who majored in what and the kinds of careers they have now. She talks to Gennifer and assures her she'll visit in the next few weeks. Once in a while, she'll try to grab a drink with Melissa and Burke, but they had both left Rosebud, and it's hard to coordinate around everyone's schedules.

Adam's mother calls one Tuesday morning, even though she probably knows her son isn't there.

"How about you, love?" Anna Zoellner asks. "How are *you* doing?"

Maybe it's because Anna seems genuinely concerned, but Phoebe isn't sure what answer to give and flirts with the honest one: that everything in her life is somehow different without Chase, even though she'd seen him only three times in the past two years.

"I went to see Adam in Vancouver," she says instead.

Hearing the joy in Anna's voice, Phoebe tells her about how friendly the cast is and how much they like her son, about how amazing he looks in costume with the Rowen makeup, and how exciting it is in BC. All the things Adam doesn't share with his mother despite loving her with a connection more fierce than Phoebe's ever felt for her own mother, even before her mom moved halfway around the world.

"That's so wonderful," Anna says again and again.

Phoebe wonders if Adam told his mother that the two of them are a couple, wonders if Anna always assumed that they were or would be. Wonders once again about why lovely and smart Anna chose to stay in small-town Florida long after her son was gone.

"Can I ask you a question?" Phoebe asks. Anna agrees. "How old were you when you went back to school?"

"Oh, I was in my midtwenties. I had Adam and I was working, so I went at odd times and took a lot of classes at night, when my parents could watch him."

"Did you feel weird being older?"

"People of all ages were there," Anna says. "Are you thinking about going to school?"

"Maybe." Like a shot of Red Bull it occurs to Phoebe she definitely is. "I kind of want to mix things up a bit."

"Well, you'd be fantastic," Anna says. "College is sort of lost on the kids who come right from high school. It's good to have experience under your belt, so you can appreciate it."

Two weeks later Phoebe flies to Chicago, where her stepmother is waiting at passenger pickup. On the ride from O'Hare to Evanston, Gennifer tries to warn Phoebe that her father isn't back to his normal routine, but nothing prepares Phoebe for the sight of Dad watching *Law & Order* on the couch in the middle of a Thursday afternoon. He's wearing jogging pants and a pharmaceutical company T-shirt, no socks or shoes; clearly he hasn't shaved in a while. On the glass coffee table, where his feet are propped up, is a plate with an uneaten sandwich.

"Lar, honey, Phoebe's here," Gennifer says tentatively as Phoebe continues to stare.

"Hey, princess." Her father turns and, after what seems like a long time, stands to hug her. Beneath her arms he feels softer and smaller than usual—the reverse of Adam. Then he's back on the sofa, eyes on the flat-screen where Jerry Orbach and the handsome Latino detective are searching for clues in a run-down apartment building.

Unsure what to do, Phoebe sits beside him. From the open kitchen, Gennifer asks if they want anything to eat. Neither one of them responds, but Gen comes back with a bag of tortilla chips and homemade guacamole, perches on the light blue love seat.

"The other day there was a *Law & Order* with an actor who was the spitting image of Adam." Gennifer's voice is cookie dough and *Romper Room*, the way she sounded the first time she met Phoebe and Chase and didn't know how to interact with her boyfriend's children. "Remember, honey?"

"Yeah," Phoebe's father says. "Looked exactly like him."

"It was him, wasn't it?" Gennifer is still bubbling. "I told Larry, 'I bet Adam's been on that show.'"

"He had a couple of small parts after college," Phoebe says, but Gennifer gives her a pleading look, so Phoebe continues, explains that in one episode Adam played the murdered victim and in another he had a few lines as a suspect's prep school friend.

"Remember which one it was, Lar?" Gennifer asks. "It must have been the school one, right?"

Her father makes an affirmative grunt. Then they sit there, and Phoebe realizes she's never watched an entire episode of the show, decides she likes the state psychiatrist. Sam Waterston gets his conviction, and the credits roll.

Another episode starts immediately after, but Gennifer turns to her husband and animatedly says, "Weren't you going to ask Phoebe about Adam's fingers?"

"Oh, yeah." Her father nods with the most energy he's shown since her arrival.

"What?" For a shocking, horrible minute, Phoebe thinks her parents are referencing her sex life.

"When he was here," her father explains, "it looked like he had mild frostbite on his left hand."

"He's fine, Dad," Phoebe says, looking at Gennifer, who nods encouragingly. "I'll ask him about it."

She does ask Adam when he calls three hours later while she's trying to nap.

"My hands are hunky-dory," Adam says. In the background someone is barking orders about camera direction, and she realizes he must be on set. "But they'd be better if they were touching my *gorgeous* girlfriend."

Giggling, she lets herself feel light. She walks to the dresser and absently plays with forgotten objects in her old jewelry box—hoop earrings, her high school class ring, a P necklace.

A few more minutes of banter about missing each other, and he changes tone, sounds serious.

"So Kathleen Turner is producing and starring in a remake of *Who's Afraid of Virginia Woolf?* with Sean Bean, and they like me for the young professor."

"Sweetie, that's great," Phoebe says. It's been years since she's read the play, but she remembers enough to envision Adam in the role, going from cocksure to confused, as the older couple play out their game.

"It would probably be really small distribution—just her passion project—but that's pretty cool, right?" Adam earnest and excited.

"It's amazing. Will you be able to do it if the show gets renewed?"

"They'd shoot in New England over the summer." He pauses. "But if the show does get picked up, would you maybe want to get a place here? We need to move anyway."

Probably true. TV stars, even stars on basic cable shows that haven't aired yet, should live in nicer apartments than their shabby two-bedroom in Studio City.

"That might be fun, right?" Adam asks.

"Maybe."

"Well, we're probably getting ahead of ourselves," Adam is saying.

Next to the jewelry box is a stack of sympathy cards her friends had sent, generic sentiments from people at her old high school and her acting workshops. There's one beige card with a simple tree on the front, postmarked from Italy.

Phoebe—
   I know that it's been a while, but I was deeply saddened to hear about your brother. My thoughts are with you and your family.
   —Oliver

It's the first and only contact she's had with Ollie since dropping him off at his father's house three Thanksgivings ago, when her brother was here with Sharon Gallaher.

On the phone, there's a commotion in the background, Adam briefly talking to someone else, words muffled.

"Okay, I gotta hop, Pheebs, love you."

When he hangs up, she realizes she's said nothing about her father and *Law & Order*, nothing about her stepmother's coddling of him. Wonders why she didn't tell Adam, hasn't told him about calling Chase's apartment or her sizzling hatred of Sharon Gallaher and all those other quiet things.

While Phoebe had lived in her father's house only a year, her brother had more time here. All of high school and breaks from the University of Wisconsin, enough years to settle in and make his room a home. Yet when Phoebe tries to picture what's on the walls or even the view from his bedroom window, she comes up blank. There might a long-abandoned guitar from his Jim Morrison phase in the corner, maybe a *Pulp Fiction* poster? She can't even remember the color of his bedspread—blue or green, something nondescript boy?

She's not sure what she expects to find when she opens the door to his room, but it's certainly not Gennifer sitting on the bed (gray plaid spread) staring out the window.

"I'm sorry." Gennifer stands, as if an explanation is needed. "I . . . sometimes I come in here."

"That's perfectly fine," Phoebe says, understanding with absolute clarity. When Chase died, her real mother blew in from halfway around the world, cried, hugged old friends, got bundles of cards and condolences. Then she was gone, back to Hong Kong, where her life hadn't intersected regularly with her son's for more than a decade.

Gennifer, who'd never had a shred of biological claim to Chase, had been the one who picked him up from track and cross-country practice all through high school, the one who sent him packages of homemade cookies while he was away at college.

Gennifer had been the one he'd been coming home to when he was having trouble with his girlfriend. She'd been the one who had to contact family members, pick a casket, and make sure her stepson was in the ground within three days, in accordance with her adopted religion. Gennifer is the one who has to babysit her near-catatonic husband. Who has to apologize for missing Chase, for sitting in a room in her own home.

Getting up, Gen starts to leave. While she still looks young, with her regular Botox and dyed hair, she has quietly slipped into middle age, forty-three, possibly too old to have her own children if that was something she ever desired.

Phoebe reaches for her arm. "Do you wanna go out to dinner? Somewhere nice, maybe?"

Her stepmother nods enthusiastically, and Phoebe feels crushingly guilty she's never asked before.

Over the years, Gennifer and Phoebe have often lobbied for French or Mexican over her father and brother's consistent vote for steakhouse dinners, but the two women agree on Gibson's and manage to get a reservation for nine. Phoebe changes into a little black dress and puts on makeup for the first time in a long time, and Gennifer, graceful in a pencil skirt and silk shirt, drives them down Lake Shore Drive.

The all-male waitstaff smiles approvingly as they take their seats in a corner booth, split a porterhouse and creamed spinach, go through a bottle of red, and order another.

Light conversation about all kinds of things that have nothing to do with her father or brother or Sharon Gallaher or the wars. Things like Elizabeth Taylor films on the classic movie station and how, though they are insanely overpriced, classic Chanel handbags are exquisite.

"My roommate at Loyola had five," Gen says. "They'd been her grandmother's."

"What was your major?" Phoebe asks, stunned she doesn't already know this.

"Communications." Gen chuckle-snorts. "I wanted to read the news on TV. Silly, right? I hardly ever watch the news now."

"Did you ever try?"

"At the college news station, sure." Gennifer looks at the last sip of Burgundy in her glass. "Then I had some entry-level thing set up with a local channel in Iowa, but a few months before I was supposed to leave, I started temping for your dad. And I . . . he hadn't even asked me out—he was sooo proper about everything—but I just knew, you know? So I canceled on Iowa."

Strange, Phoebe's older now than Gennifer was when she decided to gamble on a divorced man with two kids who hadn't even asked her out. Is that the fourteen years between them? A different generation, when love, or even the possibility of love, always trumped career?

"I'm glad you didn't go," Phoebe says, maybe the first time in seventeen years she's acknowledged that her stepmother has made her life better than it might have otherwise been.

Gennifer tears up. "Aww, honey, you know you and your brother . . ."

"I know. Chase knew, too."

One more glass of wine, and Phoebe can't help but think of the other person who should have loved Chase, should have come to his funeral. And for the first time since Sharon Gallaher hung up on her four months ago, Phoebe says the girl's name out loud.

"I don't understand how she could not come," she says.

Gennifer shakes her head. "From what he told me, they were breaking up."

"But they were together for years."

"People react to things in different ways." It's not enough, but Gennifer is too nice to say more, so Phoebe nods.

A waiter brings a giant slab of chocolate cake, tells them it's from the gentlemen at the bar—two men in expensive suits, older than Phoebe but younger than Gennifer, with the transitory look of people in the city on business—who nod from across the room.

"It's been so long since I've been out without Larry," Gennifer says, pink flush on her cheeks. "How do we tell them that we're taken?"

Adam in Vancouver, getting bruised and filming love scenes with the Jericho Jeans girl, calling when he can.

"We don't tell them anything," Phoebe says. "We just thank them on our way out."

And they do.

Her father is still on the couch in the living room when they get back, and Phoebe sits next to him after a tipsy Gennifer kisses his cheek, slips off her heels, and stumbles upstairs. The channel that reruns classic sitcoms is on—Rose, Blanche, Dorothy, and Sophia are huddled around the kitchen table eating cheesecake while a laugh track punctuates their one-liners.

"You and Gen have fun?" her father asks.

"We did. You should take her out more."

Her father bobs his head in agreement. "I will, I'm . . ." Slight shrug. "You know."

It occurs to Phoebe that she's seen this before, with Adam when the *Goners* pilot didn't go. She'd had no idea what to do then either.

"I asked Adam about his hands," she says. "He said they're great and thanked you for asking."

"He treat you well, princess?"

Phoebe rests her head on her father's shoulder. "Yeah, Daddy, he does."

"Good."

They watch syndicated episodes of *The Golden Girls* and *Cheers* into the wee hours of the morning, and Phoebe realizes she hasn't called Chase's apartment in Manhattan since noon.

Two days later Phoebe meets a very pregnant Nicole for thousand-calorie salads and garlicky bread at Leona's, where they talk about names for the new baby (a boy this time, to go with Nicole's three-year-old daughter) and how Evie wants to start her own PR shop in LA.

Both Evie and Nicole had been at Chase's funeral. Nic, bump barely showing under her long coat, had leaned on Dave's arm as they navigated the uneven sod of the cemetery. Phoebe hadn't called her, but Evie had come in from New York, shockingly demure in black boots and leather gloves, pale and visibly shaken. Only Sharon Gallaher, who'd shared Chase's life, his bed, probably whatever dreams he'd had, hadn't been in attendance.

"So how's your TV star boyfriend?" Nicole asks across the red-and-white-checkered tablecloth. "Are you guys serious?"

"I think so," Phoebe says. "But I sorta feel like I'm holding him back."

"Well, he obviously doesn't see it that way," Nicole says. "How about you? What are you looking for?"

Calling Chase's apartment, trying to remember his bedroom and what he looked like in it. Adopting a dog and the cushion of quiet. Wishing she knew how to fix her father.

"Remember how you made a million flash cards to help Evie study for the SATs?"

Nicole tilts her head in the mom way she was doing even before the babies. "You want to go back to school?"

Phoebe nods, says the tests are being offered a few times next month.

"Yeah." Nicole smiles. "I'd be honored to help you."

Coming through the garage to the kitchen, Phoebe hangs her father's car keys on the holder Chase made in sixth-grade woodshop, notices a stack of outgoing mail on the counter underneath. The top envelope is addressed to the management office of the Madison Plaza in New York City.

Flicker of recognition: her brother's building.

Ripping it open, Phoebe finds a check written in Gennifer's curly script.

And Phoebe is calling her stepmother's name, making her way through the kitchen to the living room, where her father is watching Sam Waterston deliver closing arguments to the jury on television.

"Where's Gennifer?" Phoebe asks.

Her father looks up, eyes briefly focusing in concern.

"She got back from the gym a little while ago. She might be in the shower. Everything okay?"

Out of the room and up the stairs before he finishes.

"Gen," she calls, throwing open the door to the master suite, where her stepmother is fastening a lacy bra that matches her panties, towel swaddled around her head.

"Why are you sending checks to Chase's apartment?" Phoebe demands. "Are you paying that girl's rent?"

That girl, Sharon, who'd said "Thank you" and then seemingly vanished. Sharon, who may have known that her brother was sick, could have stopped him from getting on the plane.

"No," Gennifer says, but looks at the Oriental rug under the sleigh bed. "The building manager said she moved out a few days before Chase died."

"Then why are you still sending money?"

"All of your brother's things are there—"

"You're paying four grand a month so Chase's stuff can sit in storage? That's the dumbest thing I've ever heard."

It certainly isn't a great use of cash, but Phoebe's anger isn't really about the money. Chase probably left enough to pay the rent for years, and even if her father never looks at another chest film again, it's unlikely he and Gennifer will starve or have to start driving domestic cars. It's something about the principle. About Dad watching daytime television and Gen sitting in Chase's room when she thinks no one knows. About Phoebe still calling his apartment and trying to piece together the puzzle of who her brother had become.

"Why not just have them donate everything?" Phoebe asks.

Gennifer sighs. "You've seen your dad; he can't deal with it yet. But there might be things there you guys want, things to remember him by."

And with the most direction she's had in months, Phoebe volunteers to go and sort things out.

New York is still cold in late April, and Phoebe shifts her weight from foot to foot, hands jammed into her pockets as she waits in the JFK taxi line.

"Eight Twenty-ninth Street," she tells the driver, and has to root around in her coat pocket for the scrap of paper with her brother's address when he asks if she means east or west. "East."

"Between Madison and Fifth?" the driver asks, over a grating news announcer giving traffic reports from the radio.

"I guess." Slight embarrassment that she doesn't know. From her cab window, she notices the spire of the Empire State Building.

When Phoebe was a kid, her family had gone to New York, stayed at the Marriott Marquis (before her mother worked for the Four Seasons), seen *Cats*, and taken the elevator to the top of the Empire State Building. "How long would it take you to fall?" her brother, maybe seven, had asked.

Phoebe's father stopped trying to adjust the viewfinder for her. "That's a good question," he'd said. "How long do you guys think it would take?"

"Five minutes?" Phoebe had offered without consideration, realized the answer was wrong immediately by the way her father shook his head.

"Fifteen seconds," Chase had tried.

"It's about ten seconds to the ground." Her father had smiled. "Good answer."

At her brother's building—which also juts up stories upon stories into the sky—a uniformed man with the name tag RODNEY holds open the door, and the building manager, whom she'd spoken to yesterday, comes out to shake her hand.

"Shall I show you to the apartment?" he asks, taking the handle of her suitcase when she agrees.

Two young professionals hold the elevator door for them, both about her brother's age, both wearing the kind of charcoal wool coats Chase had been partial to, carrying the same type of leather messenger bag. She wants to ask if they knew him but suspects they didn't.

The building manager ushers her off on the thirty-fifth floor, leads her down the hall to 35K, and unlocks the door.

"Let us know if we can help you with anything," he says, handing her his business card. "We're all very sorry about your brother."

Behind him the door closes with the solid precision found only in buildings less than twenty years old, not at all like the splintering wood of her own place in Los Angeles.

Though it's much nicer than hers, the unit feels strangely sterile—stainless-steel appliances and granite countertops in the galley kitchen, clean hardwood floors free of scuffs and damage. Everything paling in comparison to the glass wall of windows directly facing the Empire State Building.

The living room boasts a chocolate leather couch and armchair, a sleek television mounted to the wall. There's a glass desk with an elaborate-looking office chair and a filing cabinet. The detectives on *Law & Order* would probably start with the files or the lightweight laptop computer, but they'd be looking for the cause of death. She's looking for the way Chase lived.

File folders are labeled with headers like Warranties, Utilities, Medical, and Investments. That file should probably go home to her father. She sets it on the couch in a mental "to keep" pile.

Three tall bookcases line the wall by the desk, but they're largely empty and look as though things have been plucked out at random.

That's right: Sharon's moved out. The remaining volumes include clunky textbooks on economics and history, Malcolm Gladwell and Christopher Hitchens paperbacks, a few novels by men like Richard Ford and Bret Easton Ellis. The novels are signed on the inside flap—not by the authors but by Sharon Gallaher—in script so tortured it's almost illegible. *Thought you would love this.—S; One of my all-time favorites.—Always, Sharon.*

Phoebe wonders if Chase read them or just nodded and thanked Sharon, like he did as a child when a distant relative gave him socks or a hideous sweater as a gift.

Do the books deserve space in the pile of things to be saved? She'd known so little of her brother these past years, how is she qualified to determine the importance of his life objects?

Reaching for *The Tipping Point*, she feels something behind it on the shelf and pulls out a wrinkled, forgotten issue of *Eons & Empires*.

Adam had bought several of the collected volumes when he was auditioning for the show, but she hadn't really looked at them. She's amazed at how much Ron Brosh looks like a real-life Jason Bryce, and the Jericho Jeans girl is a dead ringer for Cordelia Snow. With Adam and Captain Rowen, there's less of a physical correlation, but flipping through the issue, she sees it in some of the panels: a cagey, weather-beaten quality that's somehow sexy. It's something she's seen in Adam before, used to see all the time in the days when they were just fucking. And Phoebe realizes *E&E: Rising* could be very good. That Adam is going to be very good.

He doesn't even know she's in New York. In all their mini-conversations, where they talked about *Who's Afraid of Virginia Woolf?* and neighborhoods they might want to live in, this trip never came up. She wonders if she'll tell him when they talk later, or if this, like all the phone calls to this very place, will remain her secret.

On the bottom shelf is a wooden cigar box that still smells of tobacco but holds ticket stubs from *Wonderful Town* and Yankees games, receipts, metal admissions badges from the Met, a ceramic turtle that might be from a tropical vacation or some junk store down the street, and a ring of keys to locks unknown. Because these things were singled out, stored by her brother (or Sharon Gallaher), she puts the box in the pile.

The bedroom is small, just enough space for a light-wood dresser and a queen-size bed neatly made with a beige comforter.

Eight crisply pressed suits and rows of shirts still in plastic film from the dry cleaner hang in the closet. There's a rack of ties ranging from conservative stripes and solids to bold patterns. Everything high-end. Nice clothes, but for whom? Did her brother dress this way for work, or did he truly enjoy the fine craftsmanship and prestige labels? Did Sharon pick them out?

For the "to keep" pile, Phoebe takes a tie with little martini glasses on it. *I can taste the difference.* She'll ask the building manager about having Veterans of America take the rest. It's fun to think of some down-on-his-luck guy looking for a passable interview suit and finding her brother's Armani; she hopes that would have made Chase happy, too.

Half the dresser drawers are nearly empty, most likely Sharon's things. The top one contains boxer shorts, a little bowl of cuff links and collar stays, swim trunks, an athletic cup. Under those Phoebe finds a nearly empty box of condoms, tube of KY Jelly, pair of handcuffs, bullet vibrator.

Had Phoebe talked with her brother about sex, ever? When she was in high school and in love with Oliver? When Chase was in college dating all those blondes? Had Chase ever asked her a question too embarrassing for their parents or his friends? Something exclusively in the territory of an older sibling? No, it was more the issue that came between them. The way he was always annoyed and hostile when his friends would say she was hot or ask for introductions. How he followed her around on her first date with Oliver and poked into her relationship with Adam on his last visit. How sad that this had been a wedge between them, that their romantic lives couldn't be something to share and bond over.

In the third drawer, there are gym clothes, a Cubs baseball cap, and white undershirts. Under those are a few of the ironic T-shirts—Oscar the

Grouch, Mr. Bubble. These she remembers Chase wearing as they fought over the television remote or when she dragged him to the mall so they could buy their father's birthday gift. When she went to visit him at college and he had the goatee. Without really thinking, Phoebe holds one shirt to her chest and curls into herself on the bed.

When she wakes (something about airplanes), the skyscrapers have come to life against the dimming sky, the city ablaze all around her.

She goes to the bathroom to pee, not to find keepsakes, but the sight makes her gasp. It looks like an actual crime scene for the *Law & Order* detectives to unravel.

Cordless phone in pieces on the marble floor above a dent in the wall. Open first-aid kit balanced precariously on the lip of the sink, gauze unraveled and hanging over the side. Reddish brown splotches pepper the white porcelain of the bathtub and the lid of the toilet seat. A plush white towel with even more red stains is crumpled by the door.

Deep breath: Whatever happened in this room, Chase didn't die here.

In the space between the bath and the commode sits a nearly empty bottle of Grey Goose.

I can taste the difference.

Another stabilizing breath.

Picking up the bottle, Phoebe holds it at arm's length and thumbs off the cap, half expecting a ghostly kind of spirit to float up from the matte glass. There's only the faint smell of alcohol. Sitting on the toilet seat, she closes her eyes and takes a sip. Warm all the way to her belly, the flavor slightly different than the Popov the restaurant uses if customers don't specify a vodka brand.

Other odd things, too, are in that small space between the tub and toilet. A box-cutting blade and black marker. A yellow Post-it note, sticky side up.

Phoebe picks it up. The ink is swollen and blurred from long-dried water, but she can still make out two sets of handwriting. First her brother's thick letters:

Had to go to work, Shar, but I love you very much. –C

Below that in the same barely legible handwriting as in the books in the living room:

I love you, too. I'm sorry.

And then Phoebe can't breathe, hands trembling. She needs air, the central heat oppressive and stale.

On the terrace she fills her lungs again and again until they calm, then eases into one of the two patio chairs—the seat webbing cold even through her jeans. From out here the skyline is different. The towers shooting up beyond the thirty-five stories and all the roofs and water towers of the buildings below. Maybe her brother stood here admiring the forest of harnessed steel and concrete? Maybe he sat in these chairs with Sharon?

The girl with the large blue eyes and the grown-up clothes, who said "adore" every other sentence. That girl, that Sharon Gallaher, whom Phoebe met only once, had loved her brother and he'd loved her. And isn't that what Phoebe really came here to find? The things that had mattered to her brother when she'd lost track of them? Phoebe likes the idea of Sharon and Chase sharing this view.

A minute or an hour passes, and the phone Adam gave her rings in her pants pocket.

"How's my best girl?" he asks. For once it's quiet in the background. He's not on set or out with his cast members.

"Good, you?" Her voice cracks a little since she hasn't spoken in so long.

"You sure? You sound weird."

His concern brings a tennis ball to her throat. Maybe it's being here in her brother's apartment, where Chase had loved someone, too.

"Yeah," Phoebe says, walks to the edge of the terrace and leans on the railing. "I was just thinking of you."

Below her, yellow cabs dart around parked cars. Small dots of people. All the sounds muted by the time they reach her. The Empire State Building is lit up green and white, and she wonders why.

Ten seconds to the ground.

"I'll actually be home for, like, twenty-four hours on Wednesday. Kathleen wants to meet with me—Marty says it's a formality."

"That's wonderful, sweetie."

"Well, you know he oversells things . . ."

"No, Adam, you're gonna be awesome." Phoebe believes this, always has.

"So I know you're looking at schools in LA, but if this thing comes through, I want you to come with me to Boston for the summer."

"Adam."

Had to go to work, but I love you very much.

"It'll probably only be a six-week shoot, but Pheebs, sometimes I miss you so much I literally can't sleep."

I love you, too.

"Well, we can't have that. I guess I'll have to come."

Adam is excited now, talking about all the things they can do in New England, asking if she can get out of work on Wednesday when he's in town.

Without really thinking about what she's doing, Phoebe holds Sharon and her brother's Post-it note over the rail, thirty-five stories above the street.

And lets it go.

8 you always swim home

MACAU

Liam Wing promised the world should you come to Macau. He claimed you could be a part of something big, get in on the ground floor. "Ollie," he's said over and over on the phone. "We can be explorers in uncharted terrain."

Because you've always been charmed by his enthusiasm (so much like Braden's), you'd agreed. So after salmon season, you'd jetted off to Beijing and taken the high-speed rails all through China. Then to Thailand and Cambodia and finally Vietnam, where you'd spent weeks zipping around dirt roads on a motorcycle and had taken up with Mai, the exotic French-Vietnamese desk clerk at your hotel. An hour ago you boarded an Airbus A320 from Hanoi to Hong Kong, where Liam and his brave new world await you.

Somewhere over Moaming the plane bounces into a patch of rough air, and passengers grumble and grip their armrests. The pilot guns the engines, seeking something smoother, and you start thinking about throttle and velocity in a way you haven't in years, not since you fled Chicago and Advantage Electric and your Ph.D. program. And you find yourself smiling, remembering how you used to be afraid to fly, even after you'd studied the mechanics and understood what kept planes in the sky—understood a little of what your father loved about the defiance of gravity.

Dad had tried to link up with you while you were in China. For days the two of you volleyed e-mails back and forth about meeting for dinner at a Mexican place he loved in Shanghai. But his flight got diverted, and then you were visiting a friend from the *Jezebel Jones* who taught English in Yangpu, and somehow you and your father couldn't make it work. You'd figured he was only being nice and wasn't all that serious about it anyway—like when you were a kid, before the Piper Saratoga, and he'd promise to take you to Six Flags or The Taste of Chicago if he was home—but this morning he'd left a voice mail about the two of you getting together in Hong Kong soon. So maybe he was serious.

Your father and aerodynamics are still on your mind an hour later when you find Liam at the baggage area and he throws his arms around you in an awkward man hug.

"You ready for the start of the rest of your life?" Liam asks, excitement and promise seeping from every pore.

And even though you're still lost in a world of jet engines and family, you have to nod and agree; Liam has that effect on you, always has. Since that first conversation on the deck of the *Jezebel Jones*, when he said the two of you were astronauts, not knowing that you had actually worked alongside people who designed things for NASA (of course, you hadn't told that to the skipper either, had simply said you'd done extensive work on engines, implying those engines were ones that powered boats).

Indeed, you *had* felt like an astronaut all that first season on the *Jones*, your life so much different than would ever have seemed possible. Liam became a true friend on that boat, and after the season—when you took off to see the world and he went home to Seattle and whatever he was majoring in at UW—the two of you worked it out so you'd be on the same boat again the next spring, and every season after. He proved better at finding the gigs, and you were a huge selling point; it turned out boat and airplane engines weren't really all that different.

Now the two of you are shuffling through Hong Kong International Airport to the Turbojet ferry in pursuit of the latest opportunity he's unearthed.

"We're making Asian Vegas," he'd explained on the phone. And from what you found on Internet searches, that seemed about right. Though significantly less publicized than the Hong Kong turnover, the Polynesian colony of Macau was also handed to the Chinese in 1999, and a few years later a handful of casino licenses were given to American developers. Liam's father was once an official, or knows someone who knows some official of America or Macau; the specifics aren't quite clear, though you're only a few slim degrees removed from importance. And there's gold in them there hills if Liam is right.

But as the two of you purchase tickets and board the ferry crossing the Pearl River, you find you're still dwelling on the intricacies of airplanes. Something that you hadn't realized you missed. Maybe it truly is something genetic, something in your blood?

"What did I tell you?" Liam asks, and the two of you slide into the waiting car and whiz from the dock over the Cotai strip. On both sides, Western hotels sprout like weeds—the Grand Hyatt, Hard Rock, the Venetian Resort—construction crews and scaffolding everywhere.

Actually, Liam hadn't told you much. What exactly you're supposed to be doing here is fairly cloudy. Liam knows you're good at stacking nets, were a tidy roommate, and can keep a seiner's inner workings from overheating; you're not sure exactly how he's sold you this time.

"Here we are," he announces as you round the gate of the Four Seasons, all marble and stone fountains and beautiful. You've barely gotten out of the car when a statuesque woman of vague ethnicity nods at you. "Good afternoon, Mr. Wing, Mr. Ryan." She smiles, introduces herself as Petra, and tells you she's come over to train with a team of people from the Four Seasons Hong Kong.

For a second you think of Mai and her weird little Vietnamese hotel that was really more like a hostel, where the guests had backpacks and were charged twenty dollars for a night's stay, including full breakfast.

"Our director can meet with you at noon, but I'm sure you'd like to freshen up first." She points to a young man in a blue uniform who's materialized from nowhere. "Joao will show you to your rooms."

The junior suite they've given you is, without a doubt, the classiest hotel room you've ever been in. King-size bed with pillows on top of pillows and a bench at the end with still more pillows. A dining table in the corner offers a basket of brightly colored French macaroons and fruit, and the enormous bathroom boasts not one, but two televisions and a Roman soaking tub.

Waiting for the stone shower to adjust, you strip off your pants and shirt, give yourself a once-over in the mirrored wall of the dressing area. Muscles from hauling lines and scars along your torso and arms, the most impressive from a salmon shark you tried to free from a net your first season—when the experienced guys had laughed and told you to kill it because it was eating half the catch.

Running fingers over the red stubble on your face (you'd cut off the beard when fishing season ended), you debate between a shave or a nap before this mysterious meeting.

Your cheeks are smooth an hour later when you, Liam, and Petra from the Hong Kong hotel reassemble in the lobby.

"So when you came in, I'm sure you saw the construction of our sister hotel," Petra is saying, gesturing toward a hallway.

That's when you notice the comely woman crossing the corridor connecting the Four Seasons to the Venetian and do an enormous double take.

You've never met Phoebe's mother, but in the year when you and Phoebe were in love, you saw the picture of Phoebe, Chase, and their mom in Hawaii so many times, it was almost as if you had. Diligently, you'd studied it—a time machine revealing future Phoebe (well, if she hadn't changed her nose). It's been more than a decade since that picture was taken, but Michelle Fisher (or whatever her last name might be now) looks completely unchanged, minus the lei. Black hair hitting at the shoulders, matching eyebrows in perfect arches, cheekbones regal and piercing.

The resemblance to her daughter is still so striking that, for a half second, you're convinced it's Phoebe herself (never mind that Braden had mentioned hearing about Phoebe living with some actor in LA). Convinced that three decades and not five years have passed since you last saw her that Thanksgiving.

No, it's Phoebe's mother.

Of course. The hotel's team is from Hong Kong, where Michelle Fisher was working.

All the things in the world that you've experienced: the cold, endless waters of the Pacific and twitching slippery fish, more creatures from a dream than anything in the animal kingdom; blood pouring from cuts on your raw hands, the color so complex and fascinating that the pain didn't really register; pyramids in Mexico and the Sphinx reclining on the Giza Plateau; your own tears of awe and faith (though you claim to be an atheist) as you said a prayer for your mother at the marble statues of St. Peter's Basilica; the broken teeth of jutting rocks in Ha Long Bay; ornate Buddhas presiding over Thai Temples; otherworldly delicacies that upset your digestive system in ways you hadn't imagined possible and fabric so fine you wanted to taste it; the smooth thick lids of Mai's eyes closing right before you entered her, entirely different than Phoebe's pale skin, than Maura's paler skin.

The whole universe that opened up when you left Illinois and stopped unconsciously waiting for everyone else to return.

Phoebe's mother turns toward you, and something like recognition streaks across her face. Maybe Phoebe had shown her your prom picture or another photo from that other life?

You could go over and offer condolences about her son. Fifteen months ago, Braden had e-mailed Chase Fisher's obituary, and you'd cried for the first time in years, thinking about the fourteen-year-old kid who'd tagged along on your first date with Phoebe. You'd sent a sympathy card and donated two weeks' salary to the Pediatric AIDS Foundation in Chase Fisher's name.

But you don't go over to Michelle Fisher and say you're sorry. Instead you break eye contact.

Five years and so many thousands of miles, other places, other worlds.

And there are things in that old life that could be worth a return trip. Turbines and exhaust nozzles, stuffed-crust pizza, a visit to your mother's grave, the Cubs, bumping into Braden's parents at Osco, regular chats with your sister, the quiet after the first snow, and maybe your father.

"You still with me, Ollie?" Liam is asking beside you.

It occurs to you that you've seen all the parts of the world that you want to see for a while. That Chicago is merely a place, and all places have their ghosts, no matter where they're laid to rest.

"I'm sorry," you say to Liam, knowing that he will strike gold out here, but it won't be with you. "I'm not an astronaut."

CINCINNATI

Sharon Gallaher was confident she'd never return to New York.

Relatively quickly, however, she realized she was going to be all right.

It didn't seem that way when she was in the bathtub with the box cutter and the Post-it note and Chase Fisher's sister called. Didn't seem that way when she said "thank you," threw the phone across the bathroom, and fled the Madison Plaza wet, shaking, and crazed. Not when she lost a day and a half wandering around the frigid city in a blank haze before finally taking a cab to LaGuardia and booking a flight to Cincinnati because she couldn't think of anywhere else to go. TSA officers had practically strip-searched her when she took off her coat, revealing the bloodstained sleeve of her sweater. It hadn't helped matters that she had bought a one-way ticket and brought no baggage. Frankly, it was somewhat amazing that they let her get on a plane at all. Even years later the whole experience remains a splotch of lights and colors, the taste of copper in her mouth, her heart in her ears the only sound she remembers. No, it hadn't seemed like she would be all right then.

She'd arrived at the Cincinnati/Northern Kentucky International Airport right before an epic snowstorm. Had she been detained by security in New York any longer, she wouldn't have made it at all, and everything might have been different in one of those *Sliding Doors/Eons & Empires* alternate reality moments. It was after nine, and she hadn't told her parents she was coming, so instead of calling them, Sharon, still trembly and liquid, headed to the row of rental car kiosks. In the Avis line, she'd been behind a bald, distracted guy who was playing with his phone and took forever. As the man asked questions about directions and the clerk took out a map and highlighter, Sharon had felt a tinge of annoyance. *It's late. People are behind you.*

That was it. A swell of frustration, and Sharon realized the world was solid again.

The first snowflakes fell as she crossed the Suspension Bridge connecting Covington to Cincinnati. Also designed by John Roebling, the bridge over the Ohio River was almost identical to the Brooklyn Bridge, and it seemed fitting as the arches and cables got smaller in the rearview mirror—a symbol of the city she was leaving behind.

Her house keys still worked, so she let herself in, climbed the stairs to her old bedroom, fell asleep in her old twin bed, and didn't wake up for nearly fifteen hours. She even slept through her mother's shriek of surprise at finding her daughter under the same purple comforter she'd had in high school.

After getting over their initial shock at Sharon's odd reappearance, her parents had been generally pleased to see her. She told them she and Chase had broken up (not mentioning why a reconciliation was absolutely out of the question), and she'd moved out of their apartment.

Had Sharon said Chase Fisher was dead, she suspected she might *not* have been okay, that her blood and guts and organs would have oozed out through that opening and puddled on the floor.

"You're welcome to stay as long as you want," her father said.

Not stay until she got back on her feet or found her own place or returned to the city, but to stay as long as she wanted. In the years since she'd left for school, Sharon had realized just how little her parents *got* about her. Every choice she'd made—taking out student loans when UC or Ohio State were perfectly good schools, riding the subway, living with her Jewish boyfriend without getting married—baffled them. But when her father told her she was unconditionally welcome, she came to the conclusion that they were actually better than a lot of parents.

For six weeks, Sharon took them up on the offer. She helped her mom make dinner and volunteered to pick up their dry cleaning and put the trash and recyclables on the corner each Monday morning. It was almost like high school, except when her parents came home from work at exactly 6:30 each night, they offered her a drink as they poured their own.

The night Sharon had run out of the Madison Plaza, she had bound her wrist tight enough that there had never been any real danger (the cut hadn't been that deep to begin with). But perhaps because she didn't get it properly stitched, it took weeks to heal—a raised scarlet slash that slowly crusted over.

It had been late January, easy enough to hide under cuffed shirts and big sweaters. But one evening, after ten days of helping her mother shake and bake pork chops and boil dry pasta for supper, Sharon accidentally ran her arm under the faucet while washing potatoes. Without thinking, she rolled back her sleeve.

Seeing the red, Sharon's mom grabbed her wrist.

Her mother looked at the uneven scab, mouth open in something that could only be described as terror—the same look she'd had when Sharon finally made it home after the *Eons & Empires* movie freshman year of high school.

"It's nothing, Mom," Sharon said.

Her mother said her name like a prayer, like it was sacred.

"It was just something that happened; it didn't mean anything."

Sharon expected her mother to tell her father or suggest she see a counselor, but her mom embraced her. Bringing her arms around her mother, Sharon hugged back—water from her wet sleeve dripping on her mother's blouse.

Of course, back in New York, there were things that had to be dealt with.

Living was a ninety-second phone call the day Sharon woke up from the fifteen-hour sleep. She told the managing editor she was quitting due to a "family emergency."

"When do you think you'll be back?" Across the line the ME sighed. "Should we bring in a temp?"

Without elaborating on the specifics, Sharon repeated that she was quitting, not taking time off.

"Well, I hope everything works out for you," the ME said unconvincingly. No one from the office followed up. It was fine; Sharon didn't think she'd be going back to New York.

After unceremoniously quitting her job, Sharon called Kristen to apologize for not showing up and to explain that she wouldn't be moving to Astoria after all.

"Do you know how worried I've been?" Kristen screamed, and Sharon apologized again. "I even called your dumb magazine looking for you."

In the eight years they'd known each other, Sharon couldn't recall Kristen being so enraged. Could almost envision her friend's pixie face blotchy and contorted and redder than Sharon had ever seen.

Sharon tried to say she'd send money until she could find Kristen a new roommate, and that Kristen could throw out her boxes of clothes and CDs if she didn't want any of it. Sharon got as far as "rent" before Kristen hung up. She sent Kristen a check and an apology (which made no mention of Chase Fisher's death) and diligently searched NYC Craigslist postings for possible replacement roommates. A week later, all of Sharon's boxes arrived at her parents' house, and Kristen called back.

"Um, I saw something on Myspace," Kristen said, unsure. "About what happened to Chase. . . ."

"I don't want to talk about it." It was actually that Sharon *couldn't* talk about it. Despite all her degrees in writing, she lacked the vocabulary. Saying the words would cause some giant snake to come through the floor and devour her whole. "I have nothing to say."

She was sure Kristen and other people in New York had lots to say about it, and that they probably said it. Sharon was okay with that; she didn't think she'd be returning to New York.

After two weeks of dinners and 6:30 P.M. drinks with her parents, Sharon determined she needed to get another job. And despite spending much of her youth alienated in Cincinnati, the Queen City seemed as good a place as any to settle into.

She thought about doing something completely different—nannying or picking up composition lecture sections at Xavier—but scrolling through online job posts, Sharon found herself repeatedly coming back to a listing for a features writer at one of the city's alternative weeklies. Her longest *Living* stories were two hundred words and most dated back to her earliest days at the magazine (when she'd been hesitant to blatantly write her novel at work), but Sharon suspected the simple fact that she'd been on the editorial staff at a major national magazine would carry a little weight. So she dug through the boxes Kristen had shipped for her clips and résumé, included a couple of the entertainment columns she'd written for *Washington Square News* in college to show range, and crossed her fingers *Cincy Beat* wouldn't actually contact anyone at *Living* for a reference.

Within an hour of e-mailing her materials, Sharon got a call from Alice in features, asking her to come to Clifton for an interview.

The *Cincy Beat* office was cramped and dusty, with depressingly low ceilings and various newspaper articles taped to the wall. Set up on long folding tables were about eight workstations, each with an old iMac, stacks of paper, books, and used food containers. Sharon instantly liked it worlds more than the shiny *Living* offices on Avenue of the Americas, which were always kept pristine for when celebrities would come by. A handful of casually dressed young people were typing or talking on their phones, and she was glad she'd worn a black wrap dress and boots instead of the suit she'd briefly contemplated.

At most a year or two older than Sharon, Alice in features was dressed like a forties housewife in a vintage jumper and cat-eye glasses. Apologizing for the mess, she led Sharon to a couch very similar to the one in her old NYU dorm.

"So *Living*, what was that like?"

Sharon told her it was fun but fluffy. "I'm looking for the opportunity to do longer pieces."

Nodding, Alice said they could definitely offer that, "a great salary, not so much, but you can pretty much get tickets to anything in town."

Telling Sharon they liked her old columns, Alice sent her to interview an area artist opening his own gallery on Fourth Street for a trial story. Though Sharon hadn't brought anything useful, such as paper or a recorder, she diligently headed out with the kind of drive she hadn't had since her early days at *Living*. The gallery owner/artist was in the space setting up for the show and was happy to talk at length about his mission: promoting his own work, which had been rejected by the city's established galleries. Sharon was able to twist Warhol's quote about fame into the lead—"Billy Franklin is creating his own fifteen minutes"—which worked well, as his pieces were all pop art prints of old comic books and starlets like Paris Hilton. By day's end Sharon had e-mailed the article to Alice in features. Within the hour, Alice called to offer the job.

A week in, Sharon had written about secondhand stores offering retro cooking classes (meat loaf and deviled eggs), the public library's funding campaign, and late-night fine dining options.

Cincy Beat didn't pay well, but the salary was enough for a used Jeep Cherokee and a weird third-story apartment in an old, chopped-up house on Mcmillan Street that came furnished with worn but interesting things—rolltop desk, kitchen table with foldout wings, tiny box television. In the bedroom, the floor was so slanted, pens and cups and most other things would fall off the desk and tumble across the room. By definition it was transitory, the kind of place you couldn't stay very long, but whenever it came time to leave, Sharon didn't think she'd be going back to New York.

Without Sharon, the city kept on going; sometimes news came her way.

There were always magazines around the *Cincy Beat* office, and she skimmed them regularly for possible feature ideas (for the meetings where she actively pitched things, something she never did at *Living*). *The New Yorker*, the Sunday *New York Times Times Magazine*, and *The New York Eye* were always good for a trend story. So she read the articles about downtown architecture and new exhibits at the Whitney, and it was okay. Her time in Manhattan felt coated in Vaseline—obscured and dreamlike.

Because of its focus on celebrities, *Living* wasn't a particularly useful source for ideas. But thumbing through one issue a few years in, she saw the annual "100 Sexy People" cover package had been written by Julie, the editorial assistant who'd been promoted the week before Chase died. Julie had apparently done all the interviews (including one with the guy who played Captain Rowen on that *E&E* origins show that Chase had mentioned and she'd dismissed), and there were pictures of her laughing and posing with the stars.

"Good for her," Sharon said to no one in particular.

She still didn't think she'd be going back to New York.

Not when Laurel Young-Griffin brought Sharon to her book club in the suburbs. The women—most married, all pinot grigio drinkers—were impressed that Sharon had lived in Manhattan. Everyone seemed to have gone to see *Cats/Phantom of the Opera/Wicked* for their honeymoon/anniversary/company convention, and they were eager to tell tales of taxicab and shopping victories.

Sharon still didn't want to talk about New York or her Vaseline-obscured life there, but she adored how, even after all those years, Laurel still brought her along with her friends, even if the book club women were no better a fit than the glossy-lipped girls from high school.

So she told them about seeing *Wonderful Town* when her parents visited and discount shopping at Century 21. On the rare occasions when she told a story involving Chase Fisher, Sharon would simply say "my ex," with the kind of war-weary gesture the women used when comparing their own husbands unfavorably to the men in the books they read. In her head, Sharon created generic, faceless figments of herself and Chase that she could talk about without sinking into the Earth's core. Occasionally that old life did sound interesting, but Sharon still didn't think she'd be going back.

Her neighbor in the old chopped-up house did something at UC Medical Center a few blocks over on Goodman and was nearly always clad in scrubs. He'd bob his head when he saw Sharon in the hall or by the bank of mailboxes in the foyer.

One night when Sharon was in her underwear and glasses transcribing notes from an interview, he knocked on the door. After checking the peephole and re-wrapping her discarded wrap dress, Sharon opened.

"I'm Scott Underwood; I live next door," he said, as if they hadn't seen each other leaving their respective apartments a dozen times. "Sorry to bother you, but I locked myself out."

"Do you need to call a locksmith?"

"Actually, I was hoping you'd let me climb out your window onto the ledge. It's pretty easy to get back in through my window."

Sharon looked at him blankly.

Scott Underwood assured her he had done this all the time with the girl who used to live in her apartment.

There were mounds of clothes and old newspapers and half-full cans of Diet Coke everywhere, but she let him in, nervously stood by as he pushed up the window and balanced on the narrow stone ledge (flicker of a memory—standing on the railing at the Madison Plaza). After fiddling with the latch on his own window, Scott disappeared to the tune of a low-level crash. Ten seconds later he knocked on her door again.

"I made it." He smiled, brown hair adorably mussed. "Thanks for your help."

Sharon nodded. "Nothing like a little B&E to get to know your neighbors."

"I owe you," he said, and she told him not to worry about it.

But the next night, he was at her door again—wearing black pants and a ribbed sweater, not scrubs—asking if he could take her out for a drink to thank her.

They went to a local bar that catered more toward grad students than undergrads and had fewer peanut shells on the floor. Scott told her he was a surgical resident who was fighting very hard to remain committed to general surgery, though medical school loans were pushing him toward plastics. She told him she had moved back from New York and worked at *Cincy Beat*.

"I read that," he said excitedly.

"Really?"

"Well, I see it in the dispensers." He smiled again. There was a gap between his front teeth, and she liked the way his tongue poked through.

Two weak gin and tonics later, Scott walked her the two blocks back to the chopped-up house on Mcmillan. At her doorstep, he bent down to kiss her.

She stopped him.

Mumbling an apology, he started backing into his apartment, but she reached for his hand.

"I had a really good time, tonight, I'm . . ." There really wasn't a good way to explain what she was. In mourning? Denial? Scared of melting should she say her ex's name aloud? "I'm not dating right now."

He nodded as if that made sense, and things were awkward until two weeks later, when Sharon forgot *her* keys and knocked on Scott's door.

He helped break into her place through his, and they forged a kind of friendship where they'd hang out in one of their apartments (usually his, he had a cleaning lady and a bigger TV) after work if they were both home at a reasonable or quasi-reasonable hour. It turned out that being a resident actually was a lot like doctor TV shows—everyone dated everyone and rarely left the hospital—and Scott was genuinely enthused to have a friend with no affiliation to UC. Some nights they'd rent a movie or play Trivial Pursuit, or she'd get *Cincy Beat* tickets to a concert or play. He ate bowls of cereal at all hours of the day and turned her on to the merits of the Frosted Mini-Wheats supper.

At first he was hesitant to talk about girls he went out with, but then he actually started asking her for advice. Sharon would occasionally see women sneaking out of his apartment in the mornings; they were almost always wearing rumpled scrubs of their own. She tried not to be jealous.

"Are you a lesbian?" Scott asked one night after six months, when they were eating Captain Crunch and hate-watching a horrible rom-com starring Kate Hudson and Jake James. "Not that it matters . . ."

"Junior year, my college roommate and I made out during a game of truth or dare. Otherwise, no."

"Just not dating." He nodded. "I remember."

While Sharon suspected their friendship may have been largely based on the fact that he was too tired after marathon shifts at the hospital to look for a social life outside of their chopped-up house, she also knew that she could have told him about Chase Fisher breaking up with her and dying. Still she kept quiet.

It took him more than a year and countless Netflix rentals before he brought up her scar.

"Did it hurt?" he asked.

"What?"

Next to her on the couch, he sheepishly ducked his head toward the thin pink mark on her left wrist. "I'm sorry; they taught us to look for stuff like that during psych rotation."

"It's fine." For the first time in a very long time, she allowed herself to think about the bathtub. About Nero. About waiting for Chase's phone call that never came. "I was drunk, but yeah, it was actually pretty excruciating. I only got to the one." Smiling flippantly, she held up her unblemished right wrist.

"Did you . . . ," Scott started.

She knew he wanted to ask what made her do it, what happened to make her stop. Knew that the moment was a fulcrum. If she was ever going to tell him about Chase and running out of the Madison Plaza, it was now. And if she did, their relationship would go one way, and if she didn't, another. Knew that they could never be more than flirty friends if she didn't tell him.

Enough time had passed that she suspected she might no longer fall through the flooring to China if she spoke Chase's name.

But she didn't.

"I never really meant to go through with it, like, not even at the time," she said, which was a chunk of the truth, if not the whole thing. "I was just being melodramatic and stupid."

"That's good, I guess," he said, and she supposed it was.

From New York, Kristen sent funny e-mails about disastrous Match.com dates she went on, people they both knew from school, and her job at the NYU Office of Annual Giving. Every couple of weeks, she'd call, and after a year, she flew out to visit.

"Who leaves New York to vacation in Cincinnati?" Sharon joked, but she was touched that Kristen used her time off to come see her.

Pulling her *Cincy Beat* connections, Sharon scored them tickets to see *Glengarry Glen Ross* at the Playhouse and a nonsensical installation piece at the Contemporary Arts Center that appeared to be nothing more than disassembled parts of a Harley-Davidson motorcycle on the floor.

Scott went with them to the Skyline Chili on Ludlow, where they gorged on three-ways and cheese conies but still managed to find room for black raspberry chip ice cream cones at Grater's down the street.

Charmingly, Scott picked up the check.

"You ladies can pay me back by playing truth or dare later," he said, and Sharon swatted his side.

"You told him?" Kristen didn't sound remotely displeased. They had both been such tragically good, good girls in college that they often recounted this very brief dalliance into Sapphism. "She tells everyone; it's her best story."

Kristen said nothing about the story of how Sharon broke up with her boyfriend and was supposed to move in with her but didn't.

After they'd sent Scott to his own apartment across the hall, the two women *did* end up in Sharon's bed together. It wasn't so they could make out, Sharon's couch just sagged uncomfortably in the middle.

"We should send Scott a picture," Kristen joked. "He's kind of cute."

Tall, gangly, and blond, Kristen looked almost nothing like her, and Sharon wondered if it was a look Scott would like. Wondered if she minded.

"So it's your turn to come visit next," Kristen said the next morning at passenger drop-off.

Sharon nodded over the lump in her throat. But she still didn't think she'd be going back to New York.

With Scott busy doing surgical residency things one Thursday night, Sharon decided to check out the *E&E* show that Julie's *Living* article had reminded her she'd forgotten about.

Like all QT shows, *E&E: Rising*'s cast was young and otherworldly attractive, and the special effects weren't particularly good. But it was relatively true to the comics, and the guy playing Captain Rowen was even better than Michael Douglas had been in the movies.

It had been nearly two years since Sharon had thought about her widely rejected manuscript or writing fiction in general. But as the *E&E* characters hopped from world to world, where things were slightly to extremely different, she began to conjure up a story: a too-pretty young man who doesn't do his own laundry falls in love with a girl in the West Village. And maybe he and the girl break up, but he gets to go on and do other things. Sharon didn't even consciously realize it was about Chase Fisher.

That's how it started.

A sentence here and there, the odd paragraph when she had the time. It wasn't something she did when she was supposed to be writing features at *Cincy Beat*, not something she told Scott or anyone else about. Six months in she had nearly two hundred pages.

Still, she didn't think she'd be going back to New York.

In Sharon's second spring in the chopped-up house on Mcmillan, Scott went to Chicago to take the medical boards. When he got back, he knocked on her door with a bottle of champagne.

"Do I have to start calling you doctor now?" Sharon asked.

"I've been a doctor since finishing med school, but, yes, I now insist."

She called him "Dr. Underwood" as they got tipsy on the Perrier-Jouët in her apartment and all through celebratory filet mignon and lobster at The Precinct Steakhouse.

"So I got a fellowship at Weill Cornell in New York," he said. "You should come, too, keep me company."

He may or may not have been kidding, but they both knew it wasn't going to happen.

"I'm gonna miss you," he said.

"Me, too." (In fact Sharon's heart would legitimately hurt the first time she saw the new tenant in Scott's apartment—an apple-shaped law student, who often blared classical music—fiddling with her keys across the hall.)

"You know, we could have been an amazing couple," he said.

And Sharon knew that, too. "In an alternate universe, I'm sure we are."

When he left three weeks later, she would give him Kristen's contact info and silently promise that she would be happy if the two of them fell in love and got married in some over-the-top affair at the Plaza. But that night, after dinner, she held Scott's hand as the two of them bumbled home drunk on red meat and red wine. Kissing him full on the mouth in the hall separating their two apartments, she felt exactly what it would be like to invite him in—a surge of lava and butterflies.

Sharon still didn't think that she would return to New York.

And she continued to think that as she had Sunday dinners with her parents, read bestsellers with Laurel's book club, got promoted to features editor when Alice left for a gig at *Cincinnati* magazine, and completed three hundred pages of the novel about the man that Chase Fisher never got to be.

But then one day, when she's in the *Cincy Beat* office finishing a piece on upcoming movies filming in Cincinnati, the music writer two workstations over rocks back in his chair to ask Sharon a question. "You know anyone at *The New York Eye*? Looks like they're hiring."

The petroleum jelly covering lifts, and it's all so clear. Scanning *The Eye*'s Happenings section with Kristen their first semester at NYU. Passing around a copy and sharing three-dollar soy burgers at Dojo on Fourteenth Street with the other MFAs. Chase bringing home copies of the tabloid on his walk back from work: *"I know you like it better than the* Voice."

And then it hits. A tingling in her nose, a mounting pressure in her bones, an overwhelming *need* to return.

Sharon waits until she's back in her apartment in the old carved-up house on Mcmillan (Vivaldi floating in from the law student's unit next door) before she checks the job posting on Mediabistro. *The Eye* is looking for a features editor/writer for their expanding Web presence. They probably want someone much younger, someone to work for nearly nothing in the impossibly expensive city.

Feeling the gravitational pull of the crooked floor in her bedroom, Sharon writes her cover letter and sends it off with her clips.

"I'm going to be in New York next week, if that works for you," she tells the editor who calls to ask if she'd be able to come in for an interview. She doesn't bother inquiring if they have the budget to fly her out, assumes they won't.

By the time Sharon books her flight and calls Kristen to see if she can stay in Astoria for a few days, she knows that, whether or not she gets the position, she's moving back to New York.

Tears and embraces with Laurel Young-Griffin.

Comped cupcakes and cheap wine at the *Cincy Beat* office.

A ride to the airport with her parents, who seem genuinely sad to see her off.

"You're always welcome to come back," says her father, and she thanks him.

As they cross the Suspension Bridge (like the Brooklyn Bridge) into Kentucky, Sharon wonders, if the cables snapped and the car plunged into the Ohio River, would they paddle to the Cincinnati side even though Covington is closer? Wonders if you always swim home. And if that means that eventually she'll come back to this city she's realized isn't half bad.

Kisses good-bye, baggage checked, and the security line (extra scrutiny because she has no return trip booked). A straight shot from CVG to LGA, baggage claim, the taxi line, and the worn leather of a cab's backseat.

As they head toward Astoria, Sharon glimpses the city skyline, and it *does* feel familiar. But when the crown of the Chrysler Building comes into view, she's once again floored and amazed.

That, too, feels like home.

9 would you tell me if you were?

Adam Zoellner is "TV's Sexiest Bad Guy."

This title is being bestowed upon him by *Living* magazine in its up-coming "100 Sexy People" issue. While most of the other selected sexies are too busy doing sexy things to speak with the poor man's *Us Weekly*, Adam's new publicist (aka Phoebe's friend Evie Saperstein, who opened her own firm in LA) has spun the honor into a two-page feature in *Living*. Adam is in the back of a Town Car on his way to meet a reporter at The Ivy, with Evie beside him going over what *not* to say.

"Don't spend a ton of time on Phoebe." Evie brushes Goth sophisticate burgundy hair from her face. "She's hot enough that we can totally sell your wedding pics, but no point in breaking all those precious fangirl hearts until it's official. Say you're in a long-term relationship and very happy, blah, blah, but you like to keep it private."

"Sure." Adam nods, whipping up a mental image of what it *would* be like if he and Phoebe got married. For Valentine's Day he'd given her a very big sapphire ring, and they'd had fun joking about which of their friends would get wasted and hook up if they had a giant wedding in

Big Sur or a vineyard in Napa. But then he was back in Vancouver while Phoebe continued her mission to take *every* class at UCLA, volunteer a billion hours at an inner-city health clinic, and (despite his numerous offers to support her) bartend at Rosebud. "So I just say enough to dispel the gay rumors?"

"Gay rumors are a good thing," Evie says, sans any shred of irony. "Why limit the number of people jerking off to you?"

That Adam even has a publicist is ridiculous. But Evie had been appalled when Phoebe told her that, after two years on a hit show and stellar reviews for the *Who's Afraid of Virginia Woolf?* remake, Adam was still letting the network handle his press. "Everyone knows you're the only one on *E&E* who's got a career afterward," Evie had said in her backhanded-compliment way that Adam is actually starting to find appealing.

"She'll ask what qualities you like in a woman," Evie is saying. "The answer is always 'sense of humor.' And you prefer curvy to too skinny."

"I'm not an idiot," Adam says; Evie doesn't confirm or deny this.

"Oh, and talk about your mom—the hardworking single-parent thing always plays well."

The driver makes the turn from Beverly to North Robertson, and the white umbrellas on the restaurant's terrace come into view. A young woman with a blond ponytail walks to the door, and Evie informs Adam she's Julie from the magazine.

"I know you think it's dumb, but have fun." Evie touches Adam's arm lightly in a more earnest way than her faux-tough persona usually allows. "This is actually a pretty big deal."

The Sexy Issue hits stands the first week in July, and Adam's phone rings off the hook with acquaintances he hasn't talked to in years. While *E&E: Rising* might be the highest-rated show in the QT Network's six-year history, a lot more people apparently follow the exploits of Jennifer Aniston and Angelina Jolie in *Living*.

As much as Adam didn't become an actor for this, it's, well, amusing when Evie tells him her assistant has dealt with no less than six pairs of panties when going through his mail. Even more exciting, his agent claims important insiders are starting to take notice. Within days Adam is on the short list to play Brick Pollitt in a remake of *Cat on a Hot Tin Roof* starring Scarlett Johansson as Maggie.

It's all going swimmingly until Phoebe comes home to their high-rise condo in the Wilshire Corridor (his first big splurge when the show got picked up) and ominously announces she has to talk to him.

Adam's stomach twists, and it seems astonishing that a few minutes earlier, he'd been excited to take her to the new Mario Batali place for dinner.

There *had* been a bit of readjustment when he returned after wrapping season three—Adam suspects it was similar to soldiers returning from deployments (if soldiers were paid significantly more and all the blood was corn syrup)—but lately Adam had thought he and Phoebe were actually really happy together.

"What's up?" He tries to sound normal. Next to him Kraken raises his furry head, sensing the change of energy in the room.

"You got a letter and Evie didn't know what to make of it, so she asked me." Phoebe bites her lip. "I'm not sure I handled it right."

So not what he was expecting her to say, Adam just looks at her for a few seconds. Finally asks, "What, like a threat?"

"No, it was from a guy in Atlanta." She pauses. "He thinks he's your father—"

Cutting her off, Adam explains it's probably someone looking for money.

"That's what I thought initially." Phoebe's voice is shaky, and it's obvious she wants to break eye contact. "But he sent old pictures of him and your mom, and . . . he looks a lot like you."

"Pictures can be doctor—"

"I did a little research; he's, like, a big corporate lawyer. I don't think it's about money." She takes a breath. "So I called him—"

"You did this behind my back?" He's on his feet, chilled with anger, grabbing keys and a leather jacket he probably doesn't need. Kraken follows, nails clacking on the hardwood.

"I wanted to check him out before I told you."

Phoebe reaches for his arm, but he shakes her off, needs to get away before he says anything he'll regret. Because in the seven years he's known her, he's rarely been this coiled, this ready to explode.

"Sweetie, wait . . ."

He's in the elevator headed twenty-four stories down to the garage before she can finish her sentence. With no actual destination in mind, he gets behind the wheel of the sleek black sports car (his *second* big splurge when the show got picked up).

He'd been two years old when his mother moved back to her parents' house in Coral Cove, and since that first moment when she'd set him up in her childhood bedroom, there'd been whispered speculation about his paternity. Busybody parents of the children from school: "Should I let Jimmy spend the night? Who knows what kind of morals Anna Zoellner has?" All those teachers who adored him, chattering in the teacher's lounge: "Look how well he turned out, considering." Girls he dated who mistakenly thought his mysterious origins made him tortured and/or poetic. He grew up doing everything right, silently challenging all those gossips to say anything to him directly. Most people, he learned, were cowards.

Because his mother never volunteered the information, Adam never asked. Not in second grade, when Mrs. Victor handed out Xeroxed copies of a family tree and he left his paternal side completely blank. Not in the genetics unit of eighth-grade biology, when Adam realized his detached earlobes—different from his mother's and grandparents'—must have been a trait of his father's. Not even after the father-son minigolf tournament junior year, when he and his grandfather finished third, and on the drive home Grandpa brought up the fact that he'd been Adam's partner. "I know Anna doesn't talk about it much," his grandfather had said, "but I'm sure you have questions."

"I don't." Adam had cut him off.

"It's only natural to wonder—"

"I don't." Adam had lived fifteen years in the same house as Wyatt Zoellner and worked in his ice cream store since he was legally allowed, but other than putt-putt and an occasional game of darts, they shared almost nothing. His loyalty was to his mother, and it was her secret to reveal. "It has nothing to do with me," he'd said and almost believed it; nobody could ever say Anna Zoellner's bastard son wasn't just as good at convincing himself of things as he was other people. Blissfully, a year later he was gone to New York and then LA, where plenty of people had parents they didn't speak to for one reason or another.

Almost without thinking he's driven to Santa Monica, a beach completely unlike the one an hour from his hometown, but a beach all the same. Weird how after all this time in California, he still associates the ocean with Florida.

He parks the car and walks to the pier, watches all the couples holding hands, riding the Ferris wheel, throwing balls into milk jugs on the midway.

He's shared more of himself with Phoebe than any person he's ever met, and in many ways, she knows him better than he knows himself. Now, his anger softened, Adam realizes what he knew from the moment she mentioned the man from Atlanta: He's going to look at the photos and whatever Phoebe found on the Web. He is going to meet this man.

It's nearly midnight when he gets home, but Phoebe is awake on the couch with the dog reading a heavy book called *Theories of Social Psychology* that she quickly sets aside.

"You're right, sweetie." She's on her feet tentatively reaching toward him. "I had no right to do this."

Telling her it's all good, he finishes the embrace for her, inhales the familiar mix of vanilla lotion and Anais Anais. A solid thirty seconds before he pulls away.

"Well." He sighs. "Let's see what you found."

A week later Adam is in the master bedroom's ginormous closet, where getting dressed is proving unusually difficult. He tries and discards four different shirts before deciding on a Thomas Pink double cuff better suited for a wedding than a meeting with a possible parent. For balance, he swaps fitted pants for a pair of distressed jeans. His off-season hair has grown to a standard military crew cut, which he futzes with to no avail.

That Michael Shipman, who thinks he's Adam's father, has business in Southern California seems far too coincidental. But Adam knows so little about this man, there's no point in calling him on the lie. Instead he simply agreed to meet at Michael's hotel for a drink. Actually, Phoebe set things up.

Adam has spent hunks of the past week studying the pictures Michael Shipman sent in his letter. The most disturbing is a strip of images from a photo booth: Michael Shipman, probably a decade younger than Adam is now (with the same Roman nose, same square chin), and Adam's mother, so young and impossibly radiant. In the pictures she's smiling, really smiling, in a way Adam has never seen. Looking at it winds his insides like watch gears.

Coming into the closet, Phoebe straightens his collar. Apparently finding an outfit wasn't all that difficult for her; she's wearing a conservative navy dress perfect for the occasion.

"This is ridiculous." He runs his hand over his scalp. "What am I possibly going to say to this guy?"

"Do you want me to cancel?" She takes his hand in both of hers.

"No," he says, but pulls her in when she starts to leave.

Backing her against a wall of shoe cubbies, he kisses her hard enough to knock down a pair of red-soled Louboutins. Presses his body against hers so tight that he'd be inside her but for their clothes. She responds equally savagely, nails down his sides, teeth on his lower lip.

And he wants to stay in this closet with her forever. To never go back to Canada, never let Phoebe attend another class, never think about the outside world and people, like Michael Shipman, who inhabit it. Just the two of them among the boots and suits and dry-cleaning bags.

There are photographers across the street when he pulls up in front of the Four Seasons Beverly Hills. Though they're probably waiting to catch Madonna, who's performing at the Staples Center that night, one of them notices Adam giving car keys to the valet.

"It's Captain Rowen!" A shuffling of feet and camera clicks, and for the first time in the eleven years he's been a working actor, Adam is blinded by flashbulbs that aren't part of a step-and-repeat on a red carpet.

"Adam, over here!"

"This way!"

"Is this your girlfriend?"

Two uniformed doormen rush from their stations to assist if necessary, but Adam holds up a hand indicating he's okay. Her own face still hidden behind giant sunglasses, Phoebe nudges him forward. Adam smiles at the photographers, gives a quick wave before entering the hotel, where the paparazzi's calls are clipped by the glass doors and ambient music in the lobby.

"I'll be really pissed if I end up in *The National Enquirer.*" Phoebe laughs, and Adam almost forgets why they're here.

Almost.

The Windows Lounge is lousy with people for cocktail hour, but Adam spots Michael Shipman instantly, tries to convince himself it's because the man is looking expectantly toward the entrance and not because Michael Shipman is a mirror into Adam's future. Phoebe squeezes his arm, and he loves her so much he wants to be stranded with her on a tropical island or in an Alaskan igloo—anywhere that isn't here.

Seeing them, Michael Shipman crosses the room. Maybe he's an inch or two taller than Adam, or it could just be that he's wearing an exceptionally well-tailored suit. Adam accepts his outstretched hand and says his name as if he's being controlled remotely.

"Phoebe Fisher," Phoebe volunteers when Adam fails to introduce her. "We spoke on the phone."

Michael leads them to a table he's reserved in the corner, and the three of them slide into winged chairs, order a round of generic drinks—vodka sodas and gin and tonics—and the waitress sets a dish of nuts and olives in front of them.

"Well, this is a little awkward." Michael Shipman smiles. It's a nice smile, an incredibly familiar smile. If this dude really is his father, Adam can expect to age well. "But like I told Ms. Fisher on the phone, my wife saw you in *Living*, and we couldn't get over how much you look like our son. When you mentioned Anna in the article, well, we did the math—"

"So your wife knew?" Adam says much more forcefully than the situation warrants. Under the table Phoebe rests her hand on his thigh.

"Knew what?" Michael Shipman is confused. "I met my wife years after I dated Anna."

"Oh." The nuts have a spice/sugar rub on them; Adam is looking at them intently enough to notice.

"I wasn't married or seeing anyone else when I was with your mother," Michael says. "Did she tell you I was?"

"No," Adam says after a while. "She never mentioned you, ever."

Something shifts in Michael Shipman's eyes—deep brown eyes that aren't like Adam's at all, actually. "Well, what did she tell you about your father?"

"My mother told me absolutely nothing."

"I see," Michael says.

Adam feels the frozen rage building in his throat again.

"So why are you here now?" he asks. Phoebe tightens her grip on his leg, but he doesn't care. "You had thirty-one years to find me, and now that I'm some famous actor you want money? It's basic cable; it doesn't pay that well."

While this is true, it's most likely irrelevant. Michael Shipman is wearing the same kind of pricey watch Adam's agent does and he smells ever so faintly of expensive cologne.

"I'm not after anything like that," Michael Shipman says gently, seems to want to reach out and pat Adam's hand.

To say they look alike is silly. Adam and Michael Shipman look like father and son—it's the wide cheekbones, the dimples. The hair on Adam's head is the same dirty blond as Michael Shipman's, and if it were ever allowed more than a few months to grow out, it would have the same wavy texture. Michael Shipman's got the detached earlobes from eighth-grade biology.

"Then what, you need a kidney?" Adam asks. "Or this magical son of yours could use a piece of my liver?"

"Adam." Phoebe squeezes his leg.

"I don't know what your mother told you, but she's the one who left," Michael Shipman says, red splotches on his cheeks and under his collar, jaw (same boxy jaw as Adam) jutting forward. "I thought we were in love, and one day she was gone—no call, no note, nothing. I looked for her for months."

Phoebe makes a sympathetic sound in the back of her throat, and Adam wants to leave her stranded on that island or freezing in that igloo.

"It's not my intention to bad-mouth your mother." Michael Shipman is visibly trying to gain control. "I'm only here to find out if I have another child in this world, period."

This seems reasonable, Adam knows, but he's seventeen and back in the car with his grandfather—someone trying to tell him what only Anna Zoellner has the right to tell.

"Look, Mr. Shipman, I already know how to play catch." Adam's using Captain Rowen's voice, hungrier and more damaging than his own, and he's saying the kinds of cutting things Rowen would say.

His napkin flutters to the ground as Adam stands and reaches into his back pocket for his wallet. He sets six twenties on the table, even though the bill is probably half that, even though Michael Shipman is on his feet, too, waving away the money.

"Please, I've got this." Michael looks inconsolable in a way Adam will remember for the rest of his life, even when he's older than his father is now.

"Really, don't waste a second feeling guilty," Adam says. "I'm *Living* magazine's sexiest TV bad guy, my life turned out fucking amazing."

Adam extends a hand to Phoebe, and for a sliver of a second she hesitates, desperate to apologize, to say something to this man. But her allegiance is to Adam, so she links her fingers in his, keeps up with his rapid pace as they make their way through the crowd back to the lobby.

"Wait," she says as the doorman holds open the glass door.

Thinking she's going to say they should go back, Adam cuts her off, tirades about how he owes Michael Shipman nothing.

"He's just some guy who may have had a fling with my mother," Adam says, loud enough that a few people at the reception desk turn.

"Sweetie." She places her palm against his chest. "I was going to say you should let me get the car. You don't want to deal with photographers right now."

Nodding, Adam takes the valet ticket from his pocket, realizes his hand is shaking, heart beating so fast he wonders if he's having a heart attack; perhaps coronary disease runs in Michael Shipman's family? "Maybe you should drive."

He waits in the entranceway until Phoebe is behind the wheel before ducking into the car.

"I'm sorry," she says. "I didn't realize this would be so upsetting."

He says nothing, and she drives in silence, does a decent job of shifting gears at the tail end of rush hour.

As she starts to make the turn onto Wilshire, Adam stops her. "Just keep going."

Phoebe wordlessly takes Santa Monica West to I-10 East. At the junction with the Santa Ana Freeway, she looks to Adam. He nods, and they drive south as fast as commuter-jammed traffic will allow. Occasionally, he feels her worried glances.

Leaning his head against the window, he closes his eyes and thinks of his mother—selfless and sacrificing and giving up so much so he could have everything. His mother, who felt the need to keep Michael Shipman from him.

Twenty miles outside Oceanside, Phoebe says they need gas. Adam checks the fuel gauge, nods again, and they follow signs to an exit ramp and a Chevron station.

"It's on the front passenger side," Adam says, the first words he's spoken in an hour and a half.

Stopping at the pump, she kills the engine and puts a cautious hand on his shoulder.

"Well, Michael Shipman seemed nice," Adam says.

A choked laugh from Phoebe. "Yeah, he did."

Her flat response strikes Adam as perhaps the funniest thing he's *ever* heard, and he starts laughing and can't stop, laughing so hard tears shimmy down his face and his stomach aches as if he'd done a year's worth of crunches.

"Are you all right?" Phoebe asks, brows upslanted peaks of concern.

"I'm fucking amazing," he manages.

Apparently unconvinced, Phoebe gets a restaurant recommendation from the attendant behind the counter. The place—one of those seaside joints with a name playing off the water—has rickety wood steps, smells of sewage, and looks as if it's closing down even though it's ten past nine. But there's a full bar, and a waitress seats them by an open window overlooking the ocean and the glow of Camp Pendleton down the road.

Adam downs his first Jack and Coke like a shot, gets a second, and chugs that as well.

"Did you eat *anything* today?" Phoebe asks (ironic, considering how little she ate when they first met, when she was just another would-be actress).

Adam shrugs, and she tells him if he's going to drink like that, they should get food. He's way too knotted to eat but appreciates her custodial care, so he orders a chicken sandwich and a soda sans whiskey.

He sips his Coke, asks, "Do you think he's telling the truth, about how things went down with my mom?"

Phoebe shakes her head. "I don't know, sweetie."

"I sorta figured the reason she never told me was because it was kind of bad—like she had a one-night stand or was raped or there were so many different guys she honestly didn't know which one it was."

"Would that make you feel better?"

"I dunno. But that guy we met, he . . . it seems like . . ."

"Like he might have been the kind of father you would have wanted?" Phoebe finishes because Adam can't say it. Even thousands of miles from his mother, he can't bring himself to betray her by speaking the thought aloud.

Clenching his eyes closed, he bows his head and nods in agreement.

Phoebe puts her hand on top of his on the table, and when he opens his eyes, she's looking at him as if working out a complex equation. Opens her mouth, then closes it again. Finally she says, "I had an abortion once."

Once again, so not what he was expecting. Adam feels his eyes grow, and that's before he does quick calculations, realizes that if this happened in the past seven years, it was very possibly his. While he's always been absently pro-choice, he's never really thought much about any choices that may have been made without his input.

This must register on his face.

"Not you," Phoebe says, far too easily.

He wonders what he would have said if Phoebe had come to him, wonders what to say now, settles on, "I'm sorry that happened."

"It is what it is," she says. "But the minute I realized I was pregnant, I made an appointment at Planned Parenthood. I didn't tell anyone, not the guy, not my parents, no one."

Adam pushes aside the unspoken *I didn't tell you,* squeezes her hand. "Pheebs."

"It's not that I regret it, I don't." She shakes her head. "I'm saying I made that decision instantly. I knew that it was right for me."

"Are you saying I should be glad my mother had me?"

"I'm saying people react to things in different ways. Maybe your mom knew what was best and that meant not telling Michael Shipman."

"Like what? She had a sixth sense he would beat me or something?" Adam sighs. "He didn't really seem the type."

"Maybe he would have. Or maybe he would have been controlling, or maybe he would have talked her out of having you. You can't know what she was thinking."

"I guess." Even in the dim light his chicken sandwich looks anemic and unappetizing, but the fries are surprisingly crisp. "I suppose I could ask her."

"There is always that."

When Adam first left Coral Cove for NYU thirteen years earlier, going home had easily been dismissed as a financial impossibility. His scholarship covered almost everything, but between plays, auditions, and studying, he usually had time for only an occasional odd job, and that money was quickly eaten up with books and food and life. As he became more established, the price of a ticket home was no more extravagant than a night out, and yet he still didn't buy those airline tickets. When he'd started doing well, he began flying his mother out to LA or Vancouver several times a year, or they would go on vacation together, but Adam can count on one hand the number of times he's gone home since he left for NYU.

As student body president, he was theoretically responsible for planning the ten-year reunion of his high school class, but he hadn't stayed in touch with a single person from CCH. The invitation arrived in California a month after the event, forwarded from his grandparents' house to his old apartment on MacDougal Street in New York, and finally to LA. The party had been held in the Coral Cove VFW Hall. The vice president, who'd apparently married the treasurer, had put it together. Even though the date had long passed, Adam had briefly felt his guts seize when he held the invite. It's the same doomed feeling he had when he bought a ticket home the day after meeting Michael Shipman.

Orlando is the closest airport, so Adam flies out with all the families going to Disney, rents a car, and drives the uneventful hour on Highway 4—all flat grass crunchy from the August sun.

With its fading smiling dolphin, the familiar sign welcomes him to

CORAL COVE, POPULATION: 25,000. Feeling the oppressive heat through the windshield, he recalls exactly how it felt to live here with that constant countdown to escape. The sensation kicks up as he turns off the state route and onto Sunflower Street. Only two more turns until Marigold Drive and his grandparents' house, with the paisley couch and love seat in the living room, the kitchen and its olive green appliances that had been so fashionable in the midseventies. Before he bought the condo or the car, the first thing he had *tried* to splurge on was a home for his mother in the newer development outside of town; she'd flat-out refused.

It's 4:00 P.M. on a Friday, and his grandparents have long since retired. They're probably sitting on the screened-in porch, the ancient metal fan teasing them with its rotating stream of air. Last Christmas he'd sent them an enormous HDTV, but he wouldn't be surprised to find them watching the same fifteen-inch set of his youth, the wires still tamped down with duct tape snaking from the outlet in the house through the window to the porch.

His mother won't be home for at least two hours. Two hours of his grandfather nodding along to Fox News or the Military Channel and his grandmother offering cans of lukewarm caffeine-free soda. Two hours of their questions about his life and what brings him home while he waits with a nervous eye on the clock, wondering how to ask his mother what he hasn't been able to ask for the last thirty-one years.

Desperately he wishes he'd taken Phoebe up on her offer to come along despite her summer term finals.

As he's about to make the last turn, he realizes he hasn't brought his grandparents anything, U-turns back toward the main stretch of town, and parks in an angled spot marked by faded yellow paint.

The downtown, with its little roundabout of shops, is almost unrecognizable. The post office is still there, and the diner, though it's pea green with a new awning. His grandparents sold Sally's Scoops years ago, and it's now a 31 Flavors with the blue-and-pink BR logo. There's a coffee shop with a sign to make it look as though it's a Starbucks and a new "art" gallery that's really a frame store with a few posters of famous paintings. Almost everything else is gone—the hardware store, the old bookshop, the pharmacy, the shoe store—all empty storefronts with FOR RENT signs in the windows.

A few years ago, his mother mentioned that the Walmart down the road was putting everything out of business. He hadn't thought much about it, because he tried so hard to never think much about Coral Cove.

Captain Ahab's Bar is still the last stop on the strip, depressing and ramshackle as always, the same neon beer signs in the tinted windows, probably full of the same drunks from twenty years ago—the ones his grandfather would call "dumbasses" and "layabouts."

He's giving serious consideration to joining them for a drink when he sees her getting out of a minivan a few spaces away. Almost unconsciously, he shields his eyes with the back of his hand to get a better look, to make sure it's really her.

It is.

Fourteen years after she left him on the beach to get beat up by Sean Dooley, there's Molly Kelly.

Jogging over, he calls her name. She turns, surprise melting into a smile.

Since high school she's gained twenty pounds and has her thick hair in a careless, unflattering length between shoulder and chin. Fine lines splinter and spread from her familiar blue eyes, and she's wearing legit mom jeans. None of it matters; Adam gets hard just looking at her.

She hugs him. He kisses her cheek.

"So what brings TV's sexiest bad guy to central Florida?" she asks.

"Please." He rolls his eyes in mock modesty. "Do they even get QT out here?"

"Oh, don't pretend your mom doesn't tell you how the whole town watches every week—you're big news." She swats his arm gently, lets her hand linger. "They do a feature on you in *The Bee* every other week."

"And no one ever calls to ask me for comment."

"Yeah, they're not the most thorough paper." Eyes lit up, she leans into him. "So you're home for a visit?"

He nods. "I forgot to bring my grandparents a gift and was hoping to grab something in town. But there's not a whole lot of town left, is there?"

"Nah." With her hand she bats away something imaginary. "There's a decent wine store around the corner on Sunflower. You could get a bottle of California wine and pretend you got it there."

"That's brilliant," he says. "Any chance I can get you to show me?"

"Sure. I was gonna grab coffee and kill time while the boys were at practice, but it's not every day I get to hang out with a TV star."

She leads him down the street and through the intersection, and he asks about her life.

Apparently she has three sons—thirteen, twelve, and nine—whom she dropped off around the corner at Martin Field for baseball, because "they all hit like Willie Mays, one good thing they got from their father." Adam assumes this means Kyle Dooley; four months (122 days) before he left for NYU, he'd seen their wedding announcement in the *Coral Cove Bee*.

He's expecting the kind of seedy liquor store that blooms in sketchy parts of Wilcox or Vine in LA, but Adam is surprised that Coral Cove Wine Shop is clean and has a sizable selection of bottles, all about 15 percent cheaper than anywhere he's been in recent years. He gets a California cabernet and a Shiraz.

"Don't forget to take off the price tags," Molly jokes.

They walk back toward the car, passing the Baskin-Robbins. It's still early, so he suggests they get ice cream for old times' sake.

"Rocky road still your favorite?" he asks, and she nods.

The teenage boy behind the counter is handsome and friendlier than most kids in service jobs, and Adam wonders if he has an escape countdown all his own—each scoop one more brick in the bridge out. Discreetly, Adam slips a hundred-dollar bill in the tip jar.

There's a Nelson bench in front, and Adam and Molly sit, licking at their already melting scoops.

"You *are* really great on the show," Molly says, more serious than before. "And in *Who's Afraid of Virginia Woolf?*—jeez."

"Thank you." A warmth on his cheeks that has nothing to do with the sun. "That's really nice to hear."

"What's it like, working in Hollywood? Is it what we thought when we were kids?"

The question is an offering, the kind he's become very familiar with since the show exploded. All it will take for him to accept is a brush of his hand along the underside of her wrist, a certain kind of crooked smile, and a tale of something grander than Coral Cove. He could tell her how the cameras and crew evaporate when he's really into a scene or about the emotional exhaustion of living in another person's skin. That's it, and he could be in her bed, the one thing in the whole god-awful town he ever really wanted.

There's Phoebe, whom he loves so much it still keeps him awake some nights. But there's more than that.

Fourteen years ago Molly had come to him with a different offer and the hope that he might save her from a life she didn't know she wanted. He couldn't do that for her then, won't do it for her now.

"It's not really very glamorous," he says. "It's all shot in Canada. Mostly I sit around freezing my ass off and trying not to mess up my makeup."

She nods, and he sends her back to the baseball diamond with a slight disappointment in her blue eyes. When she kisses his cheek, she leaves a faint smudge of rocky road.

The phone rings on the quick drive to his grandparents: Phoebe reporting that Marty messengered over an early version of the *Cat on a Hot Tin Roof* screenplay.

"It'll never be as good as our scene in Theta's workshop," Adam says.

Phoebe laughs, and Adam wonders, for the millionth time, why she's given up on acting. Now, when he's finally in a position to help her, she chooses to shy away from the spotlight and cameras when she accompanies him to premieres and parties. To modestly smile and dismiss it when people (people with the connections to make things happen) tell her she could model or do commercial work.

"That may be, but it's pretty solid," Phoebe says. "Want me to send it there?"

"Naw." He pulls into his grandparents' driveway behind the hybrid his mother *had* let him buy her last year. "I'm not going to be in Florida long."

She asks about his flight and if he's spoken to his mother yet, tells a story about their dog—the child they do share. "Kraken found a chicken bone in the canyon, and I almost lost a finger wrestling it from him."

Again, he wants to know about the pregnancy she terminated but instead tells her he loves her.

"I love you, too," she says. "Let me know if you need me to come out there."

That fantasy of living in an isolated world where the two of them are the only dwellers.

His grandparents' house is unlocked, just like when he was a kid.

Black hair still damp from a shower, his mother is on the paisley couch of his youth, reading something by Thomas Hardy. He doesn't remember a whole lot from the English classes he took at school (and probably hasn't read ten novels since graduation), but he remembers Hardy, thinks how fitting it is for his mother.

After a few seconds, she notices him and smiles, still so beautiful in her early fifties.

"Hey, baby." She takes him in her arms, her skin soft and cool despite the heat. "Your grandparents are having dinner with the Bentleys. I think they wanted to give us time alone."

"Ma," he says, realizes his hands are shaking again.

"What's on your mind?" She's still holding him lightly at the elbows. Her gray eyes (his eyes), keen as always. In all the places he's been and seen, he's yet to meet someone so genuinely knowing.

Dips his head. This is how it felt to tell her he was leaving fourteen years ago, something she'd probably been expecting his whole life. And isn't this the other thing she always had to know was coming?

"Baby, what is it?"

"I met Michael Shipman."

"Oh."

"I wasn't looking for him or anything." Adam feels the need to explain. "He found me because of a stupid magazine story."

"It's good." His mother is noticeably rattled but still in control. "I should have told you about this years ago."

Women and their choices.

Molly Kelly on the beach, agreeing to drive back to Coral Cove with Kyle Dooley. Phoebe, positive pregnancy test wand in hand, calling Planned Parenthood in Burbank. His mother packing her things in Atlanta, ignoring Michael Shipman's phone calls, fleeing the city as if it were burning a second time.

"So he is..." Adam asks.

"Yeah." His mother nods. "I'm sure you have a lot of questions."

Women and their choices and the men who may never fully understand them.

Kyle Dooley straightening the unfamiliar bow tie at the VFW Hall,
Molly already showing in her mother's yellowed wedding gown. Michael
Shipman breaking down the door of his girlfriend's apartment, finding
only empty hangers and a sad stuffed animal he'd won her at a state
fair. Some guy (him?) stuck in traffic on the 405, humming along to a
dopey song on the radio, oblivious to what Phoebe was going through
across town.

"No, there's nothing I need to know," he says, realizing this is the truth.
That despite Michael Shipman and his good intentions, Adam was right all
those years ago when he told his grandpa it didn't matter who his father
was, that it had nothing to do with him. "I'm sorry."

"Baby, it's fine."

"I'm sorry," he says, feels like he can't breathe. "I should have come
home more often. I haven't been—"

"Shh." She strokes his cheek. "S'okay. You're my good boy."

CHICAGO

Nothing sums up your relationship with your half sister better than the
random Thursday in August when the door to your apartment buzzes after 9:00 P.M., the buzzee says, "It's Natasha," and you rack your brain for a
solid half minute trying to recall if you've ever dated a Natasha or if it
might be your Russian-born landlord's daughter who came by last winter
with a space heater when the radiator was broken.

"Who?" you ask again.

"Natasha," says the voice.

You briefly wonder if you misheard, but the building's intercom system
is fairly clear, and it's not as if you'd been in a deep sleep. You'd gotten
home from Advantage Electric an hour ago and had been flipping through
channels waiting for the doe-eyed lawyer from your parking garage to get

home so you could take her for a drink. There's really no reason for your profound confusion.

"I'm sorry, who did you say this was?"

"Your sister, Natasha Ryan."

Another second passes before you ring her in.

Sliding loafers on without socks, you step into the hallway, waiting to see who will show up when the elevator doors part.

It's probably been six years since you've seen Natasha. You've been back in Chicago nine months, but since Maura and your father divorced (sometime after you left, the details of which are not quite clear), he has custody only on odd vacation weeks and never remembers to call you about Natasha's visits until they're almost over. By then it's usually too late to alter your plans (and when you're being completely honest, spending time with Natasha hasn't been high on your list of priorities). You've seen the stray picture at your father's house, but you're not sure of her actual age and find yourself doing quick math and settling on something preteen, between ten and twelve. Always, to you, Natasha will be a little girl of four or five whom you'd get down on hands and knees to play with because her life was as lonely as yours and Maura's.

While you're expecting the unexpected, it's downright dumbfounding when the young woman steps out of the elevator with a fat ponytail of red ringlets and slight swells of breasts and butt evident under her jeans and hoodie. She looks a little like Karen—the sister you *do* think of as your sister—but her skin is every bit as milky as Maura's, though less eerie and translucent. To pronounce her beautiful is probably not right, but there *is* something captivating and otherworldly about her.

"Good evening, Oliver," she says, strange and formal.

Nodding, you say something along the lines of "Hey."

Maybe it's the shock of her transformation, but you let Natasha in and offer her a soda before you remember that you weren't expecting her, and while she does look decades older than you remembered, she's still not nearly old enough to be alone in your up-and-coming-but-still-a-little-dangerous neighborhood this time of night.

Probably not wanting to hinder her good fortune at your utter lack of questioning, Natasha volunteers nothing resembling an explanation but accepts a Dr Pepper and the invitation to sit on the tan sofa you bought from the previous tenant.

"Your apartment is lovely," she continues in her diplomatic and oddly adult way. "And this is in Printer's Row?"

"Yep."

"Is it close to Wrigleyville?"

"No, that's north. Down here it's mainly old warehouses."

Her slightly disappointed nod breaks the trance, and you ask what brings her by.

"I was visiting a friend from art camp who lives in the area, so I figured I would see if you were home." Even if the story were believable, Natasha's shifty-eyed delivery tells an entirely different tale. "Obviously, I'm in town seeing Dad."

Flare of frustration that this is now your problem. That this girl you haven't known for more than half a decade is putting you in the position of calling her out on a lie, of having to find your father (if he's even available and not somewhere over India or holed up with a stewardess in Australia) or track down Maura, whom you've shared fewer than a handful of words with since you stopped sleeping with her and ran away from home at twenty-six.

"What grade are you in now?" you ask in lieu of more challenging questions such as why *she's* running away from home.

"Sixth," Natasha says. "Or I will be when school starts in the fall."

And you remember being short and hefty before growing six inches freshman year of high school. Remember spending the night at Braden's, reading his comic books and fantasizing about his mother while your own mother was lying around waiting to die. You were nothing like this precocious girl with whom you share half of your genes.

"Do you like school?" You're not sure what else to ask someone this age.

"It's fine; I earn good grades. And you? Dad says you design airplane engines. That sounds fascinating."

"Mostly it's a bunch of guys sitting around a table talking."

A sip of soda. A wish for something stronger, but you don't have any alcohol in the house.

"Does Dad know you're here?"

"Of course," she says without making eye contact. "As I said before, I was calling on a girl I met at art camp last summer, and I told him I might stop by."

Your father's parenting was definitely subpar, but it seems extremely suspect that he would let his kid wander around the South Loop after dark.

"Is that really the story you're going to stick with?" you ask.

Natasha seems very interested in her tennis shoes.

"We need to call whoever you're supposed to be with so they're not worried," you continue, with a pleasantly surprising authority.

You've dialed the first three numbers of your father's house before Natasha is on her feet telling you to wait.

"Please, I have questions to ask you without Dad around."

Flashback to your own childhood: Old Orchard Mall down the street from your mother's hospital, Karen telling you to ask her anything. Natasha is probably owed this much, an opportunity to voice her questions about sex or drugs or other grown-up things. Because you haven't been a great brother to either of your sisters, but you've at least talked to Karen since the start of the Bush administration.

"Ask me whatever you want, but we need to call Dad first and let him know you're safe."

"Fine." She takes the phone but doesn't dial. With the same watercolor eyes as her mother, Natasha looks up at you, more challenging than Maura ever dared. "Are you my father?"

Exactly the same feeling you used to get on takeoff all those years ago—testicles left on the ground ten thousand feet below.

"Excuse me?" you finally manage.

"I want to know if you're my father."

"What are you talk—"

"I remember stuff from when I was a kid," she says, and sounds like a child for the first time. "Mom was always touching you, and you slept in the same bed when Dad was gone. You'd leave before I got up, but I knew."

What you always warned Maura, that she needed to be careful. That Natasha would catch on. To be fair, not sleeping with your stepmother in the first place would have been the easiest way to avoid this line of questioning.

"I'm not your father."

"Would you tell me if you were?"

"No. I mean, I don't know. What does your mother say?"

"I've never asked her." Natasha sighs. "She's my mother. She lies to me about things all the time. I figured you don't have a reason to lie because you don't really even know me."

The logic is laughably flawed, that lies are reserved for loved ones while strangers don't warrant the effort of covering the truth. But there's a beauty to it that makes sense, makes you wonder if Natasha was perhaps the one member of your family you could have connected with had circumstances been different.

"Look, Maura and I were close, maybe too close, because Dad was away so much, but I promise, I'm not your father."

Natasha shrugs. "It's just . . ."

In many ways it's a technicality, a wiggle of fate. You *did* bed Natasha's mother, but not until Natasha was five, and it might classify as a sin of omission to answer only the specific question she's asking about paternity. But you wonder if this is really even about that or if it's actually something more universal for alienated (a girl who talks like Natasha is most definitely alienated) children everywhere.

"When I was a kid, I used to pretend I was brothers with my best friend—that Dad wasn't my dad," you tell her. "And Braden's parents called me their other son, and I always stayed there when Dad was away. I think it's pretty common to hope you've got a secret identity."

After a brief hesitation, you reach out, place your palm on her shoulder, and ask if she's okay.

Head still down, she nods, and you pray to a God you've never really believed in that she won't cry, because that would fall completely outside your skill set. When she finally looks up, her eyes thankfully are dry.

"We should call Dad now and let him know you're all right."

With a sigh beyond her years, Natasha explains that your father had to go to Singapore that afternoon and she was supposed to fly home to Cincinnati a few hours later.

"I got your address from Dad's phone and convinced him I was old enough that I shouldn't have to fly as an unaccompanied minor anymore. So after he left, I called the airline and pretended to be my mom and rebooked my flight for tomorrow morning. Then I took the 'L' here."

"What about Maura?"

"I left her a message saying I was staying with Dad one more night."

"So no one has any idea that you're here?"

So quiet it's almost imperceptible: "No."

There's a moment where you contemplate letting it slide. Natasha's already informed her mother she'll be coming home tomorrow; what difference does it really make if there were half truths involved? But with a sigh that rivals your sister's, you realize you're the ranking adult in the situation.

"We need to call your mom."

"She'll want to speak with you to verify."

So you have her dial her mother and stepfather's house in Ohio, and she hands you the phone.

"Hartlin residence," Maura says, and you remember all those times you heard her pick up the phone in your father's house and say, "Ryan residence."

"Maura?" you ask, though it's obviously her.

"Speaking."

"It's Oliver Ryan."

A pause, an intake of breath. "Oliver?" Another pause. "I've been calling Dan's about Nat's message. Did something happen?"

"Nothing bad. I just wanted to make sure you knew her flight got changed."

Another pause, and Maura asks to talk to your father.

"He had to work, but Natasha and I wanted to see each other, and there was a bit of confusion about when her flight was."

"So she's staying with you?"

For an inexplicable reason, it didn't occur to you that you were agreeing to harbor your sister when you picked up the phone and made this call. Though conceivably Natasha can hear only your end of the conversation, she looks at you with pleading eyes.

"Yes, she'll stay here, if that's all right, and I'll take her to the airport in the morning."

"I guess that's okay," she says with a bit of reserve.

"I'm so sorry for the inconvenience."

After that there's really no reason to stay on the phone. But since you haven't spoken to her in years, it's hard to hang up.

Of all the incredibly wrong things about what happened between you and Maura, the wrongest may have been that you took off without talking to her. Because the situation was inherently horrible on so many levels, it was at first an easy leap to tell yourself leaving was the best choice for everyone involved. That was likely the case for you, but when you *did* think about it—on those endless Alaskan winter nights, when there was time to contemplate so many alternate worlds and outcomes—you'd realized it might not have been the best thing for Maura. The whole affair had always really been about your father for both of you, but she was the one who had to stay behind and deal with the fallout. At the time you fled, you didn't think you cared if she told your dad (it seemed unlikely she would, anyway), but you suppose you owe her a thank-you. Her silence is probably the only reason your relationship with your father wasn't completely decimated, the reason that Dad is open to whatever it is you're building now with almost monthly dinners and discussions about airplane parts and the Bears.

"How have you been?" you ask, because it's been so long and because her daughter, who could so easily have been your daughter, is watching you as if you were an exotic bird.

"I'm good," Maura says, and it seems like forgiveness. "You?"

Certainly it's meant as forgiveness when you tell her, "Yeah, I'm doing all right, too."

And then you're handing the phone off to your sister, who is covering the mouthpiece and speaking quietly. Politely you busy yourself in the kitchen, suspecting they're having the kind of conversation reserved for mothers and their preteen daughters who have done something rash and dangerous. Even after the click of the phone, you give Natasha a minute to compose herself before coming back into the living room.

"Thanks for talking to my mom," she says. "And for letting me stay here."

You nod and sit in the chair that matches the sofa (also bought from the previous tenant). She sits on the couch and looks at the can of soda.

The digital clock on the DVD player marks the passage of another minute.

"I hope I didn't spoil any plans you had for the evening," she says, back to the formal adult, and you remember you should call the doe-eyed lawyer from the garage.

"I didn't really have anything going on."

Another minute marked on the DVD clock.

"If this was a movie, we'd bond now," Natasha says flatly, and you chuckle.

"Did you eat dinner?" you ask.

She shakes her head, so you pull a stack of menus from the kitchen drawer, tell her you're hungry, too, even though the dishes from the sandwich you made an hour ago are still in the sink. You tell her to choose whatever she wants, but Natasha is a polite girl, so she looks to you.

"How about pizza?" you say. "Tedino's is on the corner, and they deliver until midnight."

"Is it Chicago style?" she asks, and when you nod, she smiles. "Dad and I usually get it at least once when I'm here, but we didn't this time."

Giving her the TV remote, you instruct Natasha to find something good while you're ordering. Then you duck into the bedroom to call Jill and explain tonight won't work for a drink after all. She sounds skeptical when you say you're with your sister.

"I thought you said she was married and lived in Utah?"

"This is my half sister from Cincinnati. Sometimes I forget about her, too."

You suspect you and Jill will not have another date and are perfectly fine with that.

Back in the living room, Natasha is watching a show where a bald guy with a mark on the back of his head is talking to the redhead from the jeans ads. There's something familiar about the look of it, and you realize it must be that *Eons & Empires* series that started a few years ago on the cable expansion network. Natasha looks up, says you can change the channel.

"No," you say. "I used to read the comic books. Is the show any good?"

"The Ed Munn books are better, but it's reasonably well done. It looks like they're running a marathon tonight."

The episode is about the Neutrocon, which you remember from the comics, even though you probably haven't thought about them since you tried to see the movie with Phoebe Fisher fourteen years ago. Parts of the dialogue are clunky, and it's a little hard to believe that the Jericho Jeans girl is a world-renowned scientist, but the show itself is entertaining.

The pizza arrives gooey and hot, and you and Natasha sit on the couch watching back-to-back *E&E* episodes while trying not to burn your mouths on molten cheese.

Natasha points to the screen during the closing credits. "I sat next to the actor who plays Captain Rowen on a plane once."

"Really?"

"Yeah. The show wasn't even on yet, but I recognized him right away when it started. It was sad; he was trying to get to a funeral from Salt Lake City, but there was a snowstorm."

You ask if Natasha was in Utah visiting your older sister, feel an unexpected prick of sadness that she was. That she apparently sees Karen and her family at least once a year and is only a few years younger than your nieces (nieces you haven't seen in nearly as long as you haven't seen Natasha). And you think you should give Karen a call in the next week or so, just to say hi.

Natasha asks about the comic books you used to like and explains that she's pretty big into anime. And you discuss Dad a little, now that you've established he is, in fact, father to you both.

"He talks about you quite a bit," she says. "He thought it was really impressive the way you got to see the world."

You wonder if that's true, and you ask a question that's been in the back of your mind for as long as you can remember.

"Did he ever take you up in a little plane?"

"No. I asked once, but he said he took you when you were too young, and he didn't want to make that mistake again."

"He said that?"

"Yeah."

QT runs three more *E&E: Rising* episodes, and the two of you watch them all.

There's probably a time when you're supposed to tell Natasha that she should go to bed, but you're her brother, not her father. And while you don't know her well, you know enough to sense that she'll be more than prepared when you have to take her to the airport the next morning.

10 in some other world, he probably did

In the days and months that followed, Adam wondered if everything would have been different if craft services had had NyQuil instead of Sudafed and Robitussin. Despite his four-year tenure on a show all about parallel worlds, where things were a hair-fracture different one or fifty universes away, he wasn't accustomed to obsessing over small details that had the potential to change everything. But during the ten days the show had to shut filming down—and all the emptiness afterward—Adam had a lot of time to think about things in those terms.

E&E: Rising seemed to have specified in the production bible that any day Adam wasn't feeling well, filming would take no less than fifteen hours, be physically demanding, and require copious quantities of water be dumped on his head. He couldn't stop coughing and kept sweating through his makeup, which worked out fine because the whole last hour of shooting involved him and Cecily standing under a rain curtain. It didn't help matters that the scene actively sucked (a lot of scenes had been actively sucking since the series creator had stepped down as show runner after season three), and Cecily kept tripping over a giant block of exposition about the off-screen destruction of Worlds 78 and 5. Her speech ended with an overwrought turd of a paragraph: "You destroyed those worlds, if not through intent, then through neglect. You were too busy waging your war on Bryce, and you weren't watching the Neutrocon. The damage that you've done cannot be undone."

Though he considered Cecily one of his closest friends, her inability to spit it out was shredding his patience. The one time she came anywhere near getting it right, Adam couldn't contain a coughing jag. He fully expected several outtakes from the day to end up on the blooper reel in the DVD extras.

While Cecily complained to the assistant director between takes, the cute new PA brought Adam daytime flu medication. The recommended dosage of Sudafed was two pills; Adam tripled it. So in addition to feeling like he'd gone several rounds with Mike Tyson, he was oddly wired. He chugged half a bottle of cough syrup, hoping to level out.

Perhaps in some other universe (maybe World 2 or 27—just not Worlds 78 and 5, as Rowen had apparently destroyed those with horrendous dialogue), the assistant slipped him the nighttime cold stuff, and when they finally wrapped for the day he simply hobbled back to his trailer and passed out on the couch before he even had a chance to dry off. Maybe in those worlds, he returned Phoebe's call when he felt less like strangling every living creature in a ten-mile radius.

In his world, Adam went back to his trailer and toweled away ubiquitous water. He contemplated crashing because he felt achy and awful, but was too hopped up on pseudoephedrine to sleep. The idea of walking through the actual rain (in four years of filming in BC, Adam swore, there'd been all of three sunny days) to his car and driving to the generic luxury apartment he rented seemed even more unpleasant. He'd already talked to Phoebe during the break for lunch, but she'd left a message saying she wanted to discuss something. It was after midnight, but he called her back figuring the downpour would stop by the time they were done.

"Feeling better, sweetie?" she asked from twelve hundred miles away in sunny California.

Adam told her he'd survive but didn't try particularly hard to stifle another bout of hacking. "So what's your big news?"

"Poor baby, you sound terrible," she cooed. "It can wait. You should go to bed."

"Pheebs, I'm fine," he said, adding irrationally angry to achy and awful. "So I got into Michigan's grad program."

"I thought you were going to USC?"

She sighed and said that she'd already told him she was wait-listed there. "And Michigan is actually the better MSW program."

"Fucking Ann Arbor, really, Phoebe?"

"It's only a year and a half, and I think part of it can be done remotely." She sounded unsure; that annoyed him more.

"Like this isn't hard enough already? Why did you even apply there?"

On some level he realized he was being a jerk, and he did have vague memories of Phoebe mentioning Michigan (and, like, fifteen other grad programs) a few months ago. But his throat was raw, his head was killing him, and just for once he wanted a girlfriend who would be there to rub his temples and make him soup (or order—he would have been completely satisfied with a soup-ordering girlfriend). An actual flesh-and-blood girlfriend, not a disembodied voice on the phone who preread scripts and made sure that the electricity stayed on in his LA condo. Usually he tried never to play the fame card, but he was on a TV show. No, he had been TV's sexiest bad guy. Scarcely a week went by without some lady (or dude—there really was a lot of homoerotic subtext in the series) propositioning him, slipping him a number, a note, a hotel room key. At sci-fi conventions women regularly asked him to sign their breasts. And not a single time since he journeyed to Chicago after Phoebe's brother died had Adam taken any of them up on their offers. He'd pat their shoulders and say he was flattered but spoken for. Was it too much to ask that if Phoebe couldn't move to BC, she at least go to a grad school in the same time zone?

"I'm serious," he continued. "You say you love me and are committed to this, but you really do a crap job of showing it."

"Adam, you're never here anyway. You were in New Zealand all summer for that stupid slasher film."

This was true but seemed irrelevant in his mediciney head. And while for months he'd been regretting (rather loudly) his decision to star in the inauspiciously titled (and yet to be given a release date) *Murder Island*, he took offense at her calling it "stupid."

"It's my fucking job, Phoebe."

"Mine, too," she said quietly.

Also true. Plus Phoebe's work was about helping people, not making schlocky horror flicks and past-their-prime basic cable shows. Adam didn't feel like conceding that point, either.

"I'm not trekking across the country on a goddamned red-eye every weekend," he said.

"Well, I don't know, would you want to take a little break or something?"

The sentiment was a gut punch.

In some alternate *E&E* world, maybe he told Phoebe he didn't want to lose her, that he was simply scared of how her new life could change things. In his world he felt like shit and was sick of the ever-present rain. Also, vulnerability had never been a great role for him in real life.

"That's probably a good idea," he said calmly. "I slept with Cecily, anyway."

Phoebe wasn't generally the jealous type, but Adam knew she didn't *love* the fact that his best buddy was a flirty model whom he made out with several times a week as a job requirement. It was one of the cruelest things he could possibly say.

Across the line there was a pause. Plenty of time for Adam to explain that he was lashing out and probably high on cold medication (didn't Canada have different drug standards?), to say that while he and Cecily did spend a fair amount of time together, their interactions were entirely devoid of romance and/or seduction. That Cecily spent hours discussing her poop and would sometimes deliberately eat a pungent lunch on days when they had love scenes just to see if she could make him break character.

Adam said nothing.

"I don't believe you," Phoebe finally offered. "You're only saying that to hurt me."

"Am I?"

Mean was how he felt. A haunted echo of the time before they were in love, when he hated the exposed nerve of his feelings for her.

"Maybe we should talk about this when you're feeling better." She sighed.

"Oh, so we'll be allowed to talk during our break?"

"Adam—"

"No, you're right, we'll talk when we talk."

He hung up.

Whether it was the cold medicine or his anger, Adam was twitchy, muscles unsteady.

He could have called Phoebe back and told her he was sorry. In some other world, he probably flew home for the weekend or insisted that she come to BC, told her how vital she was to him. Maybe whisked her off to Vegas and finally made good on the five-carat sapphire ring she'd been wearing for two years.

Instead he dialed Cecily's cell phone.

"You out and about?" he asked.

"I'm home in my jammies," she said, but in a way that suggested it might not be a terminal condition.

"Get dressed and let's go somewhere."

"Weren't you, like, hacking up a lung and moaning about your imminent death an hour ago?"

"I'm feeling better." He chugged more cough syrup, trying to make it so. "We'll just go to Polly's, today sucked."

"It sure did."

"Come on, I know you need a drink as much as I do."

"Fine"—she sounded smiley—"but you're picking me up, and you're buying!"

Because they'd been doing love scenes in body stockings together for four years, and Cecily sometimes called to tell him about a particularly glorious dump she'd taken, Adam had long ago forgotten how genuinely stunning she was.

Quickly he remembered when he pulled up in front of her house and she bounded from the front door into his sports car, dodging the rain. She was wearing a short, tight dress made of lace, her hair tied up in a casual knot that showed off her freakishly perfect features.

Over their first few drinks, they threw darts and complained about the rain curtain scene, as well as the decline of the show in general. His cough had largely subsided, but Adam finished the bottle of Robitussin in hopes of keeping it at bay.

Though most Vancouverites were immune to all the actors filming American television shows in the area, a group of Midwestern tourists recognized them and sent over tequila shots. More shots ensued. At some point Adam switched from Jack and Coke to straight whiskey. Not long after, his darts began landing farther and farther from the bull's-eye. A few actually hit the wall next to the board and fell to the floor. Picking them up, Cecily suggested they sit at one of the high tables.

"So did you and Mother Teresa have a fight?" she asked.

Usually Adam got mad when Cecily referred to Phoebe as any sort of do-gooder, but that night he laughed. "Why do you ask?"

"Because normally about now you're having phone sex with her, not getting hammered with me."

Despite all her glib jokes about Phoebe's newfound charitable side, Cecily was a superb listener. Adam could have opened up, had her order him to call Phoebe and apologize. In one of those other universes, something along those lines likely happened.

"Naw, I just wanted to come out and blow off steam," he said. "That's all."

Perhaps it was the Sudafed/cough syrup combination, but Adam realized he was wasted; he responded by ordering a triple. The American tourists who'd sent the shots finally became brazen enough to ask for cell phone pictures and autographs. Drink in his hand, Adam looped his arm around Cecily's shoulders and blinked again and again against the flash.

After that his memory of the evening is genuinely fuzzy.

In bits and pieces he remembers the following things happening:

His arm stayed around Cecily long after the tourists left the bar.

Cecily went to the ladies' room, and he followed her down the wood-paneled hallway to the bathrooms.

Cornering her, his hands at either side of her head.

Cecily's brown eyes huge and confused.

His lips on her neck.

A voice, sadly he's pretty sure it was his, saying, "Don't pretend you haven't wanted this for four years."

Then a sharp, searing moment of pain and clarity, when Cecily kneed him in the groin. "I don't know what your deal is, Z," she said. "But you're being a total douchebag."

Adam likes to think he apologized, but he's reasonably certain he just stood there, doubled over and panting.

Things after that are hazy again:

Cecily taking his keys and saying something about him being too sloshed to drive.

Possibly puking in a puddle outside the bar.

A sad semi-smile on Cecily's face as she helped him into his car's low passenger seat and buckled the belt, everything slippery in the dark rain.

Half-formed wonder if Cecily knew how to work the manual transmission.

Brief jerk when they stalled somewhere around Sixteenth Avenue.

On the radio, that Coldplay song about the ticking clocks.

He thinks he may have drifted off.

Sensation of flying.

Something wet in his eyes, different than the rain.

Startling realization he was upside down.

Cecily contorted and broken through a film of red.

From that point on, everything is crystal clear again. Ascertaining that, despite being upside down, he was largely unharmed, Adam swatted the air bag out of the way and reached for Cecily's shoulder. She moaned in a distant, disturbing way. Even in the poor lighting, he could see her face was covered in blood.

Adam was searching his pockets for his cell phone, wondering if 911 was the same number in Canada, when a man outside started tapping on the window (Adam would later learn the guy was the driver of the other car). He could see the flashing bulbs of emergency vehicles already en route.

Firefighters broke the glass and had Adam crawl out of the hatchback, while paramedics carefully secured Cecily to a litter and slid her out through the window.

It probably didn't matter, but Adam told the emergency workers he was Cecily's fiancé and rode along in the ambulance. Someone gave him a blanket to throw over his wet clothes and a wad of gauze for his cheek (maybe he was still high on cold medication, but it struck him as hysterical that the cut was actually below his eye but blood had obscured his vision because they'd been upside down). As they were pulling into the emergency department's bay, Cecily's eyelids fluttered open, and she gave him a terrified glance. Adam took her hand.

None of the doctors and nurses who scurried around Cecily were particularly forthcoming with information. The phrases "internal bleeding" and "spleen involvement" were said a lot. A blond woman in a lab coat insisted on taking Adam into the next room and putting three stitches in his cheek. As she was covering the sutures with a bandage, he started coughing.

The doctor's brow creased. "Have you been experiencing chest pain?" she asked. "You may have broken ribs."

Adam said he had a cold and remembered a few hours ago that had seemed a completely insurmountable problem.

Cecily was out of it and still a mess—blood caked in her hair, nose twisted and swelling, IVs dripping fluids into her thin alabaster arm—but they let him spend a few minutes with his "fiancée" before wheeling her gurney to surgery for a splenectomy. Adam held her hand and told her he was sorry; she made an unintelligible sound.

A short nurse led him to an empty waiting area with an ancient television, depressing furniture, and a wall-mounted phone. She said someone would call and update him once they had a better idea of his fiancée's condition. Even though he hadn't told her his name, she called him "Mr. Zoellner" and smiled. As laid-back as Vancouver was about C-list actors, it was clear she knew exactly who they were. That seemed very, very bad, so he tried not to think about it.

There was a pot of incredibly stale coffee, and he drank cup after cup because it was warm and gave him something to do. He knew Cecily didn't get along with her mother but thought he should call her anyway. Scrapped the idea when he realized he didn't know Cecily's mother's name.

When Phoebe called his cell, Adam wasn't sure if he'd been sitting there an hour or a day. He wondered if the nurse had tipped off PerezHilton .com or one of the celebrity weeklies and Phoebe had learned about the accident online.

"Hey, I wanted to catch you before you got to work." She sounded authentically optimistic. "I was going to surprise you—"

In one of those parallel universes, he let her finish the sentence. In his world, he told her he had been in an accident and was at the hospital.

"Oh, God—"

"I wasn't hurt," he said before she could ask. "Cecily's in surgery."

Phoebe took in an audible breath, but to her credit didn't ask why

Adam had been in a car with Cecily in the wee hours of the morning. "Is she gonna be okay?"

"I don't know."

The phone on the wall rang—the surgeons with an update. Adam told Phoebe he'd call her back and hung up.

Cecily was okay . . . ish.

The doctors removed her spleen, and a few days later a plastic surgeon reset her nose, promising in a month no one would ever know the difference. They kept her in the hospital a week, and *E&E: Rising*'s producers were forced to postpone production for ten days. In one of the other worlds, Adam went home and made things right with Phoebe. In his world he stayed in BC.

Perhaps because the hospital staff still thought they were engaged, no one asked him to leave. The short nurse gave him a pair of hospital scrubs to replace his torn and bloodied clothes, and the blond doctor gave him cold medicine. Both said how sweet it was that he was so worried about his betrothed.

That first night/day/night—they all blended together—Cecily dipped in and out of confused consciousness. The hollows under her eyes were black and puffy, her lovely face distorted. There was a large bandage on her abdomen that he assumed covered a large scar. He thought about the ad campaigns she did, where she was nearly always undressed. It made him physically ill to think she might not be able to do that anymore, to think that her nose might heal wrong and she wouldn't look quite so stunning, couldn't get work.

Blaming the accident on the rain, the police hadn't cited either Cecily or the Volvo driver (apparently Cecily *hadn't* been matching him drink for drink, and her blood alcohol level had been well within the legal limit), but that seemed a technicality of the highest degree. Adam was pretty sure blame could squarely be dropped on his shoulders.

No one had bothered to clean the blood out of Cecily's hair, so he dabbed it off with a wet cloth. Standing over her bed, he whispered over and over and over again that he was sorry.

The spleen, he sort of remembered, had to do with the immune system and infections. He tried to look things up on his smartphone, but the hospital's Internet service was spotty, so he ducked out of Cecily's room long enough to call his mother in Florida. Leaving out details of the story, like the fact that it had been his car and he'd been too drunk to drive it, he said a "friend" had a spleenectomy and asked about complications. His mother confirmed everything he'd read about the greater potential risk for infections.

"Is it really bad?" he asked.

"It's not ideal, but your friend should be fine as long as she's careful. The biggest risk is after removal, but I'm sure they have her on all kinds of antibiotics."

Adam had left the pronouns gender neutral, but his all-knowing mother seemed perfectly aware that the friend was a woman, and perhaps an inappropriate one. She asked about Phoebe.

"Pheebs is doing really well," Adam said with false enthusiasm. "She got into the MSW program at Michigan."

"That's an excellent school," said his mother. "Tell her congratulations from me."

For the first time since his conversation with Phoebe, which seemed to have taken place entire centuries ago, it occurred to Adam that he could have just congratulated her. A part of him wanted to call Phoebe and do that (and maybe in one of those other worlds he did), but he went back to Cecily's bedside and apologized some more.

The QT spokesperson put out a statement saying that Adam and Cecily had been involved in an accident on their way home from a "cast hangout," but both were expected to make full recoveries.

Adam's own publicist called with advice on how to handle the situation.

"As Phoebe's friend, I think you're a dick," Evie said, blunt as always. "But as your rep, it's actually not a terrible thing if the world knows you're banging the Jericho Jeans girl."

"I'm not." Adam wondered why he didn't call Phoebe and tell her that.

"Fine, if the world *thinks* you're banging her."

He told Evie he couldn't talk and went back to Cecily.

Sometimes he slept in a reclining chair that the short nurse brought in. Sometimes he got soda and pretzels from the vending machine. Mostly Adam stood by Cecily's bed apologizing.

Phoebe left him messages, but he couldn't bring himself to listen to them. Every time he thought about what he would possibly say to her, he felt nauseated. After thirty-five hours, his cell battery died.

As the days and nights blended, Cecily became more and more aware and less and less medicated.

"Would you stop saying you're sorry, already?" she said one groggy morning. "I was the idiot who thought it was a good idea to try driving stick in a monsoon."

"Cese, I . . ." he began, but she cut him off.

"And why does everyone keep asking when we're getting married?" Her tone was light, but things felt off. It was hard to gauge true emotions with her mangled features.

She told him to go home and take a shower but didn't complain when he stayed.

By the third day, she was alert enough that they started playing checkers and Scrabble and the other games stashed in the hospital. She asked if he'd teach her to play chess, and he did, even though he hadn't played since he was a kid living at his grandparents' house.

Whenever he could, he snuck in apologies—when he checked her king with his knight, when he went to the café to get her flavored iced tea, when he helped her to the bathroom because she was "done dealing with bedpans."

"You need to stop with this 'sorry' crap and go home," she said. "You look like ass and you're seriously smelling up my room."

He apologized, but she didn't acknowledge it.

"And I'm sure Mother Teresa is wondering where the hell you are."

"I'm sorry," he said again.

The network president sent a giant floral arrangement, and Cecily cracked that Rex Stern might not have been so generous if he'd seen her face. For a woman who made a living on her looks, she was handling the black eyes and broken nose exceptionally well. Ron Brosh, Avery Lane, and a bunch of other people from the show stopped by during visiting hours. They brought cupcakes and slippers, books and magazines (the accident was a small item in both *Us Weekly* and *Living*, the latter of which had "an insider" claiming that Adam and Cecily were secretly engaged. For the first time, Adam was grateful he was on a basic cable show and wasn't a bigger star). Everyone asked Cecily how she was feeling and told her she looked great, which was an utter lie.

No one asked what happened or why Adam and Cecily were out together—everyone knew they were close and had been whispering about a torrid affair for years. It was probably a little eyebrow raising that Adam was still at the hospital, wearing a pair of blue surgical scrubs, but no one asked about that either. When one of the nurses called Adam Cecily's fiancé, Ron poked him in the ribs. Adam shook his head, and they left it at that.

Cecily told Adam the people she wanted to see and those she didn't, and he acted as gatekeeper. She refused to let him call her mother in Newfoundland the first few times he brought it up but finally consented.

Even so, things still felt off between them.

On what must have been the fifth night, he helped her to the restroom as he had been doing for days. With her arm slung around his shoulder on the way back, she turned to him and offered a serious look.

"Z," she said, and he nodded expectantly. "I haven't dropped a deuce since they cut me open."

He laughed and knew things between them were going to be okay. Though for years after, she could convince him to do almost anything by simply pouting her pretty mouth and saying "spleen."

That night Cecily's mom came in, and he finally did go home. Adam was almost to the parking lot when he realized that he didn't have a car in the city anymore and dialed a cab. It had been a frighteningly long time since he'd had a real shower or eaten anything of substance, but he picked up the phone, sat on the bed, and called Phoebe before climbing any of those rungs on Maslow's hierarchy.

"How is she?" Phoebe asked, surprisingly sincere. Adam hadn't expected her to be actively rooting for Cecily's demise, but it was still a little jarring.

"Much better, they're sending her home in a few days."

"That's great." There was clear relief in her voice. "And you?"

Adam shrugged into the phone as if Phoebe could see him. "I'm fine." It seemed a good assessment of his physical condition, anyway.

"Really?"

"Yeah." But he felt a thousand pounds. Easing onto his back, he stared at the ceiling.

"Good."

Desperately he wanted to apologize, but couldn't. It seemed he'd used all his sorrys on Cecily. There was an unappealing brown spot on the ceiling, but his head was too heavy to turn away.

"I talked to the people at Michigan, and they said if I really wanted they could get me into the program this semester." She sighed. "I'll only miss the first week, so I was thinking I'd do that."

He wondered what he said in those other worlds, where a butterfly flapped its wings slightly differently, where he wasn't made of lead.

"You know nothing ever happened between Cecily and me, right?" he finally said.

In always sunny LA, Phoebe sighed. "Adam, that's not why I'm going—"

"I know . . . but . . . I didn't want you to think I'd hurt you that way."

Maybe in some other world, Phoebe broke down or yelled at him or told him she *needed* him to come with her. In his world she said, "Thank you."

Back on the day of their original fight, one of the reasons Adam had been so grouchy was because of that last hour of filming, when Cecily couldn't get out her lines right:

"You destroyed those worlds, if not through intent, then through neglect. You were too busy waging your war on Bryce, and you weren't watching the Neutrocon. The damage that you've done cannot be undone."

At the time he'd been frustrated Cecily kept screwing up. But it was a hard chunk of text to say, and maybe not simply because it was melodramatic and full of exposition. Maybe it always seemed expository and forced to discuss incomprehensible loss.

"Honestly, I'll be done with the program in a year and a half," Phoebe said. "Maybe less if I can get part of the certification over the summer."

There were things they needed to talk about. Specifics of their break, if they were going to try that. Logistical arrangements: He was filming in BC through spring; if she was leaving in a matter of days, who would take care of condo stuff? Would she be taking their (her) dog?

Lots of exposition.

There also seemed lots of extremely important words to say. That he still loved her and she meant more to him than any person he'd ever known. That he was so very, very sorry, even if he'd used all his apologies on another woman.

Hard to get through.

He thought of all those other worlds, where maybe he did things differently, where maybe he was better.

"Phoebe," he said. "I'm really proud of you."

Having grown up in Chicago, Phoebe Fisher really shouldn't be so stunned by the cold of Ann Arbor in winter. But she'd been in LA an awfully long time—almost as long as she'd lived in the Midwest—and the frigid, wet air that chills her bones and makes her breath a visible entity is startling those first few weeks. She supposes late January is as bad as it's ever going to get, but the ice is still a shock as she sets up the apartment she found on a grad student Web site or walks Kraken in the complex's little courtyard. It's a jolt each day she treks around campus between her classes and the health center, where she starts her counseling hours for students.

The cold campus reminds her of her brother. The weekends she'd visited him at the University of Wisconsin, when Chase had bundled her up in hats and scarves and took her to football games and the strip of bars popular with undergrads. "This is good," he'd joked. "Fewer of my friends hit on you when you're wrapped up like a burrito." But she also knew how a part of him enjoyed showing off his actress sister from the yogurt commercials. She wonders what Chase would say about her moving to Michigan. If he'd be proud of her or think she was running away. Feels the familiar ball of something in her throat that she can barely remember what he looked like anymore.

Mostly the chill makes her miss Adam and his warmth. As she cuddles with Kraken under layers of blankets, she thinks of how hot it was to sleep beside him, how she used to wake up sweaty even though they had the AC on high. It makes her wonder if she's really here because it's such a great program or because in the haze of her hurt, it had seemed a good idea to put as much distance between her and Adam as possible.

It probably doesn't help that the handful of people in her program also seem cold. Everyone is amicable enough when she introduces herself in classes, but Phoebe started in the middle of the school year; friendships that were going to be formed had already been established. She doesn't fit in with any of them, anyway. There are the students right out of under-grad, a full eleven years her junior, who still swap bed partners and pound shots at the area bars. And while there are several people her own age and even older (one woman often mentions she's fifty-seven), they're all part-nered up or divorced with families of their own (an unmarried woman in her thirties absolutely unheard of outside of LA's Never-Never Land). When classes or their counseling hours end, they sprint off to pick up children from day care or hockey or ballet.

A lot of those first few weeks are spent waiting for delivery of semi-disposable furniture and staring at the phone, wondering how many times she can call Adam without violating the terms of their ill-defined "break."

That she learns Virgil's is hiring a bartender, and even of the restau-rant's existence, is complete serendipity. Lost on her way to a used-furniture sale she'd seen on Craigslist, Phoebe pulls into the Virgil's parking lot to turn around. Because the restaurant on the bottom floor of the historic inn looks out of place and reminds her a little of Rosebud, she gives it a second glance, notices the small sign in the front window: EXPERIENCED BARTENDER WANTED.

Money really isn't much of an issue. Even when she was at UCLA and essentially acting as Adam's manager, she'd worked nearly full-time at Rosebud, and Adam had refused money for the condo, so cash had piled up in her checking account.

No, money isn't the reason she parks the car and walks through the large blue door (sort of like Rosebud's famous bronzed one). Nor does she dislike what she's studying; she truly enjoys it, especially the limited time she's allowed to talk to patients. While others in her program often complain that the students who come in are self-absorbed with silly prob-lems, Phoebe understands better than most that being young and privi-leged isn't necessarily free of pain.

No, she enters Virgil's because everything is different and cold and she wants something familiar.

Probably too far from campus to cater to a U of M crowd, the restau-rant appears a mash-up of a steakhouse and a sports bar: white linens on the tables and a large bar with several HD televisions on various sports networks (and one on the channel that shows classic movies) all on mute. A mix of Rat Pack oldies—perhaps even the same station as Rosebud—floats through the empty rooms. It's forty-five minutes until they open for lunch, and she can't help but wonder if the place will actually fill up and with whom.

Waiters in white button-downs and black pants are setting tables and cleaning, and a petite college-age girl is stacking menus at the hostess stand. She hands Phoebe a generic job application without fanfare, says she can fill it out at the bar.

When the hostess sees she was head bartender at the famed Rosebud in Los Angeles, the girl gets flustered, as if she'd discovered Phoebe is someone important—the way hostesses at Rosebud kick themselves for not recognizing Steven Spielberg or Jennifer Lopez.

"Wow," says the girl, before launching into a lengthy nervous explanation about how the chef/owner has been having health problems and his nephew has been running things for the past few months. "I'll get Cole—he's, like, a classically trained chef from the city."

As the girl shuffles off into the area behind the bar, Phoebe wonders if "the city" means Detroit proper. A few seconds later, the hostess returns and leads Phoebe to a little office off the kitchen full of dry goods and boxed soda syrup.

Phoebe's application in hand, a distracted-seeming guy in a chef's tunic comes in from the kitchen and introduces himself as Cole Fleming. He looks about sixteen and has a frustrating amount of facial hair, between a beard and a goatee, that makes him look even younger.

His shake is firm, but he doesn't actually focus his attention on her until halfway through the gesture, then holds her hand too long.

"So," he says, finally letting go. "You worked at the infamous Rosebud?"

Phoebe answers affirmatively, and this Cole Fleming gives her another once-over, as if she'd clarified a point. "Well, you've definitely got the Rosebud look."

Because she'd been planning to move furniture, Phoebe's wearing jeans and a sweater under her thick coat but assumes the comment is about her general attractiveness. There seems to be no great response, so she simply nods. Something about this kid makes her uncomfortable, and she doesn't need the job. Pushing a practiced smile, she waits for the interview to be over.

But then Cole surprises her. "Is it me, or is that famous chicken salad overrated?"

Phoebe chuckles through her nose. The celebrity guests and tourists alike rave about the Rosebud salad, and it outsells every other lunch entrée by scores, but the dirty little secret to the twenty-five-dollar salad is that the chef uses canned chicken breast—the "special" marinade is salt and water.

"You don't even want to know," she says.

He laughs and invites her to sit down across from him at the little desk so they can exchange the needed information: She's a grad student with evenings free; he needs someone immediately because one of their bartenders got engaged to an auto exec and promptly quit.

"Normally I'd have you make a bunch of cocktails, but most people here order Bud Light and merlot, so you don't really need to know what's in a Manhattan."

"Rye, sweet vermouth, and bitters, with a cherry and orange twist," she blurts out, then feels heat on her cheeks.

Cole Fleming smiles again. "Can you start tomorrow night?"

Back in her car, Phoebe picks up her phone and unconsciously dials Adam because this is the kind of thing that they've been sharing with each other forever.

Heart pounding, bowels queasy, she remembers they're on a break and things don't work that way anymore. Aborting the call, she wonders again if coming here was a mistake.

The night she told Adam she was accepted at Michigan and he and Cecily got into the accident, Phoebe had been watching *E&E: Rising* (she was always working or volunteering on Thursday nights, so she DVR'd the episodes). When the phone rang, she hit pause, freezing on a tearful Cordelia Snow and Captain Rowen lamenting the loss of some other world.

Cecily's beguiling face was the first thing Phoebe saw after Adam told her they'd slept together and hung up. In disgust, Phoebe hurled her quasi-engagement ring at the screen, hitting Cecily's perfect nose.

Instantly she was mad at herself for getting upset. It was true Phoebe did occasionally want to scream when Cecily batted long lashes at Adam and pulled at his arms like a coquettish little girl. But Phoebe was certain nothing was going on between the two of them, and that Adam was only saying otherwise to hurt her, because he was hurt that she might leave.

Shaking her head, Phoebe went to retrieve the ring but stopped, noticing something about Adam's frozen image on the TV screen.

That close, she could see the tear halfway down his cheek. Her breath caught, and she realized that she'd never seen him cry in real life. At least once a season, *E&E: Rising* was determined to show Rowen's humanity by having him break down on Cordelia, and Phoebe had seen him cry in the *Cat on a Hot Tin Roof* remake, but never as Adam Zoellner. When he was upset, he got red and angry or drunk and maudlin. Petulant and pouty or stressed and shaky, but Adam never cried, at least not in front of her.

Reaching out, she put her finger to his forehead on the screen. All at once she could see him coughing and shivering, alone and sad in the generically furnished unit he rented in Vancouver. It made her insides loose and hollow. She remembered how, when her brother died, Adam drove all night in a snowstorm to see her without a thought to his own career, and she felt even sicker.

Sliding her ring back on, she decided to go to USC. If a spot didn't open up for her on the waiting list, she'd pad her résumé with more volunteer work and get in the next year. She was already a decade older than everyone else; what was the difference?

Wanting to tell Adam in person, she bought a ticket online for the first flight from LAX. Initially she planned to surprise him but figured it was best to let him know she was coming to avoid a rom-com-esque missed connection. Phoebe was already through airport security when she called his cell, hoping to catch him on his way to work. He told her he was at the hospital with Cecily and hung up on her again. She was stunned, everything she thought she knew about their relationship suddenly in question.

In a daze she'd walked back through the gate and out the door to the taxi line. It was 9:00 A.M. in Ann Arbor, so she'd called the University of Michigan from the cab, told them she was accepting their offer, and asked about starting in winter term. By the end of the week she was gone.

———

Still in front of Virgil's, Phoebe puts her phone back in her purse.

Of course she and Adam have been talking since she left, mostly practical things about the condo and Kraken and scripts she'd been looking over. The parameters of their break remain rather loosely defined—something about reevaluating when she's home in March. Deep, deep down she thinks (or maybe needs to believe?) that they'll eventually get back together after he's had the opportunity to whore around a bit as penance for her leaving. Perhaps it's a testament to how she herself needs therapy, but she misses him enough that she's pretty much okay with that (well, unless he really *does* sleep with Cecily).

Phoebe decides she'll tell Adam about her odd interview and the job in a few days.

Cole Fleming had told her black clothing was preferred, so Phoebe selects one of the short dresses she used to wear at Rosebud. It's the first time she's worn anything but jeans since moving to Ann Arbor. Because she's not sure if she's supposed to be wearing it anymore, and because her fingers are shrunken from the cold, she leaves the sapphire-and-platinum ring in its velvet box in her apartment.

She arrives early, and the other bartender—a man of about sixty named Eddie, who claims he's survived three different incarnations of the space—shows her where everything is. Virgil's uses the same computer system Rosebud did, and the layout makes sense. By the time the first early birds drift in for happy hour specials, it feels old hat. The restaurant does a consistent, if not max capacity, business, with a stream of people coming in for dinner or to drink beer and watch the hockey and basketball games.

Phoebe knows she's an excellent bartender. Part of it's simply that she's been doing it so long, but she's always had a knack for putting people at ease (a trait she hopes makes her a good counselor). Seamlessly she slips back into the rhythm, knowing which customers to pour heavy and which to pour light, which ones to flirt with and which will take it the wrong way and lean too long on the counter. Eddie sheepishly admits that he usually clocks out around ten, so she tells him she can handle things on her own.

At the end of her shift, she's tired but surprisingly content. She's starting to break down the bar—packing up the fruit and garnishes—when Cole appears and takes a seat at one of the bar stools.

"How was it?" He's still in his chef garb, now freckled with sauce splatters around the sleeves.

"Everyone ordered Bud Light and merlot."

"Yeah, there's a decided lack of imagination here."

"Can I make you something?" she asks, surprisingly nervous. It was common practice for Rosebud staff to have a drink after close, but maybe things work differently here?

"Like a Manhattan?" he asks, and she wishes she'd made the joke. "That'd be great."

Even with her odd insecurity around Cole, Phoebe's hands are steady and sure as she pours, eyeballing the right amount of each ingredient.

Taking a sip, Cole pronounces it "the best Manhattan ever served at Virgil's."

"It's the first ever served, isn't it?"

"Quite possibly." He winks a moss-colored eye.

Rumpled and sweaty, members of the kitchen crew come over to say good night to Cole. Everyone seems to like him. They're followed by the waitstaff, looking to cash out credit card tips from the bar.

A redhead named Kayla smiles and tells Cole that a group of them are going someplace in the Old Westside if he's interested. And Phoebe remembers exactly what it felt like to hang out with Burke and Melissa after long shifts at Rosebud. Those nights that spilled into mornings. Rarely eating, always drinking, and being hopelessly in love with Adam even if she couldn't admit it to herself.

"You should come, too," the waitress says to Phoebe without enthusiasm.

"Thanks, but I'm beat," Phoebe offers diplomatically.

"Not tonight, Kay." Cole gives the waitress a peck on the cheek, and Phoebe wonders if they're dating.

Cole goes over paperwork as Phoebe finishes, and when she's done, he insists on walking her to her car.

For a solid ten seconds, they stand in the cold by her Jetta. "Well, have a good night," she says, hands jammed in her pockets.

As she waits for the engine to warm up, Phoebe wonders if Cole throws her off because he's young (she'd overheard a waiter talking about his twenty-fifth birthday party last month), eight years her junior.

She's still wondering about this when Adam calls with a question about where he might find his baseball equipment.

Phoebe is tidying up the bar after midnight a few weeks later when Cole comes through the kitchen's swinging doors and plops down a plate bearing some type of grilled sandwich, says he's made it for her.

"Thanks?" she says, eyeing it curiously.

"It's grilled Fontina with onion marmalade," he says. "You're probably going to want a nice pinot noir to go with that."

Phoebe reaches for the cheaper of the two varieties they sell by the glass. Cole shakes his head, so she picks up the slightly less cheap Elk Cove and pours two glasses.

Other than a couple lingering over dessert plates in the corner and three men in suits finishing a round of beers, all the customers are gone.

Cole sits at one of the empty bar stools. There's a spot of something tomato-based on his brow and a few light freckles around his nose that she hadn't noticed before. She looks from him to the sandwich.

"Just try it. I promise it's good."

It *is* good, great even, like French onion soup on toast, and she finishes nearly half, aware the whole time that he's watching her.

"You don't like it?" Cole asks.

"It's delicious. Thank you."

"Then what? You've been here eight hours; you've got to be starving." Releasing his hair from an elastic band, he shakes out chin-length chestnut waves. "You're in the Midwest now, Ms. Fisher. People actually eat here."

"I'm from the Midwest." Phoebe feels herself smile. "I know about your kind."

"Ree-ealy," Cole stretches out the word. "The mystery deepens."

Sipping his wine, he asks where she's from, and she tells him about the Chicago suburbs. Decides she likes him well enough, even if he does occasionally look at her as if she's a high-end truffle.

"So you escaped the land of strip malls and chain restaurants for manifest destiny. Why come back?"

That's probably a good idea; I slept with Cecily anyway.

"The MSW program at Michigan."

"And what do you want to be when you grow up?"

"Something with grief counseling," she says, watches his face change.

"Really?" he asks, all affectation gone.

She doesn't have to explain, but for some reason she wants to. "My kid brother died four years ago. It sorta changed stuff for me."

"I'm sorry," he says, and she thanks him.

"You keep the important things," Cole says, seeming much older than twenty-five. "My best friend was in a car accident after prom. I couldn't tell you what color his eyes were or if he was left-handed, but he's still with me, you know?"

Phoebe nods, wishes, as always, that she felt more of her brother's presence—that she could believe all the well-meaning people who spoke of better places and angels watching over the living from beyond.

"I still have his last voice mail." Cole shakes his head. "It's him panicking because he forgot to order his girlfriend a corsage, but I play it every now and again."

"For months I called my brother's apartment to hear his outgoing message." The only time Phoebe's ever told anyone about this; a sip of wine.

Patting her briefly on the forearm, Cole nods.

Untying apron strings, Kayla comes to the bar, and Phoebe goes to the register to ring out her tips.

"You guys coming out tonight?" Kayla asks, bubbly with a hint of desperation, and Phoebe finds herself unfoundedly annoyed. Maybe it's that they both have red hair, but she thinks of Cecily.

"Maybe next week." Cole gives her a hug that seems slightly more familiar than friends.

When the waitress is gone, Phoebe raises an eyebrow at Cole. "Somebody likes you."

"Who, Kay?"

"Um, yeah."

"She's sweet, but not my type."

"Cute redheads don't do it for you?"

"Redheads, blondes, they're all swell, Chicago," Cole says. "But I'm not into girls who don't know who they are yet."

It becomes a pattern. At the end of her shift, when nearly everyone is gone, Cole brings her a snack, has a drink at the bar, and walks her to her car.

Sometimes a cool old movie comes on the TV that's always set to TCM, and they'll watch it as they shut everything down for the night. If it's anything with Humphrey Bogart, they'll stay until the end.

Cole tells her about culinary school in San Francisco, how he was actually supposed to start a job in LA, but then his uncle got sick, so he came home.

And Phoebe tells him about her family, her years as a failed actress, that moment when she can feel a patient trusts her.

"So who'd you leave behind in LA?" Cole asks one night as she's finishing one of his upscale tuna melts.

"I don't know what you're talking about," she says lightly. In all their chats, she's never once mentioned Adam, though he's always light dressing coating her thoughts.

"Chicago, girls like you are always leaving men behind," Cole says, and she wonders, no, she knows, he's wanted to ask about this for a while. "You never go out with anyone who asks—not that all the Virgil's customers are winners—but you're not rushing out to meet someone after work, either. So you must have a guy in Cali."

She says nothing, and he smiles.

"So who is he?" Cole asks, and she notices that he's had three drinks tonight instead of his usual one. He's not drunk per se, just looser. "Rich producer? Center for the Lakers? Big-time movie star?"

She means not to say anything.

"He's an actor."

"Anyone I've heard of?"

"Adam Zoellner." It might have been the first time she's said his name aloud since she left LA.

"Sounds familiar."

"He's the bald guy on E&E: Rising."

"Him? I thought that guy was gay."

Phoebe almost chokes on her wine. "You and a lot of fan fiction writers."

"But you can vouch he's not?" Cole jokes, tinged with disappointment. "So what happened? He didn't want to give up life as a TV star to come to glorious Ann Arbor?"

I'm not trekking across the country on a goddamned red-eye every weekend. Cecily's in surgery.

"Something like that." Lowering her eyes, she feels her face burn. She shouldn't be talking about this. Not with this twenty-five-year-old chef who's technically her boss and clearly into her.

Cole puts a light hand on her shoulder, maybe the first time he's touched her since patting her arm when she told him about Chase six weeks ago.

"Hey," he says gently. "I've got a past spattered with carnage and property damage, too."

Then, as quick as that, his hand is gone and he's slipping on his coat.

"You ready?" he asks. She nods, and they walk to the parking lot.

Even in the icy air, her cheeks are still warm, heart still sprinting.

Before she starts her car, she's dialing Adam. He doesn't answer his cell. It's nearly midnight on the West Coast, but she's never known him to turn in before one or two in the morning. Even if he were in bed, he'd probably answer. She wonders if that means he's out (or in) with a woman.

Seven hours later, when she's in her counseling hours listening to a sophomore's concerns that she's letting down her parents by majoring in education, Adam leaves a message: "Hey, Pheebs, sorry I missed you last night. I forgot to turn my ringer on after work, so I didn't see you called till this morning. I think you're in class, but give me a shout when you get a chance."

Maybe he's that good of an actor, or maybe it's true, but it almost sounds believable.

Saturday afternoon's patrons come to Virgil's to watch the games, the exact opposite of Rosebud's clientele. There are supposed to be no less than three bartenders on the schedule from 11:00 A.M. until close, but one calls in sick (code for a big exam the next day), and Eddie shows up with a disastrous cold that no amount of decongestants and cough syrup can make palatable to customers.

Phoebe's doing a decent job on her own—it's almost all bottled beer or sodas during the afternoon—when Cole comes through the kitchen doors, announcing he's there to help.

"Shouldn't you be, you know, cooking the food?" Phoebe asks.

Waving away her concerns, he smiles. "It's game day; the line cooks can handle burgers and wings."

He's wearing jeans and a black shirt, and Phoebe realizes it's the first time she's seen him in anything other than a chef's tunic. It makes him look taller and less like someone on the run from a mental institution. Before she can say anything, he flips a beer stein like Tom Cruise in *Cocktail* and begins filling orders.

There's a quiet harmony working with Cole. She reaches behind him for a new bottle of chardonnay; he pats her hip squeezing by her in the narrow space. Winking, he tosses the glass she needs and lets out a sigh of mock relief when she catches it. Hours pass like minutes, the changing colors of the team uniforms on TV marking time.

As the games finally end and the crowd thins, the music (so much like Rosebud's) amps up. Every now and again, Cole sings an odd line. By midnight she could easily deal with the few remaining patrons, but Cole stays until everyone's gone, and then after that to help her clean up and cash out the waitstaff.

Frank Sinatra's "My Kind of Town" comes on, and Cole points to her, raising his eyebrows up and down.

"It's your song, Chicago; you're required to dance." He reaches for her hand and keeps a nonthreatening distance as he leads her in a box step made tight by the space.

"*And each time I roam, Chicago is calling me home,*" he sings. Even though he's moving and not really trying, the tone in his voice is rich and a little rough. "*Why I just grin like a clown; it's my kind of town.*"

In her arms, he's solid but softer than Adam ever was. This close she notices his green eyes are flecked with gold. The noncommittal facial hair tickles her cheek.

"*My kind of razzamatazz, and it has all that jazz.*"

It shouldn't be earth-shattering, but Phoebe realizes it's been a really long time since she's danced with anyone but Adam. A whole lifetime since she's touched anyone but Adam in a way that wasn't perfunctory.

After Cecily recovered and Phoebe told Adam she was going to Michigan, she'd spent a lot of time thinking about the kind of women *he* would be dating during their break. Trying to make herself okay with the idea of sharing him. Not for a sliver of a second had Phoebe considered the kind of person *she* would like to date. She never wondered if she might like to feel frustrating facial hair between a beard and goatee against her skin.

The Sinatra song ends, but neither Phoebe nor Cole immediately let go. She feels dots of sweat on her brow from the exertion, sees them on his forehead, too. Her hand still in his, Cole meets her eyes and smiles.

"Hey," he says.

"Hey." She grins back.

"Don't go; let me make you dinner."

"It's two in the morning."

"Let me make you breakfast."

"Okay."

"For serious?"

She laughs at his confused look. "For serious."

Her hand still in his, Cole leads her through the swinging doors to the kitchen. When Phoebe's had occasion to go back there during the day, it's always buzzing—line cooks, expediters, and waiters shouting back and forth in cooking shorthand and Spanglish, lively music blasting from an old boom box. Now everyone's gone, everything clean and silent. Her footsteps and Cole's echo on the linoleum.

"Do you like eggs?" he asks.

"Who doesn't like eggs?" She giggles, feeling light.

"Good answer."

In a smooth swoop, he lifts her at the waist and sits her on the counter. Telling her he'll be right back, Cole disappears into the walk-in refrigerator, emerges with arms full of vegetables, cheese, and pancetta. It's the first time she's ever seen him cook, and she's entranced by the rapid, sure movements of his hands as he dices, chops, and sautés.

"What are we having?" she asks.

"Frittata Florentine." The dish already assembled, he slides it in the oven to bake and starts working on a creation in a saucepan.

"Can I help?"

"Well, we *do* need a taster." He dips a wooden spoon into the pan, holds it to her lips.

The sauce, paradoxically rich and airy, is delicious, and she tells him so. Thinks he might kiss her; he doesn't.

Instead he tells her to pick her favorite spot in the restaurant, and she selects the little banquette in the back corner. The table's already set with silverware rolled in cloth napkins, but she relights votive candles as Cole brings out the food and a bottle of wine, lamenting the restaurant's limited selection.

They don't turn on the dining room lights, instead relying on the glow from the candles and the moonlight glare off the snow through the windows. He serves her, and she's amazed at how he can make such simple things taste so divine. She's reaching for more of the sauce, but he puts his hand on hers, holds it.

"I really, really want to kiss you," he says.

She may respond, or maybe she simply doesn't object. The space between them disappears. Lips and tongues and breath. Her hands are in his hair, his in hers. Wanting more of him, she pulls his shirt up and reaches for his chest, feels the soft layer of curly hair.

Maybe it happens because the skin of his torso isn't smooth and waxed the way Adam's is when he's filming, or perhaps it reminds her of what Adam's chest used to feel like. Either way, Phoebe explodes into tears and pulls away.

Cole freezes, his expression so much like a wounded dog it makes her cry harder. Unsure, he reaches out to her and asks what's wrong, but she cashews farther into the corner.

"I can't," she says. "I'm sorry."

A part of her wants to let him wrap her in his arms and offer comfort, but that seems doubly unfair. Sliding out of the banquette, she reassembles her clothes.

"I'm sorry," she says again.

"Is it something I did?" he asks, and she vehemently shakes her head. "Then please, sit down. We don't have to do anything."

"You're wonderful, I promise, I . . . have to go. I'm sorry."

By the time he's on his feet, she's retrieved her coat and is out the large blue door. Then she's in the cold, realizes it's the first night since she started at Virgil's that Cole hasn't walked her to her car. And the parking lot *does* feel dangerous and foreboding. As soon as her engine turns, she's barreling toward her apartment, tires skidding on ice, windshield still frosted.

Phoebe doesn't check her phone until she's in bed, Kraken licking her face with a worried, wet tongue. Cole left three messages. And there's one from hours earlier in the night: Adam wanting to know if she's still coming to LA for spring break next week. Only he doesn't call it Los Angeles, he asks if she's "coming home."

The next day Phoebe should probably be working on her thesis but instead watches *The Two Mrs. Carrolls* on the classic movie station and DVR'd episodes of *E&E: Rising* that she hasn't had time for between school and flirting with Cole at Virgil's. She plays with the dog she's probably been neglecting.

In the afternoon she has counseling hours, but it's unusually quiet, with most students cramming for finals. This allows plenty of time to replay Cole's devastated Labrador look when she burst into tears. Each revisitation brings nothing close to clarity, just another spin cycle of emotions.

Around three a freshman poly sci major comes in panicked about going home to Traverse City over break because a few nights ago he cheated on his long-distance girlfriend at a Kappa Sig party.

"Do I need to tell her?" he asks. "We've been together since sophomore year of high school, and nothing like this has ever happened before."

As she advises Poly Sci to explore the reasons *why* he might have strayed (large amounts of marijuana appear to top the list, but also the notion that his life isn't limited to Traverse City anymore), it's not lost on Phoebe that, despite being nearly twice this boy's age, her problems aren't all that different.

She's not on the schedule, but she heads to Virgil's after she finishes, arrives as Cole is instructing the line cooks on preparing the day's fish special. Speaking with so much authority, he doesn't seem younger than she is.

Noticing her in the corner, a mix of surprise and happiness crosses Cole's face, but it's replaced with trepidation by the time he finishes with the staff and crosses the room to her. Asking if she wants to chat in his office, he leads her to the little room where she hasn't been since her interview, and they take chairs at opposite ends of the old desk.

"Hey?" he says, as if it's a question, as if she might turn and flee again if he hits some undefined trigger. "How are you?"

"I'm really sorry about last night."

Waving away her apology, Cole tells her not to worry, glances down before meeting her eyes. "Look, we can pretend it never happened. Nothing has to be awkward. I'll stop sexually harassing you—"

"No."

With a weary smile, he asks, "So you're okay with the harassment?"

"I kinda liked it, it's not that . . ."

"You're just still hung up on the guy from *Smallville*?"

"*E&E: Rising.*"

"I know, the one who's sadly not gay." He sighs. "Of all the restaurants in all the towns in all the world . . ."

"I walked into yours." She puts her hand on his, unsure this is the right thing to do. "I really . . ." For some reason she thinks of Chase's girlfriend Sharon Gallaher. "I adore you."

"That's good, because I'm crazy about you."

"I kinda need to figure out a few things, though. I'm sorry."

Squeezing her hand, he tells her to take her time. "Chicago, I suspect you're worth the wait."

Phoebe told Adam she'd take a cab from LAX, but he's waiting for her at baggage claim.

He hugs her, and she instinctively responds. Immediately back in his world, the way she fits against him so well known. By the time she lets go, Phoebe feels overwhelmed and dizzy.

"You look great," he says, taking her duffel bag from her shoulder.

"So do you." And it's true. Adam with short sandy stubble that's grown back since filming broke for the holidays. Adam with his sinew and muscles, the dimple when he smiles, and the gray eyes she's seen tear up only on screen.

"It's late your time," he says. "Wanna grab dinner?"

She mumbles something about not being hungry, the idea of sitting across the table from Adam, passing the salt, and not telling him about Cole is absolutely shattering.

Already he's moving them toward the exits.

"Adam, wait," she says, not clear what comes next, not at all sure the airport is the right venue, especially with two teen girls pointing at him and whispering. "I think I may have met someone."

"Pheebs." He puts a hand on her shoulder, massages the back of her neck. "You don't owe me any explanation."

When she doesn't respond, he asks, "Did you fall in love with this guy?"

"No." She looks down. "But I think maybe I could. I'm sorry."

She doesn't want to look up because either he'll be wounded or he won't, and either reaction will change things. And they've already changed so much in the past few months. Still studying the floor, she apologizes again, thinks she's said she's sorry more in the last week than at any other time in her life.

"You didn't do anything wrong." His face shows nothing, but his tone is the tiniest bit off—a slight raise in his voice. "Look, you do what you need to do in Michigan, and we'll figure this out when you're back for real, all right?"

She feels herself nod, bites her lower lip to keep from crying.

"Come here." He folds her back into his arms, and she pulls tight with all the strength she has. "No matter what, we'll always be friends."

"Really?" She clings to him in the airport. Even though they're at arrivals, not departures, a place of reunions and safe returns. Can't let go, keeps holding him, because when she releases her grip, everything will be different.

His lips on the crown of her head, words muffled in her hair: "Always . . . friends."

Maybe he's that good of an actor, or maybe it's true, but in his embrace, she almost believes it.

11   successful ditching

NEW YORK

Diana Collins hands her a copy of *The Atheist in the Foxhole*, and Sharon feels a tickle in her sinuses as if she might cry, glances out the window to the Hudson River twenty stories below. New Jersey on the other side.

"I think the cover turned out really well, don't you?" With her kitschy black glasses, Diana looks a little like Alice (no longer in features) at *Cincy Beat*.

"It's wonderful," Sharon tells her editor, and it is. Greenlee on Hudson is a smaller press, resources more limited than at the big houses, but they did an excellent job with the jacket design—shades of blue, with the Chicago skyline bleeding off the edges. Though it's not a particularly big print run, so far the few reviews have been good. Plus Julie at *Living* promised to get it in the books section when *Atheist* comes out next month.

Still, there is something profoundly sad about this moment, about this lovely book with its lovely cover and good press.

This story is completely different than the one she wrote and burned in the Madison Plaza, but it's still a published novel, the thing she'd thought she wanted above all else then. And now that seems a ludicrous waste—

the obsessing over agents and publishers—allowing the weight of that desire to buckle her relationship with Chase.

In the rational part of her brain, Sharon knows none of that killed Chase Fisher, that *she* didn't kill Chase Fisher. That if he hadn't been on that plane, he probably would have died on the hardwood floor of their apartment or in the back of a cab on the way home from a night of drinking with the sell-side guys. But it jigsaws her heart so much that, even now, she still can't let herself think too long about the tortured way Chase had looked at her when she asked why they weren't getting married, the way he'd been so defeated when he came back to get his things before going to Chicago. To think that she made his last few weeks so incredibly miserable.

In many ways, she knows, the story she ended up writing is her apology for all of that, her wish for him, for what could have been. But it's not enough. Nothing could (or will) ever be enough.

"You sure you don't have time for coffee?" Diana asks, and Sharon shakes her head.

A few weeks ago, she'd left *The Eye* for a staff position on *The Enquiring Sun*'s features desk and doesn't want to chance aggravating her new editors by being gone too long. She'd simply wanted to stop by the Greenlee office and get a few copies of the book when Diana told her they'd come in. They talk briefly about the Web site one of the designers at the paper set up for Sharon and about her scheduled readings at area bookstores and coffee shops.

"Well, I think the whole thing turned out great. Congratulations." Diana shakes her hand.

"Thank you again for every—" Sharon is saying when something through the window catches her attention. Diana follows her eyes.

"Is that a plane on the river?"

CHICAGO

You and your sister are back at Northwestern Memorial (the hospital where your mother died nearly twenty years earlier), only now you're here for your father. Dad isn't dying, but two days ago, he did have bypass surgery serious enough to warrant both Karen and Natasha flying home and you taking a week off from Advantage Electric.

Since Dad came out of the ICU yesterday, the four of you have been watching TV, playing and abandoning games of Scrabble, and talking about Karen's kids and how Natasha has to take a bus to the high school for geometry because she's two years ahead of the other eighth graders in math. All the normal family-type things you never did before as a family.

It's been sort of fun, all things considered, and your father keeps thanking everyone for keeping him company. Still, you can sense his restlessness at being stuck in bed with the nurses (well, not the good-looking young blonde) and doctors who poke and prod and talk about all the activities he shouldn't do now.

He's actually been bored and restless since June, when he turned sixty-five and had to retire from United. And you'd found yourself stopping by a couple of times a week, sometimes to watch the Bears or Bulls, but more often to share sketches of your latest compressor design or get his input on taming the machines you work to improve.

In six weeks you're scheduled to start a two-year-long project in New York, but you're considering asking for a delay until your father is up and running, even though you'd specifically asked for the job—a chance to work with other propulsion engineers from Europe and Japan.

A knock on the half-open door, and Phoebe Fisher's father walks in before getting an affirmative response.

"How's everyone doing today?" He nods politely at you and your sisters clustered in chairs around your father.

The four of you nod back, uttering some variance of "good," as Larry Fisher plucks your father's chart from the foot of the bed.

A week ago, when your father finally admitted he was going to have surgery, he'd mentioned his cardiologist knew you. "He's the father of the girl you went with in high school," Dad said. "The pretty one with black hair. He had a picture of her on his desk." While it didn't surprise you at all that Phoebe's father recognized you two days later at the pre-op meeting, the fact that your own father remembered how Phoebe once fit into your life was surprising and touching, made you once again grateful Maura had never said anything about the two of you.

Bobbing his head as he examines the clipboard, Larry Fisher smiles, says everything looks good and your father should be able to leave by the end of the week.

Turning to you, he mentions he had a conversation with Phoebe last night. "She was happy to hear that everything's going so well for you, Oliver."

"How is she?" you ask.

"Really good. She's finishing her master's at Michigan and has a job lined up in LA. And, I'm not sure I'm supposed to tell anyone yet, but she just got engaged."

"That's great," you say. "Give her my congratulations."

When Phoebe's father is out of the room, Karen rolls her eyes. "Like you needed to know she's getting married. And what? It only took her until she was seventy to finish school?"

You shrug, knowing Karen, as always, is simply trying to help.

Visiting hours winding to a close, you tell your father you'll be back the next day and ask Natasha if she is ready to go.

You'd invited her to stay with you in Printer's Row instead of at Dad's house with Karen, and she'd been contagiously excited by the idea. It means crunching up and sleeping on the couch so she can have your bed, but the two of you have actually been having a pretty good time. Tomorrow you promised to take her to Dark Tower Comics.

You're gathering your coats when Karen points to the muted television mounted on the wall, where a plane is floating on a river surrounded by emergency boats.

"Turn it up," your father says, invigorated and alive.

In silence the four of you listen to the newscaster explain how the pilot ditched the crippled plane in the Hudson and miraculously everyone survived.

"Did you ever do anything like that?" Natasha asks your father.

"No." He sighs. "We trained for stuff, had some drills in the Air Force, but nothing like that ever came up. I honestly wasn't sure you could successfully ditch."

There's awe in his voice and some disappointment that he'll never have that opportunity. And you understand this, understand *him* like you never did in your youth.

Putting a hand on his shoulder, you tell him with sincerity, "If you'd had to, I'm sure you could have done it, too."

LOS ANGELES

It's the first day of filming for *E&E: Rising*'s fifth season, but Adam is on his cell phone looking down at Bel Air from his condo in the Wilshire Corridor. In his ear, Marty is weighing the pluses and minuses of signing on for the *Murder Island* sequels. The lone pro appears to be monetary, the cons all other aspects of the project.

"It's another four months in New Zealand," Marty is saying. "And that takes you right out of pilot season if we decide to go in that direction."

"I *did* get really sick of lamb," Adam says vacantly.

The floor-to-ceiling windows—which had seemed open and freeing when Adam bought the twenty-fourth-floor unit five years ago—now make him feel trapped, like a goldfish in an aquarium.

"They'll have a bigger budget this time, but who knows if that will help," Marty continues.

By the time it was actually released, *Murder Island* had been edited down to an eighty-six minutes so slim the plot was largely incoherent. That hadn't dissuaded scores of teen fans from racing to the theater to watch Adam—wearing a not-quite-believable wig and playing a charismatic cult leader—stab, spear, and scalp a handful of young stars from other QT and CW shows. The film had opened at an astonishing number one (the *Cat on a Hot Tin Roof* remake, meanwhile, hadn't cracked the top ten, though it did make a couple critics' year's-best lists) right around the time his contract with *E&E: Rising* was up. It had made the decision *not* to go back to 5:00 A.M. calls and two hours of daily makeup for a show that was hemorrhaging viewers all that much easier. He'd told Marty he wanted to do more films; he'd hoped they wouldn't all be *Murder Island* movies.

"It's a paycheck, buddy, plain and simple. You can make this your franchise, make buckets of money—which, believe me, I got no issue with—but you're not gonna win any awards."

Reviews for *Murder Island* had ranged from mediocre to bloody, but even the harshest critics acknowledged Adam had been a "bright spot," "fun to watch," or, his personal favorite from Roger Ebert: "Zoellner, so promising in *Cat on a Hot Tin Roof*, does the best he can here but is worthy of a much better movie."

"I don't know," Adam says. "Will it hurt me?"

"Not if you want a five bed/six bath in Malibu."

Adam doesn't particularly want a five bed/six bath in Malibu. He doesn't use half the bedrooms and bathrooms in his home now, and the beach reminds him too much of Florida. Maybe some desert house in Palm Springs or a sprawling ranch in Montana or another place where they have sprawling ranches—anywhere but LA.

"Give it a few days," Marty says. "They need you more than you need them, so make 'em squirm."

"Okay, buddy?" Marty is asking, and Adam realizes an acknowledgment is required.

"Sounds good."

Hanging up, Adam checks the text messages he'd ignored while on the phone. Relief when he sees they're not from Phoebe.

Cecily: *On set, totally sux without u.*

Thirty seconds later: *Come back—Ron tired of hearing about my shits!!*

Then from Ron: *She's not kidding. You MUST guest star soon.*

Cecily again: *Yes, guest star! SPLEEN, SPLEEN, SPLEEN!!!!*

Wistful, Adam types a message for both of them, saying they should have Enchanted Ales on him tonight. Thinks about his non-fishbowl apartment in BC, tries to remember what exactly it was about Vancouver that drove him bonkers. The rain?

He's missed several e-mails as well: NYU's Office of Annual Giving looking for another donation; organizers from a charity softball event asking if they can add him to their roster again; fan letters begging him to return to the show—one of them mildly threatening.

And then, because he can't really put it off any longer, he plays Phoebe's message from this morning: "Hey, it's me. So, um, I got a job lined up and I'm coming back to LA in the spring. And I've got some other news. So when you get a chance, give me a shout."

There is absolutely no news Adam wants to hear from Phoebe Fisher.

That's not really accurate. If it was simply that she was returning, he could be persuaded to hear about that. But since she offered that as a throw-away before advertising the "other news," he'd wager eons and empires she's married or getting married, or she and her kid boyfriend are joining the circus to then get married by a clown. None of this is news he wants to hear. As long as she's happy, he's happy . . . well, happy-ish, which frankly seems like an enormous emotional maturity leap for him. But that doesn't change the fact that his grand experiment of being vulnerable and committing to someone was a spectacular failure.

Still, he knows he needs to call her back, realizes if he'd called her back last year after he'd lashed out and told her he'd slept with Cecily, Phoebe probably wouldn't even have this news to share.

Slumping on the suede sofa, he wonders if it's his couch or Phoebe's. After a decade of living together in one configuration or another, isn't it all their stuff? He should give it to her. She'll probably need furniture. If she'd take it, he'd gladly give Phoebe the whole fucking aquarium condo.

He mutes the giant flat-screen TV that's always on now that he lives alone and, for all intents and purposes, is unemployed. Phoebe is the top person on his phone's Favorites list, but he manually types in the numbers anyway.

She picks up on the second ring. Her apprehension is palpable, so he shares a story about a recent dinner with his publicist, where Evie convinced him to help poach an A-list actress at the next table and hilarity ensued. Phoebe laughs; Adam laughs.

No one could ever say Anna Zoellner's bastard son wasn't good at convincing people he felt things he didn't.

He lets her tell him about her new gig at Cedars-Sinai starting in June, and about how all the kids at Michigan can't stop talking about *Murder Island*. Lets her work up to telling him she's engaged. Without overplaying his congratulations—she *would* be able to tell that was fake—he asks polite questions. Lets her tell him "probably July" and "something pretty small, maybe the back room at Rosebud."

On the television he catches a bizarre image: a plane in the water, shivering people standing in clumps on the wings. Even with all the ships coming to help them, they look so alone and adrift.

And then, when she's finished all those things she had to say and he had to hear, she speaks his name with infinite tragedy. "Adam."

In some other world, maybe, this is the time when he makes a play, voices something dramatic and game changing.

"Phoebe," he starts, but knows that he has to get off the phone before he says more, because anything else he could say would only hurt her, and he has been trying so impossibly hard *not* to do that anymore.

"I should get going, I need to call Marty. Let's get dinner when you're back."

After hanging up, he actually does call his agent.

"I want to do the sequels."

"You're sure?" Marty asks. "An hour ago you were pretty on the fence."

"Yeah, I know. I got a craving for lamb."

12   i guess i knew that

"I fucking hate you," Evie Saperstein says as a greeting. Walking onto the patio of Chateau Marmont, she gives Phoebe's cheek a kiss. "Six months after having a kid and you look like a Victoria's Secret model."

Phoebe thanks her, but the truth is, she hasn't lost the last fifteen pounds of baby weight and is astonished, after years of starving herself and sticking her finger down her throat in the name of her "acting" career, how little she actually cares.

"Must be how you hang on to that hot young husband," Evie says. This is likely meant as a compliment, so Phoebe just smiles.

Calling Evie "Ms. Saperstein," a pert hostess leads them to a table in the shade next to scantily clad blond starlets Phoebe doesn't recognize. She never knows anyone anymore, and it seems bizarre that that used to be such an enormous part of her world. Actually, everything about her previous life in Los Angeles has felt alien in the year and a half she's been back.

As they are unfurling napkins, a waiter dips over, asks if "Ms. Saperstein" would like her usual—a crab BLT not on the menu—and Phoebe orders the chopped salad. Between counseling at Cedars-Sinai, running her group sessions in the evening, hacking out a few hours a day when her schedule meshes with Cole's, and making sure Cassie is fed, changed, and napped, Phoebe hasn't seen Evie for months, and there is much updating: the married tech billionaire Evie's sleeping with; how Cassie is starting to be more fun and less bloblike; and potential work crossovers—meeting some of Evie's clients might be nice for Phoebe's patients, or as Evie describes them, "some of your sad people."

Dishes cleared.

Phones checked.

Dessert discussed but ultimately not ordered.

Then Phoebe does the thing she tries never to do. The thing she knows puts Evie in an uncomfortable position.

"Is he okay?" she asks. There's no need to specify the "he" is Adam.

"I take it you caught his meltdown on Howard Stern?" Evie shakes her head.

"Part of it."

Her friend Melissa (who may or may not have slept with Adam a million years ago) had e-mailed her assuming she'd heard the show, the subject line, *Your Boy's Hysterical.* And when Phoebe found the Web link for the broadcast, Adam *had* been extremely witty as he bashed *Murder Island 3* and its director while Stern and guest David Arquette goaded him on. It was also incredibly unprofessional. After so many years of Adam diligently doing everything asked of him—committing to inanely written scenes, shaving his head and waxing his chest, Comic-Con panels and DVD commentaries when bigger actors couldn't be bothered—to hear him trash a project was shocking.

"Minerva and I have been cleaning *that* up all week," Evie says, and explains that Howard and Adam met at a charity softball event and Adam had stopped by the show without Evie's sanction. "Honestly, in a few days everyone will forget about it. Even New Line acknowledges the film was a shit box."

"That's good, I guess," Phoebe says.

"So you guys really don't talk at all anymore?"

Since coming back, Phoebe has seen Adam one time. Because he'd told her to call, she'd left him messages when she and Cole moved into the little Craftsman bungalow in Los Feliz. An assistant she'd never met called to set something up (and offered to ship over *anything* Phoebe wanted from the condo—actually, to sell her the place for a "very fair price" that

Phoebe suspected would have been significantly below market). Adam had canceled thrice; then he'd been in New Zealand filming. Finally they'd gotten lunch at Tavern. Looking too thin and vaguely stoned, he'd spent the majority of the meal fiddling with his phone, flirting with the waitress, and declaring everything "tight." On the drive home, Phoebe had to pull over to puke up steak salad and green-olive bread. Two days later she found out she was pregnant, but she's still not entirely convinced the vomiting was morning-sickness-related. Her wedding invitations had already gone out at that point; Adam sent his regrets and a check for too much money. She never cashed it. Though she didn't send him a birth announcement, an even bigger check arrived in a generic card when she had Cassie six months later.

"I'm sorry, E," Phoebe apologizes. "It's not fair for me to ask about him."

"It's not that." Evie shrugs. "It's just sorta sad."

There's a partially downloaded e-mail on Sharon's iPhone from Evie at the Saperstein Group, but the spinning white wheel indicates the echoy lower level of the Jacob K. Javits Convention Center is a network dead zone. Searching the costume-clad Fan-Con attendees, she finds her photographer from *The Enquiring Sun* shooting what must be his five thousandth picture of women dressed in Princess Leia's *Return of the Jedi* metal bikini. Signaling she's stepping out, Sharon weaves through tables of vendors selling old comic books and action figures, and heads out the door, shivers in the late January air as the message loads.

Ms. Gallaher—

We'd like to thank you for your interest in our client, but Mr. Zoellner is doing limited press at this time. He will be making an appearance at the "Thirty Years of *E&E*" Convention in Detroit next week, if you would like to include that in *The Enquiring Sun*.

Thank you again for your interest,
Evie Saperstein

Painful flare of disappointment as Sharon wanders back to the bustling convention floor. She hadn't *really* expected Adam Zoellner's rep to offer him up to the least respected of the three NYC dailies, but she'd hoped . . . a lot, more than was probably healthy. Maybe hoped that somehow the interview would take place not on the phone, but over coffee, hoped that she might have made Adam Zoellner smile, that he might touch her hand.

She'd gotten the media alert about the *E&E* convention in Ed Munn's hometown weeks ago, but her editors had been lukewarm about the anniversary story to begin with. There is absolutely no way they'll send her to Detroit.

Back in the exhibition hall, her photographer has moved on from nearly naked slave Leias to a pale girl, very possibly underage, in a teeny tiny Sailor Moon costume. Shoving down her gloom, Sharon is heading over to make sure Nick got the photo release form signed when a tall redheaded guy in a vintage *Eons & Empires* T-shirt puts his hand on Sailor Moon's shoulder and asks, "Nat, what's going on?"

Shifting her phone and notebooks into one hand, Sharon fishes a business card from her purse and explains that she and Nick are with the paper and would obviously *never* run photos without getting consent from a guardian.

"I'm not sure it's mine to give." The redheaded man softens, says Sailor Moon is his sister. Then, looking at the girl, "I'm thinking Maura wouldn't be on board with this."

"It does seem highly unlikely." Sailor Moon shrugs, straightens her blond wig, and goes off to talk to guys in *Star Trek: The Next Generation* uniforms. Nick starts snapping a lady in Wonder Woman's strapless bathing suit.

"Sorry about that." The redheaded brother smiles at Sharon.

"I'm the one who should be apologizing." Sharon wonders if the curious way he's looking at her means he's going to ask her out. Mentally she prepares her patented rejection.

"So, I don't mean this like a pickup line," he says, "but you look really familiar. Have we met?"

No one *ever* recognizes her author photo (more because so few people bought *The Atheist in the Foxhole* than any inherent flaw of the picture), but sometimes *The Enquiring Sun* runs her head shot when they post her stories online. She mentions this, and he shakes his head.

"Sorry, I'm a *Daily News* guy."

He glances at the card she handed him. "Gallaher, only one G." Trace of recognition crosses his eyes like water moving under ice. "I remember now, it was Thanksgiving, like, ten years ago, in Chicago. I dated Phoebe Fisher for a while, and you were there with her bro . . ."

Then it all comes crashing back: talking too much about the election; how proud Chase had been to introduce her to his family; feeling short and ugly next to his model sister. And this guy—Owen, no, Oliver—Chase had been so excited to see him (though apparently no one had been expecting him). The guy had stayed for breakfast, and everyone joked about how Chase had tagged along on his and Phoebe's first date. "He's a really good dude," Chase had told Sharon repeatedly. "So much better than those assholes Phoebe dates now."

Sharon feels her heart kick-start, sweat dripping down her spine to the waistband of her tights, and that odd sensation that the floor of the Javits Center might open up and suck her down to the molten center of the Earth's core—something she hasn't felt since she finished her book.

"Oh." She actually drops her notebooks and press badge, her phone. "Right. Thanksgiving, *Bush v. Gore* and all of that stuff . . ." Talking too much when she's nervous again.

She bends down to pick everything up, and of course Oliver follows. *He's a really good dude.*

"Right, right, right," she says. Her hands bumping his as she hastily collects her things. "Gennifer made French toast."

Even as it's happening, Sharon can see Oliver registering his mistake. This traveler from another universe trying to make it better with some mix of words: "sorry," "so young," and "tragedy."

"Well, it was a really long time ago." She's already moving away from him. "Anyway, thanks for all your help. And don't worry, I'll make sure none of those photos of your sister run."

Then she's hurrying through the tables and dressed-up fans toward the door, bumping into a man in full Batman armor and knocking a vintage Spider-Man lunchbox off a table.

Behind her someone, probably Oliver who used to date Phoebe Fisher, is calling, "Wait," but she keeps up her pace until she's out the door and in the cold January air off the Hudson.

"You're *positive* we don't know each other?" The coal-haired girl—Nikki or Nancy or was it something like Rachel—is leaning so close Adam wonders if she's stable on her bar stool. In the dim light, it's impossible to tell her age, somewhere between eighteen and thirty—younger than him, anyway.

"Pretty sure." Adam smiles, unconsciously turns so she's facing his good side, thinks about adding some line about how he'd remember having met someone as captivating as her but decides against it; if the girl's been in LA more than a week, she'll know it's crap.

"Jacqui Holland's party in Santa Monica?" She points at him, her mock accusatory finger a centimeter from his chest. "You brought a Pomeranian?"

"Nope, don't know any Jacquis, and I don't have a dog—Pomeranians are dogs, right?"

"Are you *sure*?" Nikki-Nancy-Rachel drawls. "You look familiar."

"I don't know," Adam says, as if it's only now occurring to him. "I'm an actor." From behind the counter, the bartender rolls his eyes conspiratorially.

"Someone I would know?" asks the girl.

Honestly, Adam didn't come here to pick up an aspiring actress/unemployed waitress, he didn't. He came because the place is mellow and almost always empty before ten, because he couldn't spend anymore time lamenting that god-awful *Murder Island 3* is *still* in theaters and worrying that no director will ever work with him again because he publicly admitted the film was god-awful. More time *not* reading scripts (always sci-fi, always the villain) that his manager had sent over. Not thinking about what he's going to say at next week's "Thirty Years of *Eons & Empires*" celebration in Detroit or why, after two years of trying to disassociate himself from Captain Rowen, he let Cecily convince him to appear with her at the convention in the first place.

But . . .

Nikki-Nancy-Rachel *is* cute, and if they go to his place, she'll likely continue to be a distraction. He goes for the endgame.

"I *was* on a show for a while," he says.

Wait for it . . .

Still waiting.

A sound editor might insert chirping crickets.

The bartender hums the *Eons & Empires* theme song, from the movie, not the series, but it's enough.

"You're Captain Rowen!" The girl is back in her own space, nervous, almost reverent. "My . . . my brothers watched it growing up." (Clearly putting her in the closer-to-eighteen-than-thirty camp.) "Ohmygod, I didn't recognize you with hair."

Now Adam is the one behind the wheel, telling her he's got wine at his place just down Wilshire. She probably has a car somewhere, but he doesn't factor that into the equation.

Ten minutes later they're in the Winston Tower, where Adam's opening a bottle of Barolo and Nikki-Nancy-Rachel is nervously looking around. Handing her a glass, he clinks it to his own in a toast.

"It's good," she pronounces, though she cringes at the taste; he should have opened a merlot or something sweeter. "Your apartment's really awesome."

Pretty standard reaction.

He hadn't bought a house in Malibu (or Palm Springs or Montana) with the *Murder Island* series money. Looking at property (even paying someone to look for him) had seemed a lot of work. So he'd hired Marty's decorator wife while he was out of the country and told her to make the place look completely different. Terri Minerva had gutted the space, knocked out walls, installed recessed lighting into new granite floors, and replaced everything homey he and Phoebe had picked out with derelict metals and smoked glass, dark wood, and darker stone. The place oozes sex, but all the furniture is distractingly uncomfortable, and sometimes he's actively frightened of the artwork.

They make their way to an object one might find in the Cooper-Hewitt that's actually a couch. He's about to kiss her when she points to a stack of scripts on a petrified redwood table that cost more than most cars.

"Are these movies?" Nikki-Nancy-Rachel asks nervously. "Like, for you to be in?"

"They're all pretty awful." Adam actually hadn't glanced past the first one when he saw the title was *Galaxy Warrior.* Prereading scripts had been one of Phoebe's non-jobs, anyway.

"Oh." She swallows, eyes wide and terrified—definitely closer to eighteen than thirty. "Wow."

Starting to feel like a lion circling a wounded zebra, Adam eases away from her, accepting that, despite all prior signs, he's probably not getting laid tonight. "Do you wanna watch a movie?" he asks. "I have screeners—"

She's the one who initiates the kiss, though he notices she does take a stabilizing breath before charging toward him. Hands in her hair, he can feel the bonds of her extensions. Through the floor-to-ceiling windows, Los Angeles glows twenty-four stories beneath them.

Four stories above East Seventy-fifth Street, in a rent-stabilized apartment with an excellent view into the apartment across the street, Sharon strips off her wet coat and dress, still shivering. She'd meant to go back to *The Enquiring Sun*'s Midtown office but had been so thrown by the encounter with Phoebe Fisher's old boyfriend that she'd called in her quotes instead (the Fan-Con story is the same every year, anyway—a few fun comments to go along with photos of attendees in elaborate costumes).

She'd wanted to start on the new novel Diana from Greenlee on Hudson keeps trying to convince her to write, but heart still thumping in her chest, Sharon feels completely justified sinking into the sofa and turning on the *E&E: Rising* season two DVD already ginned up.

She's probably seen the episode five times, but instantly Sharon's engaged, feels herself relaxing.

Mid-thrust, it occurs to Adam he could conceivably be tired of sex.

He wonders why he bothered picking Nikki-Nancy-Rachel up in the first place, why he does anything he does lately. To be fair, he likely wouldn't be contemplating any of this if she weren't lying underneath him like a lump of Kryptonite.

Perhaps it says something about his mental state that the image popping into his head is of his mother in her pink nurse's scrubs, her gray eyes down in the expression she has when talking about the meth heads in the Coral Cove ER. Mother image says that if he'd bothered to learn Nikki-Nancy-Rachel's name, perhaps she'd be a more enthusiastic partner.

So he strokes a stray hair from the girl's brow, lowers his lips to her forehead. Eyes fluttering open, she looks at him with a mix of confusion, hope, and something barely shy of contempt—she's really, really closer to eighteen than thirty.

"You enjoying this at all?" he asks, slowing their non-rhythm to a standstill.

"Yeah."

And he wants to tell her to go back to Kentucky/Oklahoma/San Diego, because she's *never* going to make it as an actress.

Instead he nods.

Faintly in the background, some maudlin alt-rock crap whines from the sound system, and he remembers, with a dollop of disgust, that the song had figured prominently in one of the *E&E: Rising* series montages. He'd mentioned it in the DVD commentary.

As the world comes crashing down, I just want you around . . .

I just want you around. . . .

On the screen Captain Rowen and Cordelia Snow are still kissing in a shadowy industrial space.

On the couch a blue plastic vibrator hums between Sharon's thighs.

On the screen Rowen pauses, holds Cordelia at arm's length, hesitates before closing gray eyes.

On the couch Sharon points her toes, knocking off a week's worth of newspapers and yesterday's clothes.

Through a haze of pleasure, prickly thoughts tickle, like early indicators of a sneeze. Things like how it's probably long past time she found another human being to do this stuff with.

Adam doesn't remember falling asleep, but he's got a knot in his neck, a used condom crusting on his cock, and an alarm clock that insists it's after 4:00 A.M. Nikki-Nancy-Rachel is wrangling thin hips back into ridiculously tight jeans. If she weren't much, much closer to eighteen than thirty, the jerky movements would be even less appealing.

"Hey." He props himself on an elbow, works legs out of Egyptian cotton sheets. "You taking off?"

"Yeah." She pulls on an equally sexy shirt. Her black hair may be fake, but it's pretty in the city lights flooding through open blinds.

"Don't go," he says, stunned at the desperation in his voice, stunned that he reaches for her hand. "We'll get breakfast."

"I can't," she says in a way that eclipses the fifteen years he has on her.

In a series of less-than-fluid motions, she's fully rebooted and rebuckled, and he's in his underwear unbolting the door, kissing her cheek, saying he'll call her, though they both know he never got her number (or name).

She's gone before he realizes he didn't even give her cab fare.

He picks up his discarded wineglass and finishes it off, then Nikki-Nancy-Rachel's. Taking the bottle with him, he turns on the giant TV in what used to be the den and flips through the channels, settling on an infomercial for a skin care line.

Still wearing her hiked-up dress and Fan-Con press pass, Sharon wakes up on the sofa with the unsettled feeling of having slept the night in an unintended place. Rubbing her kinked neck, she checks the time: ten past seven. Seems silly to go back to sleep, even if it is a weekend.

A jolt of terror when she realizes she hasn't checked her phone since last night. The sensation heightens when she pulls her cell from her purse and discovers several missed calls.

Scott Underwood, who had wanted her to move to NYC with him when he got a surgical fellowship at Weill Cornell: "Hey, Sharon, Blair and I haven't gotten your response card yet, and we wanted to know if you're coming. Feel free to bring a date."

The ecru invitation is sitting in a pile of undealt-with mail, and Sharon likes to think not sending it back is forgetfulness, nothing more. She's met Scott's fiancée a few times, and Blair seems a perfectly lovely person, though Sharon wonders what Scott told her about all the things he and Sharon had shared in that chopped-up house on Mcmillan Street. Wonders if Scott actually wants Sharon at his wedding or if the invite is an expected courtesy. Either way, she's sure Blair is the one insisting on the plus one.

The next message is from an unfamiliar number with a 773 area code—inhale of breath—Chicago: "Hey, Ms. Gallaher, this is Oliver Ryan from Fan-Con. You left before I could give you some notebooks you dropped."

Phone tucked between ear and shoulder, Sharon rummages through her purse and discovers several of her notepads are indeed missing. At least two of them have interviews for a story she's working on about toxic hair treatments at high-end salons.

"Not sure if they're important, but if you need them back, maybe I could meet you somewhere this weekend? And, um, I'm really sorry if I upset you this afternoon."

The message is sweet and sincere, and Sharon feels a flutter of remorse that he's apologizing for *her* weirdness. Now, in the light of day and fully prepared to hear Chase's name, it seems crazy that she sped off. She does actually need her notes and is about to call him back, when she notices one more message, this one from Kristen: "So I did find an e-mail for that actor in the NYU database, but I don't know—"

Heart alive and wild in her throat, Sharon hits call back before the recording finishes, even though it's not yet eight in the morning, something she forgets entirely until Kristen is on the phone, confused and groggy.

Apologizing, Sharon explains she was just excited by Kristen's call.

"Well, like I said, there is an Adam Zoellner who graduated in ninety-seven, but I could probably get fired for giving out his e-mail," Kristen says—part her usual nervous disposition and perhaps a teeny bit of relish that, after years of being Sharon's guest at press premieres and parties, she has something her friend wants. "Doesn't this guy have a publicist or something?"

"You're not gonna get fired." Sharon is fairly certain of this. Kristen was a sophomore work-study student when she started at the Office of Annual Giving, and now she runs the place. "I just want to set up an interview and thought, because we knew each other from school, I should contact him directly."

Kristen is unconvinced. "He was three years ahead of us; how'd you even meet?"

"Econ freshman year." She'd put off economics until she was a junior, but Kristen probably wasn't paying that much attention. "We were in the same discussion section."

Everything clenched, Sharon *pushes* into the lie, wanting Adam's contact so badly she can *make* this true, could give a seating chart for the class and a detailed description of Adam making fun of the professor's ascot during an exam study session.

A little more cajoling and Kristen agrees, reads the address, which Sharon writes down on the back of an old *Enquiring Sun*.

"A, d, a, m, underscore, z, o, e, l, l, n, e, r, at gmail, dot, com."

Sharon looks at the paper incredulously. "It's Adam Zoellner at Gmail?"

"And you didn't hear it from me. I'm serious, if anyone asks—"

"It's the guy's name; I doubt the FBI's going to get involved."

"You don't know that." Kristen laughs. "Well, probably."

Sharon's fingers are twitching to turn on her computer and write a message that could conceivably reach Adam Zoellner, but she knows Kristen has done her yet another favor, and it's been a few days since they've spoken. So she politely listens to a tale about Kristen's latest date from her latest dating Web site, and lets Kristen advise her on the Scott wedding situation. "Bring me as your guest. There may be single doctors there!"

Finally they hang up with plans for brunch the next day unless Kristen's date goes "very, very well."

Then Sharon is typing, untyping, and retyping a note for Adam Zoellner with a contemplation of word choice she's not sure she's ever employed before in all her years of writing.

It's silly, she's aware of that. The name isn't super common, but it's possible that this is some other Adam Zoellner or that her e-mail will go to an assistant or back to someone at the Saperstein Group or to a dead account no one checks. But her chest is tight as she types, and it feels important, like when she went to see the *Eons & Empires* movie freshman year of high school. It feels as if this is the kind of moment that could change her life.

Adam's housekeeper is finishing in the kitchen when he staggers out of his former den in boxers at one in the afternoon. Barely looking up from wiping down concrete counters, Elena gives a shy smile and says nothing. She never says anything. Not about the girls sometimes still in his bed when she arrives or about how the only dishes she ever has to clean are wineglasses and tumblers. Of course, she may not say much because her English isn't great.

Not wanting to watch her clean, Adam puts on a discarded undershirt from the floor, grabs his iPad, and steps out on the larger of two terraces. It's only fifty-five degrees, and the cold feels good as he reads texts from Cecily about the *E&E* convention—brief heartburn of nostalgia, remembering exactly how it felt the first year of the show, when they had filled the biggest auditorium for a panel at San Diego Comic-Con.

Most of his e-mail is crap: notes from fans who cracked his top-secret Gmail address, all beseeching him to return to *E&E: Rising*; an NYU alumni update; spam from a bank he doesn't use. And something labeled Interview Request that he's bored enough to open.

Mr. Zoellner—

I am a reporter for *The Enquiring Sun*, a fellow NYU alum, and general Adam Zoellner fan. I'm writing an article about the 30th anniversary of *Eons & Empires* and was wondering if you would be available for a short phone interview.

After years of playing Captain Rowel, you must have some great stories! I can be reached via e-mail or at 646-555-1232.

Best,
Sharon Gallaher

The letter writer has typed "Captain Rowel" instead of "Captain Rowen," and Adam wonders if she's clueless or if it's a spell-check mistake. Sure enough, when he types "Rowen," it's autoreplaced by "Rowel." After four years of shaving his head, he can't believe he never knew this.

After the Howard Stern debacle, Evie threatened to castrate him should he as much as say hello to a media outlet without her approval.

He's about to delete the message when he notices a web address in the signature, sharongallaher.com.

Something about that sounds familiar, so he goes to the site.

Apparently Sharon is the author of a novel, *The Atheist in the Foxhole*, and has written for various magazines and newspapers. In the bio section there's a picture of a cute-ish girl with shoulder-length hair and very big eyes. Her year of graduation is listed, and he calculates that she would have been a freshman at NYU when he was a senior. Perhaps that's why he feels he knows her? Someone he used to see hanging out at Main Building, using a fake ID at Finnerty's or ordering a falafel from the cart on Washington Square South?

Her site has book reviews. A few of the links are dead, but *The New York Times*, while pointing out that the book used "fairly pedestrian" language, claims it is "emotionally riveting and unsentimental." Adam orders a copy from Amazon, spends the extra fifteen dollars for priority shipping, figuring he can read it on the plane to Detroit. It's been a long time since he's read anything other than a horrible horror or sci-fi script.

Skimming *Variety* and Deadline.com, he learns about actors who are actually working on real projects. One headline makes him sit up straight and go back inside for his phone: KEVIN MCKIDD DROPS OUT OF HBO'S UPCOMING CIVIL WAR SERIES.

Adam's manager had alerted him to the project months ago and hunted down an early version of the pilot that Adam had loved. But when he'd asked his agent about it, Marty kept insisting Adam was too young to play General Grant, plus he had been committed to the *Murder Island* films; then McKidd had been cast.

It's Saturday, but Marty answers on the first ring. "You're still too young," he says, "and they're notorious for using their own people."

"Tell them I'm happy to audition." Adam feels his pulse ticking with excitement for what might be the first time in years. "Let'm know how serious I am."

"Okay, okay," Marty says, and asks if Adam has had a chance to look at the scripts he'd sent.

Adam reiterates how much he wants to be a part of *Divided*. "Seriously"—Marty sighs—"don't get your hopes up, buddy."

Flights from New York to Detroit are more than six hundred dollars on such short notice, and none of the times work with the scheduled *E&E* dedication featuring Adam Zoellner and Cecily Beissel. But according to Google Maps, it's only a ten-and-a-half-hour drive.

If Sharon rented a car after work Friday and drove through the night, she could get there in plenty of time for the ceremony Saturday evening. Maybe she could leave first thing in the morning and save a day's rental.

Even as she's pricing rental cars, Sharon doesn't think she's actually going to go. She doesn't *really* have a story for the paper, and other than standing in an autograph line for a signed photo, it's unlikely she'd have any interaction with Adam Zoellner.

And even if she had unfettered access to him, what does she want to happen? While at *Cincy Beat*, Sharon had done a whole series of pieces on different kinds of groupies, so she is aware *how* these things happen, even knows some techniques from her interviews. But after seven years of not screwing anything with a pulse, whether she *could* do it is a very different question.

And of course there's the more insurmountable impediment: Why would Adam Zoellner be interested in going along? Sharon's done some research (*not* stalking). In a few early interviews, Adam made vague references to a longtime girlfriend, but nothing in recent years. And while there are plenty of red carpet shots of him with starlets from the *Murder Island* series and Cecily Beissel from *E&E* (*Living* once ran an item about a secret engagement, but for years Cecily has been with some dude from a QT show about warlocks), the only thing Sharon's found that appears remotely personal is a series of paparazzi shots of Adam hand in hand with a tall, black-haired woman outside of a high-end hotel or apartment building—something with arches and doormen. Though Adam is clearly distracted and the woman's face is obscured behind oversize sunglasses, it's something about the way he's holding her fingers—as if he needs that connection, as if he needs her.

It seems somewhat promising, at least, that the woman is a brunette, though tall could definitely be an issue.

All Sharon really knows is that, since Evie Saperstein's e-mail, she's become convinced she *needs* to go to the convention.

She's booking an economy car when she notices the time and realizes she's running late to meet Oliver Ryan. Checks her e-mail one more time— Groupon and Living Social offers, something from a bank she doesn't use, nothing from Adam Zoellner (*but it's only two on the West Coast!*)—then Sharon hurries into her purple coat and out the door.

Because she was the one who fled and he was kind enough to contact her, Sharon had offered to pick up her notebooks from Oliver's place across town. But he was as nice a guy as advertised and insisted on splitting the difference. He told her his favorite coffee shop was on Madison and Seventy-third (much closer to her) and that she could meet him there. It starts drizzling on the way, escalates to a downpour by the time she's pulling open the door to Via Quadronno.

Oliver is at a little two-top table in the front, studying something in his own notebook. Seeing her, he stands and smiles.

Pulse of panic—Chase and the Fishers' home in Chicago—deep inhale.

Making a sympathetic sound and saying something about the rain, Oliver pulls out a chair for her. "Let me get you a cup of coffee or something." He flags down the waitress.

She'd figured he would simply return her things and she'd be on her way, but the rain has graduated to blinding sheets, and all her umbrellas are safe and dry somewhere in her apartment. Thanking him, she tentatively slips off her coat and sits. Pulling damp hair from the collar of her dress, she lets Oliver order her a latte but declines any snacks or desserts.

His notebook is actually green graph paper, where he'd been sketching something detailed and mechanical.

"It's an idea for a compressor," he says when he notices her looking.

Feeling warmth on her cheeks, she admits she's not entirely sure what that means.

He smiles and explains he works on engine designs for Advantage

Electric, tells her he would be shocked if she *did* know. "It's a really boring engineering thing."

Maybe the lighting is less harsh than in the Javits Center (or perhaps it's that he's not mentioning an older universe she sometimes pretends never existed), but Oliver is better looking than she remembers: skin golden even in late January, black glasses giving him a surprising warmth.

She asks how he got started in the field.

"My dad's a pilot," he says, quick shift of his eyes, like he's hiding something. "I guess you could say it's sort of a family business."

Perhaps it's the reporter in her, but she wants to know what the strange look meant when he mentioned his father, finds herself asking follow-up questions, forgetting his connection to the Fisher family, forgetting why she's here.

It's still pouring when the waitress comes by with their drinks. Oliver asks if she's sure she doesn't want something to eat, and Sharon lets him talk her into splitting tiramisu.

They discuss *The Enquiring Sun*, and he jokes that he'll give it a try one morning instead of *The Daily News*. He hands her back her notebooks, and she thanks him. Then he lowers his eyes, looks solemn. "I'm so sorry if I upset you the other day. I was thinking out loud."

"It's not a big deal." Sharon has never been able to articulately verbalize the compartments her brain constructed to keep her safe and guarded, even after all these years. "I . . . I wasn't expecting you to mention Chase, that's all. I sort of need to be mentally prepared for it."

"I get that," he says.

"It's just, before he died, things between us ended really badly, and I never got a chance to fix them." This is by far the most she's ever said on the topic to anyone. "I guess that sounds kind of selfish."

"I once moved to Alaska to avoid having a breakup conversation with someone."

A laugh comes out of her nose. "Really?"

"It was a little more complicated than that, but pretty much. Now that's selfish."

"It's pretty extreme."

"Yeah, probably would have been a lot easier to send an e-mail."

They talk about Hong Kong, where they both spent time. Oliver probably realizes she was there with Chase Fisher visiting his mother, but he doesn't ask, lets her say it. They discuss Alaska and Egypt, and all the places she'd like to go that he's seen.

Outside, the rain has stopped, but it's an hour and another round of coffees later when Oliver says, "I know this is really weird, but do you have any interest in getting dinner or something sometime?"

Over the past seven years, several people besides Scott Underwood have asked her out—men at her various workplaces, guys in bars, people she interviewed—and occasionally she'd thought about accepting. Yet she never did (if she truly liked the person, she'd suggest they might be friends, but most guys weren't interested in that option). At first not dating had been a way of containing her shock and grief and guilt. When those emotions faded, it may simply have become habit. And there was also the daunting idea that if she were to accept an invitation to dinner or drinks, it might lead to another and another, and at some point she would have to tell the guy about how her boyfriend broke up with her, got on a plane, and died.

"I'm going to Detroit for work this week," she says, thinking he'll forget about it by the time she returns. "Maybe when I get back."

Something poking Adam's thigh.

It's the limited-edition *E&E: Rising* action figure, which could potentially look like him if Adam had a straighter nose and spent the next thirty-six years at the gym. Gauzy tequila-blurred memories of a girl from the bar—Donna-Dana-Jamie—coming home with him, finding the toy somewhere in his bedroom, and employing it in extremely off-label activities. He should wash it . . . or throw it away.

Rolling over, he realizes Donna-Dana-Jamie is gone (should make sure his credit cards aren't), but there's a note on the nightstand saying she had fun with "big and little Captain Rowen," and he should call. Her name was Sara, not even close.

Adam sets the action figure on the table; it seems to be judging him.

It's seven in the morning, his head is throbbing, and he has a noon flight, but through the windows it's the kind of unimaginably gorgeous Southern California day that makes him feel guilty for ever moping about anything, so he puts on sweats and drives twenty minutes to Runyon Canyon instead of the gym.

City small and innocuous below him, the jog seems a decent idea the first mile of the trail—brain momentarily cleared, alcohol sweating out of his system, ubiquitous dog poop avoided. Midway through the second mile, the drawbacks of running hungover become more apparent. Just after the start of the third mile, as he's heading down the steepest part of the slope, Adam trips over a tumbleweed, sails briefly through the air, and lands awkwardly on his left foot before wiping out completely.

"Hey, man, you okay?" a young guy is asking. Maybe it's that he's hiking in swim trunks, but Adam would wager eons and empires the kid is a surfer. "Looks like you went down pretty hard."

"I'm good, thanks." Even as he says it, Adam realizes it's an entirely false statement, that his ankle has been replaced by a sack of snapped twigs and blazing fire. The Good Samaritan Surfer tries to help him to his feet, but the second there's any weight on his left leg, Adam screams and crumbles against the surfer's tan chest. Not his greatest display of masculinity; in fact, it could be the start of many of the Rowen/Bryce slash fiction stories he's stumbled upon during self-hatred-driven Web searches.

"I'm gonna call 911." Samaritan Surfer sits Adam up against a boulder.

Adam nods and concentrates on not puking. It seems excruciating pain doesn't agree with him.

A small crowd has gathered, everyone offering contradictory advice. Some douchey-looking man in new running shoes steps forward announcing he's a doctor, and Adam recognizes him as one of the plastic surgeons from Bravo's *Hollywood Docs*. Doc lays light fingers on Adam's ankle, and Adam manages to contain his reaction to a manlier "motherfucker" mumbled under his breath.

A petite blonde with absurd green knee-high socks turns to the girl next to her and asks, "Is that Captain Rowen?"

Having left at five in the morning (she *could* save a day's rental picking the car up Saturday morning instead of Friday night), Sharon's on I-80, passing through Akron, Ohio, by three in the afternoon. Plenty of time to get to the dedication at seven, probably enough to catch some of the earlier activities, and maybe even put together the story she initially pitched her editors—to justify this as work and not something else.

From the cup holder in the console, her phone signals she's gotten a text: Oliver Ryan wishing her well on her trip and asking if she's still up for going out some time next week.

And Sharon realizes that other than mentioning the trip to him over coffee, she's not told a single person about it.

Ignoring the message, she wonders if she didn't say anything to anyone else because she didn't want anybody to talk her out of the long drive on her own, didn't want Kristen to offer to come and make it into some sort of girls' getaway.

Maybe it's that words have power, and she didn't want to admit, out loud, what she's doing.

Perhaps it's the cloud of painkillers, but Adam feels oddly vindicated that two bones are fractured. He's not sure he'd recover from the spectacle of Hollywood Doc and the emergency department if he'd simply *sprained* something. Less exciting about his broken ankle is the giant temporary cast and crutches that manage to eat his armpits raw in the few minutes it takes to hobble from a cab to his building, where the doormen—still fat and happy from their holiday bonuses—rush over to help him into the elevator.

His place is its usual post-Elena surgically clean state, and she's given his signature for a package. Sputtering to the couch and propping his leg on the tree table as per the doctor's instructions, Adam opens the box: Sharon Gallaher's book.

Adam likes the cover. Yes, he's been told this is not a good tool for overall judgment, but it's a nice matte shade of blue with an image of the Chicago skyline.

Trying to read the first page, he finds himself hopelessly lost and can't even focus enough on the jacket copy to get an idea of what the book is about. He sincerely hopes this is Percocet-related; he'd been a National

Merit Scholar, after all. The author photo on the back cover isn't the one on Sharon's Web site, but it must be from the same shoot. She's wearing the same purple coat. Her hair less windblown, she looks even more familiar.

They probably had a class together, or maybe she'd lived in that run-down walk-up on MacDougal and Bleecker? Floor by floor, he tries to remember his neighbors. Briefly he contemplates contacting someone from college to ask, but realizes he hasn't kept in touch with a single person from NYU—one more place from which he's made a clean break.

Setting the book atop the unread scripts, he flips on the TV. There's a *Law & Order* marathon on TNT, and he wonders if they'll show the episodes he did after school. All in, he'd probably had a grand total of three minutes screen time; it had been far and away the most exciting thing in his world at that point. A time when the idea of going on Howard Stern and criticizing a director, even a director of something as abhorrent as *Murder Island 3*, would have horrified him.

Guilty glance at the unread screenplays as he fades.

Pain and his cell phone wake him.

His agent.

He hits "Decline" and dry swallows three more little white pills from the hospital pharmacy.

Marty's calling the landline now, and his publicist is on the cell.

This can't be good. Cell phone is closer.

"Why the fuck am I learning you broke your leg from TMZ?" Evie says, and he instantly feels that much worse. Wrestling upright, he reaches for the iPad. "I can't do my job if you don't keep me informed."

The gossip site has a few grainy cell phone pics from Runyon with the headline CAPTAIN ROWEN TAKES A TUMBLE. Praising the quick thinking of Dr. Joe from *Hollywood Docs*, the editors wish Adam a speedy recovery.

"I rep rock stars, Adam. How are you my disaster client?" Evie is saying. "Were you drunk or high?"

"I was jogging."

"So that's a no?" Evie says she'll put together a statement publicly thanking Doc and deal with the convention organizers in Detroit, which is good, since he had completely forgotten about it. Then she pauses, uncharacteristically unsure. "Want me to tell Phoebe?"

"I broke my ankle, E, I hardly think we need to alert everyone I ever dated." Adam barks, rattled by the mention of Phoebe.

"I thought . . . never mind. Let me know if you need anything, okay?"

Adam calls his agent, assures Marty he'll be ready, willing, and able should the meeting with the *Divided* creators come to fruition.

"They want to shoot mid-March; you'll be all right by then?"

In two days he has to go back to the orthopedist for a real cast that he's supposed to wear for six to eight weeks, then a brace and a cane for another few months. "Of course."

"Did you get a chance to look at *Galaxy Warrior*?" Marty says, but changes course when Adam moans. "Don't worry about it, buddy, just get some rest."

Hanging up, he texts Cecily he won't make it to Detroit.

SPLEEN! she immediately responds, and he sends her the TMZ link. Ten seconds later she's calling to make sure he's not on his deathbed.

"This is an incredibly elaborate way to blow me off, Z," she says, and he promises to come visit soon.

He's tempted to turn off all ringers and return to Sam Waterston and the parade of sexy ADAs on *Law & Order*, but his mother has a Google Alert set up for him, so he dials her number.

"What's wrong?" she asks twenty-five hundred miles away. It's been eighteen years since he left Coral Cove, and his mother can still tell all's not right in Adamsville by the way he says "hi."

"I got a little banged-up running and didn't want you to see anything online and get worried."

She's a nurse and requires a more thorough explanation, echoes the doctor telling him to keep his leg elevated and not to take pain meds without food. Then she decides he can't be trusted at all.

"I should come out there for a few days," she says, and he forces a laugh, tells her he's a grown man. "I don't want you stumbling around all alone."

"Don't worry, I've got people," he says with utterly no conviction, blames the slippage of his skills on the drugs.

"Baby," she says, wrecking him the way no other person can. "You want to come home for a while?"

His mother is someone who understands what that means. Knows at a certain moment "going home for a while" equates to never leaving again, to living in your childhood bedroom indefinitely. In all those early years of his career, when he was floundering, first in New York and then in LA, she only ever offered him the option of "coming home for a while" once— after the *Goners* pilot didn't get picked up. Then he'd gotten drunk and high and done everything in his power so he *wouldn't* take her up on the offer.

He's mesmerized that now he's waxing dangerously close to saying yes. "Ma," he says, "I'm fine."

She should probably be tired from driving four hundred miles, but the whole last hour on the road an electricity races through Sharon, and she feels she's burning thousands of calories. If she weren't buckled into her seat, she might simply float up and fly away. As traffic thickens outside the Detroit limits, it takes all her willpower not to abandon the car and sprint the rest of the way.

When her phone's GPS claims she's only two exits from the Renaissance Center, Sharon pulls off at a Shell station and grabs the cosmetic kit from her backpack. Under the fluorescent bulb, she brushes her teeth, reapplies mascara and lipstick. Sprays j'adore at her throat and wrists, slathers on deodorant, and runs a comb through her black hair—even though it's perfectly straight and flat as always. She'd chosen the blue knit dress because it's the exact color of her eyes, and people always comment on that. Plus, there's enough Lycra in the weave that it hasn't wrinkled during the long drive. Still, she straightens it and pulls back the shoulders, wishes she were taller, like the woman from the photo with Adam.

In the mirror she examines herself with the kind of cold calculation she hasn't used since her freshman year of college, when she determined she could look better than average if she wore heels and dresses instead of the shapeless sweatshirts and jeans everyone else favored. It's a tactic that still seems to be working. She's unlikely to win any beauty pageants, but there seems no reason anyone (maybe not even someone like Adam Zoellner) would outright laugh at a sexual offer she made.

Sharon had reserved a room at the convention hotel but doesn't bother checking in. The dedication ceremony—where Adam and Cecily Beissel are slated to present Ed Munn with an award—isn't for another two hours, but if Adam is at an autograph table or exploring the floor, there's a chance she might be able to approach him for an interview.

Whereas Fan-Con at the Javits Center had been a big, bustling affair, this is a much smaller event. There are only a handful of people in line to buy tickets from a lone man seated at a folding table with a metal cashbox. Through the open door of the ballroom, she can see tables of vendors with stacks of vintage comic books.

A guy ahead of her in an *E&E* T-shirt makes her think of Oliver Ryan. Pinprick of emotion—guilt? regret?—for blowing off someone so seemingly nice. Or maybe it's a different feeling, something like longing? Either way, she shoves it aside. She *needs* to focus on this, whatever it is she's attempting to do with Adam Zoellner.

Almost her turn in line, Sharon is shuffling through her purse for her press pass when she notices a black-and-white head shot of Adam clad in Captain Rowen attire with the universal "No" slash across his face: *Adam Zoellner will not be able to attend* is written in red marker.

"He's not coming?" Sharon points to the picture, as if its meaning weren't perfectly clear, as if there weren't still a person in front of her in queue.

"His rep said he was in an accident," the cashier says from behind the table. "He sent some autographed photos, though, and a statement they're going to read at the ceremony."

"Thank you," Sharon says calmly, numbly.

Get out of this car.

The ticket clerk is saying something about other activities, but Sharon just walks back to the lobby, out the door, and to the parking garage down the street.

She'd thought her car was on the second level but can't find it when she gets there. Walks up two flights along the sloping ramp, then back down. Realizes she doesn't really even recall what kind of vehicle it was, or the color—something generic and compact in a gold, or was it beige?

Late January, it's already getting dark, which casts a film of creepiness over the concrete walls splotched with grease and occasional graffiti.

Up and down the floors in her five-inch platform boots. Each time a little more panicked, a little more hurried, until she's actually running. Her breath comes in ragged gasps, her skin covered in a sickly cold sweat. Up and down and up again.

Tripping over uneven stone, she twists her ankle and falls, catching herself hard on her wrists.

And then she just sits on the cold floor, studying the rainbow in a puddle of motor oil until her ass is numb.

Dips her finger in the indigo.

After what might be a very long time, a woman in a Lexus honks behind her.

Sharon pushes herself up, gives the driver a dirty look, and almost immediately finds her own car—a Chevy Impala in metallic gray.

Starting the engine, she begins the eleven-hour drive home. Ninety minutes outside Detroit, exhaustion hits. All at once she's so drained that keeping her eyes open is positively Herculean.

There's a billboard for a cheap motel chain, boasting rooms for thirty-nine dollars a night at the next exit, so she turns off the highway.

An ancient-looking innkeeper behind bulletproof glass slips her a metal key through the slot and informs her there's a vending machine by the stairs. Fleeting thought of the room at the Marriott she needs to cancel.

Her unit, which opens onto a wooded area reminiscent of every horror film, is a smoking room, and the ghost of burned things is so overwhelming she actually coughs. She recalls her parents' house before her dad gave up cigarettes twenty years ago, how all the curtains and carpets were yellowed. Tries to remember if she's talked to her family since Christmas and realizes she's in the Midwest and hadn't even thought to stop by.

The scratchy, threadbare coverlet is just begging for a *Dateline* black camera investigation to reveal semen and other bodily fluids, but she doesn't care, collapses on top of it. A TV chained to the dresser gets only four channels, and she settles on the one airing a *Law & Order* marathon. Slipping into oblivion, Sharon remembers that no one knows where she is, wonders who Briscoe and Greene will investigate when she ends up murdered in the middle of nowhere Michigan.

Pain and the pressing need to puke wake Adam.

Getting to the bathroom isn't artful. The crutches are a useless hassle, and hopping exacerbates the nausea. He won't admit it later, but some hands-and-knees crawling is involved.

Once again, his mother in pink scrubs beams into his head telling him not to take Percocet without food, so clear he can almost see her in the toilet water.

After twenty minutes perched over the bowl, Adam determines he's *not* actually going to vomit, just going to be stuck with his stomach doing a weird slurry thing for God knows how long.

For good measure, he manages to smack his head against the side of the commode when he starts to get up.

Dizzy and sick and feeling sorry for himself, he just sits there for a while . . . a long while.

Finally he tries to pull himself up on a glass shelving unit. The piece (picked out by Terri Minerva) is designed to give the illusion of floating, so it probably shouldn't stun him quite so much when the whole system comes away from the wall.

Crashes and crashes and crashes on travertine tile, and he's covering his face with his arms as the glass shatters.

The noise stops, and he opens his eyes.

Dangerous-looking icebergs all around him, a half-dozen bloody nicks on his arms. Two steel beams and chunks of drywall have fallen on his leg, essentially pinning him down. Probably the only reason it's not excruciatingly painful is that his big honking temporary cast is acting as a buffer.

Brushing stray shards from his pants, he cuts his hand. Then he actually does throw up, more on the side of the toilet than inside the bowl. He wonders if he'll die in the bathroom before Elena comes back the day after tomorrow.

For some inexplicable reason, he thinks of Sharon Gallaher's wind-tousled black hair and the shape of her mouth.

Pulling his phone from his pocket, Adam scrolls through the e-mails for her number. Even as he's dialing, he doesn't think he'll go through with it.

It's complete melodrama. He *knows* this. His phone is chock-full of people he *could* call. Yes, some of them *do* work for him, and some might be more responsive if he'd remembered their names after they'd fucked. But there are at least ten *real* people in his contacts list who could be here, helping him off his ass in fifteen minutes.

"Sharon Gallaher," a voice says before the end of the first ring.

Who answers the phone like that after midnight?

"Hello?" she says when he doesn't respond.

Is hers a voice he heard on campus years ago?

Would his whole life be different if he'd been standing behind her in line for the falafel cart and stopped to say something about her eyes or how she looks like someone he knows from somewhere? He could have stayed in the city, waited for her to graduate, maybe done a few more *Law & Order*s, branching out to an *SVU* or *Criminal Intent*. She could have moved into his apartment on MacDougal and Bleecker, taken to writing in the pink tub in the middle of the kitchen, chewing her pen caps, twisting her fingers and pressing them to her chest when she got frustrated. She could have switched from novels to screenplays for male leads with engaging smiles and gray eyes (no sci-fi, no villains, never a *Murder Island* sequel). The two of them could have forged the kind of partnership of legends. Sure, he might have strayed with a costar or seven in a big spectacular made-for-*Star*-magazine kind of affair, but he and Sharon would have worked it out for the sake of the children—Zach and Zelda. And he wouldn't be alone and miserable on overpriced flooring.

"Hello," Sharon says, again. "I can hear you breathe."

"I can hear you," Sharon says, flipping off the television.

She realizes any other person would have hung up on Breather thirty seconds ago, or more accurately, any other person wouldn't have answered a call at three in the morning from an "Unknown" number in the first place. She could argue that she was awake anyway, watching *Law & Order* and eating Doritos from the vending machine. Could say she knows, more than most, that a middle-of-the-night phone call can be important—that an unfamiliar number could be a police station or a hospital. It could be Kristen at 26 Federal Plaza, hysterical because the FBI *did* come after her for giving out the actor's e-mail. Heck, it could be Adam Zoellner himself calling to say he'd love to give her an interview, or maybe act out some of those fan fiction stories.

None of those reasons is what made Sharon pick up or stay on so long. Sharon *always* answers in case it's the call she's been waiting for for seven years. Even if it's simply a phone call in a dream or some flirtation with an alternate universe, it would be worth it, as long as she can say the things she never got the chance to say.

"Chase?" she asks, tastes salt, and realizes she's crying. Crying like she didn't after running out of the Madison Plaza, bleeding and wet and cold.

"Is that you?" she asks inaudibly between sobs. "I love you, and I'm so sorry."

The person on the other end makes a wet sound, like he's crying, too.

"I'm sorry," he mumbles, or something close to that. It's hard to make out through his raw and haggard pants.

"I know," she says. "It's all right."

"So sorry." And it might not be her dead boyfriend, but there's something she recognizes about his voice, even so muddled.

"It's all okay," she says. "We're gonna be all right."

She keeps the line open until his breathing stabilizes, until her breathing stabilizes.

"I'm going to hang up now," she says. "Everything is going to be okay."

Adam holds the silent phone in his hand and wipes his eyes with the shoulder of the running shirt he's still wearing.

She's the first person listed on his phone's "Favorites," even now. Taps on her name and calls.

Twenty minutes later she lets herself in with old keys and follows his voice to the half bath by the den.

And it's so clear, Adam can't believe he ever missed it. The hair color and the set of the mouth, something about the forehead. Sharon Gallaher seemed familiar because she looks a little like Phoebe Fisher.

Wiping her eyes, Sharon looks around the shoddy motel room, mere minutes off the highway but completely silent at night with the television off. Her phone's clock says it's 3:30 A.M.

No traffic if she leaves now. Maybe the rental place will even give her a break and charge her for only two days if she makes it home before nightfall.

Gathering her things takes all of twenty seconds (though she'll almost certainly leave something behind, as always), toothbrush and makeup kit stuffed back in her bag. She pulls her blue knit dress back over her head and stabs feet back into boots. Grabbing her notebooks, she notices the printout from the *E&E* convention Web site with information and a thumbnail print of the stars, including Adam Zoellner dressed in Rowen's black robes. Feels herself laughing, head so clear it hurts.

Nearly two decades ago, she'd skipped school and walked to the mall to see the *Eons & Empires* movie; twenty years and she's still chasing Captain Rowen.

Leaving the convention info for some other person to find, she grabs her cell from the bed, is about to shove it back in her bag when she remembers Oliver's message from hours earlier.

It's the time of night for booty calls or drunken maudlin ramblings (even if she's never participated in these things, she's heard about them from Kristen), but she's sane, sober, and stable when she sends Oliver a text: *Yes, I would really like that.*

Getting Adam off the bathroom floor is a more challenging task than Phoebe initially anticipated. The larger glass chunks are unwieldy and treacherous. Even finding a broom to sweep up the thousands of shards takes longer than it should, because he doesn't know where the housekeeper stores supplies, and nothing is where it used to be when she lived here.

Perhaps the greatest impediment to the cleanup is the weird formal air between them. For so many years they shared everything—she used to squish the tiny whiteheads on his nose, and he knew her tampon and laxative preferences—and yet it's somehow incredibly awkward for the two of them to occupy the same space, a space that used to be theirs.

Hesitant salutations. He thanks her for coming. She asks if he's hurt.

Phoebe starts to pick up a piece of glass, but Adam stops her. "You should be wearing gloves or something."

Of course, the only gloves he has are four-hundred-dollar Gucci leather ones far too long for her stout fingers, but he insists she wear them.

Blood from one of his myriad mini-cuts gets on the thumb.

"I seem to be having an O. J. Simpson moment," she mumbles.

A laugh comes out his nose.

And things are a little better.

"So how *exactly* did this happen?" she asks, and he tells her about a run gone epically awry, followed by pain medication/food mismanagement.

Phoebe clicks her tongue sympathetically. "That stuff always makes you sick."

"I know." His smile is so much sadder than she remembers.

When they've cleared a safe patch of floor tile, Adam starts to push himself up on the edge of the toilet. Taking off the gloves, she extends her hand.

A pause before he takes it.

His skin on hers.

Adam can't stand on his broken foot, and his right leg has fallen asleep, so he lumbers into her. Everything familiar, the feel of his weight, the smell of his sweat—she's twenty-five again, helping Adam out of a different bathroom.

"I'm sorry." Letting go of her, he balances on the wall. "Can you get my crutches?"

It would probably be as easy for him to lean on her, but she does what he asks. Watches him limp to the sleek leather couch in the living room and helps prop his leg on the table. As he catches his breath, Adam repeatedly thanks her.

There really aren't many reasons to stay and so many to go—it's two in the morning, she has work the next day, her husband whom she loves—but leaving seems horribly wrong, too.

"Can I offer you a drink?" Adam asks, and they both laugh.

She sits on the sofa, a safe three feet between them.

When she first arrived, she'd been far too concerned about Adam to notice how different the condo is. Looking around now, it seems not a single piece of furniture, window treatment, or floorboard remains from the time she lived here. All gone are the things they'd picked out together, when they suddenly had lots of disposable income, when they were at long last really together. Something about that stings, but it's not her place to say anything.

Adam plucks a glass splinter from the Ace bandages around his leg.

"Maybe I should take you to the emergency room?"

"Not much they can do." The melancholy smile again. "Ankle's already broken."

"Well, you probably weren't supposed to hurl shelving at it during this phase of recovery."

"I have to go back on Tuesday. I'm sure it'll be okay for a few days."

"Fine, I'll take you then," she says before she realizes it. Remembers their lives aren't linked that way anymore. Possibly there's a friend or that new assistant who does these kinds of things? Or a woman? Even though Phoebe doesn't like to dwell on it, it would make sense that there'd be a lady in Adam's life. "I mean, unless, you'd rather . . ."

Gray eyes serious, Adam tells her that would be nice. "Thank you."

He's in desperate need of a shower—still dirty from the jog, the million little bloody scratches—but he's probably not supposed to get the plaster wet, and she knows bathing isn't something she should help him with. So she gets a damp washcloth from one of the bathrooms not full of glass and destruction.

As she hands it to him, Adam's stomach audibly growls.

"Did you eat anything today?" Phoebe asks, overwhelmed by how easy it is to ask the kinds of things she used to ask all the time, when they were together, when it was required they take care of each other.

"At some point, I think I meant to."

Suggesting they order takeout, she makes a mental list of places they used to call, narrows it to the few still open this late. "Matzo ball soup from Selma's?"

What she says makes him look up sharply. "You're ordering me soup?"

"If your stomach's still messed up, it's probably the best thing."

"That would be great." A wince, as he looks away.

"Hurts?"

Still not looking at her, he nods. "Yeah."

It's not until she's merging on the 405 an hour later that Phoebe realizes Adam might not have been talking about his broken bones.

The sun is starting to crack the sky by the time Phoebe gets back to Los Feliz, but Cole is bopping Cassie up and down in the living room.

"You were gone awhile," he says, too casually. "We were starting to get a little concerned."

It takes Phoebe longer to respond than it should, because it's so staggering to think that her husband (bed rumpled and lovable in pajama pants and bare feet) and child (the world's most delightful six-month-old) exist in the same world as Adam—these two different lives never having intersected.

"Sorry. I would've called, but I figured you went back to sleep."

"No biggie. Everything squared away?"

Phoebe starts to explain, but in the breaking dawn it seems absurd she felt the need to blindly rush over in the middle of the night. That Adam, a legitimate movie star (even if he did go on a broadcast rant about his last movie) living in a full-service building, didn't have anyone to call other than the ex-girlfriend he hadn't spoken to in more than a year.

"He broke his ankle and wasn't doing so great."

"You get him fixed up?"

"Yeah." She pauses. "Actually, I said I'd take him to the doctor Tuesday morning. Is that all right?"

"Why are you asking my permission?" Frustration percolating in his question.

An honest answer seems unwise. Poor form to tell Cole she misses Adam the way she misses her brother—a persistent, hovering ache. Probably shouldn't say she felt physically ill after reading the horrible *Murder Island 3* reviews, knowing how upset Adam would be. Not mention that thirty minutes ago, she almost kissed Adam good-bye—not because of any overwhelming passion but because that's what she always used to do.

"It's a little weird, right?" she finally offers.

"He's your friend. If he needs help, I trust you." Cole doesn't sound thoroughly convinced of this, lifts his shoulders in what's probably meant to be an unfazed shrug but comes off as simply uncomfortable.

She offers a reassuring caress of his triceps as she takes a sleepy Cassie from his arms.

"Besides," he says, "you already chose me over the famous actor, remember?"

Playfully, she bumps her nose to his because this is also true. "I did, didn't I?"

Adam is having pants difficulties and calls out a warning that he's not entirely clothed when Phoebe lets herself in.

"Please, you helpless and half naked sums up a decade of my life," she jokes. But there's a flush on her cheeks, eyes darty, when she peeks into his bedroom.

Finding scissors Adam had no idea he owned, she cuts the leg on a pair of track pants so he can pull them over the temporary cast.

At the orthopedist's office, Phoebe has zillions of questions about cast materials, future surgeries, and activity restrictions, and Adam is amazed and grateful. He can't believe he hadn't thought to ask such basic things like whether or not he can drive (he can, as long as the car is an automatic) and what kind of workouts are off-limits (pretty much any exercise that doesn't involve sitting).

"I may have called my dad," Phoebe admits when Adam raises questioning eyebrows.

Three hours and a giant blue fiberglass cast later, she's helping him back into the passenger seat of her car, and he's thanking her again and again.

"Do you maybe wanna come over for lunch?" she asks without any of the confidence she'd exhibited in the doctor's office. "You could meet Cassie and see Kraken?"

Caught off guard, Adam doesn't respond. Phoebe waves her words away, tells him that he should go home and rest.

"No." He shakes his head. "I'd love to come."

It's a half-hour drive to Los Feliz, and they talk about still-shared things, such as Evie Saperstein and the weather. She parks in front of a modest bungalow and helps him out. When Phoebe opens the front door, Kraken almost knocks her down trying to get to Adam.

Hunched over on his crutches, he's trying to maintain balance while patting the dog's head when a man, presumably Phoebe's husband, appears with baby in arms. All Adam knows of Cole has been garnered from snippets Evie rarely lets slip. He's young, a chef, Phoebe seems happy. And Adam feels strangely hollow watching this wavy-haired guy's quick, tense exchange with Phoebe.

"Babe, I'm so late." The child passed.

Then Cole notices Adam and solidifies to concrete.

Bouncing Cassie, Phoebe does a quick intro. Adam manages to shake the dude's hand while keeping his right crutch secure under his armpit. Unfreezing, Cole offers a half smile that makes no attempt to reach green eyes. A self-conscious kiss on Phoebe's cheek, a nervous wave toward Adam, and Cole is gone. For a severed second, Phoebe looks after him, something hard to read on her face.

She turns to Adam. "We need to get your leg up."

The house is small but cozy, with unique built-in storage spaces and wood trim, and there's a postage-stamp backyard with a deck and a huge old tree. Baby still in arms, Phoebe helps Adam get situated on one patio chair, his ankle elevated on another.

"Can you take her for a sec?" she says, handing him her daughter.

Adam knows nothing about babies (Cecily literally had to demonstrate how to hold one during the second season of *E&E: Rising*, when they were filming some World 7 scene where they had an infant), but Phoebe's child feels karmically sound in his grasp, as if she would have found her way there one way or the other.

"Hey there." He smiles. Of course she's beautiful.

Cassie has Phoebe's deep blue eyes and heart-shaped mouth; Adam knows instantly that he could love her, that it doesn't matter he's not her father.

Phoebe brings out a pitcher of flavored iced tea and some ridiculously delicious chowder he assumes Cole made, since he'd never seen Phoebe cook anything in all the time they lived together. She puts Cassie in an elaborate activity chair while they eat and discuss more safe topics. He suspects she's heard about the Howard Stern incident, but she doesn't mention it, only asks if he's working on anything new. So he tells her about the HBO Civil War series, about how everyone thinks he's too young to play Grant, but he can't stop thinking about the early version of the script he'd read.

"I'd love to look at it," she says.

"I'd like that."

And then they just look at each other.

"It's really good to see you." She sets her weirdly chubby fingers on his cast. "I'm glad you called."

With the chairs and his gargantuan cast between them, it's an awkward lunge, but he makes it.

Kissing Phoebe is home.

His tongue knows the crown on her right molar, his teeth know how hard he can bite before it hurts. Anais Anais perfume and vanilla lotion all around him.

Even as he's doing it, Adam is vaguely aware this isn't what she wants, that this will be one more time he fails her.

But:

She's the one who invited him over.

She's the one who wants to read scripts like she used to do.

She's the one kissing him back.

Finally, her hands on his chest, pushing him away. "Adam, stop. I'm married."

"In some forties shotgun fantasy," he says quickly, hurtfully.

"You think I'm with him because of Cassie?" Phoebe's face is flushed; of the long list of women he's angered, she's the only one who becomes lovelier. "That's really what you think?"

It might be what he'd *like*, but, no, it isn't what Adam thinks. No matter how pregnant Phoebe was when she married Cole, Adam is painfully aware she made her choice well before any of that.

"I'm sorry. It's just . . ." He gestures to the baby, the backyard, the dog, hits his hand on the back of the chair. "I wanted this."

"A Target patio set?"

"A life with you."

He studies his toes peeking out from his cast, furious at himself for saying what he had vowed not to say two years ago when she told him she was engaged, when he tried to be a better man.

"I guess I knew that." Her voice breaks into something bordering a sob. "I shouldn't have brought you here. That was unfair."

Now her head is bowed.

"But I missed you so, so much," she's saying. "It's really selfish, I'm sorry."

Thirty-five and she's still so beautiful.

"No, Pheebs." Fast as he can manage, he's on his feet (foot), a hand on her shoulder.

"I'm sorry."

He thinks of his bizarre conversation with Sharon Gallaher, whom he called because he couldn't admit he needed to call Phoebe.

"It's all okay," he says. "We're gonna be all right."

Two days after returning from Detroit and not writing any sort of article on the "Thirty Years of *E&E*" convention, Sharon is at her desk at *The Enquiring Sun* when she gets a call on her cell from a Chicago number: Oliver Ryan.

She steps into the hall to answer.

"Did you get back from Detroit without incident?" he asks.

"Yeah." She pauses, trying to remember how to do this, how it works.

"Good. So I know that we talked about going out sometime this week . . . well, I talked about it," he says, and even though Sharon's only met Oliver twice, she can completely envision him, with a hesitant smile, one hand in his pocket.

"Yeah," she says again.

"Well, I can't do this week. I got sent to Chicago for a bit."

"Oh, no worries." Bite of disappointment.

"But I do want to make this happen. I mean, if you still want to."

"I'd like that," she says, asks about what he's doing in Illinois, and he tells her how sometimes he has to return to Advantage Electric's headquarters.

"How was Detroit?" he asks.

"It was kind of a bust." She's surprised at her own honesty. "I was hoping to interview someone at this *Eons & Empires* convention, but a couple of the players didn't show."

He asks if she's a fan of *E&E*.

"I guess you could call me sort of a closet fan," she says.

And they talk about the comics and the TV show for a while. Until she remembers she's still at her office, still has stories to write.

Phoebe feels drugged and exhausted and weirdly optimistic by the time she pulls in front of the Winston Tower (where she used to live) to drop Adam off. He says he'll bring her down the *Divided* script, but he's so awkward on his crutches that she takes Cassie from her car seat and follows him in.

Her favorite of the middle-aged doormen in navy suits is at the desk. "Good evening, Ms. Fisher, Mr. Zoellner," he says, as if she hadn't been absent for years.

Up the elevator, through the foyer, and into the den, where Adam leads her to a weird table that looks like it might be a tree stump. As he's shuffling through a stack of papers, she notices a blue book with the Chicago skyline on the cover and catches the author's name—*Gallaher with one G.*

"Oh my God." Setting Cassie on the couch, she picks up the book, opens the back cover, and stares into Sharon Gallaher's enormous eyes. "I know her."

"So do I—" Adam says, and then his face contorts slightly. "Sort of."

"From NYU?" Phoebe asks, assuming what she worried about all those years ago is the case, that Adam had slept with her in college.

"Not very well, friend of a friend. You?"

"She was my brother's girlfriend, the one who didn't come to the funeral." And Phoebe realizes she might never have told Adam that. All those phone calls to her brother's apartment were something she never shared with him—all taking place in that brief part of their relationship when he was fully committed and she was the one holding back.

"Really?"

"Yeah." She flips the book over, looks at the cover again. "Can I borrow this?"

"Keep it." He pauses. "If you borrow it, does that mean we hang out again?"

There may be too many buckets of history between them for that to work. Arguably, they were never really friends in the years they shared the apartment in Studio City, before they were an official couple. Always there were glowing embers between them. Perhaps there'll always be too much electricity for them to ever be the kind of pals that Cole (or any woman Adam might love) would be comfortable with. But maybe it's possible that they can stay in each other's lives.

"I'd like to try," she says.

Oliver calls Sharon a few days later, as she's straightening her apartment—washing crusty bowls from cereal suppers and throwing out half-drunk cans of Diet Coke, old newspapers, and magazines.

"I tried to find a totally fantastic reason to call, but really, I just wanted to say hey," Oliver begins apologetically.

"That seems totally fantastic enough." Sharon feels herself smiling, sits on the couch, and turns off her TV.

"I also wanted to tell you about this great book I read," he says. "*The Atheist in the Foxhole*. I think you may have heard of the author."

"Oh." A ripple of the floor-swallowing, sucking-her-to-China sensation. All that time that Sharon was letting her relationship with Chase Fisher wilt because of her writing woes, she'd never let Chase read her work. Would shield her computer screen with her palm when she caught him looking over her shoulder, dismissed all of his offers to help.

"I'm sorry, is that weird?" he asks. "I Internet-stalked you a bit."

"No." She is pretty sure she means this. "It's actually really nice."

Setting *The Atheist in the Foxhole* on the end table, Phoebe wipes her eyes, remembers what it was like to have her brother in her life.

All the minute details that she sometimes forgets: how Chase used to rub his forehead and communicate whole worlds using only his eyebrows; the blissful look he had while running; and the way he was protective over those he loved, even if they didn't fully understand his motivations.

And the truly wonderful, miraculous, spectacular thing is that, in this book, he lives. He breaks up with the girl he's dating, but his story doesn't end there. He gets married and has kids and all the things that Phoebe's real brother didn't get. Not a life free of conflict or challenges—that would hardly make a good story—but a life nonetheless.

And Phoebe isn't quite sure exactly why she is so grateful, but she is. Wants to track Sharon Gallaher down and thank her, can't wait to share this with her stepmother.

"You cool, Chicago?" Cole asks, and Phoebe realizes that she didn't hear him come home from the restaurant, glances at the digital clock on the cable box. It's nearly two in the morning.

Phoebe nods.

"You sure?" Cole asks nervously. Sitting down beside her, he puts a hand on her thigh, and she leans against his shoulder.

"I know I've been a little weird lately," she says.

He rubs her leg, warmth seeping through her yoga pants. "I just want to make sure you're peachy keen."

"I am."

"And not going to run off with your movie star ex-boyfriend."

"He can't run for at least eight weeks."

"So you're saying I've got time?" He smiles.

"I'm not going anywhere," she says. "I'm afraid you're stuck with me."

Five weeks and Adam is no closer to mastering crutches. In Phoebe's driveway he's about to drop a sack of Bosc pears while trying to shut his car door and remain upright. Luckily Evie, top down on her M3, pulls up behind him.

"If it isn't the hobbling embodiment of my ulcer," she says, on her way to help. "Tarnish my reputation any further on the ride over?"

Kissing his cheek, Evie whispers, "If her Donna Reed shtick gets to be too much, give me a sign, and I'll have you outta here pronto."

"Thanks," Adam says, extremely touched. "I'll give you the finger as the signal."

"Wouldn't have it any other way."

Cole is the one who answers the door, gives Evie a hug, and extends a hand to Adam.

"Hey, man, how's it going?" he asks, looking all of twelve—younger than the new crop of CW and QT stars Adam had to kill in *Murder Island 3*. Adam could have seen Phoebe with someone older, maybe one of her professors or the doctors she works with, but this kid?

"Can't complain." Adam remembers the pears, hands them over. "These are for you."

"Awesome, they're Pheebs's favorite." Cole shakes his head. "Which, I guess, you knew."

But then he does smile, gets endearingly excited explaining how they can tuck a pear slice under Gruyère cheese on the burgers he's making. And Adam can see a hint of what Phoebe must.

The three of them head to the deck, where Kraken barks enthusiastically seeing Adam through the sliding door. Cassie in arms, Phoebe's parents hurry to greet him. And even though he hasn't thought about them in at least a year, he's overwhelmed by how much he *has* missed them.

"Honey, it's so nice you could come." Gennifer's golden hair tickles his nose when she tries to embrace him around the crutches.

Phoebe's father claps him lightly on the shoulder.

"Dr. Fisher," Adam says, pleased when Phoebe's father grins wide. Adam's refusal to call him by his first name had at first been ingrained politeness but had become an ongoing joke between them during all the holidays and weekends and dinners they'd shared.

"Seriously, son, you're almost forty years old," Larry Fisher says, and asks about the doctor who set Adam's ankle and the prognosis, tells him he's extremely lucky he didn't need surgery.

Coming through the screen door with a glass of wine for Evie, Phoebe offers Adam a drink, raises her eyebrows when he says he'll stick with water. He raises his eyebrows back.

Doing magical things on the grill, Cole's brown hair is long and everywhere. Adam wonders if he wears it like that at the restaurant; that's definitely got to be some sort of health code violation. Kraken stays at Adam's side despite Cole's proximity to raw meat. Periodically Evie checks in to make sure she doesn't need to instigate the great escape.

Salmon, burgers, grilled vegetables, and salads on the table, the adults take to the patio chairs while Cassie chubbles enthusiastically in the activity center.

Gennifer assures Adam there's no shame falling over one's feet and claims to have broken three toes tripping on her college roommate's cat.

Evie tells everyone how Adam wanted the role in *Divided* so badly he insisted they let him do a screen test on crutches.

"That's going to be the big story when the show starts," she says.

Adam shrugs, though he's acutely aware no one has mentioned the Howard Stern incident since the HBO execs offered him the role. "You don't need to sell me to these people, E. They're our friends."

Everyone laughs.

Adam wonders if it's true.

And it's awkward, but not.

While Cole goes inside to do something indecent with fruit and balsamic vinegar and everyone else is distracted by the baby, Phoebe puts a hand on Adam's forearm—enough chemistry remaining between them that it tingles.

"So I was thinking, if you're going to stay in town, maybe you'd want to take Kraken for a while?" she says. "Once you get your cast off?"

Flashback to the first day he saw her at Theta Tunney's workshop more than a decade ago. How he'd thought he wouldn't like her, still wanted to sleep with her. Figured she'd be just one more wannabe actress who floated in and out of his life as he plowed his way into the industry.

"That would be great," he says, swallowing over something lumpy and emotional in his throat. "Thank you."

"No, thank you for . . ." She gestures toward the kitchen.

He nods.

It hurts and it doesn't. That's not really right; it feels more like his ankle does now—active pain gone but itchy as the bones knit back together.

And Cole makes the best fucking cheeseburger he's ever had.

By the time Oliver shows up for their first date the day he gets back to New York, Sharon has talked to him on the phone two dozen times and feels as though she's known him much longer than five weeks. Thinks that she felt that way when she first met Chase, but it isn't agonizing, just interesting.

In honor of the thirtieth anniversary of Ed Munn's first *Eons & Empires* comic book, an indie theater by her apartment is showing the film version from 1992 starring Michael Douglas and Jake James. She's not entirely sure if it had been her idea or Oliver's that they see it, but he was the one who suggested they meet beforehand at the coffee shop where they'd had their sort-of date when he returned her notebooks. She arrives first this time, sits at the same little table they shared before, and takes the liberty of ordering a tiramisu to split. It arrives as he's walking through the door.

They're finishing it when he reaches for a plastic bag. Handing it to her, he explains, "So I got you a little something."

Inside is a six-inch plastic action figure still in its original packaging: Adam Zoellner in the black robes from *E&E: Rising*'s first season. Not a particularly good rendering, the eyes are especially wrong, but the head shape is right and something about the set of his jaw.

"You got me a Captain Rowen action figure?" Sharon feels tears in her eyes.

She remembers how she used to feel locking herself in the bathroom and reading the comic books while she was babysitting. Not wanting to share the world with anyone, because it would somehow be less real. But this feels real.

Ollie's hands are in the pockets of his khakis, and he slouches a little. "It's dumb. I should have gotten flowers or something—"

"No." She cuts him off. "This is the best gift ever."

"You like it?"

"I love it."

"I figured you'd be more into Rowen than Bryce or the Snow sisters."

"Seriously, this is amazing," she says.

He asks if she's ready to go see the film, signals for the check, and helps her into her coat. It's only a few blocks to the theater. Halfway there she takes his hand, and he smiles.

Maybe he'll kiss her during the movie. Or maybe she'll be the one to turn and lean into him. Perhaps they'll be too engrossed and wait until the closing credits are rolling. It's quite possible that the film won't seem nearly as good as it did when she was fourteen and longed for anything other than the safety of suburbia, for some other universe. Maybe she and Oliver will be bored, leave early, and walk the four flights up to her apartment, where she'll clear a space for them on her bed. Or perhaps she'll end up not liking him nearly as much as she suspects she will. So many different potential outcomes, nothing but options, in this world and those just one or two away.

acknowledgments

I'd like to thank everyone at St. Martin's Press, especially Katie Bassel and the incredibly insightful Laura Chasen, who has talked me down from a ledge or two.

Alex Glass is still my Jerry McGuire, and I am forever grateful to the amazing Jamie Beckman and her blue pencil.

Over the years a handful of people were kind enough to read this book in various incarnations, and I owe all of them drinks and thanks and cheese conies: Camille Sweeney, Diane Cardwell, Terri Goveia, Anna David, Taj Greenlee, Michael Ferrante, and Mandy Beisel. And a shout-out to all the wonderful writers I worked with at OSU and Northwestern, who always go above and beyond: Richard Ford, Michelle Herman, Lee K. Abbott, Lee Martin, Bill Roorbach, and Chris Coake.

Sometimes book stuff makes me grouchy, yet my family continues to put up with me. Thank you to my parents, Nancy and Michael Goldhagen, and sister, Jacqui Holland. And to my husband, Bob, and daughter, Victoria, who continually remind me what's really important.